Shifting

Shifting

BETHANY WIGGINS

WALKER & COMPANY

New York

First published in the United States of America in September 2011
by Walker Publishing Company, Inc., a division of Bloomsbury Publishing, Inc.
www.bloomsburyteens.com

For information about permission to reproduce selections from this book, write to
Permissions, Walker BFYR, 175 Fifth Avenue, New York, New York 10010

Library of Congress Cataloging-in-Publication Data
Wiggins, Bethany.
Shifting / Bethany Wiggins. — 1st U.S. ed.
p. cm.
Summary: After bouncing from foster home to foster home since the age of five, almost-
eighteen-year-old Maggie Mae Mortensen arrives in Silver City, New Mexico, to finish high
school and try to escape her reputation as a trouble-maker, only to face ostracism in her new
school and a band of evil Navajo Skinwalkers who want her dead.
ISBN 978-0-8027-2280-5 (hardcover)
[1. Foster home care—Fiction.   2. Shapeshifting—Fiction.   3. Navajo Indians—
Fiction.   4. Supernatural—Fiction.   5. Indians of North America—New Mexico—
Fiction.   6. High schools—Fiction.   7. New Mexico—Fiction.]   I. Title.
PZ7.W6382Sh 2011   [Fic]—dc22   2011005751

Book design by Nicole Gastonguay
Typeset by Westchester Book Composition
Printed in the U.S.A. by Quad/Graphics, Fairfield, Pennsylvania
2 4 6 8 10 9 7 5 3 1

For Jaime, who always believed

Shifting

1

I woke to the sun setting behind mountains and peeled my forehead from the car window.

"Where are we?" I asked the man sitting beside me.

"Almost to Silver City," Mr. Petersen said. He combed his fingers through his graying hair and buttoned the top button of his shirt.

"How long have I been asleep?"

He lifted the cuff of his blue pinstripe shirt and glanced at his watch. "Nearly three hours. Silver City's in the southern part of the—"

"Yeah. I know where Silver City is."

He studied me. "You look upset, Maggie Mae."

I gritted my teeth and glared at him, wishing he'd sat up front with the social worker. "I am. When you said you were trying something new, I had no idea you meant I'd be moved to the opposite end of New Mexico." I pressed my forehead back on the window and stared at the skyline—mountains, not skyscrapers.

"I'm placing you in the country . . . ," Mr. Petersen said.

"Yeah. I'm not blind."

"Where trouble will be harder to find."

If he knew the real me, he'd know how impossible that was. I closed my eyes.

"How many times have the police picked her up?" the man in the front seat asked. I didn't know him—he was one of the few social workers I hadn't met during my twelve and a half years in the foster program.

"More than I can count, Ollie," Mr. Petersen replied.

"But what's she doing out on the streets? You don't think she's a prost—"

"You think you can handle her case?" Mr. Petersen snapped.

"Just because I'm not from the city doesn't mean I'm incompetent."

"We'll see about that," Mr. Petersen muttered.

I sat straight up and looked at Mr. Petersen. "Wait a sec. Since I'm so far from Albuquerque, do I still have to meet with you once a week?" I asked.

Mr. Petersen stared at me a long moment. "Mr. Williams will be your new social worker," he said, nodding to the front seat. Mr. Williams looked at me in the rearview mirror.

"I mean as doctor and patient," I whispered.

"I will turn your case over to a local therapist if I see the need."

A smile lit my face, cracking through the frown that had been stuck there all day. Mr. Petersen wasn't a bad man, just freaking annoying, always wanting me to tell him my secrets. There are things a girl like me can't tell anyone without sounding insane.

We passed a billboard that said WELCOME TO SILVER CITY. Framing the words were a Navajo symbol—a red sun with a gold center—and a howling coyote. I pressed my nose to the window for a look at my new town.

In the fading evening light, the ground looked parched and red in between scattered sagebrush and crooked ponderosa pines. Wind bent the gnarled bows and whipped a funnel of dust into the orange sunset. I could see no houses, no stores, only the occasional dilapidated barbed-wire fence.

"Where's the city?" I asked.

Mr. Petersen chuckled. "You're looking at it. The outskirts, at least."

We turned off the highway before we reached civilization and drove down a deserted, pothole-filled road framed by weeds and scraggly junipers. Ollie made a sudden sharp left, sending me slamming into the door of the car and Mr. Petersen into my lap.

"Jeez Louise, Ollie!" Mr. Petersen climbed off me and straightened his tan Dockers. "You almost hit a coyote?"

"Sorry. Almost missed the turn," Ollie explained. "It's getting dark."

"Haven't you heard of a U-turn?" Mr. Petersen asked, annoyed. I knew his annoyed voice. It was the one I was used to hearing.

We bounced over an uneven gravel drive, toward lights glimmering ahead. My new home.

People say never judge a book by its cover. The same goes for families. Never judge a family by its house. I lived in a mansion once, the Simms residence. They were the worst foster parents ever. The last home I lived in, Jenny Sue's, had been small and run-down, with weeds instead of grass and plywood floors where they'd torn out the ancient carpet. I was happier there than any other place.

Ollie stopped the car in front of a big red house that looked exactly like a barn. Even the front door had big, X-crossed planks. A little farther back I could just make out another building, which looked like an actual barn.

A porch light flashed on, bringing my attention back to the house. The front door opened and a face peered out. I held my breath and studied the woman stepping onto the porch. I opened my door for a better look and cold air swirled into the car.

Her hair was white, her skin was white and laced with wrinkles, and her shirt was white. She wore a pale blue denim skirt and shiny white cowboy boots. A chunky turquoise and silver necklace hung around her neck, and matching earrings dangled from her ears. She looked like the sweet grandma from an old western movie. But then I noticed her hands on her hips, her tapping toe, the frown deepening the creases around her mouth.

"Well, it's about time you arrived, John!" she said as Mr. Petersen opened his door. "I have Sunday dinner waiting! Did you forget how to use a cell phone? Because you can't tell me you weren't raised right."

I smiled. This fragile old woman was scolding my psychiatrist. I stepped out of the car and around to the open trunk, grabbing my worn, army-green duffle bag.

"Well, where's the rest of your stuff?" the woman called, looking at me.

"Oh. This is it," I explained, glad for the darkness. My face was burning.

"I'm Mrs. Carpenter. I could be your worst nightmare if you're not careful," the old woman said as I ascended the front steps. I looked at her thin arms and doubted it. Larry Simms had been my worst nightmare, and I knew without a doubt she couldn't hit half as hard as him. I forced a smile to my dry lips.

"Dinner is getting *colder*. Come in," Mrs. Carpenter said, holding her front door wide. I stepped past a porch swing and a potted cactus plant and went inside.

Native American pottery, framed pictures of John Wayne and ancient Indian chiefs, and Navajo weavings covered every wall, every table, every shelf, door, and counter. Giant red-and-gold rugs covered pale wooden floors. There was no television in sight and the phone sitting at a small desk was the old-fashioned kind where you spin each number in a circle to dial out. Next to a massive, ancient-looking clock was a gun case holding two rifles, two handguns, and an unstrung bow. I took a closer look at my new foster mother and thought maybe she would turn out to be my worst nightmare.

"I made something special—corn on the cob, mashed potatoes, jalapeño corn bread, and grilled ribs. Sit, sit!" Mrs. Carpenter urged. I sat at an antique table set for four and watched as she uncovered a feast. My stomach grumbled as I loaded my plate.

"Now, you told me on the phone, John, that she's been acting out for attention? What exactly does that mean?" Mrs. Carpenter sat across from me and watched as I shoveled a mound of buttery potatoes into my mouth. Her eyes narrowed and the potatoes lost their flavor. "Not every meal is going to be like this," she warned. "I fixed John's favorite since he was coming by."

"Yes, ma'am," I mumbled, lifting my napkin to my mouth.

"Do you want to tell her, Maggie Mae? Or shall I?" Mr. Petersen asked.

"Go ahead," I said.

"Well," Mr. Petersen began. "Magdalene Mae, or Maggie Mae, has had close to twenty brushes with the law in the past two years." Mrs. Carpenter gasped. "She looks like an angel, I know,"

Mr. Petersen continued. "But for some reason this little angel can't seem to keep her clothes on. She keeps getting picked up for indecent exposure." He looked at Mrs. Carpenter, his bushy eyebrows raised.

"She got picked up by the cops for fighting with a prostitute over a jacket," Ollie blurted. "That's why her last family stopped fostering her."

"Where did you hear that, Oliver?" Mr. Petersen snapped.

"That's the rumor going around the office. It's the truth, isn't it?"

"What it is is none of your business," Mr. Petersen said.

My stomach clenched. I set my fork down and studied my hands. Ollie's words wouldn't hurt so badly if they weren't true.

"Is her hair really that color or does she dye it? Her eyebrows look blond," Mrs. Carpenter said, as if she hadn't heard Ollie's outburst.

"Her hair? That was actually my idea—a safety measure," Mr. Petersen explained. "She stood out at her last school, so I thought that if her hair was black, she'd blend in a little better."

"Did it work, Maggie Mae?" Mrs. Carpenter asked.

I looked up from my hands. "No, ma'am," I said quietly, running fingers through my long dyed hair, the ends swishing against the middle of my back. "I still got picked on."

"So what did you do?"

"I learned to run fast and hit hard."

She studied me. I waited for shocked outrage. Instead she said, "If you'd like, we can dye it another color. Something that suits your skin better. Red. Or blond, maybe."

I shrugged, a noncommittal gesture, as Mr. Petersen would

have said. All my life I'd had pale blond hair with a hint of red—until now. I liked my hair raven black. It made my amber eyes stand out, like a cat's eyes.

"So, how many homes have you been in and for how long?" Mrs. Carpenter asked.

"Twelve."

"You'll be lucky thirteen," Mr. Petersen said.

"Thirteen homes? Why so many?" Mrs. Carpenter asked, studying me again, searching for something dark hidden beneath my, as Mr. Petersen put it, angelic face.

"She's been bounced around since she was five. And while some of those homes were good environments, others weren't. The state had to move her out of three for physical abuse. Two of the homes began families of their own after they'd had her for a couple of years and decided they didn't have time for her anymore. She's been moved seven times in the last two years because of the indecent exposure. For six months she was moved on a monthly basis, until we found a home that was willing to put up with her bad behavior. But after ten months and nine charges of indecent exposure, they'd had enough, too. A couple of weeks ago they called me and asked that she be transferred.

"But I know she's a good kid, all appearances to the contrary. I wish something more permanent would've worked out for her." I could hear the sympathy in Mr. Petersen's voice. It pulled at my chest, making it hard to breathe.

"Maggie Mae, since you don't seem to be hungry, would you like to see your room?" Mrs. Carpenter asked, her voice soft and gentle.

I let out a breath that had been stuck in my lungs. "Yes." I grabbed my duffle and followed her past a flight of stairs and down a hall to the other side of the barn house. At the end of the hall a door led to a small, cluttered room.

It had stark white walls, a small chest of drawers, a little CD player, a closet half filled with a hundred different kinds of fabric scraps, and against the far wall beneath a small window, a foldable camping cot with a homemade purple patchwork quilt draped over it. Smack in the middle of it all was a table that took up most of the room, with a sewing machine and a half-sewn quilt on top of it.

"I'm sleeping in the sewing room?" I asked.

"It's temporary. I have an empty stable hand's room above the barn, but John says you need to be in the same living space with me until you come of age. Your birthday's just around the corner, right?"

I nodded.

"Why don't you unpack your things while John and I finish your paperwork." She turned to leave, but stopped. "I almost forgot! The laundry room is just down the hall, there. Across from it is the bathroom. It's all yours, so feel free to use the drawers for your toiletries." Her cowboy boots clip-clopped on the wood floor as she walked back to the dining room.

Toiletries? I didn't have any toiletries except my toothbrush, a little bag of drugstore makeup, and a hairbrush. I didn't even own a tube of toothpaste. Tears threatened my eyes, but I forced them to stay put. When Mr. Simms used to hit me, it was all right to cry. But tears over a tube of toothpaste?

I pulled my nicotine-scented secondhand clothes out of the duffle bag and shoved them into the drawers—jeans in the bottom drawer; T-shirts and tank tops in the middle; panties, a bra, and a nightshirt in the top. Next I hung my jacket in the empty half of the closet surrounded by a handful of waiting hangers. There—I was unpacked.

Clutching my "toiletries" to my chest, I darted down the hall to the bathroom. It, unlike the rest of the house, was empty. The vanity drawers were empty, the shower was empty—no soap, no shampoo. Even the shower curtain was a plain, foggy clear. I arranged my things in a drawer and went back to the sewing room.

Easing down onto the cot, I stared at the ceiling and wished I had a CD to drown out the quiet mumble of Mrs. Carpenter's, Mr. Petersen's, and Ollie's voices. Only a few words stood out of the many, but they weren't good words.

Sneaking out. Police. Nude. Arrested. Almost an adult. Prostitute. Convicted.

I pulled the pillow over my head.

A little while later I heard a quiet knock. I took the pillow from my head and stood. "Come in."

Mr. Petersen stood in my doorway, a frown on his face. "Hey, Maggie Mae. This is good-bye for us. You call me if anything goes wrong. And I mean *anything*." He held out his business card. "You're a good kid. Take care that you turn into a good adult."

I stood motionless and stared at him. Finally, with trembling fingers I took his business card and tucked it into my jeans pocket. He nodded, turned, and walked down the hall.

I wasn't sad to see him go, but he'd been more constant throughout my life than any of my "families" had ever been. It felt as if he were taking a part of me away with him. Who else would remember what I was like as a child, before all this strangeness started to happen to me?

I don't know how long I stood in the doorway, staring down

the hall and feeling empty. It wasn't until Mrs. Carpenter came bustling toward me, speaking as if she and I had been holding a conversation, that I snapped out of it.

"School starts at seven forty, so I recommend you get to bed as soon as possible," she said, pressing a soft, fresh-smelling bundle into my hands. I stared at it. "It's an extra blanket. In case you get cold. The cot's not all that warm," she explained. "You act like you've never seen a quilt before.

"My room is upstairs. If you need anything, just holler. I'll hear you." She stared at me for a minute. " 'Night," she finally said.

I shut my bedroom door behind her and undressed. From the top drawer, I got my nightshirt—an old oversized Michelin Tires T-shirt that used to belong to Jenny Sue's husband. I slipped it over my head and padded across the hall to the bathroom.

I washed my face and brushed my teeth with lukewarm water, used the toilet, and then stared in the mirror. Without makeup covering it, I could still see the faintest shadow of gray beneath my left eye—the last evidence of the fight with the prostitute. I looked older than seventeen. When did I begin to look so old? So tired? So hopeless?

I flipped off the light, crossed the hall, and eased onto the rickety cot.

2

I jumped awake. Years of living with strangers will do that.

I think I terrified Mrs. Carpenter as much as she terrified me. She cowered in my doorway, staring at me with wide eyes.

"We had better get you an alarm clock," she said shakily. "You nearly stopped my heart. Did you sleep well, child?"

"Yes, ma'am."

"You know, you are allowed to speak in my home. I appreciate the respect, but I wish you'd talk a bit."

"Yes, ma'am," I replied out of habit. I bit my tongue.

"Well. We need to leave for school in twenty minutes, so you'd better get ready. And dress warm. The wind's still blowing." Mrs. Carpenter turned and strode away with her hands on her hips.

Twenty minutes to get ready for my first day at a new school? I ran to the bathroom and took a shampooless, soapless shower. I brushed through my sopping hair, dabbed concealer on my black eye, and put a layer of black mascara on my pale lashes. In my room I put on a pair of jeans and a black T-shirt, pulled on socks with holes over both my big toes, then slipped my feet into Jenny Sue's old running sneakers, which were a size too big. I got my jacket out of the closet and pushed my arms into the thin sleeves. There were three minutes to spare.

Mrs. Carpenter stood waiting in the kitchen. "Here you go, Maggie Mae," she said, holding out a plate with two slices of bacon and two fried eggs shimmering with grease. I took the plate and sat at the table.

"Have you been raised with any particular religion?" she asked, sitting across from me.

"Yes. I've been preached to by everyone from Baptists to Catholics to Buddhists. When I was five, I lived with the Sharpwhites. They were Wiccan, or astrologists, or something." I could hardly remember a thing about their religion, except on clear nights we would dance under the stars. Mrs. Sharpwhite always told me that when my stars lined up, my life would be in harmony. I'm still waiting for my stars to line up.

"Well, in this house I like to say grace at every meal. Do you mind?" Mrs. Carpenter asked.

I closed my eyes, clasped my hands, and bowed my head.

"Dear Lord, thank you for this glorious morning. And thank you for blessing me with the chance to foster this child. But please, Lord, let her keep her clothes on while she's in my care. Because if she doesn't, I might be tempted to spank her bare butt. And bless this food we are about to partake of. Amen."

I unclasped my hands and stared at Mrs. Carpenter. She winked and grinned.

I ate like I was going to die—I *was* starting a new school. At least no one at my new school knew my past.

"We need to go," Mrs. Carpenter said as I stuck the last bite of egg into my mouth. She grabbed her keys from a holder by the front door. I grabbed my empty duffle bag and followed her outside.

She was right about the wind. It tugged at my clothes and whipped my wet hair into my face. I hugged the jacket to my body and shivered. And that is when the quiet morning filled with snarling and baying.

"There must be a fox in the barn." Mrs. Carpenter gasped, running toward a dark building on the far edge of the gravel driveway. She threw the door wide and the barking grew louder. Two shadows streaked out of the dark building and ran straight at me. A solid mass hit my chest and I was thrown to the ground. Muzzles snarled and snapped at my face, their breath hot on my cheeks.

I threw my arms over my head and rolled onto my side. The barking turned to whining and two slick, hot tongues began covering every inch of my exposed skin with slobber.

"Shash! Duke! Get off of her before I tan your hide!" Mrs. Carpenter demanded. She dragged the dogs from me, but I was too shaky to get up.

"Maggie Mae, I apologize!" Mrs. Carpenter said. "I don't know what's gotten into my dogs. They usually only bark like that around a wild animal. I thought they were going to eat you for breakfast, but it seems they like you well enough now." One of the dogs, hardly more than a fluffy black-and-white shadow in the gloomy morning, slunk over and licked my face from my jaw up to my hairline.

"Shash, get back here!" Mrs. Carpenter ordered. The dog took a second long lick of my face, then turned and sat at Mrs. Carpenter's feet, beside a long-eared, copper-colored dog. Finally able to move, I wiped the slobber from my cheek and pushed myself to a sitting position.

"My second husband was part Navajo. He taught Native American culture at the university, specializing in Navajo religion.

He always said animals can sense a person's true nature," Mrs. Carpenter said, her shrewd eyes studying me. "If my dogs take a liking to someone, that is a sign that I should like them, too. I can see why my son sent you to me."

"Your son?" I asked, baffled.

"My son, Dr. John Petersen, child psychiatrist and social worker. Your counselor. He called me up at the crack of dawn yesterday morning and asked if I'd take in someone special. Said he didn't trust anyone else with this particular girl and wanted to give her a chance to graduate from high school and get her feet under her so that she might make something of herself."

"Mr. Petersen is your son? But you have different last names."

"That's because John's father died when John was a teenager. Years later I married 'Bob' Bidziil Carpenter. He died, too, a few years back," Mrs. Carpenter explained. "Anyhow, Maggie Mae, let me lock the dogs back in the barn and we'll go."

I nodded because I couldn't talk. Mr. Petersen had handed me over to his own mother in spite of all my flaws? I felt a funny ache behind my eyes.

After the dogs were locked up, we got into a baby-blue Ford pickup truck that looked older than me. Mrs. Carpenter leaned toward me and plucked something from my hair. "A stick," she said, showing me a twig with a strand of black still attached.

"So, tell me, Maggie Mae—what happened to your mother and father?"

My hand froze on the seat belt and I looked at her. "I don't know. They died before I can remember."

"What about your grandparents?"

I hooked my seat belt. "They're dead, too. Child services

couldn't trace a single person who I was related to. That's how I ended up in foster care."

Mrs. Carpenter studied me for a long moment before starting the truck engine.

"John told me that you didn't enter the program until you were five years old. Who did you live with until then?" We bounced down the long gravel drive.

A child's face flashed before my eyes—brown hair, blue eyes, bright red freckles on her full cheeks—the face of Lucy Reynolds, my cousin. But Lucy didn't have freckles.

"I lived with my aunt and cousin." My voice was barely audible above the truck engine.

"What happened to them?"

"They . . . died."

"Well, Maggie Mae, you and I are alike. Seems that those closest to us die. I lost two husbands; you lost your parents, your cousin, and your aunt. We're two peas in a pod."

∽ 3 ∽

"Now, the kids in this town are different from city kids. They have been raised right, for the most part."

Mrs. Carpenter pulled into the Silver High School parking lot and bounced into a parking space. She shut off the truck engine, left the keys hanging in the ignition, and got out. I pressed my back against the seat and closed my eyes.

"Well? Aren't you coming, Maggie Mae?" she asked after a long moment. I opened my eyes. She was staring at me from her open door.

I thrust my chin forward, took a deep breath, and opened my door.

Every single person in that parking lot—student, parent, and teacher alike—stopped what they were doing and stared. I tried not to make contact with any of those eyes, but somehow my eyes locked on his. I couldn't help it. He was staring right at me and his eyes were as dark as his inky black hair. By his suddenly raised eyebrows, he was very aware that I was gawking at him. He blinked and walked past.

"Bridger O'Connell, wait!" Mrs. Carpenter called out. My heart seemed to freeze as he stopped and faced her.

"Yes, Mrs. C.?" he asked, glancing at me from the corner of his eye.

"Would you mind showing Maggie Mae around the school while I get her registered?" Mrs. Carpenter nodded toward me.

Bridger glanced from Mrs. Carpenter to me, eyeing me from my stringy wet hair to my shoes, and hesitated.

He wore all the right things—name-brand jeans that fit him like they'd been tailored to his tall body, a tan leather jacket over a button-up shirt—even his backpack looked brand-new. I looked down, hating the fact that my jeans were too long and bunched up over Jenny Sue's old running shoes, hating the rips over both my knees, hating the black T-shirt that was faded to more of a reddish gray, hating the duffle bag I used in place of a backpack. I wouldn't want to be seen with me, either.

"I don't need any help, Mrs. Carpenter. I can show myself around," I said, not taking my eyes from Bridger's.

"I don't mind," Bridger said halfheartedly, running a hand through his hair.

"I don't want to be seen with you. It might tarnish my image," I replied, tucking my hair behind my ears. It was easier to go to school when everyone thought you were a loner because you chose to be, not because you were dirt poor and dressed all wrong. "I'll meet you in the office, Mrs. Carpenter," I said, glancing at her astonished face before pushing past Bridger O'Connell. He smelled amazing.

For a small town, the school was big, with white tile walls that made it feel antiseptic. I'd been in enough new schools that finding my way around another was second nature. The students stared as I wandered by. Their conversations stopped—until I walked past. And then the halls filled with voices.

After a quick self-guided tour, I made my way to the front office and found Mrs. Carpenter talking to a short, plump woman sitting behind the front desk. The plaque on the desk read SHAUNA WINSLOW. She held a piece of paper out to me.

"Your new schedule," she said. "Your transcripts arrived this morning and I took the liberty of basing your new classes off the old. Welcome to Silver High."

"Thanks." I took the paper and scanned my new schedule. Chemistry, then Algebra II, and then twelfth-grade English followed by lunch and a free period. After that I had Animal Medicine, Health and Wellness, and Agricultural Studies. Animal Medicine sounded interesting, but everything else was just day-filler till I could get my diploma and be done with school forever.

"I'll show myself to my first class," I said, looking at Mrs. Carpenter.

"All right, Maggie Mae. I had Shauna write your bus number right here." She touched the top corner of the schedule. "It'll drop you off about a quarter mile from my house."

" 'Kay," I replied.

"She's sure an independent thing," Shauna Winslow said as I walked out the door.

I wandered down the deserted hall, scanning the closed doors for room 3. When I found it, I put my hand on the icy knob, took a deep breath, and turned.

The smell of rotten eggs and perfume greeted me—lab day.

I scanned the room as I closed the door behind me. Everyone was neatly paired at individual lab tables, doing an experiment with sulfuric acid or some other fragrant chemical.

"May I help you?" the man at the front of the room asked.

"I'm Maggie Mae Mortensen. I'm new to this school and was assigned your class," I explained. My mouth went dry as every pair of eyes in the class shifted to me.

"There must be some mistake," the teacher said, shaking his glossy bald head. "Only the brightest students who took my biology class last year are eligible for my advanced chemistry class. And besides, you won't have a lab partner."

I cleared my throat. "Well, I just got a schedule from Shauna and it says I'm in this class."

The teacher strode over to me, yanking the schedule from my fingers without a word. He scanned the schedule and frowned. I focused on his tacky brown tie. "Well. Have you taken chemistry before?"

"Yes, junior year."

"That solves it. You don't need to take it again. I'll go to Principal Smith's office and get you switched to a more . . . appropriate class."

He squeezed past me and out the door. I stood, silent and miserable, and returned the stares of the students.

What felt like a year later, the teacher came back and handed me my schedule.

"All fixed," he said smugly. Where my chemistry class had been listed was a black line. Written above it in permanent marker were the words "Track and Field—Gym." I guess I'd just joined the track team.

"Where's the gym?" I asked.

"I'll show her, Mr. Guymon!" a female voice piped out. A short, dark-haired girl hurried out of her seat.

"Thank you, Bonnie," Mr. Guymon said. I could see the relief wash over him as I turned to leave.

"I'm Bonnie Schuler," Bonnie said, holding her hand out to me as we walked. I placed my hand in hers and shook.

"Maggie Mae," I replied.

"So, where did you move here from?" she asked, voice as sweet as honey.

"Albuquerque."

She gasped and grabbed one of my hands in both of hers. "You're from the city?"

"Yeah."

"Oh, I love the city. My family goes there every fall for back-to-school shopping. I got this shirt there."

I looked at her Abercrombie T-shirt and nodded as if impressed.

"Did you know Albuquerque is the thirty-fourth largest city in the country?"

"No. Didn't know that."

"Oh my gosh! And you lived there? How could you not know?"

I shrugged.

"Well, anyway, here we are. The gym. So, do you like running?"

Do I like running? Not particularly, I thought, recalling the grueling days in ninth-grade gym class where the teacher made us run three miles. "Sure," I answered.

Bonnie started laughing. "I can totally tell you're from the city."

"You can?"

"Yeah. You're so aloof. And your freaky black hair. You totally look Goth."

I nodded. "Well, thanks for showing me the way, Bonnie," I said as I pushed the gym door open.

"Sure. And Maggie Mae—" I turned to look at her. "Sit with me at lunch if you want," she said as she hurried down the hall.

I walked into the silent gym and stared at the hall of fame jerseys tacked to the wall.

"Where are you supposed to be?"

I whirled around.

"I said, where are you supposed to be, young lady?"

A barrel-chested man in his midthirties stared me down from a door leading into what I assumed was the locker room.

"Hi. I'm new. I have Track and Field first period," I explained, walking over to him and waving my schedule.

He eyed me and frowned. "Did you bring your gym clothes?"

I didn't own gym clothes. "No, sir."

"Well, at least you wore tennis shoes," he said and motioned me to follow him.

We walked down a hallway and through a door that led outside to a football field surrounded by a track. In spite of the sun being up, a thin fog clung to the field.

"I'm Mr. Fergusson. The students call me Coach. We're doing the fifty-yard dash today, followed by hurdles. You ever done hurdles?"

"No, sir. Never done the fifty-yard dash, either," I informed him, eyeing the barely visible hurdles set up on the far side of the misty track. My stomach started to flutter.

I turned to Coach, prepared to explain that I had most definitely been dumped into Track and Field by mistake, but as I opened my mouth to speak, he blew the whistle that hung around his neck.

A small group of students dressed in gym shorts, hoodies, and sneakers materialized out of the mist hovering around the bleachers. They began lining up at a line painted across the track.

"Maggie, put your bag down and join the other students," Coach said gruffly.

I slipped the empty duffle from my shoulder and lined up with the other students. They studied me, their eyes lingering on my jeans. I felt more out of place here than I ever had before. One pair of eyes caught and held mine. It was the boy from the parking lot—Bridger O'Connell. He nodded as if to say hello. I swallowed and looked away.

Coach hustled fifty yards down the track, put the whistle to his lips, and fiddled with a stopwatch. The whistle pealed out and the students burst into action, leaving me in their dust. I blinked, realized I was supposed to be running, too, and dug my toes into the rubbery track.

Mist clung to my face, coating it with a sheen of moisture. My feet pumped, barely touching the ground, and within two seconds I had caught up to the track team. Then I passed them. All of them. I breezed by Coach—and the finish line—and kept following the curve of the track, my feet light as feathers. A grin lit my face. Running, when bullies weren't after me, felt like flying. And I *liked* it.

As the first hurdle solidified out of the mist, I leaped and soared over it. The second hurdle was the same. I glided over, hardly impacting the ground when I landed, took a step, and leaped over the next. And the next, until I'd gone all the way around the track.

I couldn't stop grinning as I skidded to a stop a few yards from Coach and the team.

"Show-off," someone murmured. "We're doing the fifty-yard dash, not hurdles." My smile faltered.

"That was . . . impressive," Coach said, eyeing my sneakers. "Have you ever done any type of sprinting before?"

"No, sir." I panted. "Except when I'd run away from the mean girls at my old school. They couldn't catch me."

He studied me for a minute with curious brown eyes. "All right. Maggie, let's have you and Bridger go to the start line and race the fifty-yard dash again."

I looked at Bridger and caught the tail end of a scowl scurrying over his face.

"You afraid she's going to beat you twice, O'Connell?" Coach taunted.

"Not likely," Bridger said, running a hand through his glossy black hair.

As Bridger and I walked to the start line I studied his long, muscular legs. *Not likely* was right. I don't know how I beat him the first time around.

Bridger positioned his toe just at the start line, touching his fingertips on the track, and stared straight ahead. I stood with both my toes on the line, my arms hanging at my sides, and listened for the whistle. And when it blew, I took off.

I never saw Bridger, even in my peripheral view. As I approached Coach I saw the stopwatch in his hand, heard the rhythmic sound of the watch's ticking until I crossed the finish line and his thumb clicked down on it. But of course that would have been ridiculous, hearing the stopwatch, with my heart pounding in my ears.

Coach started jumping up and down and hollering, punching the hand holding the stopwatch into the air over and over again. "You set a new school record!"

"Are you serious?" I asked, completely dumbfounded. I knew I was fast, had learned to be out of necessity, but setting a new record?

"She beat the school record! She beat your dad's thirty-year-old record, Bridger!" Coach hollered. "I can't believe it!"

Bridger stood just past the finish line with his hands on his knees and his head down, breathing hard and studying me out of the corner of his eye. The rest of the team hovered around Coach and his stopwatch. A couple were smiling, but the others were frowning, looking between Bridger and me. I guess they weren't hoping I'd lead the school to victory.

We never raced hurdles that day. Instead, Coach had me individually race the fifty-yard dash with every person on the team. Twice. I beat them all.

"You're a natural," Coach said, slapping a hand on my shoulder as we walked back to the lockers. "Tomorrow, bring your gym clothes. We'll do hurdles. I promise."

I nodded, trying to catch my breath.

News of my running traveled fast. In my next two classes, the students were whispering about it before I sat down. And most of them were scowling at me, as if setting a new school record was like infecting everyone with head lice.

At lunch, I looked for Bonnie and found her looking for me. I sighed with relief. There's nothing more embarrassing than sitting alone at lunch while everyone stares at you.

"Hi!" Bonnie chimed. "Are you buying lunch or did you bring something?"

I scowled. Mrs. Carpenter and I had completely forgotten about my lunch and I didn't have a dime I could call my own. "I'm not hungry," I lied, eyeing her tray. The cafeteria was serving tacos, applesauce, Jell-O, and cookies. My stomach grumbled.

"Not hungry? After all your running this morning, you don't even want a Sprite or anything?"

"No. I'm good."

I followed her to a long row of noisy tables where the seniors sat. Bonnie sat on the second-to-last seat at a narrow rectangular table, and I filled the last. Everyone stopped talking and turned to stare at Bonnie and me.

"What?" Bonnie asked, baffled. "This is the new girl I was telling you guys about. From *Albuquerque*? I told her she could sit with us."

I studied the students. Bridger O'Connell sat at the center of the table, surrounded by the school's prettiest girls and best-dressed boys, and they were all shooting daggers in my direction. Bridger was obviously still mad that I'd beat him, and beat his dad's old track record. And, apparently, so were the students sitting with him. In fact, his dislike seemed contagious. Everyone in the cafeteria was glaring at me—not just the seniors.

As one, every single person at the senior table, except Bonnie, turned their backs to me. Bonnie, her face as red as the tomatoes on her taco, looked at me as if I might be infectious. She was faced with a choice. Be my friend and lose all her others, or ditch me and keep her reputation intact.

"Um," she mumbled, studying her lunch. She was nice. Too nice to tell me that she didn't want to be friends.

"Gee, Bonnie. You know, actually I am a little bit hungry. I think I'll go check out the vending machines. I'll see ya," I said. She looked at me, relief plain in her eyes.

"Oh. All right, Maggie Mae. Maybe I'll see you around or something."

"Yeah. Probably," I answered, forcing a smile to my face as I stood from the table and walked away. Of course she'd see me around. She just wouldn't notice me.

I found a quiet spot by the girls' bathroom and leaned against the brick wall, waiting for lunch to end. I had eaten at just such a spot at my last school.

"This spot's taken," a voice said.

I turned and stared into a pair of chocolate eyes framed by sleek black hair and olive skin.

"What?" I said.

"That's my spot." She motioned to the wall I was leaning against.

I crossed my arms and gritted my teeth. Was a spot by the girls' bathroom worth fighting over? She crossed her arms over her chest and glared.

"Wait a sec," the girl said, a smile tugging the side of her mouth. "Are you the new girl? Who kicked the entire track team's asses this morning?"

"Yeah. That's me."

She let her arms fall to her sides. "That rocks. I wish I could have seen it. I'm Yana." She looked at the brick wall and shrugged. "I suppose there's room for two."

"Yeah. That would be nice." I let my arms relax and sank down to the floor.

Yana sat beside me and pulled a plastic fork and Styrofoam box out of her camouflage-print backpack—the kind of box you get from a restaurant for leftovers. She opened the lid and took a bite of something orange and lumpy.

"Where did you get that?" I asked.

"From my grandpa's restaurant. He sent it home with me last night after my shift."

"You work at a restaurant?"

"Yeah."

"Does it pay well?"

Yana shrugged. "I mostly get paid in tips. Some nights it doesn't pay all that well, but on a good weekend night, I've come home with more than a hundred dollars."

That sounded like a fortune. I could imagine having my own money. "Are you guys hiring?"

"Why? You need a job?"

"Yeah."

Yana pulled a piece of paper from her backpack and jotted down a name and address. "Stop in and fill out an app. Ask for Naalyehe. He's the tall leathery guy with a heart of gold—and my grandpa. You can't miss him. Tell him Yana sent you."

4

The bus dropped me *half* a mile from Mrs. Carpenter's house, not a quarter mile. By the time I got home my stomach felt like it had been replaced by a black hole. I stumbled through the front door.

"Coach called this afternoon. Said to make sure you brought gym shorts tomorrow. I am guessing you don't own any?" Mrs. Carpenter asked, putting her denim jacket on.

I shook my head. "I don't, but, um . . . actually . . ."

"Spit it out, child! What's the problem?" Mrs. Carpenter asked with a grin.

"The problem is I don't have any money to buy gym shorts. I was wondering if you could take me job hunting. This girl at school told me about a restaurant that's hiring. And I could pay you back after I started working."

"A job is a brilliant idea. After you apply we'll stop by the Wal-Mart for gym shorts. I noticed you need some shampoo and toothpaste, too. But as for paying me back, that's nonsense. I get paid to foster you. That money is meant to buy you what you need." She got her keys and walked out of the house, cowboy boots echoing hollowly on the front porch. I took a wistful look toward the kitchen, set my duffle by the front door, and followed.

"Holy crap! What is that?" I asked, my feet skidding to a stop on the gravel driveway. Mrs. Carpenter came to see what I was staring at and chuckled. A palm-sized spiky reptile was baking itself on the warm gravel drive in front of me.

"I know you're from the city and all, but haven't you ever seen a horny toad?"

I tilted my head to the side and studied her. Did she really just say that? "A *what* toad?"

Mrs. Carpenter chuckled harder and the reptile scurried away. "They're horned lizards but we always called 'em horny toads," she explained. "It doesn't mean they're horny. Just covered with horns."

"Okay."

We got into Mrs. Carpenter's truck.

"So what's the name of the restaurant that's hiring?"

I took Yana's paper from my back pocket. "It's called the Navajo Mexican. The address—"

"Don't you worry about telling me the address. I can find it blindfolded," Mrs. Carpenter said with a wink.

We drove to downtown Silver City. Tall trees with new green buds on winter-bare branches lined the streets, and shops and businesses lined the sidewalks. Cars, many of them with college students behind the wheel by the look of it, were filling those streets. Western New Mexico University was close by.

Mrs. Carpenter parallel parked in one of the oldest parts of town. I peered out and frowned at a narrow two-story building sandwiched between a bank and a Navajo jewelry shop. The building had floor-to-ceiling windows on the lower level and THE NAVAJO MEXICAN was painted on the front door.

"What type of restaurant is the Navajo Mexican?" I asked.

"The best in town," Mrs. Carpenter answered. "Are you going to go in and apply on your own, or do you need me to hold your hand?"

I held my hand out and forced a pout to my face. Mrs. Carpenter's eyes grew round and I grinned. "Just kidding. I'll do it all by myself."

"Watch your step getting out. The curbs are high, built that way from horse-and-buggy times. I'm going to swing by the fabric store. I'll be back in about fifteen minutes."

"Sounds good." I opened the car door and a gust of something delicious swirled on the cool spring air. Stepping up onto the knee-high curb, I walked past three metal tables set up on the sidewalk, tables where people could sit at dusk and eat their dinner, and entered the restaurant.

It was bigger inside than I thought it would be, long and narrow, with about twenty brightly painted tables and booths. White Christmas lights, dried red chili peppers in braided ropes, and Native American weavings decorated the walls. Quiet music played, Navajo chanting accompanied by pipes.

A server burdened with two plates and a hugely pregnant belly hurried past me. "I'll be right with you," she called over her shoulder. She set the plates on a table in front of two customers, wiped her hands on the white apron tied below her bulging stomach, and came back to me. "Table for one?" she asked. She was short and dark haired, and above her heart was a name tag that read *Maria*.

"I'm here to see about getting a job," I said, turning my voice sweet and, I hoped, compelling. "I was wondering if I could fill out an application?"

The woman's shoulders sagged. "How soon could you start?" she asked.

"Um. Tomorrow?"

She smiled. "Come with me." I followed her to the other end of the restaurant and through a swinging door.

"José! Naalyehe! Come see what the cat dragged in."

Two men turned to face me. One was shorter than me, with thick black hair and a mustache that hid his top lip. The other man stood nearly as tall as the ceiling, with a gray braid that hung down to the small of his back, a strand of bear claws around his neck, and a potbelly.

The short man stepped up to me. His mustache twitched and fine wrinkles creased the dark skin around his eyes. "The cat dragged in a *gringa*?"

"She's looking for a job," Maria said.

"I am José Cano, co-owner of the Navajo Mexican." He held out his flour-dusted hand and I shook it.

"Magdalene Mae."

"Have you ever waited tables, Magdalene?" he asked, looking me up and down.

"No."

"Are you eighteen years or older?"

"I turn eighteen at the end of the month."

He scratched his head. "Do you speak any *Español*?"

"No?"

"Do you speak Navajo?"

"No, but I'm a fast learner." I tried to give him my most pitiful, pleading puppy-dog eyes. They worked on my old foster mother, Mrs. Montgomery, when I wanted to use the Internet or stay up late watching movies.

"We close late on weekend nights—eleven p.m.—and I need someone who can work every single Saturday. Plus, we get a lot of college kids and, with those eyes, I am guessing you will be harassed by some of the rowdier *gringos*. But on the other hand, you might be a big draw. . . ." He rubbed his pointer finger and thumb over his chin, studying me in a whole new light. "Unfortunately the state liquor laws prohibit a minor from serving alcohol."

I batted my eyelashes. "I'm almost eighteen. And Yana said you were hiring."

The tall man stepped up beside José, casting a shadow over me. "Yana? How do you know my granddaughter?"

"I'm new in town. She let me sit with her at lunch."

The two men looked at each other. José shrugged and Yana's grandfather smiled.

"I am Naalyehe. It is a pleasure to meet one of Yana's friends. Are you familiar with Navajo cuisine?"

I shook my head.

"What do you know about *comida mexicana*? Mexican food?" José asked.

"I love Taco Bell."

Naalyehe burst out laughing.

José's cheeks flared red. "Taco Bell is not Mexican food!" he said vehemently. "Where are you from, that you are so deprived, *gringa*? Canada?"

"Albuquerque," I answered.

"Aye aye aye," José muttered, turning around, taking a plate and filling it. "You are from New Mexico and you think Taco Bell is Mexican food." He sprinkled a handful of cheese over the loaded plate, turned back around, and held the plate and a fork out to me. I stared at it.

The plate was slathered from edge to edge with pureed beans and melting, greasy orange cheese. Beneath the beans and cheese were lumps of something, but I had no idea what, and I was almost scared to find out.

José stood with a huge, expectant grin on his face. Naalyehe took a folding metal step stool from against the wall and set it behind me. I sat down on the stool, took the fork and plate, and stabbed one of the unidentifiable, bean-covered mounds. It made a squelching noise as I lifted it from the plate. I studied the gooey blob for a moment, then closed my eyes and shoved it into my mouth. It was hot and salty and mushy. I made myself chew and my eyes flew open. "What is this?" I said through a full mouth, trying not to drool.

"That is my specialty. It is a fish taco, breaded with blue corn, fried, cut into bite-sized pieces, and smothered with beans and goat cheese. You like?" José asked, though I'm sure he already knew the answer. I was shoveling the food into my mouth as fast as I could swallow.

"It's great," I said, my mouth still full.

"What do you think?" José asked, turning to Naalyehe.

Naalyehe studied me, his eyes locking on mine. "What is the last animal you saw?"

I raised my eyebrows. "A *horny* toad? It was sunning itself on Mrs. Carpenter's driveway."

"The horned lizard. It symbolizes perseverance." His eyes narrowed. "And keeping secrets."

His eyes bored into mine. I blinked and studied my short nails.

"Keeping secrets isn't a bad thing. It means you can be trusted," he said.

Hope made my blood speed through my veins and I looked up.

José grinned. "Welcome to *la familia, gringa*. As soon as you turn eighteen, I'll put you on the schedule."

"So I got the job?"

José and Naalyehe nodded.

I stood in the bathroom that night, brushing my teeth with Crest and looking in the mirror. I still looked old, but not as old as I'd looked the night before. My black-dyed hair was fading to a dull greenish brown, the roots almost copper against the dye. But my hair was clean, since Mrs. Carpenter had bought me some Suave shampoo and conditioner.

I looked at my new watch—a seven-dollar designer knockoff from Wal-Mart—and set the alarm for a quarter after six. Mrs. Carpenter was convinced that I'd sleep through the alarm. I wouldn't.

My new sweatpants, gym shorts, tube socks, and sports bra were packed in a new gray backpack. Laid out on my bed was a brand-new outfit: jeans without holes, a long-sleeve red sweater, and a heavy gray jacket—a "welcome to Silver City" gift from Mrs. Carpenter. I was almost excited to go to school. And honestly, I couldn't wait to kick some butt in track.

As I climbed into bed and snuggled beneath the two home-made quilts, I smiled. Things didn't seem so bad. I had a job. I liked Mrs. Carpenter. And she liked me.

∽ 5 ∽

"Maggie Mae, you look beautiful!" Mrs. Carpenter said as I walked into the living room the next morning. "Red suits you. Makes your black hair look thick and glossy."

"Thanks," I answered, grinning. I put on my new jacket and grabbed my backpack. Mrs. Carpenter handed me a brown paper bag.

"Your lunch," she said. "I apologize again for forgetting to send you with something to eat yesterday. I hope you like peanut butter."

"Sounds good." Peanut butter was definitely not my favorite, but beggars can't be choosers.

I walked the half mile down the lonely country road to the bus stop and groaned. I was the oldest student there. Probably the only senior who had to ride the bus to school. The students filed onto the waiting bus. I followed and sat in an empty seat.

Nervous jitters zipped around in my stomach as the bus approached Silver High. I kept telling myself that since I looked nice and my hair was clean and dry, today would be better than yesterday.

I made my way through the busy halls more or less unnoticed, arriving at the locker room as the tardy bell rang. The other girls on the track team stopped talking the minute I entered, eyeing me warily. They dressed in silence and hurried out before I had my jeans off.

"Good morning, Miss Mortensen," Coach called as I strode out onto the track. "Why don't you go and warm up with the other kids."

I nodded and headed toward the bleachers, studying my track mates as I approached. And then I copied.

Heel resting on the bleacher, I leaned over my shin and placed my hands to either side of my shoe. With my eyes closed, I breathed out and deepened the stretch. I'd never made a point to stretch before and was shocked at how good it felt, almost as relaxing as stepping into a hot bath. The image of a cat stretching its long, flexible body jumped into my head. My eyes popped open and I backed a step away from the bleachers.

"Did you pull a muscle?"

I spun around. Bridger stood behind me, morning sun gleaming off his black hair. He smiled. I stared at him and tried to think of something intelligent to say. A whistle blew, saving me from my momentary inability to speak.

"All girls line up for hurdles," Coach called.

I stepped past Bridger and trotted over to the start line with the other girls. Three of us were seniors, the fourth a junior. Esponita was a short, muscular Hispanic girl; Danni Williams was dark haired, tall and lanky, with legs as long as a horse's; and the third girl, short and wiry-thin like she didn't eat enough, was Ginger, a junior from my math class.

The whistle screeched and I was off. The three other girls

were left in my dust, but as I reached the hurdles, the noise of feet slapping the ground and heavy breathing was creeping up behind me. I glanced to my left. Danni leaped over a hurdle right beside me. It was her long legs—they gave her a huge advantage. I looked forward again and focused, pushing myself to go faster, run harder, jump quicker.

My muscles responded. I began to pull ahead of Danni, gliding over each hurdle. But then something happened. I could see everything perfectly, down to the tiniest detail, as if looking at the world through a microscope—each blade of grass, the splintering white paint on the hurdles, a grain of sand on the track, an ant carrying a crumb on an anthill across the field. Then my ears changed. I could hear the ticking of Coach's stopwatch—from the other side of the track. The sound of Danni's pounding heart almost matched my own. In fact, I could hear the heartbeats of everyone on the field, mixing and meshing into one noisy throb.

Then my nails began to grow, pricking sharp against my palms. I panicked. Midleap over a hurdle I froze and my toe collided with wood. I tipped forward and soared through the air before crashing to a painful, bloody stop.

Instantly, my claws shrank back into short, blunt nails, my ears heard nothing but my own heart, and my eyes were squeezed shut against pain. Fear was holding me on the ground. This sort of thing had never happened to me during the daytime, and if anyone saw . . .

My eyes flew open and stared straight into a pair of hazel eyes, brownish with a circle of green around the pupil.

"Are you hurt?" Ginger asked. She touched my chin and I gasped. Her fingers felt like acid.

"You have road rash on your chin," she explained, showing me the glimmer of blood on her fingertips.

"Maggie Mae! Are you hurt?" Coach yelled as he ran across the football field. I rolled onto my side and started to push myself up, but groaned and fell back to the track. My palms looked more like raw hamburger than human flesh.

Coach knelt at my side, forcing me to my back as he looked me over, paying special attention to my ankles, rolling each in his hands and asking if it hurt.

"I'm just scraped up," I said shakily, noting the hole in my new track pants and the bloody knee beneath.

"Good. Scratches won't slow you down. But these ankles are a secret weapon. I'm glad they survived the fall unscathed. O'Connell," Coach barked.

I looked at Bridger in time to see the smile slip from his face.

"Yes, sir?"

"Help Maggie to the nurse's office."

Bridger rolled his eyes, but came over and helped me to my feet, pulling me up by my wrists.

He strode across the field. I followed a shaky pace behind, and he neither looked at me nor said a single word until we entered the school. Inside, he slowed his pace and eyed my chin.

"So, why'd you freak out like that?" he asked.

"What are you talking about?"

"Right before you tripped on the hurdle, you freaked."

I ran my finger over four tiny punctures in my palm and was glad the skin around them had been shredded, masking them. "I didn't freak," I lied. "Just didn't jump high enough."

"Does your face hurt?"

He reached toward my chin and I pulled away before he could touch it. "I've had worse."

"Like that scar in your eyebrow," he mused, studying my face.

"Yep. That hurt." The scar, a crescent through my left eyebrow, had come from the big, fat class ring on Mr. Simms's pinky finger. It had split open my skin when he'd backhanded me across the face—I was twelve years old.

"Well, we're here," Bridger said, holding the door to the nurse's office open. I stepped past him and breathed in his cologne. "Maggie." I paused and looked at him, thinking how unfair it was that some people were born as gorgeous as Bridger O'Connell. He grinned. "If you need a ride home, I could . . ." His voice trailed off. I stared at him for a long moment but he left his offer incomplete.

"I don't want to ruin my reputation," I finally replied, wondering if I'd heard him right. Had he just offered me a ride home? Maybe, unlike his friends, he had a conscience.

By the time I got out of the nurse's office and changed into my new outfit, Algebra II was more than halfway over. No big deal since I was repeating the class. I sat through the end of a lecture and pretended to listen.

Instead of hearing the teacher's voice, though, I kept reliving the incident on the track—not the fall, but what led to it. Even though the damage to my hands should have hidden them, I could see the four pinprick scabs, where my nails had punctured the skin when they turned into . . .

"Ms. Mortensen," someone said and I snapped back to the

present. Mrs. Tolliver was staring at me from the front of the classroom with that annoyed look teachers get when they realize they're being ignored. An unanswered problem was written on the dry-erase board. I did the problem in my head and spit out the answer.

Mrs. Tolliver's satisfied eyes sought out her next victim.

I sat through the rest of the morning as an anonymous presence. No one acknowledged me in any way—not even the teachers—as if I didn't exist. It was a lonely feeling, almost worse than being outright picked on.

At lunch, I ate my peanut butter sandwich with my back pressed against the brick wall by the girls' bathroom, staring at a prom announcement taped to the opposite wall.

"So, are you going?" Yana sat down beside me and opened a can of Coke.

I shook my head.

"I'm not going, either. Every school dance I've ever been to ended in disaster. And I have to work."

"I've never been to a school dance. I got invited to homecoming last September, though."

"What happened?" Yana asked.

"He never showed up," I lied.

The date had lasted five minutes because the instant I got into his car, he tried to tear my dress off. I slapped him and jumped out of his car. We never even made it out of the driveway. And then I had to do chores to pay to get the stupid dress fixed because I'd rented it.

Yana laughed. "Wow. That's brutal."

"I know."

She studied my face, her eyes lingering on my scraped chin.

"If you put piñon sap and calendula on your chin, it will heal better."

"If I put what on it?"

"Piñon sap and calendula. Navajo herbs. Naalyehe mixes them into a salve and sells it. I'll bring you some tomorrow."

"Thanks." I smiled. Yana hardly knew me. Was she a friend? Did I dare have friends? I wondered. I'd never stayed in one place long enough to have friends.

The bell rang and we went our separate ways.

My three afternoon classes were just like the morning. Aside from Yana, no one in the school talked to me; no one said hi. And only one other person noticed I existed at all. Every time I passed him in the hall, Bridger stopped talking to his friends and stared as I walked by, making me antsy in my own skin.

It lasted the whole week. By Friday I felt like a ghost in a school filled with the living, like I had learned to disappear completely unless Bridger or Yana was around. Even though I was dressed like the other students, I was still different.

6

Saturday afternoon, six days since I'd moved to Silver City, Mrs. Carpenter had me out in her future vegetable garden, hard at work tilling the dry earth, with her dogs keeping me company. A cool breeze blew, forming a halo of gold pollen around the ponderosa pines, and milky clouds hid the sky. Even with the breeze, sweat glistened on my skin, making my threadbare T-shirt cling to my back.

The rumble of an engine broke the afternoon silence. Shash and Duke's ears perked up. I looked toward the driveway, expecting to see Ollie's sedan. Instead a shiny black SUV with extra-high ground clearance bounded up to the house and stopped a few feet in front of the porch. The engine cut off.

I sank the tip of the shovel into the loose dirt and stared at the vehicle. When he stepped from the SUV, my stomach dropped into my hips. Shash and Duke went ballistic. I grabbed both dogs' collars and started dragging them toward the barn before they had the chance to attack.

Footsteps thudded on the ground behind me.

"Maggie Mae."

I stopped and peered over my shoulder. The dogs growled and struggled against me, nearly yanking me off my feet to get at Bridger O'Connell. He held his hand out and stared at the dogs. *"Beh-gha,"* he said, his voice deep and quiet. Shash and Duke whimpered and sat. "Um . . . hi," Bridger said, thrusting his hands into the pockets of his fashionably worn jeans and looking at me. Duke's tail thumped on the dirt.

"What did you say to them?" I asked, looking between Bridger and the calm dogs.

"I told them that was enough. And they listened."

"Enough? In what language?"

Bridger smiled. "Navajo." He scanned the dirt I'd been working. "You're tilling a garden?"

I nodded.

"Want some help?"

I looked at his leather shoes, his expensive jeans, and short-sleeve button-up shirt. Without a word he turned from me and unbuttoned his shirt, revealing a white V-neck T-shirt beneath. Just above the neckline of his shirt, a necklace hung on a leather strap against his golden chest—a glossy black claw of some sort, mounted in silver, with a turquoise stone embedded in it.

Bridger tossed his button-up shirt onto the hood of his SUV, walked to my upright shovel, and dug it into the ground, flipping the dirt over on itself. Leave it to Bridger O'Connell to make me feel underdressed to do gardening—even if he was wearing a plain T-shirt.

Shash broke away from me and wagged his way over to Bridger. Bridger grinned and scratched the dog's ears, then dug the shovel back into the hard earth. I watched him work for a full minute, absolutely shocked that he was seriously going to help me dig, before going to the shed on the side of Mrs. Carpenter's house for a second shovel.

We tilled the garden side by side, the dogs our silent companions. I stole glances at Bridger when he wasn't looking, watching the way his broad shoulders moved and his biceps flexed as he lifted and turned shovels full of dirt.

More than once, I caught him staring at me, too.

With Bridger's help it didn't take long to till the entire garden. When the last scoop of dirt was turned, Bridger and I leaned on our shovels and stared at each other. When neither of us said a word, Bridger took the shovel from my hands and carried it to the shed. I dragged the dogs to the barn and locked them in.

We met back at the edge of the tilled earth and Bridger wiped a hand over his brow. I stared at him for a long, awkward moment, wondering why he was here.

"That was hard work. I'm thirsty," he said.

Yeah, I could take a hint. "You want something to drink?"

"That would be nice."

I nodded and walked to the house. On the front porch, Bridger and I removed our dusty shoes.

"Do you want juice or . . . ," I asked as I stepped into the house. I stopped walking and turned. Bridger stood framed in the doorway, watching me. "Do you want a drink or not?"

"You didn't invite me in," he said, folding his arms over his chest.

"Come in," I said.

"Thanks. Can I get a glass of water?"

I filled two glasses with ice and tap water and sat down at

the dining room table. Bridger sat in the chair beside me and our knees bumped.

"So, why are you here? Do you need to see Mrs. Carpenter? Or do you typically drive around on Saturday looking for gardens to till with girls you hardly know?"

"I wanted to talk to you, Maggie Mae, so I called your house. Mrs. Carpenter answered and said if I had something to say to you, I could come over and say it while I helped you till the garden." A slow smile spread over his face. I couldn't help but smile back.

"So, what do you want?" I asked with a laugh.

"A rematch. Fifty-yard dash."

I stopped laughing. "If I win, are you going to turn the entire school against me as payback? Oh, wait. You already *did* that."

He leaned closer and I stared into his dark eyes. "I might have been mad that you beat me, but *I* didn't turn the school against you. Danni Williams did. You're a faster runner and she can't stand it," he said. He moved a strand of hair from my cheek and tucked it behind my ear. I prayed he couldn't see the pulse pounding out of control beneath my neck.

He grinned and leaned back in his chair. "So?" he asked quietly.

"If I beat you again, will you tell the school?"

"If you win, I'll do better than that. I'll take you to prom to prove to the entire student body that there are no hard feelings between us."

"And if *you* win?"

"I'll have my dignity back."

I rolled my eyes. Like I could take away his dignity. He was overflowing with dignity.

"So?" he asked.

"I can't go to prom. I don't own a dress."

He leaned toward me. "Wait, did I hear you right? We're talking prom dresses. So you'll race me?"

I studied his midnight eyes. He knew as well as I did that I'd beat him. The real question was: if I owned a dress, would I go with him? Yeah—in a heartbeat. Any girl in her right mind would. He was smart, athletic, and totally hot. "Sure," I said before I realized the word was out of my mouth. I couldn't help it. He was the first decent guy that had ever asked me out, even if the date depended on me beating him in a race.

Bridger opened his mouth to speak, but the doorbell chimed.

Floorboards groaned overhead.

"I'll get it, Mrs. Carpenter," I called toward the stairs. She'd gone to her quilting circle the night before and been out until midnight, so had gone upstairs with the excuse of an afternoon nap. And besides, it was for me. Ollie was right on time.

I glanced at Bridger as I stood. "You should probably go."

Bridger downed his water and followed me to the front door.

Ollie stood on the threshold, my file tucked under his arm. Without a word, he turned and spat a glob of black tobacco into the bushes.

"Hello, Magdalene Mae." He pushed past me and into the house. "Why, hello, Bridger!" A chill raced up my spine. "What in the wide world are you doing *here* of all places?"

"Hanging out with Maggie Mae," Bridger replied as if he thought it was pretty obvious.

"Oh. I see," Ollie said. "Tell me, how's your dad doing?"

"He's fine. He and my mom and sister moved to France in January," Bridger replied.

"They left you here alone?"

"They moved the day I turned eighteen," Bridger said with a shrug. "But they're probably coming home to see me graduate. What are *you* doing here?"

I tried not to cringe as I waited for Ollie's response.

"I've come to visit with Ms. Mortensen, too," Ollie explained, holding my file up. My shoulders slumped.

"You mean Maggie Mae? But I thought you were a social worker. That you dealt with foster chil . . ." Bridger's voice trailed off as his eyes met mine. "Oh."

"Ms. Mortensen's been in the fostering program since she was five," Ollie said.

I wanted to punch Ollie. Wasn't my life, contained in the file under his arm, supposed to be private?

"Oh," Bridger said again, studying me as if we had just met. "I'll see you later, Maggie Mae." He shook Ollie's hand before practically running from the house. Seeing Bridger's hand clasped in the hand of my new social worker made me physically ill. They knew each other. And Ollie knew details about my past, about the indecent exposure. What if he let something slip? What if Bridger learned the truth about me?

"Seems you moved away from Albuquerque just in time," Ollie said, pulling me from my thoughts. He spread my paperwork on the dining table. "A pack of wild dogs has been attacking bums and killing pets in your old neighborhood. The authorities have never seen anything like it." He shivered and pulled an envelope from his breast pocket. "This is for you."

I took the envelope. It was from Jenny Sue and had been

mailed to Mr. Petersen's office. I tucked the letter into my back pocket.

Ollie removed his glasses and cleaned them with his white button-up shirt before scanning my paperwork. He asked basic questions about how Mrs. Carpenter was treating me, how I liked school, if I was fitting in with the students.

When we finished, he asked to see Mrs. Carpenter. I ran upstairs and tapped on her door. "Ollie's here," I called through the wood, and ran back downstairs.

After a long moment, she came ambling downstairs.

"Why are you pulling an old woman from her bed, Oliver? I was trying to take a nap," Mrs. Carpenter grumbled, squinting at him from bleary eyes.

"I need to interview you about Maggie Mae," he said.

"Well, she's the best kid I've ever met. I wish John had been half as good as her! And I already told him that. He called this morning just to see how she's doing," Mrs. Carpenter retorted, turning back toward the stairs.

Ollie and I stared at each other for a long, awkward moment after she'd gone. He cleared his throat, took off his glasses, and began cleaning them on his shirt again.

"Well, Miss Mortensen, you turn eighteen in a week and graduate in a month. Are you making the necessary arrangements to live on your own?"

"I applied for a job. I mean, I *have* a job."

"Good. Well, I'll let Mr. Petersen know that things are acceptable here. And don't worry about seeing me to the door. I'll show myself out. Take care of yourself."

As I walked to my bedroom, I heard the front door close. I pulled Jenny Sue's letter from my pocket and tore it open.

Dear Maggie Mae,

I hope life is going good. Mr. Petersen told me he found a real good home for you. Paul and I miss you and hope that you get the help that you need. You're a real sweetheart.

The reason I'm writing this letter is because some guy has been by the house looking for you, but he won't say why he wants you. He came the very day you were taken from my custody, and he has been coming almost every day since, even though I told him that you don't live here no more. He's been hanging around the house and neighborhood a lot, too, usually in a real fancy car. He gives me the heebie-jeebies. I am worried that he'll follow you to your new house. That's why I mailed this to your counselor. So please be real careful.

—Jenny Sue

I read the letter five times. Who'd be looking for me? And in a nice car? Some pervert who saw me naked and wanted to see more? I got a pen and piece of paper from my backpack and wrote a quick note.

Jenny Sue,

Stop worrying. I'm good. I live with a sweet older woman in the southern part of the state. I got a job at a restaurant called the Navajo Mexican. Totally weird name, I know, but the food rocks.

Thanks for warning me about Mr. Creepy. I'll keep an eye out, but don't worry. I can take care of myself.

—MM

I stuck the letter in an envelope and wrote her address on it, but hesitated. Just to be safe, I left the return address blank.

I got a stamp from Mrs. Carpenter's desk and walked the letter out to the mailbox.

7

On Monday morning, when the bus pulled into the school parking lot, the energy level in the air doubled. The sophomore and freshmen girls started jabbering and pressing their noses against the windows facing the school.

The words "totally hot," "prom," and "staring right at this bus" carried over the low rumble of the engine.

I stayed in my seat as the freshmen and sophomores filed out. When the bus was empty, I stood and choked my way through the fog of diesel exhaust that had filled the bus. As I stepped into the cold morning air, I knew what had gotten the girls so excited. Bridger O'Connell stood leaning against the school, staring at the bus. He looked picture-perfect wearing expensive jeans and a tan leather jacket, with the wind tousling his black hair. But there was something more about him. He seemed different than other guys—always still, always aware of everything around him.

He waved. I looked over my shoulder to see who he was waving at, but the only thing behind me was the bus.

"I'm waving at you, Maggie," he called, striding toward me. Though it was nearing the end of April, the morning still held a hint of winter. Then Bridger smiled and the air seemed to warm ten degrees. He fell into step beside me.

"How do you know Ollie?" I asked as we walked.

"Ollie Williams? He's Mike and Danni Williams's uncle. You know—Danni who runs hurdles, with legs like a moose. Ollie comes to our track meets every now and then," he explained.

A wave of panic made it hard to breathe. What if Ollie mentioned my past to Danni, his niece? Danni, who already hated me without knowing my past? Or her brother, Mike?

A hand clasped mine and pulled me to a gentle stop. Panic was replaced with warmth.

"Maggie? Are you okay?" Bridger asked.

"I'm fine," I said, my voice disbelieving. I looked at our clasped hands, marveling how something so simple could send a wave of warmth through my body. "So, why were you waiting for me?" I eased my hand from his.

"You think I was waiting for you?"

I smiled. "Weren't you? It was pretty obvious, Bridger." He returned my smile and took my hand again, pulling me past the stairs leading to the front entrance to the school.

"It's time to race," he said.

"Right now?" I looked down at his feet. He wore running shoes.

"Yeah. Prom's in five days. I figure *if* you win, you'll need time to shop for a dress."

Something clicked in my head. Five days . . . Monday, Tuesday, Wednesday, Thursday, Friday, Saturday. Saturday night. I thought of the moon, a waxing gibbous, and my heart started pounding. The full moon was five days away. My birthday was on the eve of the full moon.

I stopped walking and yanked my hand from Bridger's.

"Maggie?"

"What?" I snapped. Speechless, I stared at him. I couldn't go to prom. It was absolutely, ridiculously impossible. Saturday night was a bad night for me. Really, really bad. I wiped my damp palms on my jeans and shook my head. "I can't go to prom."

Bridger lifted an eyebrow and studied me. "You haven't won yet."

We walked to the rear of the school in silence. The track was empty. Bridger and I took our backpacks off and set them on the bleachers and then moved to the fifty-yard dash start line.

We lined up side by side, each of us in a pre-sprint lunge, and stared at each other. His face was so close I could see his pupil surrounded by the coal-dark iris.

"You ready?" he asked, studying my eyes just like I was studying his.

I nodded and looked forward.

"Just so you know, I've been practicing. On your mark, get set . . . go!" he yelled. I dug my toes into the track and felt my muscles respond. Wind rushed through my loose hair, my pulse sped up, and my feet hardly touched the ground. I knew he couldn't beat me.

Until I caught a flash of movement out of the corner of my eye and almost tripped. Bridger was keeping up with me. I focused straight ahead and pushed myself. So did Bridger. The finish line sped into view and we both crossed it and continued on, sprinting around the bend in the track before our legs were able to slow.

I gasped the dry morning air and looked at Bridger.

"You beat me." He panted.

I shook my head. "It was a tie."

"Nope, you were one pace ahead. You won. And I'm okay with that. You're the first girl I don't mind losing to," he said with a gleam of satisfaction in his eye. "I'm man enough to admit when someone's better than me at something, which rarely happens. So it looks like we're going to prom."

"No, thanks. You don't have to feel obligated to take me," I said, thinking of the full moon. No way I could go!

"Maggie?" I looked at him. "I want to take you. I knew all along you'd win."

"Whatever! You are so full of crap!"

"Okay, maybe I thought I stood a chance at beating you. But even if I won, I was still going to ask you. And you already agreed to go. So what time should I pick you up?"

My mind came alive with options. Maybe I could go to the dance and be back before ten. Maybe I was wrong about the moon. Maybe I was freaking insane and nothing bad was going to happen on Saturday night.

But maybe not.

With the word "no" on the tip of my tongue I looked up into Bridger's eyes. He put his fingers against my cheek. The newly risen sun gleamed off his dark hair and silhouetted him in light.

"Please?" he whispered. I melted beneath that touch.

"Fine. *If* you promise to get me home by ten." Insane or not, I was crazy to go along with this. But when he touched me like that, I couldn't think straight. I stepped away from him and dug my hands deep into my jeans pockets. The tardy bell rang and I turned toward the bleachers.

"There's one more thing," Bridger said, walking beside me. "I was wondering if we could be friends. You know, say hi to each other in the hall, you could actually smile at me during track, sit by me at lunch . . ." His eyes got a wicked gleam. "Unless you're still worried about your reputation."

I frowned and slung my backpack over my shoulder. "Whatever," I said. But inside I was smiling. "Except I sit with Yana at lunch. So you're on your own there."

"What's up with you and Bridger O'Connell?" Yana asked.

We sat side by side, our backs against the brick wall by the girls' bathroom. She took a bite of pizza.

"We're friends, I guess." I washed down my PBJ with a swig of milk.

"Friends? I overheard some girls talking in the bathroom. They said he's taking you to prom?"

I glanced at the prom flyer on the wall. "Yeah. He's taking me to prom." Saying the words seemed surreal. Even though I was only going with him because I won a race, a smile jumped to my face. I looked at Yana and it fell off. "What? Is he a juvenile delinquent or something?"

"Juvenile delinquent? Aside from streaking last year's graduation ceremony totally nude, not that I know of. But he's a jerk. He's got some rich girlfriend from France that he's practically engaged to. Well, there's a problem. France is on another continent. So when Bridger's hormones rage, he finds someone local to use as a temporary replacement. And then he tosses her aside."

I sagged against the wall. Bricks dug into my shoulder blades through my T-shirt. "Are you serious?"

Yana nodded. "Danni was his last victim. And just a heads-up, but he was originally going to take her to prom. So watch out. That girl's got claws."

"What happened with him and Danni?"

"She's had a crush on him since junior high, even joined the track team to get him to notice her. And he finally did notice her when she beat him at hurdles," Yana said. I cringed—this was starting to sound all too familiar. "They dated for a little bit," she continued, "and when he dumped her, she stopped eating and didn't come to school for a week. When I told Naalyehe about it, he said Bridger's parents want him to marry someone in their *social class*. Therefore, he only gets serious with girls in his *social class*."

"What social class is that?"

"The über-rich, world-traveling, university-graduate social class."

"Wow."

"Sorry to have to tell you, but that's what friends are for."

"Yeah. Friends. Thanks for letting me know." I looked at my T-shirt, purchased from a thrift store in Albuquerque, and felt as if I'd been punched in the stomach. If Bridger's social class had an opposite, I would be it.

Yet a little part of me hoped Yana was wrong. Okay, a big part of me hoped. Mrs. Carpenter's dogs liked him, after all.

Even though I had been warned, my heart beat like a galloping horse every time Bridger said hi to me in the hall. When he smiled at me, or talked to me during track, I couldn't stop grinning. The few times we walked the same direction to class, he took my hand and interlaced his fingers with mine, and my blood raced through my veins.

I started counting the hours until prom.

.　.　.

On Thursday, when I got to third period, Senior English, I noticed the female half of the class was staring at me, as if noticing the new girl for the first time—again. Their eyes and whispers clung to me. When I sat down at my desk, a loud snickering filled the classroom. Danni, who sat directly behind me, was in full hysterics.

I turned around to see what everyone was laughing at, and they laughed harder. The girls did anyway. The guys were studying the walls or ceiling.

Class passed normally, with me struggling to hold my eyes open. We were discussing *The Scarlet Letter* by Nathaniel Hawthorne, a novel about a woman who had to wear a red *A* on her dress so that everyone knew she'd had sex out of wedlock. It was one of my least favorite books and, to make matters worse, I'd read and dissected it junior year. The urge to let my eyelids sag shut was almost overwhelming. The rest of the class seemed just as bored, antsy for class to end. Yet when the dismissal bell rang, no one made the usual mad dash for the lunchroom. They all stared at me.

My palms became clammy and my stomach started to churn, the same feeling I got when I knew the girls at my old school were planning on jumping me in the hall. My eyes met Danni's. She grinned from ear to ear. Did Ollie tell her about me?

I stood to leave.

The class burst into raucous laughter. I reached between my shoulder blades, expecting to find a paper with *Kick me* taped there, but felt nothing. The class laughed harder. I clenched my teeth and left.

Laughter followed me down the hall. Every person I passed

exploded with it when they looked at me. They pointed at my back and whispered, told other people to look, and they laughed, too.

Panic clawed at me. I started to run toward the girls' bathroom. It felt a mile away. By the time I reached it, tears were filling my eyes and I was gasping for air.

When I looked in the mirror, though, nothing was wrong. It was just plain old red-faced me staring back. I don't know what I had expected—a clown nose, maybe? Footsteps echoed in the empty stalls and Yana walked into the bathroom.

Her eyes met mine, and then wandered down my neck, over my red sweater, and to my jeans. She cringed.

"You riding the crimson wave?" she asked delicately.

I didn't know what she meant. Crimson wave?

"You've bled through your pants," she croaked, as if the words hurt her throat.

I turned around and looked at my butt in the mirror. Crimson smeared the seat of my jeans. I touched the stain and brought my fingers to my nose. Nail polish. I had sat in bright, blood-red nail polish.

My hands balled into fists and my blood started to boil. I saw the pink-and-gray-tiled bathroom through a fog of red. As I ran from the bathroom to the crowded lunchroom, I told myself what I was about to do was worth the consequences I would face.

Danni was watching for me, perched atop a table surrounded by her friends. Bridger was there, too, talking to Danni and smiling. My heart sank. He was in on it. I didn't know who to hit first—him or Danni.

But then Bridger saw me and frowned. He met me halfway

across the lunchroom and grabbed my fist. I kept walking, pulling him with me.

"What's wrong?" he asked, trying to uncurl my fingers. I glared at him and stopped.

"Tell me we're friends," I growled, clenching my fists tighter. "Tell me you wouldn't do anything to hurt me."

He studied me. "We're friends. I *wouldn't* do anything to hurt you."

"Good." I yanked my hand from his and strode over to Danni. She was gloating, laughing as I approached. When she opened her mouth to say something, I shoved my balled fist into it as hard as I could, knocking her backward off the table. She lay frozen on the grimy lunchroom floor, staring up at me. But when I started for her again, she scrambled to her feet and hid behind a couple of big senior guys. I pushed and shoved them out of my way and grabbed the back of Danni's shirt as she tried to run away.

She whirled around to face me and the fight was on.

She didn't know how to fight—just sort of hugged me, pulled my hair, and buried her face in my shoulder—making it impossible for me to punch it again. I started punching her in the ribs and pulling her cropped brown hair. She tried to kick my shins and bite me, but in the middle of a fight, you don't feel little things like that.

When she was suddenly yanked away, I swung hard and fast and my fist clipped her just below the eye. Arms came around me. I could smell Bridger and knew he was the one restraining me, but I wasn't done beating the crap out of Danni Williams. I struggled against his iron embrace, but couldn't break free.

Then I saw Danni wrapped in a backward hug by the school nurse. Danni wasn't struggling to get free, like me. She was struggling to put Ms. Opp in front of her. Danni was terrified. Of me. I froze.

All the steam went out of me and I leaned into Bridger. I had become just like the girls that used to corner me and beat me up. I couldn't believe I'd sunk so low.

"If I let go of you, do you promise to leave her alone?" Bridger asked, his mouth against my ear.

I nodded because I knew if I tried to talk I'd probably start to cry. His arms fell from me and my body heat seemed to fall with them.

"What is going on?" The gathered students moved aside as the principal strode over. He gasped when he saw Danni. Her chin was streaked with blood from a split lip and her eye was swelling shut. His astounded, glasses-framed eyes turned to me. "Did *you* do that to her?"

I nodded, still unable to speak. Bridger's hand found the small of my back and lingered there. I closed my eyes and leaned against him.

"To my office, girls." I squared my shoulders and stepped away from Bridger. Dr. Smith started herding Danni and me out of the cafeteria. "We don't need your assistance, Mr. O'Connell," he said when Bridger tried to follow.

Slowly, like the onset of a really bad headache, my bruises and scrapes became painfully obvious. My shins hurt, my shoulder throbbed from Danni's biting, and my right hand was burning. I looked down and saw blood on my knuckles—my blood. Danni's tooth had split my knuckle and beneath the skin I could see pale bone. I pressed the knuckle against my jeans.

The three of us walked to the office in silence, and once we were inside, the interrogation began.

"Maggie Mae, what happened?" Dr. Smith asked stonily.

I shrugged. "I hit Danni."

"Why?"

I glared at her but she was staring at the floor. "Because she is a malicious witch who deserved it."

"And why do you feel she deserved it? You are the one dating her ex-boyfriend. I thought *she* would have swung the first punch."

Danni finally looked at me. Her eye, the one that hadn't swelled shut, was full of hate.

"Danni deliberately put red nail polish on my chair and I sat in it without knowing. She made it look like I'm having my period."

Dr. Smith winced. "Please stand up, Ms. Mortensen," he said, though he looked less than thrilled.

I stood.

"Turn around," he prodded, spinning his pointer finger in a circle. I turned and stared at the wall while he inspected my butt. Dr. Smith sighed heavily. "You may sit."

I turned and sat back down.

"Danni, what do you have to say in your defense?" Dr. Smith asked.

Danni looked at Dr. Smith with a wide eye and batted her eyelashes. "I would *never* do something like that to a fellow female. I don't know what Maggie Mae sat in, but I didn't have anything to do with it. She hit me for no reason."

"You're saying she hit you unprovoked?"

Danni sniffled. "Yes."

My face started to burn and I clenched my fists. One swift punch and both her eyes would swell shut.

Dr. Smith's lips thinned. "Ms. Mortensen, we have a no-violence policy at this school. A first offense is punished with suspension. You are suspended for the remainder of today and tomorrow. And this will go down on your permanent record."

"Does that mean she can't go to prom?" Danni asked hopefully.

"No. The dance is on Saturday, not Friday. You are excused, Danni. Go to the nurse's office. I'll call your mother and have her come and get you."

Danni left without looking at me, and Dr. Smith sat back down.

"Ms. Mortensen, you need to leave the school premises immediately. I'll have the attendance office call your guardian and explain what has happened."

Without a word I left the principal's office and found Danni waiting for me in the hall. She held out an empty nail polish bottle and smirked. "He only wants to take you to prom because you're a slut," she hissed. "And it's every guy's dream to get laid at senior prom."

I bit my tongue and walked past her, hurrying through the empty hall. As I approached the front doors, my feet slowed. Bridger stood leaning casually against the wall beside the exit. When I saw him, a dam broke inside of me. Tears began streaming down my cheeks.

"Hey, you want a ride home from a friend?" he asked, putting a finger under my chin and tilting my face up to look at him.

"Yes, please. That would be great."

He wiped the tears from my cheeks with his thumbs, took my good hand in his, and pulled me toward the door. I glanced over my shoulder and caught Danni staring at us, eyes full of fire.

8

I could feel the pull of the nearly full moon before the sun reached the middle of the sky. It made my skin crawl. I lay atop my covers, chewing on the tip of a pen, trying to write a stupid essay on symbolism in *The Scarlet Letter*.

The phone rang. I heard the floor creak and the quiet echo of Mrs. Carpenter's voice.

"Maggie," she called. "Phone."

I rolled my eyes, assuming it was Mr. Petersen calling again to lecture me on how important it was to graduate—he'd called the night before. I climbed from the bed and went to the living room. Mrs. Carpenter, white hair hidden beneath a red bandanna, handed me the ancient receiver and started to dust the gun case.

"Hello?"

"Hi. It's Yana. You recovered from the fight?"

I glanced at Mrs. Carpenter. "More or less."

"Good. Are you still going to prom?"

"Nope. When Bridger brought me home yesterday, Mrs. Carpenter told him I'm grounded."

"Good. O'Connell doesn't deserve you." There was a pause. "This is going to sound totally paranoid, but I promised my grandpa I'd call."

Curious, I pulled the desk chair out and sat. "What's up?"

"Some guy came into the restaurant last night asking about you. My grandpa didn't like him, said he had negative energy."

"That's weird. What was his name?" I asked, twirling my finger in the spiraled phone cord.

"He wouldn't say. But after he came in and asked about you, even though we said we had no idea who you were, the dude sat out front in his car and watched the restaurant. My grandpa ended up calling the cops."

Goose bumps shivered up my arms. "Weird."

"Yeah, totally. We thought you should know."

"Thanks, Yana."

"Sure. I'll see you at school."

I hung up the phone and felt Mrs. Carpenter hovering, so I looked over my shoulder. She was still dusting the gun case and watching me.

"Everything all right?" I asked. The feather duster stopped.

"I've been thinking. Since today is your birthday, I'm going to unground you until midnight."

"Why am I getting a Cinderella vibe?"

She chuckled. "I have no intention of being your fairy god-mother. But you'd better call Bridger and see if he can still take you. And then let's go birthday shopping at Wal-Mart. You can pick out a new pair of jeans, a dress for prom, and some heels. My gift to you."

"Really?"

"Absolutely."

I jumped up and hugged her.

It was the second dress I'd worn since I was twelve years old. Every time I moved, air swirled up the skirt and against my thighs. The dress was beautiful—creamy white and made for warm weather, with thin straps and an empire waist, and a skirt that fell right above my knees.

I also got new hair dye, a dark auburn almost the color of a plum, but not quite so purple. I leaned in close to the mirror and attempted to put on mascara, but my hand was trembling. It took two tries.

Danni and Yana's warnings about Bridger kept running through my head. Even so, I was hoping Bridger would kiss me after the dance—just a simple good-night kiss. It seemed like my stars were finally lining up. My first real date. My first school dance. My birthday. A guy I liked a little more than I should. A full moon. A beautiful dress. My first kiss would be the perfect end to such a night.

I took a step away from the mirror and looked at myself. Mrs. Carpenter had helped me curl my auburn hair and pile it on top of my head with a gazillion bobby pins; plus she'd loaned me a pair of real pearl earrings that matched the dress perfectly. I could hardly believe the girl in the mirror was me, Maggie Mae the foster child. A smile spread over my glossy lips.

I went to my room and checked the clock. It was five to seven, five minutes until Bridger was to arrive. I took a deep breath and left my room.

Mrs. Carpenter was waiting in the living room with a camera.

"Oh, Maggie Mae, you look absolutely picturesque!" she exclaimed, putting her hand over her heart. "Let me take a photo."

She pointed the camera at me and I smiled just as the flash burned splotches into my vision.

"Why don't you sit down and wait," she said. I shook my head. "Do you know where he's taking you to dinner? You've got to tell him it's your birthday so your server sings to you and brings you a slice of complimentary birthday cake."

My hollow stomach growled at the thought. Chocolate cake was my favorite food. "I don't know where we're going to eat, but I'm starving."

"Sit down," Mrs. Carpenter urged again, patting the sofa beside her.

"I don't want to wrinkle my dress," I explained, wringing my hands.

"How's your hand feeling?" She eyed the gauze bandage wrapped around my right knuckles.

"Fine." The split knuckle, held together with several butterfly bandages, was tender to the touch and hurt if I made a fist. But other than that, I hardly noticed it.

Mrs. Carpenter and I waited in silence for a few minutes, both of us darting glances between the grandfather clock and the front window. Each time I heard the drone of a car engine, my heart whirled double-time. Yet no headlights bounced and flashed in the yard.

"He's late," Mrs. Carpenter said disapprovingly when the clock read one minute past seven. "I guess your generation doesn't place the same stress on punctuality that mine does."

We waited in silence some more. I stepped from foot to foot, having to move so I wouldn't burst with pent-up energy.

"Well," Mrs. Carpenter said when the clock read eight minutes past seven, "I'm going to go heat up some leftovers. Not all of us have the luxury of eating dinner at a restaurant tonight. I'll take another picture when he gets here."

She stood and walked from the room. I could hear her banging around in the kitchen. The phone rang and Mrs. Carpenter answered it, dragging the long spiraled cord into the kitchen. I could hear her chatting with someone about the right tension to set a sewing machine to if you're sewing quilt patches, could hear the hum of the microwave, and eventually could smell reheated beans, rice, and corn bread. My stomach rumbled.

At twenty past seven, I gave up on not wrinkling my dress and sat delicately down on the edge of the brown leather sofa. I kept my eyes glued to the window, but all remained dark in the moonless night outside. I thought that was pretty ironic, that darkness. I could feel the full moon pulsing inside of me even though it was buried behind a thick wall of clouds.

It wasn't until seven thirty, when Mrs. Carpenter came out of the kitchen to hang up the phone, that I finally began to doubt. Mrs. Carpenter looked out the window and frowned. Her silence spoke louder than words.

She went back into the kitchen and I stopped staring out the window. It was obvious he wasn't coming. I stood, hating the feel of the dress as it swished around my knees, and turned toward my room.

Light flickered against the glass face of the gun case. I looked out the window just in time to see a red sports car skid to a stop in front of the porch. My breath caught in my throat and I stared, hoping Bridger was behind the wheel.

The car door opened, Bridger stepped out, and I started

breathing again. He smoothed his hair, straightened his bow tie, and walked up the porch steps. The doorbell rang and, as if on cue, my palms started to sweat.

Please don't try to hold my hand! I swung my moist hands through the air, trying to dry them.

"I'll get it," Mrs. Carpenter called, hustling out of the kitchen with a smile on her face. She opened the door wide. "Please, come in." Bridger stepped inside, one hand hidden behind his back.

My heart flip-flopped at the sight of him. He wore a black tuxedo that matched his hair and made his shoulders look twice as wide as normal.

"Sorry I'm late. The florist was running behind, since I called in my order so last minute. I tried calling you—twice—but the phone was busy." He pulled his hand out from behind his back and handed me a bouquet of yellow tulips and white daisies. "And this is for your wrist," he said, removing from the base of the bouquet three tulips attached to an elastic bracelet. I held my hand out and he slid the elastic strap into place.

"Let me make this a permanent memory," Mrs. Carpenter said, holding her camera up. Bridger put his arm around my waist and pulled me close. I didn't need to hear the word "cheese" to bring a smile to my face.

I wasn't going to need a photograph to remember this night forever.

We went to Long John Silver's for dinner—fish and chips had never tasted so good. Bridger apologized for the informal restaurant, said he'd made reservations somewhere nice but had canceled them when he thought I was grounded. Long John's was the only place that wasn't booked.

After dinner we drove to the high school. As we crossed the parking lot, Bridger took my hand in his and I silently prayed it wasn't damp. His fingers tightened on mine and I looked up at him.

"You look really beautiful. Did I already tell you that?" he asked.

I smiled. "No."

"Sorry. It's the first thing I thought when I walked through your front door, but I was stressed from running late."

We walked into the school through the gym doors and I froze, like a deer staring at headlights. My hand fell from Bridger's.

The other girls weren't dressed like me. Not at all. To say they wore dresses was like saying I was poor. I was destitute. And they all wore gowns. Gowns that showed flashes of bare shoulders, cleavage, and thighs as they sparkled beneath disco balls.

Stepping in front of me, Bridger blocked my view of the gowns and placed his hands on my shoulders.

"Maggie," he said, leaning close so I could hear his voice over the music. "I want you to promise me something."

I looked into his eyes, wondering if he was as embarrassed about being seen with me as I was to be wearing such an inappropriate dress.

"What promise?"

"Don't worry what anyone in this gym thinks about you except for me. I'm the one you're with. I think you're beautiful. That's all that matters."

His words stirred something deep in my chest and I found it hard to breathe, let alone maintain eye contact. I looked down at my white sandals and wiggled my toes, wishing we'd never come to prom. A warm hand cupped my chin and Bridger angled my face up to look into his eyes.

"Do you want to leave? We can go to a movie or something."

I nodded, relief flooding me.

"Okay. I have one favor to ask first."

"What?" At this point, I'd grant him just about anything.

"One dance."

My eyes flickered past him, to the crowded gym. To the other students.

"Please?"

"Okay," I whispered, though the word scraped out of my mouth.

Bridger led me onto the dance floor and everyone stared. Girls snickered and pointed at my dress.

"That is the cheapest dress I've ever seen," someone called. "Where'd you buy it? The Wal-Mart clearance rack?" Bridger's hand tightened on mine. "This is prom, not a church picnic," someone else called. Bridger's hand tightened more.

He stopped in the middle of the dance floor, right beneath the biggest disco ball, and took me in his arms.

"Don't listen to them," he said. "And if you don't want to see their faces, just look into my eyes."

I nodded and stared into his dark eyes, trying to find the pupils in the irises, but it didn't matter. Sure, I couldn't see the other students. But I could still hear them.

". . . embarrassed to be seen with her."

"So shoddy, especially next to O'Connell."

"I hear he doesn't have to rent his tux. He owns it, and it's Armani."

"The least he could've done is buy a halfway decent dress for her."

I closed my eyes and laid my head on his chest. One of his hands left my back and moved to my ear, gently pressing the voices away. So he could hear them, too. My heart seemed to double in size at his small gesture and I smiled.

Yeah. I might have been wearing the wrong dress. And the wrong shoes. And I didn't have a teeny, sequin-covered purse to clutch. But when it came to a date, I had the best one in the entire room. I lifted my head and looked into his eyes again.

He smiled and my gaze moved to his lips, to his white teeth. I licked my lips and prayed he'd kiss me good night.

"Not so bad anymore, is it?" he asked.

I bit my bottom lip and looked back into his eyes. "No. Not bad." The song ended and I let go of Bridger, ready to bail. Prom was way overrated. But his arms tightened and he pulled me closer.

"One more song?" he asked. I looked around the gym. For the most part, I'd been forgotten. I put my hands back on his shoulders and got lost in his eyes. More than one song passed, and if the other students were talking about me, I couldn't hear them over the music and my drumming heart. My gaze moved between Bridger's eyes and his mouth. Once, when I'd been staring at his lips so long I could almost imagine how they'd feel on mine, he leaned closer to me and his lips parted. My eyes met his and we stopped moving to the music. But then he looked away and stared toward the doors we'd come in through. His hands left my lower back.

"Bridger?"

"Sorry," he said, shaking his head. He took me in his arms again, gazing into my eyes. We swayed to the beat for half a song and then he slowed, no longer moving to the beat, his eyes far away. He tilted his head to the side and I wondered who he was listening to. Who was verbally beating me to a pulp this time? I strained my ears but couldn't separate one voice out of them all. Bridger frowned and he stopped dancing.

He took a step away from me and said, "I'll be back in a couple of minutes. Want some punch or a cookie or anything?"

"No, I'm—" Before I could finish, he turned and wove his way across the dance floor, disappearing through the door that led into the main part of the school. "—fine."

I folded my arms over my chest and stood in the middle of the dance floor, waiting and trying not to make eye contact with anyone. But I could hear them.

"Look, he couldn't stand her dress anymore. He ditched her."

"Dude, O'Connell's got more guts than you could string on a fence—he left her on the dance floor."

I tried to shrink out of existence. When that didn't work, I dodged dancers and found a shadowed place close to the refreshment table to disappear. The song ended and another started. And then another.

Finally, when more than twenty minutes had passed with me skulking in the shadows, I went to the door Bridger had left through and entered the dark school. The loud music muted as the door closed behind me.

I stood with my back to the door, waiting for my eyes to adjust. And when they did, I started down the long, empty hall.

The hidden moon did little to light the window-lined hall, seemed to create more shadows. My sandals echoed with every step I took and my heart started to pound. I caught myself jumping at nothing and looking over my shoulder more than once.

"Bridger?" I called as I approached the end of the hall.

A dark shape moved up ahead, framed by an inky window. I stopped walking and squinted.

"Bridger?" I whispered.

A female chuckled. She stood and the eerie gray window silhouetted an ample Cinderella ball gown.

"Who's there?" I asked, taking a step backward.

"You're not so tough in the dark, are you." The person moved away from the window and a swishing sound followed her.

"Danni?" I guessed.

"Uh-huh."

I turned to go back the way I'd come. There was no way I wanted her to know I couldn't find my date.

"If you're looking for Bridger, he left," she said. So much for her not knowing.

"You're so full of crap," I said, my feet slowing.

"I'm serious. He ran out of here like his dad's car was on fire. Go check the parking lot if you don't believe me."

"He wouldn't leave without telling me," I said, but my statement sounded weak, even to my own ears. I wiggled my toes in my cheap sandals. Would he leave without telling me?

"He would if he knew about your past."

9

I ran back to the gym door, shoved it open, and pushed my way through the crowd, ignoring their condescending looks and mocking remarks as I searched for Bridger. Not finding him, I burst through the doors leading outside and gulped the cool, damp air.

I trotted through the parking lot to where Bridger had parked the red sports car. And found an empty parking space.

Tears filled my eyes and anger burned in the pit of my stomach. I wasn't angry with Bridger, though I had every right to be. But I was too busy being furious at myself for caring about him. Mad that I'd started to count on his interest in me making life a little bit nicer, because now that things would be going back to not so nice, I'd feel the difference every single day.

I looked down at my inappropriate dress and hated myself for wearing it, for giving in. Yanking the tulips from my wrist, I chucked them across the parking lot as hard as I could.

My anger mixed with the pull of the moon and the hair on the back of my neck bristled. My nails began to sharpen. *Bring it on*, I thought, reveling in the fact that my stupid Wal-Mart dress was about to get shredded.

I stepped between two cars and crouched. My skin shrank and squeezed against muscle and bone. I gasped and fell forward on my hands and knees. My ribs expanded and the dress strained against them. The fabric, unable to withstand the pressure, ripped noisily and the dress hung limply against my shoulders. The night sounds intensified and my brain filled with sharp, primitive instinct. The change was complete.

But something was different. I *tasted* every scent on the air—new things growing, a distant skunk, a hundred different scents of car air freshener, rain trapped in the clouds. My eyesight and sense of sound weren't as acute as normal, either. I looked down at my paws and whined. I wasn't a tabby cat. I had big, black, furry paws and short, blunt claws.

Even though my brain flowed with dog-instinct overload, my appearance was a shock. Since the very first change I had always been a cat. But tonight, judging by my shaggy black-and-white-spotted coat, I was probably the spitting image of Mrs. Carpenter's border collie, Shash.

I turned my nose to the sky and inhaled. The desert smelled alive despite its lack of vegetation, as if it held secrets in its dirt, air, even rocks. Another smell mingled with the desert's scent and my stomach rumbled. I trampled my prom dress and left it, torn and filthy, in the parking lot, and ran to the cafeteria Dumpster. With my front paws braced against the Dumpster's side, I inhaled, drooling over the thought of eating rotting corn dogs and Tater Tots wriggling with maggots. If I could just jump high enough . . .

Desperate to withstand the temptation, I started running again. As I passed from the school parking lot to the suburbs, I knew a dog was going to start barking, as if our minds were connected. The night exploded in barking and howling. A flicker of worry danced in my mind. What if the other dog attacked? But then the night called to me.

I ran with a grace and agility no human can understand, past houses and farms and into the uninhabited desert. Even in the tar-black, fog-coated night, I could sense each tree as I approached it, could leap over fallen logs and fly over uneven ground. Cactuses and sage grabbed at my fur, poked me, tried to find flesh, but my fur kept me protected.

When the clouds dropped, releasing a deluge of fat, soaking drops, I hardly noticed. My outer fur shed the water before it came close to my skin.

Rain turned the dusty desert to a bed of mud. With my nose to the saturated ground, I continued exploring, discovering new scents—coyote, fox, snake, human, and dog. Once or twice I even overlapped my own scent.

I ran down country roads that led back toward town, through neighborhoods and across grocery store parking lots until I was in downtown Silver City, dodging the occasional car and running after cats. I spent hours with my nose to the street—it was like another world—when I sensed rather than heard the approach of another canine.

My head lifted, my front paw came up, and I pointed in the direction of the approaching animal.

Shash, his black-and-white fur slicked against his narrow body, loped down the road and stopped at my side. A low, pitiful whine echoed from his throat and he began pacing back and forth.

Where in the world did you come from? I thought at him. I have no idea if he heard me, but he yelped and trotted off.

Before he was a block away, he turned and looked at me over his shoulder, tail wagging. Waiting for me to follow.

We ran through the town and back into the country. It was easy to stay behind Shash because his scent, musky and strong, saturated not only the muddy ground, but every single twig, branch, rock, and blade of sagebrush he touched, not to mention the very air. I could have followed him with my eyes closed.

We wound our way through the bushes in a steady direction— home—when I smelled something that made me stop dead. With my snout held up toward the falling sky, I inhaled. My fur bristled and a sudden, primitive instinct overtook all human control: *Evil—RUN!*

Up ahead Shash started barking—ferocious, murderous barking. As one, we resumed our sprint through the scraggly brush. And that is when I spotted the gleam of wet, mangy bodies through the narrow gaps in the trees.

Shash and I darted through the underbrush. Fear lent fresh speed to my legs. But whatever chased me was so unnatural, so malicious, it took sheer willpower not to lay on the ground, frozen with terror, and let them have me.

They were not the glossy, wet-coated dogs that they appeared to be. They were something more, something different. Wrong.

Though Shash and I ran at top speed, I could feel them behind me, could smell them when the wind shifted and hear their ragged breathing.

When one got so close I could hear its pounding heart, teeth snapped and pain seared my ankle. I fell, rolling on the muddy ground. The animal was on me before I stopped moving, its snarling, long-toothed mouth searching for skin through my thick fur. I bit back, something so natural I hardly gave it a second thought as wet fur filled my mouth. My teeth came down hard and I smelled blood before a single drop touched my tongue. And then the creature was off me and Shash was at my side. We tried to run, but my ankle was useless, my tendon severed.

Side by side, my head by Shash's tail, Shash's head by my tail, we waited. A large, menacing pack of doglike creatures crept out of the underbrush and circled us. There were all sorts of breeds, all larger than us. My lips pulled away from my teeth in a snarl and I tensed my hind legs, ready to spring. When a solid Doberman-looking animal leaped at me, I leaped, too, and we met in midair, both of our mouths finding the other's neck.

We crashed down and I landed on top of the rock-hard creature, shaking its neck with all my might. Hope, that I might actually kill the unnatural thing beneath me, lent power to my jaws and determination to my tired body—until the rest of the dogs pounced on my back.

Hundreds of teeth sank into my flesh, from my shoulders to my haunches.

A yelp screeched into the rainy night, the sound a dog makes right after it is hit by a car, a split second before it dies. When another yelp ripped through the night, torn from my throat, I realized *I* was the dog about to die.

With every ounce of strength I possessed, I bit and scratched the motley, stinking mound of animals smothering me, but I was outnumbered. The weight of death pressed me down and I couldn't get up.

An ear-deafening boom rattled the night, vibrating my bones and swallowing the rumble of animals snarling. Time seemed to pause as every set of teeth so intent on ripping my head from my body paused inside of my skin. The boom sounded again. A dog yelped. Teeth released my flesh and the creatures scattered so quickly, so silently, I almost wondered if they had existed at all.

A third shot rang out, this time from the opposite direction, and Shash whined a low, pitiful sound.

I whimpered and struggled to get up but was too hurt to move. A new scent entered my nose and a copper shadow loped over and began licking my snout. Duke. He whined and pushed at me with his nose. Slowly, shakily, I found the strength to stand. Duke began trotting away. Shash and I followed, though my hind leg dragged behind me, as useless as a stick caught in my fur.

I hadn't gone ten paces when I froze. A rottweiler, eyes glazed, mouth gaping, lay in a growing pool of blood. I shuffled around the dead body and followed Shash and Duke.

We passed the school bus stop and loped toward home. It wasn't long before Mrs. Carpenter's brightly lit barn and house came into view. On three legs I hobbled toward the open barn door. Inside, I fell onto a pile of straw, every inch of my body hurting, and slid back into my own shape. I lay curled in a trembling, naked ball and wondered how I was lucky enough to be alive.

Beside me Duke and Shash whined.

"Dear Lord almighty, if you're a Skinwalker, I'll shoot you before I ask questions." It wasn't until Mrs. Carpenter spoke that I realized she was in the barn, too.

Shocked and horrified, I looked up to see her standing over me with a rifle in hand.

10

"What's a Skinwalker?" I asked, waiting for her to kill me. Duke whimpered and, ears flat against his head, slunk in between Mrs. Carpenter and me.

She lowered her gun and grunted.

Something soft and rose scented draped my shivering body, stinging the scrapes that covered my skin.

"We need to get you inside, child, before you catch your death," Mrs. Carpenter said, as if I had been out working in the garden on a rainy afternoon. She pulled me to my feet and helped me slip my arms into a bathrobe. Her bathrobe. She wore nothing but an old, thin nightgown. Without a word, she tied the pink terry cloth belt around my waist.

Mrs. Carpenter tilted her head to the side. After a silent moment, she picked up the rifle and walked over to shut the barn doors.

"Shash, Duke, come," she commanded. The dogs left my side and ran to her. "Is it safe? Is that pack of mangy animals gone?" she asked the dogs and pushed the doors wide. Both dogs sniffed the air and wagged their tails. In spite of this, Mrs. Carpenter dropped another shell into the rifle and pointed it outside. "You go first, Maggie Mae," she said, motioning me outside with the gun barrel.

As I passed her, I couldn't help but wonder if she was going to shoot me in the back.

"Hurry, Maggie Mae. Before that pack of unholy mongrels comes back!" I hobbled to the house. Shash and Duke ran with me, Mrs. Carpenter a step behind. When we entered the dark living room, Mrs. Carpenter slammed the front door and locked it before flipping on the light.

"Now let me take a look at you, see if we need to go to the emergency room," Mrs. Carpenter said, setting the gun on the dining room table. "Some of those bites looked pretty deep."

I dropped the robe to the floor around my bare feet. After being picked up nude so many times by random police officers, modesty wasn't really an issue anymore. Naked was naked.

Mrs. Carpenter's eyes grew wide as she took in my bare form, and I wondered if I had gone too far, standing naked in front of her.

"Turn around," she instructed, staring. I turned. "Lord have mercy! Let me see your knuckles." She grabbed my hand, examining the wound I'd gotten from Danni's tooth. "I can hardly believe it," she muttered, looking at my body again. "Your hand . . . it's still hurt. But the rest of you . . ."

I looked down and gasped. Not a single scratch remained on my pale, mud- and blood-streaked skin. I lifted my leg and twisted my injured ankle. It was good as new. I was healed.

"You may not be a Skinwalker, but you're something unnatural," Mrs. Carpenter said, stepping away from me. "If my dogs didn't seem to like you so well . . ." Her voice trailed off as she

studied me with wise, yet terrified, eyes. But there was something else there. Shock.

I looked at my naked self again and tried not to cry, but I
couldn't help it. I looked so normal, so human. But I was an
abomination. An animal. A freak. Loud, ugly sobs joined the
tears. I covered my face with my hands and tried to hold it all in.

"Oh, Maggie Mae, forgive my hasty words." The soft robe
enfolded my naked body, and then her arms, warm and gentle,
embraced me. "Dear child, what are we going to do with you?"
she whispered, running her hand over and over my wet hair.

I hadn't been held this way—like I was loved—since my
last family member had been killed. Not only loved, but loved
by someone who felt nearly like a mother.

She tugged my hands from my face. "Maggie Mae, dear,
why don't you take a shower."

I nodded. With the robe held tightly in place, I hurried to
the bathroom.

After a scalding shower, I put on my nightshirt and, in spite of
the predawn hour, went to the kitchen. The light was on and I
could smell food. I was so ravenous, my stomach was trying
to turn inside out.

Mrs. Carpenter eyed me warily, like the day I'd come to
live with her, but she didn't say a thing—just passed me a bowl
of boiled wheat farina with cinnamon and raisins. I took it to
the dining room table.

The bowl was empty in less than a minute, warming me
from the inside out. Mrs. Carpenter refilled it and sat beside
me, searching my face, my clean hands, my eyes.

"I'm still the same girl I was yesterday," I said, my voice ragged from crying. "You just know more about me now. But I haven't changed."

Mrs. Carpenter shook her head and squeezed her eyes shut. "I keep telling myself that. But what exactly is it that I now *know* about you?"

I shrugged and swallowed farina before answering simply, "I change at the full moon."

Mrs. Carpenter looked at me in exasperation. "Why, thank you for stating the obvious, but *what* are you? Why do you . . . *change?*"

"I've asked myself that very same question every single day for the last two years. Since this started happening. I don't know why I started to change or what I am."

"Well, who else knows about this? This changing?"

"No one. I'd be turned into some sort of top secret medical experiment if anyone did. Unless, of course, I was lucky enough to be locked away in an insane asylum for the rest of my pitiful life," I snapped. "Your son already thinks I'm crazy without that little tidbit added to my mental shortcomings."

Mrs. Carpenter nodded, her face thoughtful. "I see. Now, tonight you looked just like Shash. I couldn't tell the two of you apart. Why's that, do you think?"

I shrugged again. "Ever since I started changing, I always looked like Mrs. Montgomery's big orange tabby, my foster mother's pet. Maybe I turn into whatever animal I'm closest to." A smile tugged the side of my mouth. "It's a good thing you don't own a cow."

"Well, at least you weren't a wolf. Or a grizzly bear," Mrs. Carpenter said with a shiver. "I would have shot you without hesitating if that had been the case." She looked at me with a frown. "Tell me about how all this started."

"I changed for the first time one month after my sixteenth birthday. I was fostering with the Montgomery family and had gone to a party with some kids from school. They were totally bad kids, but I was desperate to fit in. There was alcohol at the party and I wanted them to like me. So I tried alcohol for the first time—tequila." Mrs. Carpenter's eyebrows shot up. "Don't worry. It was the biggest mistake of my life.

"I got wasted and passed out. When I woke up, it was the middle of the night. I had been dumped in someone's front yard and all I wanted to do was catch rats. I didn't even realize I wasn't human at first—just slunk into the night, dragging my shirt with me. I killed and gorged on rats till dawn." My stomach turned as I remembered the taste of rat fur, blood, organs, and bones.

"When I changed back to myself, I was standing in some slummy alley between two buildings, naked, and vomiting up undigested chunks of rat mixed with tequila. I couldn't remember how I got there, thought maybe I was lying in bed having a really horrid nightmare. Until a dirty homeless man tried to attack me. I kicked him in the crotch, ran out into the road, and was almost hit by a police car. That was the first time I was picked up for indecent exposure." I looked at Mrs. Carpenter. She was leaning toward me, eager to hear more.

"I thought it was the alcohol that made me change. I haven't touched it since, but when the moon's full, I still change. And I can't control when I change back.

"That's why I have a police record, why I am found naked in the streets. I don't mean to change, don't even want to. But it is as unavoidable as my period, and when I change, I can't take my clothes with me. I leave them behind, if I don't accidentally drag them away."

Mrs. Carpenter looked positively smug. "Well, I knew you weren't up to no good when they found you naked in the streets. My gut told me you were a decent girl, and my gut has never been wrong. And Ollie thinks you're a prostitute!" She began laughing, a full-bodied chuckle. "You, a prostitute!"

I smiled. I'd never even been kissed.

"So, can you only change when the moon is full, or any time you want?"

"Only at the full moon," I said, but then remembered the day in track when I'd tripped on the hurdle. My vision had sharpened and my nails had grown into claws. "Honestly, I've never *tried* to change. I try to *avoid* it."

"Well, mercy, Maggie Mae. You've been dealt a hard lot in life. I hope you make sense of it one day, because I sure can't. I don't know what to do with you now." She looked at me with haunted eyes. "Aside from calling animal control about that pack of wild dogs, I suppose there is nothing to do, is there? Unless you want me to lock you in the barn on the night of the next full moon?" She shuddered. "You're a good girl. I'll just keep reminding myself of that."

She looked rather dazed as she took my empty bowl to the kitchen. When she came back, she said, "Let's not move you out to the barn just yet. Not until animal control has taken care of the dog problem."

I sighed. I might have been brave when it came to taking a punch, but I was relieved at the thought of staying in the house. Taking a deep breath, I asked the question that had been troubling me since she'd found me in the barn. "What's a Skinwalker?"

Her lips thinned and she wouldn't meet my eyes. "Forget I said that name. Speaking of them draws them near."

11

The bus pulled into the school parking lot. I stared at the tan brick school through the rain-streaked window and wished I could shrink down into my seat and disappear. When all the students had filed off, I dragged myself to the exit and stepped into the rain. My feet refused to take another step.

The parking lot was awhirl with students. They hurried past me so intent on themselves that I was invisible again.

By the time I mustered up enough courage to make my feet start walking, I was soaked clean through. My bra was visible beneath my thin, sopping wet black T-shirt and my drenched hair looked blacker than black despite that it wasn't black anymore. I hugged my sodden jacket closed over my shirt and trudged forward.

As I pushed the school door open, the tardy bell rang and students evacuated the halls. My shoes squeaked and squelched on the linoleum. I turned a corner toward the gym and my feet screeched to a stop before the rest of my body. Hands clamped down on my shoulders and held me in place. I took a step back and glared up at Bridger.

"Can I talk to you?" he asked.

"Nope."

"I need to talk to you. I tried calling your house yesterday, but Mrs. Carpenter said you were grounded from the phone."

"Yeah, I was grounded. Leave me alone." It was easier not getting attached to someone. Because that way, I couldn't get hurt. I turned toward the locker room, but his long arm came up, hand resting on the wall, barring my way.

"Something really important came up," he said.

"Something so important you didn't have the decency to give me a freaking ride home? *What* came up?"

"I can't talk about it."

"Whatever. Just leave me alone, Bridger. As far as I'm concerned, we never met." I shoved his arm away and strode into the girls' locker room.

The locker room was empty. I wiggled out of my drenched jeans and jacket, then pulled the soaked T-shirt over my head. From my locker I got dry running clothes and yanked them on, shoving my jacket and backpack inside.

Instead of stuffing my jeans and T-shirt into the locker, I laid them out over the bench to dry.

I stood tall, wiped the smeared mascara from under my eyes, and walked into the gym.

It was hard, but I did not let my eyes wander, did not allow myself to scan the gathered students for any sign of Bridger.

"We'll hold class indoors today because of the rain," Coach bellowed as he entered the gym. "All girls, line up for sprints. Boys, stretch."

I followed Ginger to the far end of the gym. We were the only girls in track that day.

"Hi," Ginger said as we lined up.

"Hey."

"All right, ladies, to the other side and back twenty times. And hustle," Coach said and blew his whistle. As I sped past the bleachers where the boys stretched, I couldn't help but search for black hair. He was there, as studiously avoiding my eyes as I had been avoiding his. All the other guys, though, stared at me. I looked straight ahead again and ran.

The whole class passed that way, with me straining to avoid any type of contact with Bridger, even eye contact. A wall of tension loomed between us. The students must have sensed it. No one spoke. No one smiled, even at each other. And everyone seemed to be glaring at me. Except Ginger. And Bridger, who acted like I was nonexistent.

When Coach excused us to shower and change, I practically ran from the tension.

"Maggie Mae," someone called when I was only a step from the freedom of the girls' locker room. My heart thudded in my chest as I turned to see what Coach wanted. My track mates pushed past me a little too roughly, jostling me with their shoulders. Bridger was last in line. As he brushed by, his eyes flickered to mine and he paused.

"I think something might be up," he whispered, glancing toward the boys' locker room. "Be careful." His fingers touched mine and I had to fight the urge to jerk my hand away. Then he was gone.

"Maggie Mae?"

I blinked.

"I need to speak with you," Coach explained. "I'll give you a late pass for second period."

I followed him to his office, a small room next to the locker rooms, decorated with trophies and ribbons of years past.

"Have a seat," he said, motioning to a metal folding chair squeezed into the corner. I sat. "You're the best sprinter I've ever had," he said as he sat behind the desk. His chocolate eyes, with their thick caterpillar brows, studied me. "I'd hate to lose you."

"What do you mean, 'lose me'?" I asked, though I pretty much knew what he was going to say.

"We can't be a team if two of our members are trying to kill each other." I raised my eyebrows, wondering if he was referring to Bridger and me, or Danni and me. "It would be a darn shame if I had to kick you and Danni off the team for fighting. This is the only warning I'll give you."

So he meant Danni.

He stared at me for a long time. Could he tell that I didn't care if I was on the team or not? Running track had never been an ambition of mine.

"Do you realize that with your fifty-yard dash time, you could get a track scholarship to any major university?" he asked. "You are planning on going to college, right?"

"Not really." Everyone seemed to make such a big deal about college, like if I didn't go, I'd be a complete failure.

As if to convince me of the importance of gaining a higher education, Coach told me all sorts of stories about when he ran track at Arizona State. It wasn't until the dismissal bell for second period rang that we realized how much time had passed. He scribbled an excusal note for me to give to the attendance office and I hurried out of his office.

Back in the girls' locker room, I began to tremble with cold, as if the rainy morning had made its way to my bones. I stripped out of my gym clothes and grabbed a towel from my locker, then darted to the deserted showers.

The water, even when turned to full hot, was barely warm enough to feel good. It did nothing to melt away the ice that coursed through my blood and made my teeth chatter. The third period tardy bell rang, but I ignored it, standing under the tepid water, letting it spray the top of my head and trickle over my body.

Long after my skin had turned prunelike with wrinkles, I turned off the shower, wrapped the towel around my freezing body, and went to my locker.

My clothes were exactly where I'd left them—draped over the bench and dripping puddles on the locker room floor. I put my jeans on first, hardly able to get my legs into the cold, stiff fabric. Then I grabbed my black T-shirt and paused. Something had caught my eye—a burst of color. I held the shirt up.

My heart dropped to my stomach and seemed to explode. On the front of my T-shirt was a giant scarlet letter A, paint fumes oozing from it. I thought of Hester Prynne from *The Scarlet Letter*, thought of the A that marked her as an adulterer for everyone to see. I had been marked, too. I studied the A on my shirt and my blood started to boil.

Absolutely furious, I threw the T-shirt onto the bench. There was no freaking way I was going to wear it. I'd wear my smelly gym shirt because, seriously, it's not like anyone got close enough to smell me.

I opened my gym locker and gasped. It was empty. Nothing— not even my gym shorts, not even my backpack—was in it.

I sat heavily on the locker room bench and stared at the

empty locker, thinking maybe I'd opened the wrong one. I double-checked the number—117. Nope, I had the right locker. My things had been stolen.

I looked down at myself, at my damp, dingy white bra and low-rise jeans. I couldn't go out into the halls wearing that, so I grabbed the black shirt and turned it inside out.

As I pulled it over my head, I cringed. The paint had soaked through. Even inside out the A was visible. I felt branded.

My shoes and socks, still soaked, sent a shiver through me as I pulled them on. With nothing to carry, nothing to cover my scarlet letter, I folded my arms over my chest and crept from the gym, out into the cafeteria-food-scented hall. I stared at my feet, my wet hair shielding the sides of my face, and slunk toward the front doors. I was going home.

My shoulders sagged with relief as the doors came into view—until I realized someone was standing beside them. Mike Williams from track stepped in front of the doors and folded his arms over his thick chest. I knew the look in his surly brown eyes all too well. He was not going to let me get past him without a fight.

My steps slowed and I let my arms dangle at my sides. Could I fight my way past him and then sprint home? I was a faster runner, and if I got a solid punch in before he did . . . I perched on the balls of my feet and gritted my teeth. But there was a problem. If I fought him, I'd be expelled and I was so close to graduating that I could almost taste it.

A bell blared.

Bodies filled the hall. A horde of hungry students stood between me and the freedom of those front doors.

People started noticing me and the chatter in the hall died

down to the swish of whispers. Everyone stopped walking and stared, pointing to the scarlet letter on my shirt. As if they had been waiting for me. As if they had been told what to look for.

A shrill laugh pealed through the quiet hall, sending a fresh shiver down my spine.

"Didn't I tell you?" a female voice said. "She's a prostitute. Has been picked up by the police for streetwalking more times than I can count on both my hands." Danni strutted down the hall toward me, smirking in spite of the black bruise circling her eye. My hands balled into angry fists. "Yep. She is a whore. A parentless, streetwalking, professional whore who can't keep her clothes on. Just look at the letter on her shirt." Danni smiled and started laughing.

"Leave her alone, Danni." Yana pushed through the crowd, her eyes locked on mine. Danni stepped in front of her and blocked her way.

"Get out of here, little squaw. This has nothing to do with you."

Yana shoved Danni, but a guy I didn't know grabbed Yana, yanking her into the crowd. It didn't matter. If Danni wanted me to fight, she was out of luck. Not even the satisfaction of pounding her face in again could induce me to jeopardize graduating.

Danni slid through the crowd to stand in front of me, and that is when I saw what she held snug under her arm. A rectangular, dog-eared file folder bulging with papers. The sight of it made my ears ring and my knees knock together. I pinched myself, hoping I was in a nightmare and about to wake up.

She raised her hand and slapped me across the face. My cheek flamed with pain and I knew this was no nightmare. It was something worse.

"That's for giving me a black eye. I couldn't get prom pictures because of it," Danni said.

"You're so full of crap," I snarled. "You couldn't get pictures because you didn't have a date. Your *ex*-date was with me."

"Yeah, only until I told him about your police record!" she replied loud and clear, taking the folder from under her arm. "Maggie Mae has been arrested at least a dozen times. Listen—" Graduation at risk or not, I couldn't let her read what was in that file. I lunged for her, fists primed for some serious damage.

Hands cinched in a death grip on my shoulders before I could swing. I turned, expecting to see a teacher, and looked right into the eyes of Mike Williams, Danni's brother.

A paper rustled. I looked back at Danni. She scanned the sheet of paper in her hand and started reading. "June 24, 4:37 a.m., Albuquerque. Magdalene Mae Mortensen found nude in an alley with homeless man. Picked up by police." She flung the paper aside and pulled out another from the file. "December 3, 3:17 a.m., Albuquerque. Magdalene Mae Mortensen found nude wandering city street. Picked up by police." She threw that paper aside and got another. "This one's from a month ago," Danni announced.

I lunged for her again, fighting against the fingers digging into my shoulders, but couldn't get away.

Danni looked at me and smirked. "Looks like you already know what it says." She cleared her throat and read, practically yelling, "March 26, 5:55 a.m., Albuquerque. Magdalene Mae Mortensen found nude on city street, assaulting a prostitute for possession of a jacket. Picked up by police." She looked at me. "Do you have anything to say in your defense?" she asked, tossing the paper aside. Someone caught the paper—someone I didn't know—and started reading.

"No way, man! It's true," the someone said, passing the paper to someone else.

"Slut," Mike said. "I bet that's why you left prom. You had to go out and make some money!" Wetness splattered my face and something thick and warm slowly slid down my cheek. I touched the warm goo, pulled my hand away to look at it, and almost gagged. Mike had spit on me.

Someone else spit, this time hitting me on the ear. Then everyone started spitting. Mike let go of me, running for cover. The halls might as well have had rain clouds in them for how much moisture was flying through the air, all aimed at me.

"Leave her alone!" Yana yelled. She was pinned against the white tiled wall, thrashing against the guy holding her there.

I turned to leave, but my way was blocked. I shoved someone aside, a guy from my English class, but he grabbed my wrist and flung me back into the middle of the riot. Well, I wasn't going to stand for that. I turned and socked him in the nose and strode past him, but he grabbed the back of my shirt and flung me down onto my butt in the center of the students. That's when things went from really bad to freaking horrible. Everyone started throwing things at me—pencils, crumpled paper, a banana from someone's lunch—anything they could get their hands on.

I jumped to my feet and shoved through the tightly circled mass of bodies imprisoning me in my own personal hell. But Mike shoved me back into the frenzy.

Panic and anger swirled in me, making me feel too big for my body. My animal instincts kicked in and I started attacking

Mike, scratching, kicking, hitting—anything to get away. Until my nails pricked into fine claws and I heard the underlying throb of hearts. I was about to change into an animal, right here in front of everybody. For the briefest flash of a second, I debated what would be worse—to turn into an animal and fight my way free, or give up?

I stopped fighting.

I crouched down on the floor, pressed my forehead to my knees, and covered my head, waiting for the interruption I knew must be coming. Someone tapped me on the shoulder and I made the mistake of looking up. I only saw Danni's face for a split second before she smashed a bowl of hot chili into my face.

"What is wrong with you people?" a voice boomed. The hall became hushed. "Danni, get away from her now, or so help me, I'll pummel you!"

"But she's a prostitute!" Danni protested weakly.

"I don't care if she's a murderer! Leave her alone! Get out of here and leave her alone! All of you! Get out of here!"

Feet shuffled over the food-spattered floor as people moved away, and then Coach was with me, pulling me to my feet and wiping chili and melted cheese off my cheeks. He cursed under his breath and began wiping my face with the hem of his shirt.

"Bridger, run and get a wet towel from one of the lunch ladies," Coach barked. He hugged me to him, not minding that he held someone wet with saliva and juice and spattered with all sorts of cafeteria food.

I didn't mean to cry, but I couldn't help it.

"Oh, no. Are those tears from my best sprinter?" Coach asked. "You can take a fall on the hurdles and not even blink, but when you get a little chili in your eye, you cry?" His voice sounded strange. I looked up and saw tears trickling down his bristly cheeks. "I'm so sorry, honey," Coach whispered, hugging my head to his chest.

Bridger appeared with two damp washcloths. One was pressed to his nose and soaked with blood. Coach took the other and began wiping my face and arms. "Let's get you home, Maggie," Coach said when the foulest things were wiped from my skin. "I'll drive you."

"I'd rather walk. I need to be alone," I told him between sniffles.

"But it's raining," Coach protested.

"Rain isn't going to hurt me."

"Maggie Mae, I can't let you leave without calling Mrs. C. first. Wait right here." Coach trotted toward the office.

I didn't wait. Bridger's dark gaze followed me as I made my silent, humiliated way to the front doors.

The day was uncommonly cold, yet I didn't feel it. I was glad for the icy rain washing the filth from me as I slowly trudged through the mud puddles on the side of the road.

I hated my life. I hated school. I was so miserable I stuck my thumb out as cars passed, eager to hitch a ride with anyone, anywhere, if it meant never having to go to Silver High again.

Several cars passed, splattering me with mud, when a truck pulled to a stop in front of me. My heart started pounding as I asked myself if I was brave enough to get into that truck and go, empty-handed, into the wide world and fend for myself. I had nothing, not even my jacket—just the shirt on my back.

Someone wearing a bright yellow rain slicker got out of the truck and splashed through the roadside puddles to my side.

"Coach called me," a familiar voice said. I peered beneath

the slicker hood, into the anxious eyes of Mrs. Carpenter. "Let's get you home. I'll draw up a nice hot bath for you and make hot cocoa." She put an arm around me and guided me to the car.

I couldn't decide whether I was happy to see her or not.

∽ 12 ∽

Shash must have felt the anxiety coursing through my body and causing my stomach to hurt. He stuck to me like a shadow as I walked through the barn to the chicken coop.

The chickens either couldn't sense my inner turmoil or they were too plain dumb to notice. They didn't protest in the least as I reached beneath them and stole the warm brown- and green-speckled eggs from their nests and put them in a basket.

With the eggs gathered, I threw a cupful of grain onto the ground and locked the coop. Walking to the other side of the barn, I sat on the bottom step of a flight of stairs leading up to a padlocked door and sat. Shash followed.

"Trust me," I said, stroking his soft forehead. "I'd trade places with you in a heartbeat."

It was Tuesday morning, and I had to leave for the bus in twenty minutes. Mrs. Carpenter hadn't said anything about me *not* going, so I was thinking up all kinds of excuses to keep myself away from Silver High. My throat hurt, I was having cramps, my vision was blurred, appendicitis . . . they were all lies, but I didn't care. I couldn't go back and face all of those students. I didn't have it in me.

I would drop out and start a new life, maybe back in Albuquerque, working a minimum-wage job for the rest of my uneducated existence—if I could keep out of jail now that I was eighteen, legally an adult, and running the risk of getting in some real trouble for my indecent exposure. Even flipping burgers at McDonald's till I was able to retire didn't sound nearly as daunting as going back to school.

Shash whined.

"I know. Looks like I'll be making another fresh start. Again." I left the barn and trudged to the house. It was warm inside and scented with bacon. I carried the eggs to the kitchen, where Mrs. Carpenter was hanging up the telephone.

"That was my son, John," she informed me.

Great, I thought, *she's called my psychiatrist.*

"He's glad to finally know the reason behind your indecent exposure," she continued.

I almost dropped the eggs. "You told him?"

Mrs. Carpenter pursed her lips. "He says he can't imagine why you didn't tell him yourself. Nude sleepwalking isn't common, but it's nothing to be ashamed of." She chuckled and took the eggs. "He says there's a cure."

"Oh, really?"

"Stop sleeping in the buff."

I smiled and some of the knots in my stomach loosened.

"I thought I'd drive you to school today," Mrs. Carpenter said as she cracked eggs into a bowl. The knots in my stomach retied themselves. "Thought we could go meet with the principal."

"I can't go back," I whispered.

"It seems you need to make a choice today. You're eighteen. You can do whatever you want with your life." She faced me and put her warm hands on my cheeks. Peering right into my eyes, she said, "But never let another person's actions dictate how you are going to live your life, Maggie Mae. You are a strong, smart girl. If you never return to Silver High, what kind of message is that going to send Danni Williams?"

"That she won." The words hurt coming out, because the way I saw it, she had.

"Smart cookie, you are. I'll be darned if you let her win." Mrs. Carpenter dropped her hands from my face and started whisking the eggs.

"Is that what Mr. Petersen told you to say?" I asked.

"No. He told me to send you to the school in the next town over. Let you make another fresh start. I told him it was time you stood up for yourself and stayed put. So chin up. It's time to show Silver City what Maggie Mae Mortensen is made of."

Mrs. Carpenter and I arrived at the school fifteen minutes after class had started. The halls were silent. When we got to the principal's office, Dr. Smith wasn't waiting for us alone. Coach was in one of the chairs opposite his desk, and standing beside him was Ollie.

"Good morning, Opal," Coach said to Mrs. Carpenter, standing so she could have his chair. "And Maggie Mae."

"Hello, Maggie Mae," Ollie said, holding his hand out.

I forced myself to stop wringing my icy hands and nodded at Coach, then shook Ollie's hand. I took a seat beside Mrs. Carpenter.

"Good morning," Dr. Smith said, adjusting his glasses.

"Well, Raymond, would you like to tell her or shall I?" Mrs. Carpenter, never one to beat around the bush, asked him.

"I want to tell her," Coach interjected. He had a gleam of satisfaction in his eyes, the same look he'd gotten when I beat the school's fifty-yard dash record. "Dave Whitlock and Mike Williams are suspended." Coach smiled grimly. "They will not be returning to school for the rest of the week."

"What about Danni?" I asked, my breath quickening.

"Danni's not suspended," Coach said. I opened my mouth to protest but Coach held up his hand. "She's been expelled. If she wants to graduate, she has to find a new school to attend. She *planned* the attack on you, Maggie Mae. Got Mike and Dave to help her."

A chill shivered down my spine.

Ollie cleared his throat. "Danni came over to visit me Friday night and asked about you, but I wouldn't tell her any details of your case. She must have snuck into my office and stolen your file. I'm really sorry."

"What about Bridger? What part did he play?" I thought of his bloody nose and wondered who'd given it to him. I wished it had been me.

"He was in the chem lab finishing up an assignment. When he heard the fight, he tried to get to you, but Dave fought him away, so he came and got me," Coach said. "Dave hit him. That's why his nose was bleeding."

I bit my lip and tried to ignore the guilt bubbling up in me.

"Do you have anything to add, Raymond?" Mrs. Carpenter asked.

I looked at the principal. He didn't need to add anything—I could see it in his eyes. He was cursing the day I came to his school. If I hadn't come, none of this would have happened.

"I'm sorry for the unfortunate events that have surrounded

you, Ms. Mortensen," he said. "We have done everything in our power to maintain proper behavior at this school. No one else will harass you, but if they do, they will suffer consequences. You had better get to class."

" 'Kay," I said, and stood.

Mrs. Carpenter and I left the office. "Do you want me to walk you back to the truck?" I asked.

"No, thank you, Maggie Mae. I'll see you after school." She wrapped me in a hug. "I'm proud of you," she whispered. And then she strode away.

The bell rang and the halls filled with students, though there was such a subdued air about them, you'd think they were on their way to a funeral, not second period. I swung my duffle to my shoulder and started weaving my way through the crowd. But when I saw glossy black hair above square shoulders, I stopped.

Bridger must have felt my eyes boring into the back of his head. He turned around and his eyes met mine. I looked away and took a deep breath, and walked past him.

"Hey, Maggie Mae." I stopped walking and found Ginger hovering behind me. "I just wanted to tell you how sorry I am about what happened."

"Thanks," I said, stunned.

"Yeah." She smiled and hurried away.

I took two steps when a hand came down on my shoulder.

"You survived." Yana fell into step beside me, her eyes lingering on a purple bruise on my forehead.

"I suppose I did," I said.

"I wanted to thank you."

"For what?"

Yana grinned. "Getting Danni's ass kicked out of school."

I couldn't help but smile. "Whatever."

"So, you wanna work tonight?"

"Seriously?"

"Seriously. The motocross is in town and I have tickets. Naalyehe said if you'd cover for me, I can go."

"Sure. What time?"

"Be there at four. I'll walk you through the basics."

" 'Kay."

"Awesome. I'll see you at lunch."

I walked the rest of the way to math alone. If I had been invisible for my first two weeks of school, I wasn't anymore. I might as well have been in a cage with *Warning! Keep your distance! Dangerous creature!* signs on it. Because I was now Silver High's main attraction.

I looked at myself in the mirror and winced, and not because the bruise on my forehead had turned ten shades darker. The Navajo Mexican had a dress code: black shirt and jeans without any holes, and long hair had to be in a ponytail or hairnet. Like that was a hard choice. Pretty easy dress code to follow, except the only black shirt I owned had a giant scarlet *A* painted on the front of it.

I grabbed my old thin jacket and walked into the living room, ponytail swishing against my shoulders.

"You ready?" Mrs. Carpenter asked, eyeing the shirt.

"Yep."

We got into her truck and drove downtown.

"Do you mind asking one of the other servers for a ride home?" Mrs. Carpenter asked as she parallel parked in front of the restaurant. "I have my quilting circle at the retirement home tonight and sometimes it goes pretty late."

"Yeah. No problem," I said.

"Did you bring your house key?"

I patted my pocket.

"Good." The wrinkles between her white eyebrows deepened. "On second thought, maybe I should pick you up. I called animal control to see if they'd found any of those dogs, but they didn't find a trace of 'em. If they decide to attack you again . . ."

"I'll be fine." I got out of the truck and waved as Mrs. Carpenter pulled away.

The Navajo Mexican had only four customers when I arrived, their voices mingling with the soft drums and chanting played over the speaker system. Yana was at a table taking an order. She smiled and mouthed, "Thank you!"

"Magdalena!" a voice called. I jumped. José came bustling out from the kitchen, wiping his hands on a rag. "Magdalena. You're right on time. Here, come and get an apron and a name tag."

Magdalena? I looked at Yana. She shrugged.

I followed José into the kitchen and my eyes started to burn. Naalyehe was chopping onions faster than I could see. He paused and looked over his shoulder. Our eyes met and he set the knife down.

"Yana told me what happened at school," he said. My face started to burn. Naalyehe reached into his pocket and pulled something out. "This is for you. *Yo-ih.* It means 'beads.'" He held a bracelet up. It was made from red and white glass beads interwoven with three larger, brown beads. "Those," Naalyehe said, touching the brown, "are cedar berries. They will keep you safe."

I reached out to take the bracelet, but before I could, Naaly-ehe hooked it onto my left wrist and whispered something I couldn't understand.

"Thanks," I said, wondering if he had a mild case of dementia.

He nodded and turned back to chopping onions.

José handed me a white apron, which I tied around my hips. I looked up to find him studying the letter on the front of my shirt.

"I'm sorry. This is the only black shirt I own," I said.

"It's fine," José said. "You can have anything except profanity on your shirt, as long as the shirt itself is black. I was just wondering if you bought it that way or made the *A* yourself. *Es interesante.*"

"That means 'interesting,'" Naalyehe said over his shoulder.

I looked down at the scarlet letter, at the spattered spray paint. Maybe it was sort of interesting.

"Are you ready to work?" José handed me a pin-on name tag.

I stared at it blankly. "This isn't my name."

"I thought you needed a bit of Latino flare, *Magdalena.* When my wife heard I was hiring a *gringa* . . ." José's voice trailed off and he carefully pinned the name tag over my heart.

"Nervous?" he asked.

"Very."

He smiled. "Well, just do your best and hustle. Even if your serving isn't too good, your pretty face and the food will make up for it. You'll do fine."

With a pad of paper and a pen, I went out into the dining room. For thirty minutes Yana showed me how to seat people, where the menus were, how to use the pop machine, and how to take food orders.

I can't say waiting tables was easy. It was actually really hard. And even though the restaurant wasn't very busy, I ran the floor alone after Yana left. Midway through my shift I was sticky with sweat and my back ached between my shoulder blades. But I was getting tips. Not a lot—five dollars here, a few ones there. And people actually talked to me, unlike at school. At the restaurant I wasn't invisible, and I wasn't the main attraction. I was just me.

A little after nine o'clock, after my last customers had gone, José came into the dining room with a broom and dustpan, and turned the OPEN sign to CLOSED.

"Magdalena," he said, "good work. Why don't you take the trash out, then come and see me. Dumpster's out back."

"All right, boss," I said, wiping my damp forehead.

I carried the restaurant's sticky, leaking trash bags through the kitchen. Naalyehe held the back door open for me and watched as I crossed a small parking lot to the Dumpster.

"Thanks," I said as I walked back into the kitchen.

He nodded and locked the door.

I took the tips from my apron and put them into my jeans pocket, then went back to the dining room. José was finishing sweeping the floor.

"Ah, *gringa*. How was your first night?" he asked, handing me the dustpan.

"Tiring!" I said, rolling my aching shoulders. I put the dustpan at the edge of a junk pile and José swept it into the pan.

"You did surprisingly well for having no experience. I'll put you on next week's schedule."

A smile danced onto my face. "Sounds good." I dumped the dustpan's contents into the trash and handed it to José.

"All right. *Buenas noches*, then, Magdalena."

I stared at him.

"It means 'good night,'" he explained.

"Oh. 'Night," I replied, taking a step toward the front door. I paused. "José?"

"*Sí?*"

"Aren't you going home?"

He laughed. "There's work to do. Naalyehe and I will be here another hour at least."

"Oh. All right." I didn't bother to ask for a ride home. I knew the way.

I stepped out into the cool, dry New Mexico spring night. The air felt amazing on my sweat-dampened skin. Overhead, the stars shone brilliant, looking close enough to touch. I stared at them as I started the slow walk toward home.

I'd gone two blocks when I realized I had forgotten my jacket. I wouldn't have cared, would have just kept going, if it didn't have my house key in it. Groaning, I turned around and began walking back.

Naalyehe was mopping the floor when I walked into the restaurant.

"Why are you back?" he asked, glancing at the bracelet on my wrist.

"Forgot my jacket and house key," I explained, hurrying to the back room. "Bye," I said a second time.

"Be safe, Maggie Mae," Naalyehe said.

For the second time, I trudged wearily toward home. The occasional passing car lit up the dark night as I hurried along the city streets. It wasn't until I was out of downtown and walking along a lonely, deserted stretch of road that I realized a car kept driving by—the same car. My palms started to sweat.

The car crawled by a fourth time. My blood flowed double-time as I stared at the glowing red taillights. When the brake lights flashed crimson, I stopped walking and watched the car pull to the side of the road fifty yards ahead. It flipped a U-turn.

I was off the road and crashing through dry, brittle weeds. The car inched to a stop at the very place I'd been standing.

I crouched behind a narrow-trunked juniper and listened. A car door opened and slammed shut. Feet thumped on cement and then began snapping sticks and swishing through weeds.

My blood turned to ice as a dark figure picked its way toward my hiding place. Who in their right mind would follow a lone female into the woods on a dark night? Only a murderer or rapist. I needed a dog for protection. Or pepper spray.

I had a thought. An epiphany, actually.

Call me freaking crazy, but I unhooked my new bracelet and then tore off my clothes, right there in the woods, in spite of the fact that I was alone with a (possibly) murdering rapist. I was mad with fear and totally desperate.

And I had a plan.

I closed my eyes and thought of Shash, his lean body, long black-and-white fur, the smell of him, the sound of his barking. Then I willed myself to become him. *Forced* myself to change. My hearing sharpened, then my sense of smell. My fingers shrank, claws replaced my nails, and my teeth grew long and sharp. I fell to all fours, growling at the shadow slinking through the trees, then darted forward, barking.

A shrill scream broke out in the night. The shadow turned toward the road and started to run, but fell with a heavy thud and noisy expulsion of breath. The scent of soap and lavender drifted on the air, but I couldn't quite place where I'd smelled it before. Then I heard the voice.

"Please, good doggy, don't hurt me!" she begged. It was Ginger. I could hear her heart jumping in her chest, hear her labored, terrified breathing, smell the acrid tang of fear. "I was just trying to find my friend to see if she wanted a ride somewhere! Don't hurt me."

A high-pitched whine left my throat. I had to make sure she wasn't hurt. With my ears flat against my head and my tail wagging, I slowly walked toward her.

Ginger jumped to her feet, ran to her idling car, and drove away.

I hung my head and tucked my tail between my legs. If I had just stayed on the side of the road and found out who had been following me, I would be in a car on my way home at this very moment. Instead, I was a smelly old dog three miles from home.

Joy filled me and my tail began to wag so hard my entire butt wagged with it. Had I been human, I would have danced a jig, would have jumped for joy, screamed with elation. I had changed! It wasn't the full moon, yet I had changed! Because I wanted to! And not only that, I had changed into Shash . . . on purpose.

I trotted over to my pile of clothing and picked up my jeans and T-shirt, careful not to spill the tips from my jeans. Somehow I managed to get my shoes by their untied laces, but couldn't get the jacket into my mouth. Although, with a dog's sense of smell, I could come back for it another time. And besides, I was clothed in a fur coat.

I ran home.

In Mrs. Carpenter's yard, I willed my body back to its normal shape and I . . . changed back.

"Yes!" I whispered, silently clapping my hands. For two years I had been shifting at the most terrible times. I had no idea that it could be a voluntary transformation.

I got dressed in the dark, grinning, until I remembered my key was in my jacket pocket. The smile fell from my face and my shoulders slumped.

The house was dark and Mrs. Carpenter's truck wasn't in the driveway. I walked to the front porch and rattled the door handle. Locked.

I sat on the porch swing, weighing my options—wait for Mrs. Carpenter, or go back for the jacket? Then another brilliant idea came to me. I had changed into a housecat before, and a dog. What if I could change into something really *fast*—a natural runner. Like a cheetah?

For the second time that night, I stripped, folding my clothes into a neat pile and setting them on the swing.

I tried to remember exactly what a cheetah looked like—the long, rangy, superthin body and gold, feral eyes—then willed myself to take its form. Slowly, agonizingly, I felt myself begin to change. The shifting of shapes felt awkward, like trying to fit a square package into a round box. And then I was a big, lean, spotted cat with really long sharp claws, amazing night vision, and a tail as thick as my human wrist.

Then I ran.

I don't mean ran, but flew, glided, soared over the land with more speed and grace than I'd ever imagined. I was like water rushing over a smooth surface. My body was so fine-tuned and fast, I could imagine how it would feel to drive a Ferrari one hundred miles per hour. Trees blurred as air slipped over my speeding form.

In mere moments I was at the spot where I'd left my jacket. I picked it up carefully, for I had felt my razor-sharp teeth, had licked them with my sandpaper tongue.

I started the gliding sprint toward home and arrived long before I was ready to stop running. The desert night called to me, begging to be explored, but exhaustion clawed at my muscles and hunger gnawed my feline belly. If I kept running, I would find a wild animal to track and eat, raw and bloody and still alive as my teeth tore into it. The thought made me queasy. It was definitely time to change back.

The transition from big cat to human was so easy, I lost my balance and fell to my knees on the front porch. Not bothering to get dressed, I got my clothes from the swing, unlocked the door, and stumbled inside.

∾ 13 ∾

Over the course of that week, I discovered three things.

First, it was better being invisible than the main attraction at school. Everywhere I went, girls whispered about me behind their hands and boys whistled and leered. The male half of the freshman class thought I was something pretty special, daring each other to ask me for my panties, or out on a date, or standing as close to me as they dared while someone covertly snapped our picture with a cell phone.

Second, Bridger O'Connell treated me like we were perfect strangers, like I'd asked. And it was miserable.

Third, I could change into *almost* anything.

By the time Friday rolled around eleven different boys had asked me if they could have a pair of my panties. Seriously, even if I'd had a pair or two to spare, there was no way they'd be getting them.

I went directly to work after school, so by the time I walked out of the Navajo Mexican, I was dead on my feet and aching to get home fast so I could fall into bed until noon the next morning. The last table I'd waited on was a group of cowboys wearing sweat-stained cowboy hats who'd talked nonstop about their horses. Horses were fast.

Behind a screen of scrawny bushes that grew in front of a bank, I stripped down to my birthday suit and thought of a beautiful black horse—black to blend with the night. I told my body to change, felt my long hair start to grow longer, my front teeth lengthen . . . then I hit a brick wall, metaphorically speaking. Nothing else changed. With my tongue, I prodded my very horsey teeth. My fingers trailed through my new waist-length hair. The change had definitely started.

I tried to change into a horse again, *forcing* my feet into heavy, rock-hard hooves, even though they didn't want to change. Again, I got stuck. I thought myself out of horse shape, back to me, but my hooves did not turn into the soft human feet I was born with. And my teeth didn't shrink back to normal, or my hair—as if I'd tried so hard to shift, I was stuck that way permanently.

I forced myself not to freak out and started getting dressed. But when I tried to shove my hooves into my jeans, they got stuck.

"You've got to be kidding me." I whistled through my horse teeth.

I slung my jeans and useless tennis shoes over my shoulder and clopped along the road, praying no one would stop to offer me a ride. I couldn't have explained walking home with hooves. Or wearing nothing but a T-shirt and panties while carrying a perfectly good pair of pants. Where were the freshman boys with their cell phone cameras now?

Finally, I reached Mrs. Carpenter's house. My hooves echoed like thunder on the front porch. Inside, I stomped to my bedroom as fast as I could. My feet shook the whole house—you can't tiptoe with hooves. I worried Mrs. Carpenter would wake up and investigate. But she didn't.

I didn't bother showering; I was too upset. And besides, I didn't know how stable horse hooves would be on the shower floor. Instead, I stared at my face in the dresser mirror for hours, watching my buckteeth slowly, millimeter by millimeter, shrink back to their normal size. My hooves grew into regular human feet again, too. And by the time sunlight was squeezing into my bedroom window, my hair was its normal length, halfway down my back.

Mrs. Carpenter went to church on Sunday while I slept in, still exhausted from the horse incident. After church she planned on doing service at a soup kitchen by feeding the homeless, so I had the house to myself all day. I folded laundry. Did homework. Worked in the garden. Cleaned the bathroom. The day wasn't half over, and I was stuck in a house with no TV, no computer, and a bookcase filled with western romance novels older than me.

I lay on my bed and stared at the ceiling, listening to the lazy tick of a clock, and fell asleep.

I jumped awake, pulse hammering, as if someone were standing over me, breathing on my face. The cot groaned beneath me as I struggled to sit. My room was nearly dark, the only light a pale evening glow squeezing into my room through the closed blinds. And the room was empty.

"Hello? Mrs. Carpenter?" I called out. The ticking clock was my only answer. I pulled the purple quilt under my chin and wondered what had woken me—until I heard the hoarse, raspy howl of a hound.

"Duke?" I whispered. As if they'd heard me, Duke and Shash started barking bloody murder, like there was a fox in the barn. And I was the only one here to chase it out.

I scrambled up off the cot and jammed my feet into shoes, then ran through the shadowy house and out the unlocked front door. But when I got out into the long-shadowed evening, I realized my mistake. It wasn't Duke and Shash barking—the barn was silent. The noise was coming from the woods that surrounded Mrs. Carpenter's property.

I stood frozen in her driveway, listening. Evening wind ruffled through my hair and danced through the pine boughs, and the barking stopped. And then, as if my animal instincts tapped momentarily into my human brain, I understood what was happening. The dogs that had attacked me were trying to track my scent. And they were close.

Without warning, the howling and yapping started up again, lots of dogs this time instead of two, the noise coming from all directions. The wind had carried my scent to them.

Duke and Shash started barking and scratching at the barn doors. A light shone on me, followed by the sound of something approaching on the gravel drive. I whirled around, certain I was about to be eaten.

Mrs. Carpenter's baby-blue truck crawled along the driveway. She parked it and shut off the lights.

"Maggie Mae, how are you, dear?" she asked, climbing from the truck. Her feet crunched on gravel, the only sound left in the darkening evening. "Maggie?"

"We've got to get inside," I said, my voice trembling. I steered Mrs. Carpenter to the front door and bolted it behind us.

"Is everything all right?" Mrs. Carpenter asked, her eyes wide.

"Yeah. I mean no—I don't want you to catch a chill. It's a bit windy out there." I glanced out the front window. "Have you heard anything from animal control?"

"Nothing new," she said, frowning. "But I'll call them tomorrow morning if you'd like. Have you had dinner yet? I'm famished."

I shook my head. But I had no appetite.

Due to a sleepless night, with Duke and Shash restless in the barn and barking half the night, I passed Monday morning in a groggy daze. Students watched me, but their whispers didn't register. Only cobwebs filled my brain. By lunchtime I could hardly keep my eyes open. Instead of sitting with Yana, I wandered outside to the rear courtyard and sighed, for the sun's warmth seemed to soak into my skin and make it impossible to keep my eyes open. I took ten steps and lay down in the sunny grass.

Like a reptile, I curled up and fell asleep.

I mentioned before that I am not usually a deep sleeper. But I slept like a rock on that grass. It wasn't until a shadow blocked the sun that I jerked back to consciousness, flinging my arms in front of my face, expecting to smell dog breath and feel fangs.

"Are you all right, dear?" a white-haired man asked, staring at me and holding a rake.

I slowly eased my arms down from my face. "Just taking a nap," I explained, blinking sleep from my eyes.

"A nap during class?"

Class? It wasn't still lunchtime? I looked around the courtyard and felt embarrassment creep through me. Beneath one of the farthest trees sat a spectator.

"Um . . . thanks for waking me," I said to the groundskeeper. I walked toward a shady circle of grass and sat down, then peered toward the farthest tree to see if I had been forgotten. He was still staring right at me. Well, two could play the staring game.

He sat perfectly still in the shade of the tree. His skin looked unnaturally white against his midnight hair. And even though he'd ditched me at prom, it didn't hurt to look at him. Seriously, he was a visual feast. Pure eye candy.

He raised his dark eyebrows. I felt my cheeks start to flush, so I looked at my watch.

"Dude!" I blurted, shocked. It was almost one thirty, way past the end of lunch. I had been asleep a long time. I stood and started walking toward the school, making a point not to glance at Bridger again. Behind me I heard a shoe scuff cement and then someone fell into step beside me. My heart started to flutter. I knew if I looked up I would be gazing into a pair of black eyes.

Don't get attached, I thought.

"What I don't get is why Danni's so convinced you're a prostitute."

Of all the conversation starters, he would have to pick that one. I stopped walking and looked at him with a smirk, ready to brush him off, but my heart lurched and stuttered. Standing so close, I realized how much I had missed his friendship. I glared into his eyes, eyes so dark a shade of gray, his pupils got lost. A smile danced across his face and I realized I was staring at him again. I blinked and cleared my throat, trying to remember what he had asked me. Oh, yeah—prostitute.

"Well, it's a long story," I said sarcastically. A warm breeze blew my hair across my face and I breathed in the smell of Bridger O'Connell. I took a second deep breath and fought the urge to close my eyes. He smelled . . . wonderful, like clean clothes and soap and joy.

Don't get attached!

I took a step backward. He was cramping my personal space and making it impossible to think.

He took a step forward and leaned toward me. "I could use a good story," he said, grinning. My heart started to patter, like rain hitting a window.

"I never said it was a *good* story," I corrected.

"So, it's a bad story? Even better."

"It's not a bad story, either. I'm not like that, Bridger. Look, I have to get to class," I snapped, turning toward the door. He walked beside me and our fingers touched. I tucked my hands into my pockets.

"I'm really sorry about prom, Maggie. Is there any way I can make it up to you? Any way you can forgive me?" he asked.

I paused and looked at him again. The way the sun hit his hair made it look as shiny and black as a crow's feathers, but there were hints of gold in it, too. He raised his black eyebrows and I realized I was gawking at him. Again.

"Well?" he prodded, the smile gone from his face.

Well what? I wondered, tearing my gaze away from his. "Oh. Yeah. Whatever. You're forgiven." I bit my tongue and groaned inwardly. Had I seriously just forgiven him?

"So, we're friends again?" The breeze was back, stirring the scent of Bridger into the air and blowing my hair into my eyes. He brushed my hair from my forehead and tucked it behind my ear. I had to fight the desire to press my cheek against his hand.

Don't get attached! I mentally screamed.

I shrugged and pushed the door open. He didn't follow me into the school.

∾ 14 ∾

You would think that after the horse incident I would stop experimenting. But obviously I hadn't learned my lesson.

It started because of my skin. New Mexico is dry—the air, the ground, everything. Including my skin. It was dry to the point of looking a little scaly, and when I looked at my skin, I could almost feel the forked tongue fluttering against my teeth. So I thought, *Why not turn into a snake? I have an hour to kill before work.*

I stood in front of the bathroom mirror, closed my eyes, and imagined sleek, green, pearly scales instead of skin, a forked tongue, and eyes with long, narrow pupils. Then I tried, very gently, to change.

My tongue thinned and split, darting out between my smiling lips. My skin changed next, turning from dry and semi-pale to metallic green scales that shimmered in layers of thin, translucent disks. I leaned closer to the mirror and studied my eyes, waiting for them to change, too.

They didn't. I was stuck. Again.

"Crap!" I hissed through gritted teeth, fervently trying to

change back into myself. I glared at the freaky scales covering my entire body and tried to visually force them back beneath the surface. They didn't budge. At closer inspection, I realized the problem might be washed away—I was coated in a silky powder, as if the scales were slowly deteriorating into a fine, pearly dust. It floated off me in shimmering clouds and drifted down to the floor.

I stripped and got into the shower.

With half a container of body wash squeezed onto a washcloth I vigorously began scrubbing. Milky white water dripped from me, water that reflected the bathroom light in translucent rainbow colors, like motor oil in a parking lot puddle.

After scrubbing my body at least eight times, my skin looked halfway normal and the slit in my tongue was substantially smaller.

I toweled off and groaned as puffs of opalescent dust wafted from my skin. A bottle of lotion would have been ideal, cementing the powder to me. Unfortunately, I didn't have any; otherwise I never would have gotten into this mess in the first place. I tried applying a thin layer of conditioner to my skin—bad idea—and got back into the shower.

Five minutes later, I got my black T-shirt from the bedroom floor and pulled it over my wet hair. "No!" I groaned, looking at my reflection in the mirror. My shirt was no longer black. It sparkled and gleamed dark bluish silver. Even the *A* on the front looked rosy pink instead of scarlet. I rolled my eyes. I was such an idiot!

I pulled a brush through my wet hair and slicked it into a high ponytail, grabbed my house key, and went to the living room.

"You ready to go?" Mrs. Carpenter asked, peering over the

top of a romance novel. Her eyes grew wide and she closed the novel. "What in heaven have you done to yourself?"

I took a deep breath. "Don't ask," I grumbled, the *s* in *ask* coming out in a hiss. Her eyes moved over my entire body and she started laughing.

"Maggie Mae, you have a knack for finding trouble," she said, standing.

"I sure do." I followed her out the front door.

The afternoon sun gleamed, making the snake-scale residue glow in shades of rose, baby blue, and grass green.

"You are such an idiot!" I whispered.

Mrs. Carpenter peered at me over her shoulder. "Did you say something?"

I shook my head and was blinded by my own glow. And that is when my toe caught on a knobby tree root and I crashed to the ground in a giant cloud of snake-scale dust. I sneezed once and climbed back to my feet.

"Maggie Mae!" Mrs. Carpenter clasped my elbow. "Are you hurt?"

"I'm fine," I muttered. My palms stung and my knees felt bruised. I looked down at my jeans and groaned. This really wasn't my day. My jeans, the only hole-free pair I owned, now had tears over both of my scraped, bloody knees, and, yes, even the blood oozing from the shallow scrapes shimmered like gold. Brushing myself off, I climbed into the truck.

As we drove through town, Mrs. Carpenter kept glancing at me from the corner of her eye and laughing under her breath.

"You don't mind if I drop you off across the street from the restaurant, do you? It's hard to make a U-turn in rush-hour traffic."

I peered out the window at the busy road. "No problem." Mrs. Carpenter pulled to the side of the road. "Have a nice night," she called as I climbed from the truck.

I smiled and shut the door, watched her merge with traffic, then walked half a block to the crosswalk and waited for the light to change.

Every single person on that city block stopped what they were doing and pointed at me. Their scrutiny made me sweat, and, with that sweat, dust seeped out of my pores. The sun magnified the effect, giving me a full-body halo. Cars slowed and people rolled down their windows to stare. I pulled my hair out of its ponytail and let it hang around my face, shielding my identity from view.

The light changed. I kept my head down and crossed to the other side of the street. And plowed into Yana.

"Maggie Mae!" she blurted. She clutched my shoulders and shoved me into the cramped space between two buildings, staring at me with wide brown eyes. Scared eyes.

"It's only glitter dust," I began to explain self-consciously, brushing my arm for effect, but she didn't notice.

"Someone's looking for you again," she said, peering toward the road. "A stranger—same guy that I called you about. He's sitting in a Cadillac parked in front of the restaurant. He's been there all afternoon . . . waiting. Naalyehe is nervous."

I stared at her, dumbfounded. "Who is it?"

Yana rolled her eyes. "Didn't you hear what I said? My grandpa is afraid of him. Afraid! And he can sense things about people." She bit her lip and studied me.

"What does he look like?"

"Totally normal—your average middle-age man, someone

you wouldn't look at twice. Not too tall, thin, brown hair, receding hairline."

I shrugged. "Whatever. I don't care. He's probably got me mixed up with someone else." I stepped toward the street.

Yana grabbed my bicep. "Naalyehe is afraid of him! You can't come into work," she insisted. "At least not yet. José just called the cops and reported the guy for loitering. As soon as the cops pick him up, you can come to work. Go to the park and hide out for now. I'll come get you when it's safe."

Yana pulled me into an unexpected hug. A shiver of fear danced down my spine. That hug scared me more than news of the stranger. I had the sinking suspicion she was hugging me in case this was the last time she'd ever see me.

"Be careful," she whispered into my ear. When she let me go, her black motocross T-shirt shimmered with color. She dashed back to the sidewalk.

"Thanks," I called in a shaky voice, darting glances all around.

I slunk out from between the shops and peered both ways down the street before sprinting back the way I had come, dust trailing after me like a rainbow-hued comet's tail. I covered two blocks before the dust settled, then circled back another two blocks before making my way to the park.

With spring warming the air, the park was packed. I sighed with relief—where better to hide than out in the open, camouflaged by other people? College students partied at one end of the park; at the other end the playground bustled with children and people crowding the winding cement. Cotton fell from the giant trees lining the park and filled the air with the illusion of snow.

I wandered past the college party, ignoring the catcalls and invitations to join them, and found an empty section of sun-flooded lawn close to the playground. I looked in all directions, making sure no one could sneak up on that spot, then sat, trying to ignore the anxiety making me feel like the ham sandwich I had for lunch might make a messy return.

A thousand questions were shifting uneasily through my head: Was I in trouble? Had someone in town seen me naked and tracked me down? Was it someone from my past? A previous foster parent? Did he ask for me by name, or show a picture, or what?

I was so wound up in my thoughts, I didn't realize anyone was sitting beside me until he spoke.

"You're glowing. It's beautiful."

His voice was little more than a whisper, but I was on my feet, staring down at him and ready to sprint.

"I didn't mean to scare you. Are you going to run away from me again?" he asked with mild amusement. Curiosity danced in his dark eyes.

I swallowed a lump of fear and answered, "Someone's looking for me."

He stood. "What do you mean?"

"Someone was at the restaurant today looking for . . . me?" I said uncertainly, wondering if that was a piece of information I should be sharing with Bridger. "Never mind. It's no big deal."

"You're glowing," he said again, reaching out to touch my dusty cheek. His fingertips came away from my skin alive with reflected sunlight. "Wow. Where did you get this stuff?" He blew on his fingers and the dust sparkled a hundred different colors in the air before settling on his jeans.

This *stuff? Oh, I tried to turn into a snake with scales and a forked tongue this afternoon and it backfired*, I thought sarcastically. I wondered how long he'd stick around once he found *that* out.

"I don't remember," I mumbled, turning my back to him.

"So, you want to go get something to eat?"

I looked at him over my shoulder. "You mean you and me? Together?"

"Yeah, you and me. Remember, we're friends." He glanced at his leather-banded watch. "I know this place—"

"I'm working tonight."

"Where do you work?"

"The Navajo Mexican, with Yana."

"What time do you get off?"

"Sorry. I've got to go," I blurted, striding away. Yana was on the other side of the park looking for me.

"Creepy dude's gone," she called. "Police came and picked him up. They'll hold him overnight while they do a background check."

My shoulders relaxed as if the weight of the world had been lifted from them. As Yana and I walked toward the restaurant, I glanced over my shoulder. Bridger was staring at me, a frown on his face. I felt a feathery touch on my skin and forgot about him—Yana was running her fingers over my forearm.

"What are you doing?" I asked.

"This glitter crap is really freaking me out. It looks like it's coming *out* of your skin." She brushed her fingers over her eyelids and they shimmered.

"Pretty," I said, wondering how she'd feel if she knew she

was putting disintegrating snake scales on her eyelids. "What's the occasion?"

She blushed. "José hired a new dishwasher. He rides a motorcycle and has a tattoo of a tarantula on his hand," she said with a smile.

∞ 15 ∞

It was a bad night. Not only did I drop a tray of drinks on myself, I slipped on the spilled soda and beer and landed in it. The liquid soaked into my freshly torn jeans, clear to my panties. I also managed to crash into Yana while carrying a scalding plate of fry bread smothered in refried beans and greasy cheese. The beans and melted cheese clung to my shirt, burning me through the fabric. I tore my shirt off in the middle of the dining room. The college boys I'd been waiting on cheered and clapped, and left me a really good tip.

I got orders all wrong, accidentally giving a child an alcoholic margarita, serving a vegetarian college professor the mutton platter, and serving lukewarm coffee—I had forgotten to put the pot back on the hot plate.

To make matters worse, I'd been too busy to ask Naalyehe about the stranger.

At a quarter past ten, when most of the patrons were gone and no more were coming in, I made my way to the kitchen.

José, Naalyehe, and two part-time cooks were cleaning up the dinner rush, talking and laughing.

"Can I talk to you, Naalyehe?" I asked.

All four men turned to me and their mouths snapped shut.

"Maggie Mae," Naalyehe said. He put down his washcloth and steered me out to the dimly lit parking lot behind the building. José's car was the only vehicle parked in back.

Naalyehe studied me for a moment before asking, "Are you hiding something I should know about?"

I sighed, blowing loose wisps of hair away from my face. I was hiding all sorts of things.

"You do not need to fear me," Naalyehe said, his voice soft. "But I need to know why that man is looking for you."

"I don't know why." That question had been running laps through my brain all night. "Did he tell you his name?"

"I asked. He refused."

"Well, what exactly did he say?"

"He said, 'I'm looking for a young woman, goes by Maggie Mae Mortensen. She has black hair and pale eyes and is eighteen years old. I was told that she works here. Have you seen her?'" Naalyehe repeated in monotone.

"What did you tell him?"

"I said no one by that name works for me, *Magdalena*, and my only employees with black hair have dark eyes."

I ran a hand through my faded plum-colored ponytail and smiled. "Thanks."

"Are you sure you do not want to tell me anything?" Naalyehe asked again.

"I'm an orphan. Is that what you want to hear?"

His lips thinned. "I am sorry. That must be hard at your age."

Yeah, I thought bitterly. *But not as hard as it was when I was a little kid.*

"You wear the *yo-ih?*" he asked. I held my left arm up for him to see. "Good. Do not take it off."

He opened the door and I walked into the steamy kitchen, Naalyehe a step behind.

"*Gringa,*" José said. "Yana restocked the condiments before she left for the night, so you get to empty the trash. Then go home and put your feet up. You worked hard."

"Sure, boss," I said, faking a smile. I hated trash duty. My feet dragged as I went back into the restaurant.

Since I was already covered with soda and beans, I figured it was only fair that I tackle the trash. The bags dripped soda and beer as I dragged them out back. The smell of old Mexican food, stale beer, and rotting meat wafted from the Dumpster. I held my breath and slung the trash up over the side.

Light flickered beside the Dumpster. A face, red against the small flame of a lighter, glowed to life. I stumbled backward and almost tripped.

"*Hola,*" a stranger said, taking a drag on a cigarette. The lighter died and his face went dark.

"Hello," I squeaked, ready to run to the restaurant.

"I'm Tito. The new dishwasher."

"Oh!" Yana's motorcycle guy. I took a calming breath. He chuckled and took another long drag on his cigarette, the end glowing red.

"Nice to meet you. Have a nice night," I said, turning to leave.

Back in the kitchen, I studied myself in the bright light. Refried beans plastered my shirt, mashed into the fabric. The drinks I'd spilled and then sat in were almost dry and getting stiffer by the minute, and the scale dust, though hardly visible on my skin anymore, clung to the sticky fabric, making the spill brilliantly obvious.

"Ugh. Thank you for sending me home, José," I whispered.

Just then Penney and José burst into the kitchen, José speaking about a mile a minute in Spanish, fanning his face with his hand.

"I *already* gave him a seat in the best booth!" Penney interrupted, flinging her hands about as she spoke.

"Well, go out there and see what he wants to drink . . . and don't mess it up!" José barked.

Penney nodded, put her hands on her curvy hips, and hurried out the door to the dining room.

"What's going on?" I asked. Naalyehe watched us from the other side of the kitchen.

"An important customer." José's voice was a little too loud. He looked at Naalyehe. "If the town knows he's eating our food, this will be the most popular restaurant around!"

"I thought it already was," I said.

José smiled, walked over to the sink were I stood, and gave me a one-armed hug, squeezing the air from my lungs. "Oh, you sweet little thing! If only my sons weren't already married . . ."

Just then the kitchen door burst open. Penney walked in with her hands on her round hips and stared at me like I'd stolen her favorite lip gloss. José let go of me.

"What?" José and I asked at the same time.

"He wants *Maggie Mae* to wait on him."

José took one look at my filthy clothes and started spewing Spanish again.

"Who wants me to wait on him?" I asked.

"Bridger O'Connell," Penney answered.

"What?"

"Don't panic, Magdalena," José said in obvious panic, handing me a damp washcloth and motioning to my filthy shirt. "You've become a fabulous server. Just don't mess up! And don't drop any drinks on him!" He turned to Penney. "Can you fix her up a little or is it a lost cause?"

Penney studied me and yanked the washcloth out of my hands. Pulling the hair tie from my ponytail, she let my hair spill around my shoulders. She tugged her fingers through it a few times, fluffed it around my face, and then looked at me.

"Better," she said. "But wait!" She fished in her jeans pocket and pulled out a tube of glittery red lip gloss—as if I didn't have enough glitter on me. Without a word, she coated my lips. "Hopefully he won't notice the stain on your pants," she mused, cringing. "On second thought, hopefully he won't care." She smiled apologetically at me. "All right, *chica*. He's in the booth by the window. Go take his order."

My hands were trembling as I stepped into the nearly empty dining room. I felt like José and Penney had thrown me out to appease a hungry pack of wolves. The booth by the window is the one farthest from the kitchen. Bridger sat facing the front window. I approached slowly, studying his back.

He was wearing black pants and a dark blue button-up shirt with the sleeves rolled around his elbows. He must have seen my reflection in the window, because he turned around.

"Hey," he said. I watched his eyes slip from my face to my shirt to my spattered jeans, and my cheeks started to burn. Then his eyes lingered on my name tag. "Magdalena?" He studied me a moment before I remembered to speak.

"Can I get you something to drink?" I asked nervously.

"Coke."

I nodded and headed toward the kitchen. Penney and José were peering at me from the kitchen door.

"So far, so good!" José said, giving me a thumbs-up.

"What does he want to drink? I'll get it for you," Penney said. I wondered if she was afraid I'd spill it.

"Coke. But why are you guys freaking out? He's my age."

"He is an O'Connell," José snapped. "His family owns the old mine."

"There's an old mine in Silver City?"

"Why do you think it is called Silver City, *gringa?*" José answered, tugging his mustache. "Now go back over there and recommend my fish tacos."

I strode over to Bridger. He'd been watching my reflection in the window with an amused grin on his face. "Do you want to order, or would you like to try our chef's specialty?"

"What's your favorite entrée?" he asked.

"The fish tacos. They're awesome." And the only thing I'd ever eaten.

"All right. I would like two servings of fish tacos. And another Coke. I'm expecting company."

My shoulders slumped. I looked at him, so gorgeous and dressed to kill. Of course he'd be expecting a date.

"You're frowning," he said.

I forced a smile to my mouth. "Two fish tacos and another Coke coming up."

"Wait. May I speak with José, please?"

"Two fish tacos, one Coke, and one Hispanic chef, coming right up," I amended and hurried to the kitchen.

"José, he wants to see you. And he wants fish tacos. Two plates. He's expecting company."

"Ah! Good girl. Penney, go home. Magdalena will finish up

tonight," José said before removing his apron and hurrying out to the dining room.

Penney looked at me and shrugged. She removed a wad of tips from her apron pocket and crammed them into her jeans pocket. "Good luck with Bridger," she said, pulling her denim jacket from a coat hook on the door.

"Thanks."

She studied me for a moment. "Yana told me about the creepy dude. Be careful."

"Don't worry about—" I started to say, but José came running into the kitchen all frantic and out of breath.

"Change of plan!" He gasped, tugging the jacket from Penney's shoulders and handing her a clean apron. "Penney, you stay and wait tables. Magdalena, go talk to Señor O'Connell." Without a word, he untied my apron and set it on the counter.

Penney and I exchanged confused looks. "Well, go on," she prodded.

My palms turned cold and damp as I approached Bridger's table. When he saw my reflection in the window, he stood and watched me. I stopped in front of him.

"Maggie?" he said.

"What?"

"I was hoping you would have dinner with me. I've taken the liberty of ordering your favorite entrée."

I swallowed hard and studied him for a moment. "Are you serious?"

"Totally."

"Did you get stood up? Am I your last resort?"

"No. You're my first choice. And José said you're done for the night."

He was so gorgeous, I would be a total idiot to say no. And it had been hours since I'd eaten. But on the other hand, I didn't want to get attached. I looked down at the *A* on my shirt and felt the sting of tears in my eyes.

I bit the inside of my cheek in an attempt to stop the tears and turned my back to him, blinking furiously. I turned back around.

"Thanks, but I really don't think dinner would be a good idea," I said. "I'm tired."

"So . . . we'll eat fast and then you can go home to bed," he reasoned.

"Look, I don't want to . . . I don't want to date anyone."

"Anyone? Or me?"

"Anyone."

His eyes narrowed. "Why not?"

"Because I don't want to get attached. Every time I get close to someone, I get hurt." And I didn't mean cute boys. Every time I got close to a foster family, I was removed from their house, never to hear from them again.

"And what makes you think that eating a meal with me is going to hurt you? All I want is to get to know you a little better."

Well, that right there's the problem, I thought. Knowing me better is what makes everyone despise me. All right, I told myself, just dish and he'll never want to see me again. I rushed in before I had time to chicken out.

"You want to get to know me better? I'm a dirt-poor orphan that has been passed around to more foster homes in the past thirteen years than I can remember. I had fifteen run-ins with the law before the age of eighteen. Yana is my first and only friend. I've never had a boyfriend. The only date I ever went on, my date was so miserable he *ditched* me and left me standing on the dance floor. The scar in my eyebrow? I got it from an abusive foster father. Wanna know why I stayed with his family for two years even though he hit me? His wife was southern and cooked the best food I ever tasted . . . on a regular basis. You think I look like a nice person, and I am nice, but I come with a lot of nasty stuff." I crossed my arms and hardened my face into my best "I won't take crap from you" look.

"Interesting. So tell me the part that is going to make me hurt you," he said sarcastically. "Don't you realize that everything you've said makes me think you have the potential to be one of the most interesting people I've ever met?"

I struggled to keep my jaw from hitting the floor.

José arrived with two steaming bean-and-cheese-covered plates of fish tacos. My stomach rumbled.

"Sit, Magdalena!" José ordered, setting a plate down on the table.

"Come on. Just one painless meal," Bridger coaxed, sliding into his seat.

I looked between José and Bridger, then gave in and sat across from Bridger. I didn't know what else to do. This totally hot, smart guy wanted me to eat dinner with him, even after I gave him the dump truck version of my past? Well, minus the turning into an animal. Maybe I hadn't made it clear enough?

"So, if you've never had a boyfriend, have you ever been kissed?"

I caught my bottom lip in my teeth and shook my head.

"Huh. If the *A* on your shirt is for 'Adulterer,' but you've never even been kissed . . . isn't that the slightest bit contradictory?"

A smile lit my confused face. "Yeah. Ironic, isn't it?"

"Very. So, tell me about your foster families."

"Seriously?"

"Yeah. And sorry I ditched you."

I talked while we ate, yet even with me doing all of the talking, I finished my food long before he did. Penney kept our drinks full and asked if we'd like to see a dessert menu when our plates were empty.

"Would you like dessert, Maggie?" Bridger asked.

I looked at my watch. It was past eleven.

"No, I'm good," I said.

After Bridger paid for the meal and left a pile of bills on the table for a tip, we left the restaurant.

"So, where are you parked?" he asked, pausing beneath a streetlamp. In the dim light, his eyes were sparkly black.

"Parked?"

"Your car?"

"Oh. I don't drive myself home from work. I walk—"

"You walk to Mrs. C.'s house? Alone? In the dark?" Bridger asked incredulously.

"No, I don't walk. I . . ." I change into an animal. That slip of the tongue would have gone over well.

"You ride a bike?" he guessed when I didn't continue.

"No, I . . . run," I said awkwardly. It was true—I did run. Usually in the shape of a mountain lion or a coyote. They were faster than other animals.

"In your work clothes? In the dark? Aren't you afraid you'll trip and fall?" Bridger glanced at my freshly torn jeans and frowned. "Aren't you exhausted by the end of the day? Aren't you afraid some psycho will see you and hurt you? There are really dangerous people out there."

Every single thing he said was true. Were I a normal girl, I'd worry about those things. But I was abnormal. "I run fast," I said lamely.

"I know you run fast, but still. It seems dangerous. Can I drive you home?"

The night was dark, a thin layer of clouds hiding the moon. I thought of the man looking for me and wrapped my hand around the bracelet. "I suppose you can give me a ride," I told him.

Relief softened his beautiful face and my heart felt full of sunshine.

"Let's go." He looked me over once, his eyes lingering on my hands, before he shoved his own into his pockets and walked down the sidewalk. I walked half a block beside him till we came to his car. It beeped, the lights flashed, and the doors unlocked. I opened the passenger door and climbed in, hoping my dirty jeans wouldn't ruin the seat.

"What kind of car is this?" I asked. I'd never seen anything like it.

"Toyota FJ Cruiser. And it is definitely *not* a car. It's an SUV."

His FJ Cruiser was really nice. If I had to choose between some of the foster homes I'd lived in or Bridger's SUV, I'd live in his SUV in a heartbeat. The seats were soft and lined with pale gray leather, and when he turned the car on, Native American music filled it. I was immersed in sound, swimming in music.

Eagle feathers and beads hung from the rearview mirror, swinging with the movement of the car as he pulled away from the curb. We drove to Mrs. Carpenter's house in silence, just listening to music. When the car stopped in front of the porch, he glanced at me and turned off the engine. The car became pitch black inside.

"Why did you turn off your car?" I asked, instantly nervous.

"It's dark out. I thought I'd walk you to the door," he said as if this should have been pretty obvious. I glanced at the house. The porch light flooded the night and the windows glowed.

"I'll be fine by myself. Thanks for dinner. And the ride. It was nice, not . . . running . . . home in the dark."

"Are you sure you don't want me to walk you to the door?" he asked, unhooking his seat belt.

"No!" I blurted, reaching for the door handle.

"Wait," he said.

"What?"

"Thanks."

"For what? You paid for the meal."

"Thanks for giving me a second chance."

"You're welcome." I opened the car door and the interior light flashed on, giving me one last look at his face. My gaze lingered on his lips and the truth was, I wanted him to walk me to the door. Really wanted it. Because I could imagine him kissing me good night.

I climbed out of the car and darted to the front door. "Don't get attached, don't get attached," I chanted as Bridger pulled out of the driveway.

∾ 16 ∾

It was Sunday morning and I couldn't sleep. Thoughts of Bridger O'Connell were sprinting through my brain. Thoughts like, if I were a smart girl, I'd stop being friends with him. Because I felt a lot more than plain friendly every time I thought of him.

I rolled out of bed and put on grubby clothes, then went outside to work in the garden. It needed a good weeding.

The day was warm, the air utterly still. The screech of a bird filled the morning as I dug the tip of a shovel into the soil at the base of a weed. It screeched again, swooping overhead. I looked up and a small gray bird soared to the far end of the property and into the branches of a knobby pine. Something at the property's edge caught my eye. It shone white in the morning sun, like a bleached tree skeleton with branches pointing to the sky.

I walked to the edge of the property and paused, noticing for the first time a pattern in the trees. A perfect circle of pines had been planted around a central location, like planets orbiting the sun. Only these trees were orbiting Mrs. Carpenter's house. And they were perfectly spaced, as if someone had used a tape measure to get them all the exact distance apart.

But it was what lay perfectly spaced between the trees that caught my attention. Skulls. Not human—animal. The skull to my right was a horse skull, to my left a cow. The one in front of me, which had caught my attention, came from an animal with tall, branchlike horns. I clasped my hand around the rough, gray horn and lifted. A centipede slithered in the wet indentation the skull had left, and earthworm trails lined the dirt.

I examined the skull's empty eye sockets, then turned and went back to the garden, skull in hand, to resume my weeding.

A few minutes later, Mrs. Carpenter walked out of the house in a white denim dress, tan nylons, and rubber-soled pumps with her white hair pulled back in a bun and turquoise earrings dangling in her ears. I leaned on my shovel.

"Are you sure you don't want to go to church with me? And feed the homeless after?" she asked, pausing to look at the pile of weeds I'd pulled out of the freshly sprouting garden.

I wiped my hand across my gritty forehead. "I'm a mess. I'd make you late."

"I don't mind being late. The Lord forgives such things. I feel bad leaving you alone all day again."

I shook my head. "No thanks."

"The garden's coming along real nice."

I looked at the straight rows of sprouts coming out of the ground and smiled. "Thanks."

"If you want, you can get some of the chicken manure and sprinkle it around the plants. That'll help 'em grow." Her eyes moved over the garden and paused on the animal skull. "Where did that come from?" she asked.

"I hope you don't mind . . . I found it on the edge of your property. Thought it might look cool in the garden."

She frowned. "My second husband must have put it there—he's the one who planted the trees. It looks lovely in the garden and will probably scare scavengers away." She smiled and got into the truck. As the door slammed shut, I almost called out to her to wait. A whole day alone with no one for company but my sprouts didn't hold much appeal.

The truck crawled down the driveway as I hacked at the roots of a weed and pulled a fragrant piece of sage from the ground. I tossed it into the growing pile of weeds and felt so lonely my body seemed hollow.

I'd pulled three more weeds when an engine rumbled, growing steadily closer, and a vehicle turned into the long driveway. Mrs. Carpenter must have decided to try again to convince me to go with her. And I'd say yes this time. I dug my shovel into the ground and saw it wasn't Mrs. Carpenter's baby-blue truck that stopped in front of the porch.

I let go of the shovel and smoothed my hair, aware that I was a sweaty mess.

"Gardening on a Sunday?" Bridger asked as he stepped out of his SUV. He walked toward me, slow and leisurely, his hands in his jeans pockets. He wore a simple T-shirt, but the way it fit him, it looked like T-shirts were invented for his body. At my shovel he stopped and peered down into my eyes. "Hi."

"What are you doing here?" I asked, forcing myself to ignore the urge to wipe under my eyes in case I had mascara smeared there.

"I forgot to get your cell number."

"No cell phone. Sorry."

"Seriously?"

"Yeah. Why'd you want my number?"

He grinned. "Why do you think? So I can call you."

"Call me about what?"

He shrugged. "I knew the Navajo Mexican was closed today and thought you might like some company. I figured you'd be lonely, being new in town and having no family." My eyes grew round. I was so lonely it was driving me mad.

"Do you have lunch plans?" he asked.

"Lunch?" I looked at my watch. It was barely past ten. "No. No plans. I figured I'd finish the garden and then warm up some leftover chili and corn bread," I replied.

"Mind if I join you?" he asked.

"For leftovers or weeding?"

"Both."

"You eat leftovers?"

"If I'm lucky enough to be in a house that has them."

"All right. But just to warn you, I'm going to be dabbling in chicken manure before I eat lunch."

He laughed and pulled the shovel out of the ground. "How about I dig and you pull," he said.

" 'Kay."

He sunk the shovel into the dirt at the base of a weed and paused, frowning. "Where did you find that elk skull?" he asked, nodding toward the side of the garden.

I pointed to the edge of Mrs. Carpenter's property.

Bridger's eyebrows shot up. "You've broken her ring of protection. You should put it back."

"Her ring of *what*?"

"Protection," he answered, his eyes darkly serious.

"Whatever. It's just one measly animal skull, not an electric fence. And there are at least a hundred more. They make a huge ring around the entire property."

"Yeah. A ring of protection. I think you should put it back."

I rolled my eyes. "And what makes you the ring of protection expert?"

He leaned closer to me, looking right into my eyes as if he could see my soul. "My ancestry. I'm Navajo, remember?"

"Mrs. Carpenter didn't care that I moved it to the garden," I said, acutely aware of how dark his eyes were. "And besides, it's protecting my garden."

Bridger looked between the skull and me. "Just don't take anything else from the ring."

When we finished the garden, we went to the barn for the manure. An ancient wheelbarrow with a flat tire sat just outside the chicken coop, used to clean the coop out on a semi-regular basis. I shooed the clucking chickens away from the door and stepped inside, but Bridger didn't follow. He stood just outside the coop, completely preoccupied.

"What's up there?" he asked, pointing to a narrow flight of stairs with a dead-bolted door at the top.

"I've never been up there, but Mrs. Carpenter says it's an old stable-hand room. She says I can move up there if I want."

"Why don't you? It'd be a cool place to live."

I shrugged. There was no way I was going to tell him I was too scared to live up there, away from the safety of Mrs. Carpenter and her guns.

"Did you know Mrs. C. used to do barrel racing?" Bridger asked. "She competed at rodeos when she was younger. This barn used to be a stable before her first husband died."

"What happened? To the horses?"

"She couldn't keep up with the bills on her own, so she sold them."

We filled the wheelbarrow with rancid chicken manure, and then Bridger helped me spread it at the base of my sprouts. When we finished, he shaded his eyes and peered at the sky.

"You know," he said, "it is a gorgeous day. Why don't we pack your leftovers and go on a picnic?"

"That sounds nice."

He followed me to the front door and paused.

"You're invited in," I said, remembering the last time he'd come over and stood in the doorway waiting for a formal invitation. I left him in the living room and went to the kitchen to wash my hands and dig around in the fridge. Instead of getting chili, I got two yogurts, two apples, and two plastic spoons, and put them in a used Wal-Mart bag.

I walked into the living room. "I hope you don't mind—" He wasn't there. "Bridger?" I called, wondering if I'd been ditched again. I looked out the front window. His SUV was still there.

"Back here." I followed the sound of his voice to my bedroom. He was perched on the edge of the sewing table holding a photograph, studying it with a frown on his face.

It was the picture of me in my "prom dress." I'd torn up and thrown away the one with both of us before I'd decided to forgive him. I snatched the photo from his hands and forced down a surge of anger. And humiliation.

"I'm sorry how that night turned out. I wish things would have worked out differently," he said, studying me.

"Not me," I snapped, tossing the picture back onto the dresser. "Things worked out just how they should have."

"Why do you say that?" he asked, standing.

"I got to see the real you. You saved me from liking you as more than a friend." At least, it should have. But I liked Bridger more every day.

One black eyebrow slowly lifted. He stepped up to me and leaned in so close I could feel his exhaled breath on my face. His eyes lingered on my lips before looking into mine. I turned around, my heart hammering and my lips burning, and strode out of the house. Bridger followed.

"So, where should we go to eat?" he asked as we got into his SUV.

"I haven't thought ahead that far," I admitted. Because my brain was too full of Bridger.

"I'll choose then, since you're providing the food." Bridger started the engine. We drove through town and ended up on a sparsely populated road. The houses we passed, while few and far between, were growing nicer and bigger by the minute. Then the biggest house I have ever seen came into view on the left side of the road, surrounded by a tall stone fence. I stared at it as we drove past, trying to take in all the details.

"That house is huge!" I craned my neck to get one last look at it.

Bridger peered at me out of the corner of his eye. "You know, you should never judge a person by his house."

"Yeah. I know."

The paved road turned to dirt, and we entered uninhabited wilderness. About two miles up the dirt we were surrounded by dry, dusty mountains. There was a strange feel to the area, as if it should be teeming with life, yet it was silent and still.

"What is this place?" I asked.

"It's the old mine. No one ever comes up here anymore," Bridger replied. "I know a perfect spot for a picnic."

We circled around to the back side of a mountain and he stopped the car. I stepped out, looked around, and a smile washed over my face. The air smelled of dust and juniper and sunlight. The dry land was dotted with patches of green and shadowed in places by scraggly junipers and ponderosa pines. The trill of birds filled the air and wind rustled the trees. And that was it. Absolutely no human noise.

"How did you ever find this place?" I asked.

"I go biking up here all the time," Bridger explained. "And that"—he motioned to a tall hill of brown dirt where a red flag, faded and threadbare, flapped in the wind—"that is Evening Hill."

With the grocery bag picnic in one hand, Bridger grabbed my hand with his other and began pulling me up the dirt hill behind him.

"Why do you call it Evening Hill?" I asked, trying my best not to let the loose dirt spill into my shoes.

"Because if you sit here at sunset, you can actually see the evening descend over the world. See, look." He pulled me to a stop at the top of the hill.

"Oh." I could see for miles and miles. The sky stretched overhead brighter and bluer than I had ever seen it. A juniper-filled valley expanded out before us, ringed by distant purple mountains. There were no signs of humanity in that valley, no roads, no houses, no power lines.

"When a storm's coming, you can see lightning on the horizon before you see a single cloud," he added. He dropped my hand and casually draped his arm over my shoulders.

His arm felt good there, like I fit perfectly beneath it, like I should wrap my arms around his waist and lean against his chest. The view forgotten, I searched his face, trying to see what he was thinking. His face was turned to the horizon, alive with memories.

"I've been all over the world, but nowhere is as beautiful as the New Mexico desert," Bridger said quietly. Finally, he looked down at me and dropped his arm to his side. "Hungry?"

"Very."

We sat cross-legged, side by side, atop Evening Hill. I handed him his lunch and opened my yogurt.

"An apple and yogurt? What happened to the homemade chili and corn bread?" Bridger asked.

"I figured this would be easier to eat on a picnic. No dirty dishes."

"You realize this doesn't count as a *meal*, right?" He bit into his apple.

"Why not?" I replied, wondering if I should be offended.

"Because it's a *snack*. I'll be hungry five minutes after I eat this. But there's this place I want to take you. The food is awesome. You game?"

"What? Right now?"

"No, not right now. Around dinner time, preferably. Do you have plans?"

I looked away from him, at the beautiful view. My tongue felt tied in a knot and my brain zoomed through excuses I could give to turn him down.

"What? You already have a date tonight?"

"It's not that."

"Well, then, why don't you want to go?"

Because I like being with you too much and that's going to lead to a broken heart. Mine, specifically. "I don't want to date you," I said. "But don't get me wrong, you're pretty cool to hang out with and all. Only, I don't want a boyfriend or anything. Just a friend."

He studied me for a long minute. "Good. I'm not supposed to date local girls. Family rule."

He stood before I had a chance to ask him why.

"I want to show you something else," he said, gathering up our lunch trash from the ground. I took a bite of my apple and followed him down the hill, past the car, and over to the base of the mountain. A breeze, cold and mysterious as an autumn night, blew the hair away from my neck.

"Did you feel that?" I gasped, holding my hands out in front of me. "There's cold air right here."

Bridger smiled and pointed to a dark, jagged gash running from the base of the mountain all the way to the road. Gnarled tree roots jutted out of the side of the gash, dangling down into the darkness. I wanted a better look, so I took a step closer, but he grabbed my wrist.

"Whoa! Don't go any closer. The ground has caved in there, falling into the ancient mine shaft. This whole area is riddled with them." He bent and picked up a small rock, then threw it into the black shaft. I strained to hear it land and looked at him when it didn't. He put his finger to his lips. Then, unexpectedly, a hollow thud echoed up out of the sunken earth.

"That is so deep," I whispered. "What would happen if I fell in?"

"Best-case scenario, if you weren't lucky enough to grab hold of one of those tree roots, you'd crash to the bottom, break your neck, and die. Worst case, you'd trigger a rockslide and we'd both fall in, be buried under a ton of earth, and search and rescue would have to come and try to save us. We'd probably still die, but slowly and painfully. So be careful." He tugged me a pace farther away from the mine shaft. "The whole mountain is covered with places where the earth is caving into the mine. If this wasn't private property, I have no doubt something would be done to seal the mine and the collapsing shafts. Come here. I'll show you another."

We walked along the dirt road, the mountain to our right and the open valley to our left. We hadn't taken a hundred steps when Bridger took my hand in his and pulled me into a clump of scraggly trees. Before I saw the gaping hole, the cool air touched my arms and face, and then I was looking down into blackness. We stopped a good five feet from the edge. I picked up a rock and threw it, counting in my head while I waited for it to land. I counted to six before the hollow thud reached my ears.

"That's more than half a mile deep." I breathed, remembering a math lesson on measuring distance with sound. Picking up an entire handful of rocks, I chucked them down the mine shaft. They scattered, eventually sounding like the thud of fat raindrops landing in mud. I smiled and looked up to see Bridger's reaction. He was staring at me, studying me with serious eyes.

"So, are you going to save me from eating alone again tonight, or am I going to be turned down? I'm not used to being rejected when I ask someone out. And it doesn't have to be a date. We'll go as friends," he said, stepping so close I could smell him. He looked right into my eyes.

"Um, well," I stammered. He took my hands in his and my heart seemed to turn into a hummingbird's frantic wings.

"I can see your answer in your eyes." He dropped one of

my hands and we strolled back out to the road. "Do you want to go home first? To freshen up, or anything?"

I was still wearing the grimy clothes I'd weeded and manured the garden in. "I need to shower and put on something nicer," I answered, trying to figure out how he had gotten me to consent.

∽ 17 ∽

Later that afternoon, I climbed into Bridger's SUV and my face
started to burn. He wore dark gray dress pants, a pale blue
button-up shirt, and glossy black shoes. I had on torn jeans, a
purple cotton tank top, and Jenny Sue's worn running shoes.
My damp hair was loose around my shoulders, and I had put on
makeup after I'd showered, yet I felt put to shame beside him.
A dandelion compared to a rose.

"Do you mind if we stop by my place for a minute?" Bridger
asked as we pulled away from Mrs. Carpenter's house.

"Whatever." I rolled down my window and stuck my arm out
into the breeze.

We drove through town and started up the road to the abandoned mine. "You live up here?" I asked.

"Yeah. My great-grandfather owned the mine when it was
still running. My parents' house is on mine property."

That is when I knew exactly which house had to be his, and
I felt even more underdressed than before. I wanted to turn into
a cat, slink out of my clothes, jump out the open window, and
never see him again. Instead I sank down in my seat and stared
out the windshield.

I was right about his house. We passed all the really big houses on the road and then came to the enormous stone-fenced mansion that I had stared at earlier. Tall, wrought-iron gates barred the entrance to the mansion's driveway. Bridger pushed something that looked like a garage door opener and the gates slid to the sides.

We drove along the tree-lined driveway in silence—I was rendered speechless by the size of the three-story stone house. It looked like something out of a British movie, some kind of English country estate complete with a rose garden, a fountain, and a pristine white gazebo. Cotton floated in the air like a million fairies dancing their way to the ground.

When Bridger stopped the car, I turned to him to tell him to take me home. I didn't fit into his world.

He glanced at me with anxious eyes. "Don't say anything," he pleaded. "Just wait here."

He jumped out of the car and ran to the front door, which I noticed had a keypad beside it instead of a lock. He pushed some buttons, opened the door, and went inside.

I stared at his towering house and felt lost in its shadow, completely out of place. I didn't know what Bridger was thinking, wanting to take me out to dinner. Again.

I had my hand on the door handle, ready to open it and run home, when he burst out of the house wearing a pair of jeans, flip-flops, and no shirt. With shirt in hand, he sprinted to the car.

"Don't you dare leave!" he yelled.

My hand froze. He yanked the driver's-side door open and looked at me, his mouth a grim line.

"You were about to ditch me, weren't you!"

I wondered how he could possibly know that.

"Admit it," he said.

"Fine! I *was* about to ditch you. I don't know why you want to be friends with someone like me when you come from a house like this." I pointed out my window.

He stared at me for a long time, emotions playing across his face. "You have been through a lot of crap, haven't you?" he finally said, climbing into the car.

"I have been through enough crap to know I don't want some rich boy to try and save me," I replied, trying not to stare at his bare chest. His skin was golden, like he'd recently been in the sun, and his shoulders were square and strong, his torso covered with lean muscle. I jerked my eyes away before I lost my train of thought. "I don't need you, Bridger. I've already saved myself."

"Good, because the last thing I want is some stupid girl dating me because I live in a big house. I am *sick* of that. And besides, does it matter, since we're just friends?" He was practically yelling.

"I don't know. I haven't had much experience with friends," I yelled back.

"Well, friends accept each other for what they are, rich or poor, happy or sad, weak or strong. So do you want me to take you to dinner, or do you want me to take you home so that you can wallow all alone in your bedroom?" he said, his voice hard.

"I don't wallow," I retorted.

The anger faded from his eyes. "But you could."

"What's that supposed to mean?"

"It means that you have been through enough crap to have a very good excuse to feel sorry for yourself. Yet you don't." He fiddled with his shirt and pulled it over his head. It was a simple, worn gray T-shirt with some faded words across the front.

"Why'd you change clothes?"

"I was embarrassingly overdressed. Not to mention, I'm more comfortable in a nice worn pair of jeans." He started the engine and glanced at me as the car pulled away from the house. I couldn't help but smile. All of a sudden, I felt comfortable in my own clothes. Exactly, I imagined, how one should feel in the presence of a friend.

We drove to Deming, a town almost an hour away. When Bridger pulled up to the restaurant, an old, stately house surrounded by beautiful gardens and hedges trimmed to look like animals and shaded by tall trees, I was speechless. I had never seen anything like it. The sign above the door read TARA'S—SOUTHERN CUISINE AT ITS FINEST.

Bridger opened the restaurant door for me. I stepped past him and paused. The woman playing hostess was dressed like a man, in a fitted black suit with a bow tie, but she was beautiful and elegant and wearing enough eye makeup for three women. She took one look at me and pursed her lips.

"I'm sorry, but we only take customers who have reservations." She glanced at my worn sneakers and raised one pencil-darkened eyebrow. I felt my cheeks grow hot, was about to stammer an apology and leave when Bridger's hand pressed against the small of my back.

"We have a reservation," he said. "The name's O'Connell."

The woman studied him and smiled. She batted her fake eyelashes and jealousy surged through me.

"Right this way, Mr. O'Connell," she said, grabbing two menus and leading us into an old-fashioned dining room with a real fire burning in a hearth, regardless of the air-conditioning pouring out of the vents on the floor. "Will this be all right?"

She motioned to a candlelit table for two by a window overlooking a hedge sculpted into the shape of a giant bunny.

"Maggie Mae?" Bridger asked.

"Sure. Looks dandy," I replied, pulling a chair out and sitting down with my back to the dining room.

Bridger sat and passed me an open menu.

"When did you make reservations?" I asked.

"This morning."

"This morning? But you . . . we . . . Were you originally planning on taking someone else?"

"I was hoping to take you."

Warning bells chimed in my head. "Why?" I asked warily. There had to be some underlying motive. For a nanosecond I wondered if, maybe, he believed Danni and was hoping I was easy. It had happened with other guys.

While all of these thoughts raced through my head, he studied me. Finally he said, "Do you want the truth, or do you want the safe version that assures I won't hurt you?"

"The truth," I stated, bracing myself for some creepy, perverse answer.

He leaned across the table and stared right into my eyes.

"She was a Phantom of delight
When first she gleamed upon my sight;
A lovely Apparition, sent
To be a moment's ornament:
Her eyes as stars of Twilight fair;
Like Twilight's, too, her dusky hair;
But all things else about her drawn
From May-time and the cheerful Dawn;

A dancing Shape, an Image gay,
To haunt, to startle, and way-lay.

"That's Wordsworth."

"Yeah. I know. We memorized it for English last week, moron." My voice trembled.

"Maggie, that poem might as well have been written for you. 'To haunt, to startle, and way-lay' . . . You're the most captivating person I have ever met." His eyes were serious and so dark they looked like storm clouds on a moonless night.

I grabbed my menu and put it in front of my face, hoping he hadn't seen the blood burning my cheeks.

"Maggie," Bridger said gently. I lowered my menu so only my eyes showed above it. "You asked for the truth."

"Thanks," I squeaked. I put the menu between us again and began looking it over. The prices! I couldn't believe it! My stomach started to hurt—twenty-two dollars for chicken fried steak and baby potatoes? And the fried chicken and collard greens—twenty dollars? I could hardly believe my eyes. The worst was the vegetarian plate: beans, rice, corn bread, and salad, for seventeen dollars.

"What's the matter?" Bridger asked quietly.

"The prices! Twenty dollars for pork chops and string beans?" I whispered, afraid someone might overhear. "Mrs. Carpenter could make that for probably eight dollars, if not less! If you wanted southern food, I could have made you some."

Bridger's concerned face broke into a grin of amusement. "Maggie, I'm not here because I want southern food. I'm here for you. You said your foster mother used to make it and it was the best food you'd ever had. Since I'm paying, ignore the price."

"I just don't see how a twenty-dollar plate of fried chicken can taste any better here than what they serve at Kentucky Fried Chicken for five dollars!"

Bridger laughed.

"May I bring you something to drink?" a female voice interrupted.

I looked up, dismayed to see that the woman who'd seated us was also our server. "What do you want to drink, Maggie?" Bridger asked.

"Water. It's free, right?" I asked.

The server pulled her eyes away from Bridger and looked down her nose at me.

"Of course the water isn't free. We are a five-star restaurant. Our water is imported from Europe." Her eyes lingered on my faded tank top. "If you can't *afford* imported water, we have a wide range of soda. Or milk."

A familiar burn started beneath my skin, like when I'd get picked on at school and knew I had to fight back. I glared up at her. She lifted one drawn-on eyebrow and smirked.

"Whatever. Coke. But just so you know, there's nothing wrong with drinking water from the tap," I snapped.

"Well, then why don't you go eat somewhere that is better suited to trailer trash," she mumbled under her breath. But I heard every word. My hackles rose and my skin felt too tight. The urge to pounce on her and scratch her black-lined eyes out made my entire body tremble.

Bridger stood. "You know, Maggie," he said lightly, "I think I would rather have Kentucky Fried Chicken after all." He wrapped his long fingers around my upper arm and yanked me to standing, then looped his arm around my waist and literally forced me out of the restaurant.

I struggled against him as he opened my car door—I wanted to go back into Tara's and start a fight with that stupid self-righteous waitress. But Bridger more or less tossed me into the SUV and slammed my door. My hands were shaking so badly I couldn't buckle my seat belt. When Bridger got into the SUV, he leaned over and hooked it for me.

As he backed his big four-wheel drive out of the parking space, he asked in a stiff voice, "Are your previous brushes with the law for fighting?"

I took a deep breath and forced my tense muscles to relax. "No. I've only been in two fights I started myself, and one was with Danni. So thank you for getting me out of that place before I did something monumentally stupid."

"You're welcome." He glanced at me again. "So why exactly do you have a juvie record?"

I sighed and pressed on my temples. "You know, I'd rather not talk about it. Just know it had nothing to do with hurting another person, or drugs, or prostitution, or anything like that."

To my relief, Bridger nodded, as if he knew how much I didn't want to talk about it. As if he knew exactly how I felt. . . .

"Okay, Bridger," I blurted, feeling really bold all of a sudden—probably a by-product of the adrenaline zooming through my blood. "I need to ask you something."

"Ask away."

"There is this . . . thing . . . about you that's bothering me. Something unnatural."

He pulled the car to the side of the road, turned off the engine, and looked at me as if I'd just admitted I had a forked tongue. "What?" he asked. If I didn't know any better, I would have said he was scared.

"Are you psychic? Because you keep doing things that make me feel like you know what I'm about to do."

"What do you mean?"

"Well—" I paused, thinking where to begin. "When we went to your house tonight and you ran in to change. I had my hand on the door, ready to leave, and you ran out and yelled at me not to. And in the restaurant just now. You made me leave when I was about to snap. I might have pounded that woman's face in for no good reason if you hadn't pulled me out of there. And you changing your clothes as if you knew I felt—"

"Underdressed?" he asked.

I nodded.

Relief flooded his face and softened the fear in his eyes. "Is that all?"

"No, you do it all the time. Like the day Danni and her friends planned the attack on me. You warned me something might be up. Like you saw the future."

"It's nothing like that. I can feel what you feel if you are close to me, like if you're scared, or happy . . . or lonely. It's not just you—I'm like that with about half of the people I meet— though somehow I can feel you almost as well as I can feel my sister." He shrugged. "I was born with it. It's sort of a gift and a curse wrapped up in one. I call it my *nah-e-thlai*, my *guide*."

"Can you give me an example of how it works?"

He leaned back and thought for a minute before answering. "Do you remember your first day at school, when Mrs. C. asked me to show you around and I hesitated?"

"Yeah. I remember." How could I forget? "You didn't want to be seen with me."

He laughed under his breath and shook his head. "Wrong.

You didn't want to be seen with *me*. In fact, you couldn't get away from me fast enough."

I thought back to my first day of school and looked Bridger square in the eyes. "I didn't want to be seen with you because you were looking at my wet hair and torn jeans like you'd die if you had to walk in with me. I was sparing you the embarrassment, and me the insult."

Bridger shook his head. "Actually, I was checking you out."

My face started to burn. I looked out the window.

"I learned the hard way not to judge a person by appearance. In elementary school, I could tell a lot of the kids and some of the teachers detested me because I was an O'Connell and wore nicer clothes to school," Bridger said, his voice somber. "I'd never done anything to deserve their prejudice, yet I felt it all the time. And the two times I took Danni Williams out to dinner, I could feel her greed, and just knew she only wanted to date me because my dad is wealthy. So I never asked her out for a third date. Sometimes . . ."

I turned to look at him.

"Sometimes I can feel the violence in people," he continued, "and sometimes it scares me, like tonight. I thought I was the one who wanted to pound our server's face in, and it freaked me out until I realized your feelings were overpowering mine. I can feel evil in some people, too. That is the worst thing about my ability." He shuddered and closed his eyes for a minute. When he opened them again, he looked at me. "The first time I saw you, you radiated fear so strongly my knees almost buckled."

I frowned. "When did you first see me?"

"In the school parking lot, right before you gave me the

shaft. You were terrified and didn't want to get out of Mrs. C.'s truck. But then you got out. I've never met anyone as brave as you," he said, leaning closer. I could feel his breath on my face as he continued. "The morning after prom, I could feel how much I'd hurt you. I've never regretted anything more." He leaned closer. "You like it when I hold your hand. I can feel the heat rise under your skin when I get a little too close to you. And the fear. And the mistrust. And I know that if I kissed you right now, you'd *probably* kiss me back." He stopped talking, slid his hand under my hair and against the bare skin on the back of my neck, and leaned even closer. Our noses almost touched. "But I also felt how scared you were in the restaurant a few minutes ago when I said you're captivating," he whispered. "And right now fear is your strongest emotion. I don't mean to scare you." He pulled his hand away, turned, and started the car. I started to breathe again.

"And now, I feel your relief," he said and smiled, though his eyes were dark and stormy.

We ended up eating fried chicken from the local KFC. And while I enjoyed Bridger's company way more than I should have, I worried that I might accidentally give something away to him, like the fact I didn't want the night to end, or that he made me really happy. Or that I kept wondering what his lips would feel like against mine.

I tried to feel nothing.

When he brought me home, he didn't turn off the car engine or attempt to walk me to the door.

"Maggie," he called out his open window as I made my way through the moon-bright yard. I paused and looked at him. "How about I drive you home from work tomorrow?"

"All right."

"And don't be afraid of me," he said, running a hand through his dark hair.

"I'll try."

18

I was awake long before my alarm went off, my body too wound up in Bridger O'Connell to go back to sleep. It was like I'd been eating bread and water my whole life, and then one day someone gave me chocolate cake. Bridger was the cake. And I liked how it tasted so well, I never wanted to go back to bread and water. But bread and water was safe. Chocolate cake? Totally dangerous.

What if Bridger could sense how I craved him?

Yesterday had been a big mistake. I was getting attached . . . again. No, that was a definite understatement. I was beyond attached. I groaned and pulled the pillow over my head, forcing myself to think Bridger-free thoughts, like how much fertilizer the chickens could produce in a week.

A knock at my door woke me. I pulled the pillow from my head, blinked my bleary eyes, and tried to remember why I was thinking of chocolate cake and chickens. Someone knocked again.

"Yeah?" I called.

The door opened and Mrs. Carpenter peered at me. "You've slept late," she said.

I sat up and looked at my watch.

"Crap!"

I sprinted through empty halls to the deserted locker room and put on my running clothes.

Class had been in session fifteen minutes by the time I left the locker room. I pushed through the door to the track and found Bridger staring at me. As if he knew I was coming out at that very moment. A smile softened his worried face.

"Nice of you to join us, Maggie Mae," Coach said, looking at his watch.

I walked to the gathered students, careful to keep my distance from Bridger, and dug my toe against the track. A pair of running shoes stopped beside mine, but I didn't look up.

"Are you all right?" Even his voice made me hungry.

"I slept through my watch alarm," I blurted, not taking my eyes from my foot.

"I guess I kept you out sort of late."

I dug my toe harder against the track, as if watching my gym shoe rub the dirt from it was the most amazing thing I'd ever seen.

"Maggie?" His voice was so gentle, so full of concern, I had to grit my teeth and dig my nails into my palms to keep my eyes from wandering to his face. He reached out and put a finger under my chin, tilting my face up. When I met his gaze, warmth flooded me and time stopped. So much for not letting him know how much I liked him. "Sooner or later you've got to stop letting fear be the ruling emotion in your life," he said.

I caught my bottom lip in my teeth and stared back at him. And then I nodded.

"Maggie Mae, Bridger, I hate to break up your precious moment," Coach said. Bridger's hand left my chin. "But since you were tardy, Ms. Mortensen, you're running laps." The whole track team was gawking at Bridger and me, and my face felt so hot it probably glowed. But before I could say a word Coach blurted, "There's no use arguing with me, Ms. Mortensen."

I ran.

That night, Yana and I worked the dining room at the Navajo Mexican. It was too busy to talk much, but when we were both refilling drinks at the soda dispenser, she managed to say, "Why are you being such an idiot?"

"What are you talking about?" I asked.

"O'Connell. The story is he practically kissed you in front of the track team—*during class*—so Coach made you run laps. Have you forgotten he walked out on you at prom? That's totally unforgivable."

"I know, but he's . . ." *As tempting as chocolate cake.*

"He's what? Hot? Rich? Smart? Smells really good?"

I groaned. He was all of those things. But something more.

"You need to ask Naalyehe about his family," she said, and strode off with her refilled drinks.

When the evening turned to night and all the customers had gone home, I went to the kitchen.

"Naalyehe?" He looked at me. "Yana says you know the O'Connell family. She said I should ask you about them."

Naalyehe frowned. He turned his back to me and began

chopping. All right. Guess he wasn't big on gossip. I turned toward the dining room but stopped, straining my ears. Because it sounded like he said something. Maybe my imagination was going wild?

"Never be out past dark with Bridger O'Connell," he said again. Nope. My imagination wasn't going wild. Was he joking?

Totally confused, I went back to the dining room, pondering Naalyehe's warning.

"You'll never guess who's here," Yana said, voice full of sarcasm. I glanced around the empty dining room. "Speak of the devil and he appears." She nodded toward the window. A big black SUV was parked out front with its parking lights on.

My heart thrummed beneath my ribs and I wasn't sure if it was the effect of Naalyehe's warning or Bridger's appearance.

"I'll finish up—you go on," she said. "Don't want to keep O'Connell waiting. But don't say I didn't warn you."

I crossed my arms and stood beside the door, Naalyehe's warning hovering in my brain. The window came down and Bridger peered at me from the dark car interior. His car smelled just like him. I took a deep breath.

"So, are you getting in?" he asked. And smiled. A smile that instantly overrode Naalyehe's warning. What harm could a ride home do? I returned Bridger's smile. He leaned over and opened the passenger door. "Get in."

I glanced over my shoulder at the lamp-lit sidewalk, then back at Bridger, and climbed into his car.

"Does Naalyehe know you walk home at night?" he asked, putting the car into drive.

"No. Why?"

"He's Navajo. *Traditional* Navajo. He's got superstitions about the dark."

That's not the only thing he's got superstitions about. "How do you know?" I asked.

"He's my dad's third cousin."

"Really?" That bit of info made Naalyehe's warning even more bizarre.

"Is something bothering you?" Bridger asked.

"Um . . . yeah. If you're Navajo, you're not very tan." I lied. I couldn't bring myself to tell him what Naalyehe had said. "At least not compared to Naalyehe and Yana."

Bridger laughed. "I'm also part Irish. And English. But believe me, I'm more Navajo than anything else. My great-grandpa . . ."

His words lost meaning. I pressed my face to the window. A man stood on the side of the moonlit road. He was staring at Bridger's car with eyes that glowed like an animal's. The stoplight changed and Bridger eased the car forward. I squeezed my eyes shut and a warm hand came down on the back of my neck under my hair.

"Maggie, what's wrong?"

"Did you see that guy?" My voice trembled.

Bridger slowed the car.

"No! Don't stop!" I peered out the window again, but the sidewalk was empty.

"What did you see?" Bridger asked, kneading the muscles in my neck.

I studied his shadowed profile. "There was a guy standing over there. And his eyes glowed."

"His eyes glowed?"

"Yeah. Like an animal's."

Bridger laughed. "You must have imagined it."

"Gee. Thanks for the vote of confidence."

He took his hand from my neck, trailed it down my arm, and found my hand. His warm fingers intertwined with mine. Instead of pulling away—my first instinct—I held on. "So what other nights do you work this week? I'll pick you up."

"Wednesday and Saturday, but Saturday I get off early for graduation."

"What are you doing after graduation? Wanna hang out?"

I looked at him. His hand tightened on mine, and my heart seemed to grow inside of my chest, pressing against my throat and making it impossible to talk.

"You know what hanging out is, right?" he said. "We could get hamburgers and fries and *hang out* at the mine. I'll bring my telescope and we can look at the stars."

"Yeah. That sounds . . . nice."

"Really?" he asked, glancing at me. "I don't have to talk you into hanging out with me this time?"

I shrugged. "I guess not."

We pulled into Mrs. Carpenter's driveway and Bridger stopped in front of the porch. He let go of my hand and turned off the car. And unhooked his seat belt. He turned to me, where I sat frozen in my seat, my eyes glued to the windshield. "Maggie."

I licked my lips and looked at him. And practically had a heart attack when his phone rang, shattering the moment.

He pulled the phone out of his pocket and looked at it. "I've got to take this," he said and answered. "Hi, Dad."

I unhooked my seat belt and put my hand on the door handle.

"What? Right now? At this very moment?" Bridger said,

glancing at me, his eyes uncertain. "No, I *am* excited. That's great. I'm on my way home right now. . . . What am I doing out at this hour on a school night? Just out running an errand. . . . Yeah, a late errand. I'll see you soon." He hung up and put the phone back in his pocket. "Hey, sorry about that. About Wednesday—my family's home. I'm not going to be able to pick you up."

"That's okay," I said, struggling not to feel disappointed. I opened my door and got out, and he pulled out of the driveway before I had Mrs. Carpenter's front door open.

∾ 19 ∾

Bridger was different at school the next day—nice as always, but nothing more. It lasted all week.

Saturday came. I worked my butt off at the Navajo Mexican, and when my shift ended, I got a ride home from Yana.

"See you tonight," I said as I climbed out of her car.

"Yep. No more homework, no more books, no more teachers' dirty looks. Ever!" Yana waved and drove down the driveway.

My aching feet thumped on the front porch. I stepped through the front door and my mouth started watering.

"Surprise!" Mrs. Carpenter said, spreading her arms toward a table covered with way more food than she and I could eat in one sitting. In the middle of the table sat a giant cake with thick chocolate frosting. "Thought I'd whip up something special for your graduation," she said, laughing. "I even called Bridger to see if he'd come and help us eat, but he said he already had dinner plans." She clicked her tongue and shook her head. "That boy doesn't know what he's missing."

After dinner, I put on my—thanks to Mrs. Carpenter— freshly ironed white graduation gown, brushed through my hair, and touched up my makeup. Then I was ready to go.

The dogs were restless, whining from inside the barn and scratching at the door as we walked to the truck.

"It's just us," Mrs. Carpenter called. Shash yelped and scratched the door again. Duke howled, a hoarse, guttural sound that had me peering warily toward the edge of the property. "I swear. Those dogs have taken to you like you're their alpha." She looked at me sidelong. "Speaking of dogs, tomorrow is the full moon. What can I do to help?"

"Lock me in the barn," I said, wiping sudden tears from under my eyes before they could ruin my fresh makeup. I had help. For the first time in my life, I wasn't doing this alone. And it felt amazing.

We got into the truck and drove to Silver High. The school parking lot was packed, every space taken. We parallel parked two blocks away, in front of a stucco house with a cactus growing in the yard, and arrived at the ceremony five minutes early.

"You can go home after the ceremony," I said as Mrs. Carpenter and I walked toward the outdoor bleachers.

"You have plans?" she asked, a gleam in her eyes.

"Yeah. Bridger and I are going out for hamburgers." I couldn't help but smile as I said the words.

She grinned and started humming. "You have fun," she said. "And speaking of Bridger, why don't I take a picture of the two of you in your gowns?"

I blushed and nodded.

We made our way to the O section of students, and Bridger stood out like a tree among shrubs. "My goodness, Bridger looks handsome in traditional Navajo garb. That's what Navajo men wear for formal ceremonies," Mrs. Carpenter explained, looking him up and down.

He wasn't wearing the navy-blue graduation gown all the other guys wore. And he wasn't alone. A stunning girl with silky black hair, an oversized leather shirt with fringe, skintight jeans, and high-heel boots was tugging his head forward. She ran her black-polished nails through his hair, and then slipped a red headband around his head so it fit snugly on his forehead. Next she adjusted the shoulders of his bright blue velvet shirt, then fiddled with the chains of turquoise hanging around his neck. Bridger's eyes flickered to me and he winked.

The girl must have seen it. She turned and looked at me, her ice-blue eyes wild with curiosity.

I stood where I was, frozen with confusion, staring. Someone bumped me and a warm hand clasped my elbow.

"Excuse me," a deep voice said. I turned and looked into a pair of dark, semifamiliar eyes. The man continued past me, a blond woman dressed in a suit-dress at his side, and stopped beside Bridger and the girl. The man took a palm-sized camera from his suit pocket and snapped a photo of Bridger and the girl.

"Go on over there," Mrs. Carpenter said, nudging me forward. Bridger grinned at me and motioned me over.

"Hey," he said, clasping his hands behind his back. "I want you to meet my family. This is my sister, Katie." He nodded to the girl with slick black hair.

"Kat, not Katie," she said, her eyes taking in my every detail.

"My mother." Bridger nodded to the blond woman. "And my dad."

The man who'd bumped me a moment before studied me with curious dark eyes. He held his hand out and I shook it. "Nice to meet you . . ."

"Maggie Mae," I said.

"And how are you and Bridger acquainted?" his mother prodded, her eyes never leaving mine.

"She's my friend, Mom. From school," Bridger said hurriedly.

One of Kat's black eyebrows slowly rose, and aside from having pale blue eyes, she looked just like her brother for a second. "Nice to meet you, Maggie Mae—Bridger's friend," she said with a mischievous grin. She gave Bridger a look.

"Hello, Aidan. Vivienne. Nice to see you again," Mrs. Carpenter said.

Bridger's mom nodded at Mrs. Carpenter, a slight bob of her head. His dad smiled and said, "Opal. How are you?"

"I'm doing real good. Thought I'd take a picture of Maggie Mae with her friend Bridger." There was an icy tone to her voice.

Kat moved away from Bridger without a word and looked sideways at me. I stepped to Bridger's side, yet he eased away from me, making sure there was a good gap of space between us.

"Say 'cheese,'" Mrs. Carpenter said. Before I had a chance to smile, the camera flashed. Mrs. Carpenter patted my shoulder. "I'll see you later tonight," she said, and got lost in the crowd.

I looked at Bridger's family, all staring at me as if I weren't good enough to be his friend, and I needed to get away. "Good luck. Don't trip when you get your diploma," I muttered to Bridger and walked toward the M section of graduating seniors. I could feel his family's eyes boring into my back the entire way.

The sun set and I sat through two speeches and a choir performance. When the principal started reading the names for diplomas, all the graduating students stood. I got to my feet and took a deep breath of evening air. I'd been waiting for this moment since my first day of kindergarten.

The students at the front of the line started walking toward the stage, but paused, whispering and looking around, pointing toward the darkening skyline. The whispers traveled back, eventually reaching the M section.

"Did you hear it?" someone whispered.

"Hear what?" someone else replied.

"I don't know!"

"Shh!" someone behind me hissed, and everyone fell silent and still, staring up at the purple sky. And that's when I heard it. A shiver of ice trilled down my spine as the low, lonely howl of a wolf carried through the dusky air. Everyone started whispering again.

"It was a coyote," someone behind me said.

"Coyotes yap, not howl," another student answered.

"But there aren't wolves around here. There haven't been for years."

"No, that's not true. They tried to reintroduce them into the mountains a while ago. Maybe one or two survived?"

Mrs. Tolliver walked down the line of students, glaring at us. Everyone shut up as the line began to crawl forward. I took a deep breath and forced myself to relax and forget about the wolves and Bridger's family.

I made my slow way with the other students toward the podium. And then Dr. Smith was reading my name. "Maggie Mae Mortensen, a new student who set a new Silver High fifty-yard dash record." Coach stood and started cheering. Bridger and Mrs. Carpenter followed, along with Yana and Ginger. And then the male half of the freshman class joined in. Their cheering seemed contagious, as eventually the majority of the stadium was cheering for me.

My cheeks started to burn and a smile tugged at my mouth. I took the diploma from Dr. Smith, blinked against the flash of a camera, and hurried from the stage. I'd done it.

When I got back to my seat, a long, low howl echoed through the dark night. The students sitting beside me glanced around nervously. Dr. Smith stuttered through the name he was reading. When he got to Bridger's name, I stood and cheered along with every other person at the graduation ceremony. The noise was incredible. Dressed in full Navajo garb, he took his diploma and waved to the crowd.

Within minutes it was over and everyone was throwing their caps, a snowstorm of white and navy-blue squares silhouetted against the almost dark sky.

I made my way to Bridger, excited about the prospect of having him all to myself for the night.

"Congratulations," he said when he saw me, but he was distracted, looking over the tops of graduates' heads. "I'm so sorry—I know we were going to hang out tonight, but my mom's made other plans. I've got to cancel. So . . . I guess I'll see you around. I'll call you sometime. Or drop by and help you with the garden." He smiled and then wandered away.

My jaw dropped open. "But . . . I . . . don't have a ride." My voice was swallowed in the noise of the crowd. Bridger never looked back. He found his family and left with them.

I stood for a long time in a mass of ecstatic graduates before I had the energy to pull my gown off and put it in the massive bin marked WHITE GOWN RETURN.

I wandered toward the place where Mrs. Carpenter had parked her truck. Of course it wasn't there. Surely she was long gone.

Not wanting to walk home and explain why I wasn't out with

Bridger, I rummaged through someone's trash can and found a used grocery bag. Next I located a dense patch of shrubs in front of an adobe house and forced my way into the center of it. I took my shoes and socks off and then unfastened my watch and the yo-ih, and set them all into the bag. Next I took off my jeans and T-shirt, removed my bra and panties, and dropped them on top of the watch, bracelet, and shoes.

I landed on all fours and the sounds haunting the night intensified—police sirens, dogs barking, people cheering, howling, laughing, screaming. My heart pounded against my cougar rib cage. I picked the bag up in my teeth and ran from the sounds, ran from population.

I prowled the uninhabited outskirts of the city, as far away from humanity as I could get. When the sounds of sirens and howling finally stopped, I made my leisurely way toward home, making sure to take a long time—as long as it would have taken to eat hamburgers, fries, and a milk shake at the mine, and then look at the stars.

In some bushes across the street from Mrs. Carpenter's house, I shifted back to human and got dressed. When I crossed the street and stepped onto Mrs. Carpenter's driveway, my feet skidded to a stop. Bridger's SUV was blocking it. And so was yellow police tape.

My hands started to tremble. A shadow moved at the far end of the driveway and I leaped into the shrubs hugging the side of the driveway, just in case I was in danger. The shadow solidified into a police officer holding a dim flashlight. I stepped out of the bushes.

"Is everything all right?" My voice quavered. "Where's Mrs. Carpenter?"

"Are you Maggie Mae?" he asked, stopping beside me and shining the light in my eyes.

I shaded my eyes and nodded, suddenly sick to my stomach. Something was wrong. *Really* wrong.

"I have some bad news for you," the officer said. My windpipe constricted and I could hardly draw breath. "Mrs. Carpenter's in the hospital."

"What happened?" I gasped.

"Come on. I'll show you."

I followed him past Bridger's SUV and under the police tape. At the front porch I paused. The porch light was on and something was . . . different. Deep scratches had been gouged into the red front door. Flakes of paint and wood littered the porch next to the cactus, which lay overturned on its side accompanied by its shattered terra-cotta pot.

Paint and wood chips clung to the soles of my shoes as I walked through the front door. Inside I stopped, too stunned to move. White fluff covered the floor, the furniture, the top of the gun case, even the blades of the ceiling fan—the stuffing from Mrs. Carpenter's brown leather sofa. The cushions had been torn to bits.

I made my legs carry me down the hall to my room. The sewing table looked untouched, but my small dresser was tipped on its side beside my toppled clothes hamper. My clothes, underwear, and pajamas lay shredded on the floor beside them. The cot was bare and ripped down the middle, my two quilts part of the underwear-and-clothes mess.

"What happened?" I asked.

"Seems some wild dogs got into the house."

Wild dogs? *Demon* dogs was more like it. Instinctively I knew—they'd come for me again.

"Tore everything up searching for food," the officer explained, running his thumb and finger over his goatee.

I looked at my toppled dresser and questioned the food theory. There hadn't been any food in there. Not even chocolate. And if my bedroom looked like this, what did Mrs. Carpenter look like?

"Is Mrs. Carpenter all right?" I whispered.

"She's been injured, but it's not life-threatening."

"How'd she get hurt?"

"She tried to shoot the dogs and got bit on the leg. Practically tore her calf muscle clean off the bone. She'll be in the hospital for a few days. In the meantime, do you have somewhere to stay for the night?"

"Um. I . . . well . . ."

The floor creaked outside my bedroom. The officer pulled the gun from his belt and pointed it out the door, sidestepping in front of me.

"Who's there?" he barked. Bridger walked into view, his hands up. The officer lowered his gun. "Good gracious, son! I might have shot you! What are you doing here?"

I stared at Bridger, dressed in jeans and a hoodie, red headband still around his forehead, and wondered the same thing.

"I came to get my SUV, but wanted to make sure it was all right if I moved it."

The officer nodded. "That should be fine."

"Maggie, you can stay with me tonight," Bridger said, glancing at my ruined cot.

I shook my head. "No. I'll stay . . ." Where? I *couldn't* stay here, not with the wild dogs roaming the area.

Bridger crossed his arms over his chest. I bit my bottom lip and looked at him. He raised one eyebrow.

"Do you want a place to stay or not?" he asked.

I sighed. "Yeah. Just give me a sec to see if any of this is still wearable." I sifted through the pile of my shredded things and held up the black T-shirt—at least I held up half of it. The other half was somewhere in the mess. I closed my eyes and fought the urge to groan. It looked like I'd be clothes shopping at Wal-Mart in the very near future.

"Are you all right?" the officer asked.

"Yeah. Fine." I stood and kicked the pile of shredded stuff. "Let's go, Bridger." We walked through the stuffing-filled front room and into the dark night.

"So, why are you really here?" I asked.

"I already told you. I'm here to get my SUV." He rubbed his eyes and sighed. I folded my arms over my chest and shivered. A chill had crept into the night and seeped beneath my skin. Bridger unlocked his SUV. "Climb in. It's warmer in there." He pulled off his hoodie and handed it to me. I tugged it over my head and thrust my arms into the sleeves. It was filled with his warmth.

I got into the SUV, but Bridger, instead of getting in, too, walked to the vegetable garden and picked up the elk skull, ghostly white beneath the heavy moon. He carried it to the edge of the property and placed it back between the two trees. The exact spot I'd taken it from.

As he walked back to the SUV, his eyes met mine. He opened the door and the interior light flashed on.

"Don't mess with the ring of protection again," he said, and got in. He shut the door and the light stayed on while he put the keys into the ignition. The sleeve of his long-sleeve T-shirt lifted as he cranked the engine, and then the interior light dimmed to dark.

"Wait!" I turned on the light and leaned toward him. Taking his hand in mine, I pushed his sleeve up, revealing three bloody gashes on the back of his wrist. He sucked a breath of air in through his teeth and pulled his arm from me. "You're hurt. What happened?"

"It's nothing."

"What happened? Why are you here? And why are you bleeding? I want the truth."

He looked at me and lifted his hand. I shrunk away, thinking of Naalyehe's warning. But all he did was turn off the interior light. "When I got home from dinner, I could feel someone's fear—really feel it like I was experiencing it myself. It was so strong, I could even tell whose fear it was—Mrs. C.'s. I knew something was wrong. So I left and came straight here. When I got here, there were three wolves in her house."

"Wolves? The police officer said it was dogs."

Bridger shook his head. "Wolves."

"And one of them bit you?"

"No. Those are claw marks. I was chasing them from the house and one lunged for me."

"You were chasing *wolves* from the house, bare-handed?"

"I had Smith and Wesson backing me."

"Who?"

"Mrs. C.'s Magnum. You know, her gun."

I leaned back in my seat and stared out the front window. Wolves—not the pack of dogs that had attacked me a month ago. Was that a good thing or a bad thing? "That is freaky."

"Yeah." Bridger put the SUV into drive and pulled out onto the quiet road. We passed a parked car wrapped in police tape. I pressed my nose to the window.

"Whose car is that?" I asked.

"Danni's," Bridger said, his tone nonchalant.

"Danni Williams's?"

"Yeah."

"What's her car doing parked in front of Mrs. Carpenter's property?"

Bridger glanced at me. "She came to vandalize Mrs. C.'s house. The cops found shaving cream and rolls of toilet paper in her car—her graduation gift to you, Maggie. Only, she got a bit of a surprise."

"What do you mean, 'bit of a surprise'?"

He pulled the SUV to the side of the road and looked at me. "She's in the hospital. She was attacked by the wolves, too. They don't know if she's going to live."

∞ 20 ∞

I fell back against my seat and closed my eyes, fighting the churning in my gut. Danni Williams almost died?

"Your work clothes got ruined, didn't they?"

I blinked twice, trying to make sense of Bridger's words.

"Maggie? Your work clothes? Are they ruined?" he asked as if he hadn't just told me Danni might die.

"You're trying to change the subject."

"Yep. Do you have anything to wear to work?"

I groaned. "Not until I go to Wal-Mart. Stupid wolves shredded every piece of clothing I owned." Right down to my last pair of threadbare panties.

"You need to buy more, right?"

I looked at Bridger. "Right now? It's freaking two in the morning. There aren't any open stores," I snapped. I might as well have drunk five cups of coffee, I was so wired.

We drove to Swan Street and stopped at the gates barring entrance to the brightly lit O'Connell mansion. Bridger pushed his garage door opener thingy, and the gates parted.

"I want you to promise me something," he said as we drove down the long tree-lined drive.

An alarm went off in my head. I folded my arms and studied his profile. "Tell me what it is and then I'll let you know if I can promise."

"I'm going to offer you something, but promise me you won't get mad." He glanced at me.

"Sorry. No promise until you tell me what I'm getting myself into."

He exhaled loudly and shrugged. "You have major trust issues. Never mind!"

We got out of the SUV and I followed him to the front porch. He punched numbers into the keypad on his front door and opened it. "You're invited in," he whispered, and pressed a finger to his lips for silence. We stepped inside a well-lit room.

I don't know what I expected to find inside, but it was definitely not what I saw.

The mansion felt eerily dead and was so quiet I had no doubt I'd be able to hear a pin drop across the giant room I stood in. A massive fireplace was at the far end of the room, framed in stone that reached to the top of the two-story ceiling. Elegant sofas and tables were centered in front of the fireplace. Stone sculptures of animals and birds, and cases filled with ancient Navajo beadwork and weaving lined one wall. Cases filled with guns lined another. Warm light from lamps with bases made of deer antlers flooded the room, highlighting giant framed paintings of open fields and mountain valleys.

Bridger led me to a flight of stairs, dark and wide. He turned on a light and pressed a finger to his lips for more silence, and I followed him up to a spacious hallway lined with shut doors and ancient-looking portraits.

"Who are these people?" I whispered, studying each painting as we walked past.

"My grandparents and great-grandparents. This woman here—" He pointed to a young woman with black eyes and mocha skin, wearing beads and feathers in her slick dark hair. "She's my great-grandmother. She was Navajo. She married this man here." The man in the picture had pale skin, red hair, and green eyes. "That is my great-grandpa, Niall O'Connell. He came to America from Ireland, broke and penniless, and ended up one of the richest men in the country by the time he died. He started the mine."

We passed a door on the right and I paused. Quiet sobbing was coming from the other side. I looked askance at Bridger and he rolled his eyes.

"It's only Katie, my little sister," he whispered. "My dad decided she needs to stay in Silver City for a while and she's having a tantrum."

"Why does he want her to stay?"

He paused for a long time, studying me before answering. "To keep an eye on me. And you."

"What do you mean?" I asked. He held a finger up to his lips and opened a door on the left.

I followed Bridger into a giant room with pale gray walls decorated with framed pictures of galaxies. There were double doors on the far wall leading out to a balcony. To the right was a sofa facing a flat-screen television. And to the left, a queen bed. My spirits sank.

Bridger went to the bed and looked at me expectantly. "Come here," he said. Then he must have felt what I was feeling, because his eyes became guarded and panicked, all at once. He took one look at my wide-eyed face and started laughing. "You have a dirty mind! My parents are asleep just down the hall! I brought you up here because Katie, being her typical, overly indulged self, gutted her closet first thing when she got home to make room for the new wardrobe she bought in Europe. Said she's outgrown her *alternative* dressing phase. I . . ." Bridger looked away and ran a hand through his hair.

"You what?" I asked.

"I think you guys are about the same size. I thought, if you wanted to go through her old stuff before I take it to the second-hand shop . . ."

As if to prove himself, Bridger pulled a bulging trash bag out from behind the far side of the bed and tipped it over the black quilt. Clothes spilled out. He lifted another bag and dumped it onto the contents of the first. Then another. And another. The bed was completely covered with stuff—jeans, dresses, shirts, sweaters, hats, scarves, purses, shoes, shorts, swimsuits, belts. They were all flamboyant, too—I felt like I knew his sister just by looking at her clothes. Almost everything was either black, bright orange, hot pink, or dark purple. And half of it was way too sexy for me. There was also a large assortment of crazy tights: fish-nets, black and orange stripes, cobweb tights, glitter tights. And most of the shoes had heels at least three inches high.

I looked at Bridger, thinking maybe I should have been a little bit offended by the offering, but I'd been a secondhand girl all my life. I walked to the bed like I was under a spell, like a fool finding the leprechaun's pot of gold, and picked up a pair of Diesel jeans. They looked like the right size. I tried on a pair of strappy red sandals. They fit—almost. Maybe half a size too big, but I didn't mind. I felt like a kid in a candy store, and every kid knows, if you get offered free candy, you don't care what kind it is.

"Can I try some of this stuff on?" I asked.

"And I thought you'd be mad at me for offering you Katie's stuff," Bridger said with relief. "You do realize it's the middle of the night?"

"I wouldn't be able to sleep even if I had a bed to sleep in." I stifled a yawn.

"Why don't you try them on in the morning? Let's veg and watch a movie," Bridger said, sitting on the sofa. I sat down beside him. The sofa was so soft, it might as well have been trying to swallow me.

Bridger scooted a few inches away from me and said, "We need to talk."

My heart started to hammer, and not in a good way. "We do?"

"Yeah." Bridger took off his shoes and put his feet up on an ottoman, his eyes never leaving my face. "I know how you feel about me."

I sank into the sofa and pressed my hands over my eyes.

"Maggie." His fingers clamped down around my wrists and tugged. I met his gaze and wished the sofa *would* swallow me. "Let me just start by saying I really like you, too. A *lot*." He let go of my hands and folded his arms across his chest. "You're one of the most intriguing, unique, beautiful people I have ever met. But I haven't been fair to either of us. I'm not supposed to date local girls. I've been taught that my whole life—so having my family come home has made me realize that I need to rededicate myself."

I couldn't look at him. I found a string on the sleeve of his hoodie and began running it through my fingers.

"Now that school's out, we won't see each other anymore," he said.

My heart sank with the thought of never seeing him again.

"The thing is," he continued, "I wanted to let you know I'm still here for you, as a friend. Nothing more, nothing less. So if you can forgive me for misleading you, maybe we can hang out sometimes. Nothing major, just the occasional movie, or hike, or something."

Why had it always been my lot in life to be removed from the people I cared about? I wondered. I could already feel Bridger slipping away forever.

"Hey, I'm not bailing on you. And I'll never ask anything of you but friendship. I just . . . can't *date* local girls."

Yeah, I got it. No dating.

"Why *don't* you date local girls?" I asked. "Yana told me the same thing."

"I'm supposed to marry someone who has a similar background as me."

"You mean religious background? You have to marry a Navajo girl?"

He scowled. "Not quite. More like the same social background. So that my kids are . . . like me."

I rolled my eyes. Yana was right. Rich people always wanted to produce rich offspring. I definitely didn't fit into that stereotype. "Sounds like your parents are breeding you. Like a race-horse," I said, my voice full of all the bitterness I felt.

Bridger frowned and nodded.

"Well, invite me to your wedding. 'Cause that's what friends do, right?"

A slow smile spread across his face. "You don't hate me?"

"I suppose not."

Smile still plastered to his face, he turned on a movie. With twelve inches of very obvious space separating Bridger and me, I let the sofa absorb half my body and zoned out, letting the movie blur.

I snapped awake as light shone on my closed eyelids, but I didn't open my eyes. Someone walked into Bridger's room, two sets of feet tiptoeing over the hardwood floor. A woman gasped.

"She's here!" she whispered. "And wearing the sweatshirt I got him in Italy. I knew it was more than a casual friendship when I saw how he looked at her."

"You need to trust him," another voice mumbled—Bridger's dad. "He is eighteen and he knows his duty. I can tell he has every intention of following what he's been taught."

"I'm so glad you're making Katie stay. But what if—?"

"Shh—I think she's awake."

I opened one eye a crack, watching through my lashes as Bridger's parents came to the sofa, bent over the back of it, and each kissed Bridger's forehead. His dad looked at me. I froze on the other end of the sofa, closing my eyes and making my eyelids as soft and supple as if I were fast asleep.

"Good-bye, son," his mother whispered.

They left the room and shut the door.

∞ 21 ∞

Something vibrated against my ribs. I shifted and inhaled, relaxing into a dream that smelled just like . . .

My eyes popped open. A warm and heavy weight draped my shoulder. The pillow beneath my cheek moved up and down and smelled like heaven. My ribs vibrated again and I practically jumped out of my skin in my hurry to scramble to the other side of the sofa.

Bridger's black lashes fluttered against his cheeks and he peered at me with glazed eyes. His hand went to his jeans pocket and he removed a vibrating cell phone. He pushed a button.

"Yeah?" he said, voice groggy. His eyes lost their gloss of sleep and he sat up, glancing at me. "Yes, ma'am. She's here, Mrs. C. Give me a minute to go get her."

He put a finger to his lips and handed me the phone, then stood and left the room. I put the phone to my ear.

"Hello?" I said.

"Maggie Mae, how are you?"

"How am I? How are *you*? I've been so worried."

"I can honestly say I have been better. But I've also been

worse." Mrs. Carpenter chuckled. "Would you come to the hospital? We need to talk."

I didn't know what to say. Hospitals were the place where people never saw each other again.

"Maggie, dear?"

"Okay." I would do anything for Mrs. Carpenter, even go to the hospital.

The sliding doors parted and I got a whiff of disinfectant and sick people. Memories started flashing in my brain. Blood. Pale skin. Blue lips. Silence.

Kat O'Connell strode past me, adjusted her oversized sunglasses, and flopped down in a waiting room chair.

"Are you all right?" Bridger asked me. I looked at my feet, cemented to the sidewalk outside the hospital doors, and forced myself to proceed.

"I can't believe you guys are up so early. I'm sixteen. I need my sleep," Kat mumbled, standing as we walked past.

"Then you should have stayed home," Bridger snapped. "You're the one who insisted on coming."

She stuck her tongue out at him.

We walked through a waiting room, past people staring in a daze at a tiny television mounted in a high corner. They had no idea what they were watching. At least, that's how it was when I sat in the waiting room.

As we made our way deeper into the hospital, the beep and hum of life-reading machines came out of hospital rooms and made me sick to my stomach. When I was five, I'd sat in a hospital room staring at a pale face with blue lips, listening to that very sound—the staccato beep of a pulse machine. It was when the sound stopped that my life changed for the worse.

I stared at my feet as they passed over white linoleum, too scared to look into the rooms.

"What's wrong?" Bridger asked, slowing to walk beside me.

I swallowed and shook my head.

"You know, Maggie, friends tell each other stuff. It makes life easier if you have someone to confide in. Did someone you love die in a hospital?"

I looked at him, wondering how he knew. "My aunt."

"What happened? How did she die?"

"A freak accident in a national park."

"Really?" Kat chimed in.

I nodded and touched the scar in my eyebrow. "And when I was twelve, I had to come to the hospital to get this sewn shut." As if it were yesterday, I could still see Mrs. Simms, her eyes brimming with tears, sign the papers that released me from her care while police officers led her husband out of the ER in a pair of handcuffs.

"You know, I bet a plastic surgeon could make that scar disappear," she said.

"Katie, shut up," Bridger snapped.

We arrived at Mrs. Carpenter's room and knocked.

"Come in," she called, her voice full of sunshine and cheer. She lay semireclined in a bed, her left leg wrapped in layers of bandages and propped up on a mountain of pillows.

"Hello, Maggie Mae, Bridger . . . Katie," Mrs. Carpenter said, studying Kat's bare shoulder poking out of her oversized wide-neck sweater.

"I go by Kat now," Kat said, walking to the chair in the corner of the room and sitting.

I forced a smile to my face. "Hi. How're you feeling?"

Mrs. Carpenter didn't mince words. "Maggie, I'm going to need some help with getting my house put back to rights and taking care of the animals. I was wondering if you're ready to move up into the stable-hand room above the barn, and I can use your room until my leg's better?"

The dark cloud of hospital memories receded with her words. "I think that would be a good idea," I said with a smile.

She sighed and squeezed my hand. "Bless you, child. Now, if I can just convince them to release me. These hospital gowns are ridiculous."

While Kat sat silent in the corner, Bridger and I chatted with Mrs. Carpenter as she ate her breakfast. She told me where the key to the barn room was located. When a nurse came in to check her vital signs, we left.

"Do you mind if we make one more stop?" Bridger asked as the door clicked shut behind him.

"You mean at the hospital or on our way home?" Kat asked. "Because I'm all for stopping for breakfast."

"Here, Katie," he said.

She sighed, adjusting her oversized sunglasses again. "I'm going to find some coffee. See you at the car." She strode away and I wasn't sorry to see her go.

"So where are we going?" I asked.

"I'd like to see how Danni is."

I laughed a humorless laugh. "Please say you're not serious."

"I'm serious, Maggie."

Filling my lungs with a breath of recycled hospital air, I answered, "Lead the way."

Bridger got the room number from the woman at the information desk and together we walked to the other side of the hospital, to the intensive care unit. But when we got to Danni's door, we were told by a nurse to stay out. ICU patients got visits only from immediate family.

We stared at Danni through a window. Bandages wrapped her arms, a heart monitor beeped with her pulse, and she lay utterly still beneath a white blanket. She could have been my aunt, except Danni's lips weren't blue. And the heart monitor was still registering life.

Movement from the side of the room forced my eyes from Danni's slack face. A haggard-looking woman with brown hair and bloodshot eyes stood from a chair and opened the ICU door.

"Bridger." She closed the door behind her and forced a smile to her face. Opening her arms, she took a step forward and wrapped Bridger in them. "Thanks for coming."

"How is she?" he asked, returning the hug. The woman let go of Bridger and glanced at Danni through the window.

"She's in stable condition. The doctors hope to move her out of ICU in the morning. Who did you bring with you?" she asked, turning to me.

I clenched my jaw shut.

"This is Maggie Mae," Bridger said.

Danni's mom frowned, as if trying to remember where she'd heard my name. "Oh. Maggie Mae. Mortensen? I'm sorry if you're looking for your jacket."

I looked between Danni's mom and Bridger.

"What jacket?" I asked.

"Gray jacket with your name on the tag. Danni was wearing it last night when she got attacked. The doctors had to cut it off of her. I'm so sorry. I can buy you a new one if you want." A film of tears glazed the woman's eyes, making them look even redder than before.

"No. It's no problem. It's summer. I totally don't need a new jacket."

Mrs. Williams pulled a wadded tissue from her pocket and began dabbing her eyes.

"Let me know if there's anything I can do to help," Bridger said.

"Thank you, but at this point all you can do is pray." She sniffled and went back to Danni's room.

Bridger and I walked through the hospital in silence. When we got to the sliding doors and stepped out into sunshine, my entire body sighed.

"What was she talking about?" Bridger asked.

"Who?"

"Mrs. Williams. Danni was wearing your jacket?"

I shrugged. "She stole it from my gym locker. I'd written my name on the tag. Guess Danni liked it."

Bridger didn't say a word the whole drive home.

As I opened the barn doors, a whiff of chicken-scented air hit me and I prayed the barn room didn't smell the same.

Kat started coughing. "Are you seriously going to live in a *barn*?" she asked. "Like a homeless vagabond?"

"Yep," I said. Being a foster child felt like being a homeless vagabond at times. My own snug, sound room above a barn didn't sound so bad.

Shash darted past me and jumped on Kat, trying to lick her face. She kneed him in the gut and brushed off her shirt.

"Stupid dog! He got dirt on my new Pierre Cardin sweater! I'm waiting in the car," she insisted, striding away.

With Bridger at my side, I crossed to the far side of the barn and stopped at a narrow wooden stairway. I thrust my hand under the bottom step. My fingers snapped spiderwebs and I cringed, hoping the web didn't belong to a black widow. I rummaged through the dirt and produced a grimy key.

Wooden stairs groaned beneath my feet. At the top of the stairs I paused, inserted the key into the door handle, and twisted. The door swung silently open and the smell of dust and sage and wool wafted out. I stepped inside and gasped, pressing a hand over my mouth.

"What's wrong?" Bridger asked from the doorway. His first words since the hospital parking lot.

A wrinkled black face with wide, hollow eyes was staring at me. Matted hair framed the face and stark white outlined the eyes. I slowly lowered my hand and took a step closer.

"Did that scare you?" he asked, lingering in the doorway and pointing to a mask hanging from the wall.

I nodded. "Totally freaked me out."

"It's a ceremonial Navajo mask of Haschebaad, the goddess," Bridger explained. "And it is probably a priceless antique."

"It's creepy."

"Yeah. It's supposed to be. It's made to scare evil spirits away."

"Do you really believe that?" I asked, looking at Bridger.

"Have you seen any evil spirits while you've been living here?"

I laughed under my breath. Evil spirits? No. Demon dogs were another story.

"So, can I come in?" he asked.

"Yeah, of course. Why are you so paranoid about being invited in?"

He stepped through the door. "Because I'm Navajo."

"And the Navajo people are . . . vampires?"

He laughed. "No. But we have certain beliefs. If I enter your house uninvited, I run the risk of bringing all sorts of bad stuff in with me."

"Bad stuff? Like what?"

"Anything. Death, *chindi*, bad luck . . . anything."

"*Chindi?*"

"Evil spirits."

I studied him for a hint of insincerity. "You're serious."

He nodded. "Warriors are often haunted by *chindi*, by the spirits of those they killed."

"And this applies to you how?"

He shrugged. "It's just a Navajo belief," he said, and started walking around the room. I followed. There were more masks, one on each wall, and all of them were freaky beyond belief. They were made from leather, which looked like shriveled human skin, and had ratted, human-looking hair coming from the tops of their heads.

"I've got to get those out of here. I won't be able to sleep with them watching me," I said.

"You're giving me a hard time about my beliefs, yet you're the one too scared to sleep with them in the same room?"

"Sorry."

Bridger carefully took the four masks from the four walls and laid them on the bed. "I'll find somewhere safe in Mrs. C.'s house to store them," he said.

I walked to a door on the right side of the room and opened

it. "Thank goodness," I whispered under my breath. Through the door was a small bathroom with a toilet, sink, and stand-up shower. I shut the door and went back to exploring the bedroom, pausing at a wide dresser.

"What is that?" I asked. A wooden bowl filled with pale gray powder sat on the dresser's edge. Bridger dipped his fingers into the powder and blew on them. Dust filled the air and I sneezed.

"This is ash. Another form of protection."

"Protection from *what*? I don't get it. Protection *masks*, a protection *ring* around Mrs. Carpenter's property, protection *ashes*, even a protection *bracelet*." I held up my wrist. "Is Silver City located on top of an opening into hell or something?"

Bridger laughed and shook his head. "No. Silver City's a good place to live. But evil is everywhere. You can never be too safe. Mrs. C.'s husband obviously loved her very much." He looked at the door. "How about I go get Katie's old clothes out of my SUV and bring them up."

I nodded. "Thanks." Bridger reverently picked up the Navajo masks and left. I kept examining the room. Sunlight streamed through the window, lighting dust particles that floated silently through the air. Burned sticks and bird feathers were nailed above the door and window. Bowls of crystals and turquoise sat on the dresser beside the bowl of ash. Inside the drawers I found individual bundles of twine-bound sage as long as my forearm and a little thicker than my thumb. I leaned my face into the drawer and inhaled. Something about this room spoke to me, making me feel calmer, stiller than normal. I'd been in this room for only a couple of minutes, yet already it felt like home. I picked up a bundle of sage and held it beneath my nose.

Bridger's voice echoed up into the room from below. Not

bothering to put the sage down, I walked to the door and opened it a crack. Bridger stood just outside the open barn door, cell phone pressed to his ear.

". . . totally serious . . . I don't know why they would, either, but the sooner you can come, the better. . . . That soon? Yeah. I'll arrange it." He took the phone from his ear. I stepped back to the dresser, holding the sage beneath my nose and inhaling again. A minute later the stairs thumped and Bridger walked into the room, two black trash bags in his hands. He set them on the bed.

"You like the smell?" he asked, looking at the sage.

"Yeah. It's really nice. Calming."

"Certain things have spiritual properties, like the beads in your bracelet. Sage has spiritual properties, too," he explained. "That's a smudge stick. Medicine men light them and purify a residence. Or a person."

"How do you know all this stuff? Like about the masks. And the ashes and sage."

"Family heritage."

"Yeah, but your house isn't like this room—there are no freaky masks."

He shrugged. "You haven't seen my whole house. And besides, a person's religion and beliefs aren't always visible to the naked eye. My family has always passed down Navajo teachings. Knowledge is power." The way he said it, I could tell he believed it wholeheartedly. "Hand me that." He held out his hand. I placed the smudge stick into it. "You didn't happen to see a lighter in any of those drawers, did you?"

"Actually . . ." I reached into the sage-filled drawer and pulled out a silver lighter.

Bridger took it, then removed one of the feathers from above the door. "Eagle feather," he said. He lit the smudge stick and began fanning the pungent smoke with the feather. In a deep, quiet voice he began to chant:

"May this room be filled with peace,
From ceiling to floor, may it be happy,
From wall to wall, may it be happy,
May all who enter dwell in safety,
May all who leave return in safety,
All around me, may it be happy."

He stuck the smudge stick into the bowl of crystals and the pale smoke curled toward the ceiling.

"What was that?" I asked.

"A Navajo house blessing." Bridger replaced the eagle feather above the door. "So, what are your plans for the rest of the day?"

"Clean Mrs. Carpenter's house, feed the dogs, shovel manure, collect the eggs—"

"You're sleeping up here tonight, right?" he interjected.

"Yeah, I'm sleeping up here. Why?"

"Because I don't know if her front door will lock, so you'll be safer up here. You know what you should do?"

I studied Bridger. "What should I do?"

"Let Bear sleep with you. He's tougher than he looks."

I scrunched my eyebrows together. "Who in the world is Bear?"

"Mrs. C.'s dog. The black-and-white one?"

"You mean Shash?" I asked, wondering if he was feeling as sleep deprived as me.

He grinned. "*Shash* means 'bear.' It's—"

"Let me guess. Navajo?"

Bridger nodded. "I've got to go. Some family friends are coming into town this afternoon and I need to arrange a place for them to stay. I'll try to get someone over to fix Mrs. C.'s door."

"All right. Thanks. For, you know, the clothes, the house blessing, everything."

Bridger smiled and I had to fight down a sudden surge of butterflies. "That's what friends do, Maggie."

When it started getting dark out, I grabbed a box of crackers and a jar of peanut butter from Mrs. Carpenter's pantry. With food in hand, I went to the barn.

I brought the crackers to my room, a snack for later. The full moon shone in through the window, creating a steel-blue square of light on my bed. I pulled the curtains closed, and even though I didn't feel the moon's pull as strongly as usual, I undressed and shifted into Shash's twin.

Ears perched and heart pounding, I sat by the door that led out of the barn and waited. Waited for wolves. Or wild dogs. Anything. But nothing came. After half a night of waiting, I gave in to canine instincts and played.

22

Someone pounded on my bedroom door and I jumped awake. Shash, cozy atop my feet, lifted his head and wagged his tail.

"What in the . . ." I looked at my watch and knew something must be wrong. Only bad news came knocking at a quarter past six in the morning. "Oh, no!" I gasped, imagining all sorts of bad news, Mrs. Carpenter's death topping the list.

I yanked my feet out from under Shash and leaped from bed, completely unconcerned that all I wore were panties and a black wifebeater, and pulled the door wide.

Bridger's eyes filled with relief when they saw me. "I was worried about you—worried the wolves might have come back," he said. And then his eyes moved from my face to my legs, then to my tank top and back to my face. He took a small step back.

"What's wrong?" I asked. "Is Mrs. Carpenter all right?"

He cleared his throat and focused on my eyes. "Yeah. She's great. I talked to her last night. She tried calling the house first, but you didn't answer, so she called me and asked me to relay a message. She is doing well and hopes you had a nice night, and found the barn to your liking." His eyes narrowed the slightest bit. "She sounded worried about you, but made me promise to wait until morning to give you the message."

"Oh." A smile tugged at the corner of my mouth. Found the barn to my liking? Yep. I'd chased chickens and rolled in the dirt with the dogs for hours.

I glanced down at my pj's and closed the door halfway, hiding behind it. Shash, thrilled to see Bridger, tried to nose the door open. "Shash, stop it," I said, nudging him away with my knee. "If Mrs. Carpenter's fine, then why are you here so early?"

"You don't have a phone. I came to see if you wanted to go mountain biking with me."

"You mean right now?" For the first time I noticed he was wearing biker shorts and a jersey.

"Yeah, right now," he said with a laugh. "Sunrise is the best time to go; plus this is the only activity I could think of where Katie couldn't tag along."

"Your plan is flawed. I don't have a bike," I said, stifling a yawn.

"I know. I brought Katie's bike—hence the reason she can't come," he said with a wicked grin.

I laughed. "I've never been mountain biking."

"Do you know how to ride a bike?"

"Of course. I'm a foster child, not an invalid."

"Then you'll be able to mountain bike. Get dressed and meet me in the driveway."

"But . . . Mrs. Carpenter's house. It's a disaster. I need to clean it."

"Do it this afternoon. Hurry up and get dressed. And in the future, lock the barn at night."

With that he turned and left.

.   .   .

Mountain biking was like discovering a new world, riding trails where hardly any human ever walked, seeing lizards, chipmunks, hawks, and the occasional snake. Bridger took me on a tree-shrouded trail that switchbacked up the side of a steep mountain. And believe it or not, I was pretty good at mountain biking—until it was time to ride back down.

"I'll meet you at the bottom," Bridger said. He stuck his shoes into the clipless pedals of his bike and was gone, yelping and hollering as he sped out of sight.

Thirty minutes later, I finally made it down to the bottom of the mountain, my hands cramping from gripping the brakes so tight. Bridger was lying on a giant shaded boulder, shirt off, eyes closed, no helmet, and hands behind his head. His bear claw necklace gleamed against his tan skin, and I thought about what he'd said the day before—that you can't tell a person's beliefs just by looking at them. There had always been something slightly different about Bridger, something more than the eye could see.

"What took you so long?" he asked, cracking one eye to look at me.

"That trail was so steep, if I squeezed the brakes on my front tire, my bike started tipping forward."

Bridger laughed and sat up.

"Did your friends arrive all right?"

"Who?" he asked, pulling his jersey back on.

"The people you were finding a place to stay?"

"Oh. Yeah, them. They made it." He put his helmet on. "So, you want some help cleaning up Mrs. C.'s house?"

"You mean from you?"

He looked left and then right. "Who do you think I meant?" he asked with a grin.

"You'd seriously help me clean her house?"

"You're surprised. Why?"

"I don't know. Because you're rich. And rich kids usually don't help clean old ladies' ravished houses."

"Oh, really? And how many rich kids are you basing this observation on?"

I bit my lip and grimaced. "One?"

"Just because my dad makes lots of money doesn't mean I don't know how to work. The day I turned sixteen he made me go out and get a job. At his insistence I assembled kids' bikes at Wal-Mart for two years for minimum wage. He believes the only way to learn to work is by working. There's a lot you don't know about me, Maggie."

"Ditto."

"And just to warn you, Katie's going to insist on coming, but she's not big on cleaning."

Cleaning the house with Bridger and Kat made it seem more like a pleasure than a chore. Kat followed me around and watched me clean, talking nonstop about Europe, or telling me what pants and accessories I should have been wearing with her hand-me-down shirt, because apparently I'd worn the wrong pair—and no accessories. Bridger did all the hard work, like hauling the destroyed sofa out into the driveway and getting the cushion stuffing off the ceiling fan blades. Kat, finding a way to be useful without actually having to clean anything, called a trash service to remove the sofa and the black garbage bags Bridger and I had piled up on the front porch.

With the living room clean, Bridger helped me move the

sewing machine and table where the destroyed sofa had been. Then we took Mrs. Carpenter's double bed apart and brought it downstairs to the sewing room.

Bridger, with Kat trailing on his heels like a lost puppy, came over every day. And by the time Wednesday came, the house, minus the brown leather sofa, was in pristine order. Bridger had even repaired and painted the front door.

"Are you all right?" Bridger asked as I was fluffing the pillows on Mrs. Carpenter's love seat, the final touch before she came home. Kat, sitting at the dining table, looked up from the magazine she'd been reading, her eyes moving between Bridger and me.

"You seem sort of . . ." Bridger trailed off, glancing at his sister.

"I'm fine," I said, pounding the pillow into submission. Kat went back to reading.

"Would you mind doing me a favor?"

"Yeah, what's up?"

"Go to your room and get a smudge stick and one of the eagle feathers. I'm going to bless the house before Mrs. C. gets here."

I ran to the barn room—my room—and stopped inside, giving in to the frown that had been trying to dominate my face all morning. I took a deep breath and grabbed a smudge stick and feather.

Back at the house I removed my frown and handed the smudge stick and feather to Bridger. He lit the sage and began walking from room to room, saying;

"Bless this house, these walls north, east, south, west,
May this be a good place to live again,

May peace enfold the inhabitants,
May harm never pass through the doors,
May joy and love grow within these walls,
May it be a place of healing,
May the sun, my mother's ancestor, shine upon this house."

After we'd walked through every room, Bridger laid the smudge stick on a plate and placed it on the dining room table beside Kat's magazine.

He looked at his watch and then his eyes met mine. "It's time to pick her up. Do you want to come?"

Kat looked from Bridger to me again, her eyes curious.

"No, I'll wait here," I replied.

Kat stood. "I'll go. I am *so* bored that even driving to the hospital sounds fun at this point. See ya, Maggie."

I smiled and watched them go, but as soon as they got into the car, the smile fell from my face and I let the feelings I'd been trying so hard to hide flood to the surface.

I was glad Mrs. Carpenter was coming home—thrilled—but I knew with her return, I wouldn't see Bridger as much. I'd been with him from sunup to sundown for three days. But now that the house was back in order, I was certain his talk from the night of graduation would come into effect. I could still hear him. . . .

I wanted to let you know I'm still here for you, as a friend. Nothing more, nothing less. So if you can forgive me for misleading you, maybe we can hang out sometimes. Nothing major, just the occasional movie, or hike, or something.

He'd be busy hanging out with Kat and his friends from out of town.

Yet it was a good thing. Because I was seriously, undeniably attached. Way more than friends.

I opened two cans of chili and dumped them into a pot, then put the pot on the stove. While the food heated, I made sure for the tenth time that Mrs. Carpenter's new bedroom looked perfect.

Convinced everything was flawless, I stood in the window, breathed in smoldering sage, and stared at the gravel driveway. When Bridger pulled up, I forced a smile to my face and opened the front door.

Bridger got out of the car and opened Mrs. Carpenter's door. Her voice carried to me.

"If you'll get the wheelchair, Bridger, I'll just—"

"There's no need for the wheelchair yet," Bridger said. He leaned into the car and lifted Mrs. Carpenter out, carrying her like a baby. Mrs. Carpenter's pale cheeks warmed to pink and she grinned as she put her arms around Bridger's neck.

"If I knew it would take a wolf bite to get a young man like you to carry me across the threshold, I'd have got bit years ago. You're a strong boy," she said.

"You hardly weigh a thing, Mrs. C.," Bridger said with a laugh.

He carried her into the living room and gently laid her on the love seat. I stacked pillows beneath her leg. Kat came inside with the wheelchair and sniffed the air.

"Do I smell canned chili?" Kat asked, scrunching up her face. Bridger chucked his keys at her, which she snatched out of the air without blinking.

"If you have a problem with the food, go get dinner somewhere else," he said.

She glared at her brother. "Why are you so grouchy? I never said anything was *wrong* with canned chili. And besides, it's not like we were invited to eat dinner here."

"Kat, you and your brother are invited to eat dinner with us whenever you are available," Mrs. Carpenter said with a sly look in my direction. Bridger grinned at me.

With Mrs. Carpenter's return, Bridger didn't disappear from my life, like I'd assumed. And neither did Kat. He and I went mountain biking Thursday morning—without Kat—before Mrs. Carpenter woke. On Thursday night, he and Kat drove me to work, hung out with their visiting friends until the end of my shift, and then drove me back home. On Friday morning, Bridger and I went mountain biking again, and that night Bridger, Kat, and I played a card game called Rook with Mrs. Carpenter.

Saturday morning found Bridger and me in the mountains again. But this time Kat was tagging along. On the brand-new mountain bike she'd purchased since *someone* was always using hers.

With my hands clenched on the brakes, I dodged gnarled tree roots and rocks and maneuvered the bike down a steep, narrow trail. When the ground leveled out, I sighed with relief.

Bridger and Kat sat shaded in some bushes beside their bikes, helmets off, eating trail mix with more chocolate chips than nuts, and sipping water from matching Camelbaks.

". . . say you had to stick to me like glue," Bridger was saying, glaring at his sister.

"I'm keeping you out of trouble. Better safe than sorry," she said, a self-satisfied grin on her face. I pulled my bike up beside them and yanked my feet out of the pedals, then shook out my cramping hands.

Bridger wiped the glare from his face, held up his hand, and started counting his fingers.

"What are you doing?" I asked, plopping into the weeds beside Kat.

"Counting. We've gone biking seven times and you're still gripping the brakes like a five-year-old every time we lose elevation. I sorta thought you'd catch on by now, but don't you know that you're supposed to go *faster* on the downhill?"

"He's right," Kat said, yawning. "You're slow. We've been sitting down here for at least half an hour."

"I'm scared of going fast," I explained, a completely reasonable fear. The look of consternation that filled Bridger's eyes made me laugh.

"This from the girl who sprints faster than the speed of light?" he said around a mouthful of trail mix. "You've got to be kidding! Don't you know that cruising down a mountain at dangerously reckless speed is just like flying?"

"No, there is a freaking huge difference," I argued.

"Oh, really?"

"Hello! You can't crash into a tree when you're flying!"

One black eyebrow shot up. "I beg to differ. When a bird flies through the forest, there are trees all around," Bridger said. Kat glared at him.

I opened my mouth to argue, but snapped it back shut. He had a point.

"Don't you want to know how it feels to be a bird soaring through the air, Maggie? Get back on that bike so you can do the downhill again. Flying is quite amazing."

"You want me to ride back up to the top of that mountain?" I asked, looking at the steep, pine-cloaked path.

"You've got to be kidding," Kat whined. "I refuse to do it."

Bridger smiled wickedly. And, silly me, I couldn't resist that smile, couldn't deny him anything. Somehow he'd become my best friend.

"Let's get this over with," I said with a sigh.

The ride up was at least ten times harder than the first time around, and I was gasping for air as I neared the top. But I made it. Bridger didn't seem to think it was any harder, but one glance at his legs, sculpted with muscle from years of biking and track, showed why.

"Okay, my little Magpie, are you ready to fly?" Bridger asked, straddling his bike beside me.

"No," I answered. "I need a drink of water first." He looked at the water bottle fastened to the frame of my bike, and then at me like I was stalling. "I'm out of water. Wanna share yours before I keel over from dehydration?"

I climbed off my bike and Bridger climbed off his. He held the straw end of his Camelbak out to me and I took a tentative step forward, practically stepping on his toes to put it in my mouth. I drew in a deep swallow of the warm water, letting it wet my burning throat, and sighed. And then I realized the air between us felt charged with electricity. Being so close to Bridger made me aware of every inch of my body, and every inch of his. I stared at his neck and could see the pulse pounding beneath his skin.

Since our little chat on graduation night, he hadn't flirted with me. At all. Hadn't touched me once. I wondered if he could feel my reaction to him, so I looked up at his close face. The breath caught in my throat.

He was staring down at me, frowning, his entire body still as stone. Something in his eyes told me he knew exactly what I was feeling.

Behind us, Kat's voice interrupted the silence. "Are you guys still up here?" She gasped.

He yanked the rubber straw out of my mouth and turned away. "Yeah. We're about to start down," Bridger called. "So move out of the way."

Kat rode into the clearing at the top of the hill, her face red and slick with sweat.

"Time for you to fly, Magpie," Bridger said, winking at me.

I took a deep, unsteady breath. "Fine. But if I fall off my bike and get hurt, you're going to carry me back to the car." *And that means you'll have to touch me.*

"Fair enough." He climbed onto his bike and looked at me. "What are you waiting for? Go!"

I got off to a wobbly start, struggling to clip my shoes into the pedals. Once they were in, I pointed my bike down and started to bump along the path. It was hard not to cling to the brakes, but I made myself let go and careened down the trail. Trees and foliage began to blur past, wind whipped my face, and tears streamed from my eyes. My delighted scream echoed far and wide, my hair blew out behind me, and for a glorious moment I *could* imagine how a bird must feel gliding through the air.

Then I was at the bottom, smiling, pulse racing, and ecstatic. I had done it, and while it was a little bumpier than I imagine flying would be, it had been positively exhilarating.

Bridger came to a stop beside me, his dancing eyes studying my face.

Kat zoomed past. "I'll meet you at the car," she called.

"So, what do you think of flying?" Bridger asked.

"Awesome."

A satisfied grin spread over his face. "I knew you'd like it. Let's go."

He pedaled hard, leaving a cloud of dust in his wake. My

legs were so rubbery I could hardly snap my feet back into the bike pedals. But somehow I managed and began to follow.

The winding trail was narrow, shaded by tall pines and fringed with yellow and purple wildflowers and waist-high weeds, making it impossible to see far. Birds chirped and chipmunks chattered at me.

The farther I rode, the thinner the trees got, the sparser the weeds. I rounded a sharp bend and had my first clear view of the trail. Bridger and Kat were out of sight—probably already at the SUV. I forced my exhausted legs to continue pedaling when something niggled at my senses—I seemed to catch a whiff of an unusual odor. Or maybe I heard something, or saw a flash of color out of the corner of my eye. I wasn't sure what it was, but . . . something had changed.

I glanced at the sky, thinking a storm must be blowing in, but it was clear as glass. And then I realized. The only sounds disturbing the woods were my tires scrunching along the ground and my panting.

I jerked the brakes and jolted to a stop. Popping my foot out of the pedal, I placed it on the ground and looked around. I knew this feeling. When I lived with the Simmses and Mr. Simms had been drinking too much, he'd get violent. When he stomped down the hall to my bedroom, I hid under the bed because I knew he was searching for someone to hurt. The way I felt right now, Mr. Simms might as well have been stomping down the hall to get me.

Breathing turned to a chore, the dense air hardly fitting through my constricting windpipe. I needed to hide. Or run.

I put my foot back on the pedal and pushed as hard as I could. Well, I didn't clip the sole of the shoe into the stupid clipless pedal all the way. Ten feet down the trail I lost control of my bike and totally wiped out. In a daze I stared up at the sky. A big black bird circled overhead, hunting something. Struggling to get free of the bike, I saw a gleam of black in the woods and froze. Someone was there, watching. Me. I was being watched.

My brain decided to freak out, filling with thoughts of the man who'd been looking for me at the Navajo Mexican. Maybe he'd found me. . . .

In a flash, I was back on my bike and pedaling as fast as I could, my butt not once touching the bike seat. There was a disturbance in the woods behind me, the crash and snap of something big careening through the underbrush. Peering over my shoulder, I caught a glimpse of gold fur. I pedaled harder.

Bridger's SUV came into view, two bikes beside it. I'd never been so glad to see a big, expensive hunk of metal. I rode up to it, gasping for breath, but Bridger and Kat weren't there.

Close by, a stick snapped and I flinched, staring at the woods. Bridger emerged from the trees, shirt in hand, pulling a twig out of his midnight hair. Kat followed, eyes wide, face pale.

Bridger looked at me and frowned. "Are you all right, Maggie? Your knee's bleeding."

I pressed my lips together.

"You're scared. What happened?" he asked. Kat stared at me with rapt attention.

I took a ragged breath. "I thought I saw something in the woods."

Bridger studied me, dark eyes calculating. "But you didn't?"

I shrugged. I had seen something. I just didn't know exactly what.

"We need to hurry and get out of here. It's almost ten o'clock. Mrs. Carpenter's going to wonder where we are," he said.

I nodded and looked around. The forest was noisy again, alive with birds and chipmunks. With the appearance of Bridger and Kat, everything seemed to go back to normal.

23

A week later, Bridger talked me into playing Ultimate at the city park, whatever the heck that meant. I was just happy to be doing something without his little sister.

We got out of his car and I followed him across the grass to a group of guys, half of them white, half dark skinned, with Kat in their midst. So much for doing something without her.

My heart dropped when I realized these big, tall, muscular *men* were Bridger's "friends" that I was going to play Ultimate with. I was tiny beside them. I hoped there was no physical contact in Ultimate, because if there was I'd be toast.

"Hey, guys," Bridger called a greeting. "I made good on my promise and found one more player." He nodded at me as if I were some sort of a peace offering. "Guys, meet Maggie. Maggie, meet the guys."

Their eyes went from my face, to my fancy black tank top, to my hand-me-down designer jeans, to my running shoes. More than one of them started to complain. I couldn't blame them. They all wore sporty exercise clothes—even Kat, dressed in teeny skintight shorts and a matching tank top, with gym socks pulled up to her knees. One guy, the oldest, even had on a knee brace.

"Um, Bridger?" I said, tugging on his T-shirt. He was wearing workout clothes, too.

"I know you're nervous. Just trust me," Bridger whispered, never taking his eyes from the "guys." He looked awfully pleased with himself, like the cat that swallowed the canary. "So," he called out. "Whose team are Maggie and I on? Walt's or Alex's?"

Two men, one white, one dark, stepped out of the group and eyed each other, then eyed Bridger and me, sizing me up all over again. They looked at each other once more, and the dark guy started talking.

"With those two added, we can't play dark on light. Unless—" He looked at Bridger. "You wanna be on my team, Atay? You've got enough color in your skin to still look Navajo."

"I don't care whose team I'm on, but Maggie has to be on my team. She and I work well together," Bridger said. Kat barked a laugh and rolled her eyes.

"But we dark boys are skins." The guy looked me over once more and then took his T-shirt off, exposing washboard abs and smooth golden skin. "Unless she's taking her shirt off, you two'll have to stick with Walt and Kat."

I glared at the guy and folded my arms over my chest. He laughed and looked at Bridger. "*Ne-zhoni*," he said. Bridger shrugged. "Walt, give me one of your pasty white guys."

"All right, you're on my team. I'm Walt. That's Alex." The blond man with the knee brace held out his hand. I pulled my eyes away from Alex's abs and shook Walt's hand. Before Walt could say another word, Bridger grabbed the back of my tank top and towed me out of hearing distance from the other players.

"Maggie, whatever you do, don't tell them you've never played before, because I said I wouldn't bring a beginner. Now, when the game starts, you run to the end zone as fast as you can and catch the Frisbee I'm going to throw to you. You got that? As soon as you catch it, you freeze—you can't move, because that is the rule. If you aren't in the end zone, throw the Frisbee to Kat or one of the guys with a shirt on. Any of them will do. You got that?" He looked at me expectantly.

I nodded. "Sure. Run to end zone, catch Frisbee, throw Frisbee if I'm not in end zone. Got it." I didn't mention my hands were shaking and I wasn't sure if I could catch a Frisbee, since I had never tried.

"You'll do fine," he assured me. "Otherwise, I wouldn't have brought you."

We walked back over to the guys and lined up for a game of Ultimate. My team, the ones wearing shirts, had the Frisbee, so when the game started I sprinted, easily clearing the defense of Alex's shirtless golden-skinned team and headed toward the end zone. Before I was quite there, I looked over my shoulder in time to see Bridger fling a fluorescent pink Frisbee clear from the other end of the field. It soared through the air, high over the heads of the running defense, and floated down right into my hands. I happened to be standing in the end zone.

We played for a good half hour, with me scoring several points because of my speed, but that was about all I did—run to the end zone, catch the Frisbee.

The more I watched the other players, though, the more I understood the game. I started using my speed not only to run to the end zone for points, but also to intercept the Frisbee when the other team had it. Alex would have the Frisbee and throw it toward one of his guys, but I would sprint as fast as I could and snatch it out of the air a split second before Alex's guy could catch it. Boy, did that make me a popular player. My weakness was throwing. Half the time when I intercepted the Frisbee, I gave it right back to the other team. "Learn to aim," Kat would snap. But when my throws were successful, all the guys on my team would whoop and holler and high-five me.

Bridger wasn't the least bit surprised. He'd just nod and have a look of pure satisfaction in his eyes when they met mine.

After my team had won three games to none, it was four twenty-five—five minutes till work. I was sweaty and panting, and my hair, I am sure, needed to be redone before I set foot into the Navajo Mexican.

"I've got to go to work," I told Walt, who was ready to play again even though he was winded and soaked with sweat.

"Oh! Come on, Mag! Play one more!" some of the guys called.

"Another time, guys. I've got to go, too," Bridger said. He pulled his T-shirt off and wiped a sheen of sweat from his brow. My eyes latched onto his body. His shoulders were like airplane wings, his arms corded with long, lean muscle. Some of the guys bumped their knuckles against his and said, "Nice game, Atay." Then he came and stood beside me, pulling his shirt back on.

"So, Mag, where do you work?" Walt asked. I don't know where the nickname Mag had come from, but I didn't mind it.

"She works at a little restaurant, serving people," Kat said, as if it were the most demeaning job in the world.

"Wait a sec! Are you *Magdalena*?" Walt asked incredulously.

"Yeah. How do you know me?"

"I'm Maria's husband," he said, smiling. "She's away on maternity leave. You're covering for her?"

"Wow, small world," I said. I reached up and unbound my hair, shaking it out.

"Small town," Walt corrected. "Well, come and play again, Mag. We play every Tuesday and Thursday at three thirty."

"Yeah, come back again, Mag. Anytime," Alex said, his eyes holding mine.

"Thanks, Alex." He grinned as he watched me comb my fingers through my hair. A hand came down on my shoulder and I jumped. Alex scowled and stopped staring. Kat, standing beside Alex, shook her head the tiniest bit.

I glanced at Bridger in surprise. He was smiling at Alex, but his eyes were hard as rock.

"Thanks for the invite, Alex. I'd like to play again," I replied, feeling sorry for the guy. I turned to go, shrugging Bridger's hand away.

Bridger called his good-byes to the guys, told Kat he'd be back in five minutes, and caught up with me.

"What was that about?" I asked as I pulled my hair back into a tight ponytail.

"Huh?" He didn't look at me—just stared straight ahead.

"You don't like Alex looking at me."

He turned toward me, making eye contact. "I don't know what you're talking about."

"Whatever." I rolled my eyes. "So, how do you know them and why do they call you Atay?"

"Atay's a nickname. Alex is my second cousin. He and the other Navajo guys just moved to town for the summer, from the Navajo reservation. The guys I told you about the day after graduation, who I hang out with when you're at work. They're doing some work for my dad."

"What kind of work? Because, no offense, but they look like they do hard labor."

"Don't judge a person by the color of his skin," Bridger snapped.

I looked at him, confused. "What are you? Oh. I get it. I didn't mean they looked like they do hard labor because they're dark skinned. I mean, Alex is way beautiful." Bridger barked a laugh and my cheeks started to burn. "What I meant is they're ripped—all of them. It looks like they spend a lot of time in the gym. Or mowing lawns. Or herding cattle or something."

"They're doing some security jobs for my dad," he explained.

"Even Walt?"

"No, just the Navajo boys. Walt's a banker. He handles my dad's money."

"He looks like a banker. So, what are you doing tonight? Hanging with your cousin?"

"Stuff for my dad, actually."

"But I thought he was in France."

His dark brows drew together. "That's the problem. He's not here, so when things go wrong, I'm the one who gets to sort out the local crap."

"Is everything okay? You look worried."

The expression melted from his face, replaced with nonchalance. "It's just family stuff. No big deal." He smiled. "You're a fast runner. I can't believe you picked up on Ultimate so easily. Katie felt pretty annoyed that you're better than her." He reached his hand toward me, as if to pat me on the back or ruffle my hair, but it stopped halfway and dropped back to his side.

"Yeah. Alex seemed pretty surprised, too."

Bridger's lips thinned the slightest bit. If I hadn't been looking for his reaction, I would have missed it.

"Well, I'll see you after work," I said. We'd arrived at the restaurant. Bridger stared down at me, his eyes questioning, his face
darkly serious. The breath caught in my throat and I couldn't
move. He blinked and ran a hand through his dark hair, and the
moment was gone.

"I'm coming in for dinner. Tell Yana and Penney that I want
you to be my server."

"That drives them nuts, you know."

"Yes, I know. I can feel their jealousy," he said.

"So, why don't you let us take turns serving you?"

He leaned closer to me. "Because, Maggie, the food seems
to taste better when you bring it to me. You are what draws me
here." I felt myself blush. He shrugged and got that serious look
in his eyes again. "I'll see ya later." With that he was gone. I
watched him walk away and felt empty, like there was something he forgot to tell me, like he was leaving our good-bye
undone. I shook my head to clear it and walked into work.

I rearranged my schedule with José so that I didn't work the
lunch shift on Tuesday or Thursday. Bridger, Kat, and I met up
with the guys on those afternoons and played Ultimate. Now
Bridger and I together were like a secret weapon. We just worked
well as a two-person team—we were like chips and salsa, or
bacon and eggs. He had amazingly good eyesight and aim, and
I had speed and agility. We were unbeatable. Alex and Walt
fought over whose team we were going to be on every time we

played, since Bridger insisted he and I play on the same team. And while I still caught Alex checking me out when Bridger wasn't looking, he never hit on me.

I felt so human around Bridger I nearly forgot how different I was.

I spent every waking moment with Bridger, Kat, Naalyehe, or Mrs. Carpenter, and I didn't have the time or need to turn into an animal, not with Bridger driving me home from work every night.

Because I stopped changing, I stayed alive longer than I should have.

And because of this bitter irony, Bridger was the one who ended up shooting me.

∽ 24 ∽

The streets were unusually empty for midafternoon and the desert sun blazed down on the top of my head and seared my bare arms. Bridger couldn't drive me to work because he had to help Alex with some sort of crisis, and I didn't want to bother Mrs. Carpenter for a ride.

Even though I was sweating like a sinner at confession when I walked into the air-conditioned restaurant, I had a smile on my face.

"Maggie Mae," José said as I entered the kitchen. "Have you been out in the sun? You look rosy! Healthy!" He waggled his bushy eyebrows. "You look like you're in love!"

My face started to burn and it had nothing to do with the fact that I'd gotten a sunburn walking to work. He chuckled and started singing in Spanish, something about *amor*.

Naalyehe put his dishcloth down and peered at me over his shoulder. His eyes focused on my wrist, on the bracelet, and he frowned. "I need to talk to you," he said, voice barely audible over José's opera. I followed Naalyehe out the back door and into the rear parking lot. Even standing in the shadow of the restaurant, the air was searing hot.

"Everything okay?" I asked, wondering how twenty seconds ago I was blushing about an accusation of being in love, but now felt like snakes were wrestling in my stomach.

"That man," Naalyehe said quietly. "Remember the man who was looking for you?"

A chill ran down my spine. "Yeah, I do. Is he back?"

"He's been in the local jail. A deputy mentioned it today at lunch."

"Really? Jail? Did you catch his name?"

Naalyehe nodded. "I also got a picture." He pulled a three-by-five photograph out of his back pocket and handed it to me.

It was a mug shot, a man standing by a ruler, holding a black plaque that had writing on it. I studied the words but couldn't make them out.

"The deputy gave this to me to see if you might recognize the man. His name is Rolf Heinrich. When he was arrested, the police did a thorough background check and found an outstanding warrant."

"Rolf who?" I asked, squinting and studying the unfamiliar face. I was absolutely certain I had never seen the man before.

"Heinrich," Naalyehe said more slowly. "He is American, but his name is foreign."

"Hmm. I have no clue who he is," I said, handing the picture back with unsteady fingers. I thought of the afternoon I'd been mountain biking with Bridger, when someone had been in the woods. I opened my mouth to tell Naalyehe about it, but then thought better of the idea. No use worrying the man.

Back inside, I put on an apron.

"Business has been slow," José warned as I pinned my name tag into place. "But any day now the tourists will be coming to town and it will pick back up."

"Well, thank goodness for that," I said distractedly and hurried to the dining room.

Bridger came in for dinner that night—alone—though he came earlier than his normal eight o'clock. It was half past five when he strode through the door like a restless wind and sat down in the booth by the window.

"You're early and you forgot your shadow," I said, instantly aware that my hair was slipping out of its ponytail and framing my face in a wispy mess. I tucked the loose strands behind my ears and smiled. He smiled, but it hardly touched his eyes. "Everything all right?"

"No. My dad called this afternoon. We had a huge fight." The muscles in his jaw clenched and released. I wanted to put my hands on his face and steal away the tension. His eyes met mine and anger was replaced with concern. "I'm sorry. Don't worry about me. I don't deserve your worry." He made a second, much more convincing effort at smiling.

"Are you hungry?"

"Not really."

"Then why are you here?"

His eyes met mine and held. "I needed to get away from Katie, and I need someone to talk to."

It took a minute for his words to make sense. When they did, I couldn't help but smile.

"Since I'm here, I might as well eat, but I need a change. How are the nachos?" That was possibly the only thing on the menu he'd never eaten.

"I've never had them. They look good, though. They're made with stone-ground blue corn."

"That's what I want. And a Coke."

"I'll be right back with that."

As José had predicted earlier, business was slow. Penney and I were running the dining room. Actually only Penney was—I didn't have any customers besides Bridger, so when I brought his nachos out, I sat across the table from him. He was so consumed with something other than hunger that he didn't notice me, or the plate of food steaming beneath his nose.

"Bridger? Earth to Bridger!"

He looked at me, puzzled; then a grin split his face and wiped the worry from his eyes. "Sorry." He looked at his food and his eyes fogged over again.

"Bridger?" He didn't respond. I rolled my eyes and stood. If he was too distracted to hold a conversation, I'd leave him alone with his thoughts.

Quick as lightning his hand shot out and grabbed my wrist. "Don't," he said, the brooding back in his eyes.

"Don't what?" I asked.

"Please don't leave."

I sat back down and he let go of my wrist. He passed his half-full Coke to me and leaned back with his arms folded across his chest to watch me drink.

Just then, an older couple entered the restaurant. I passed Bridger's half-empty Coke back to him and jumped up to seat them.

"What can I get you to drink?" I asked the couple as they sat down in a corner booth.

The man opened his mouth to speak, but I didn't hear the words that came out of it. My ears were muted, as if blood had pooled around the eardrum. My skin became sickly hot and clammy all at once, and I had the sudden urge to flinch. A flash of memory assailed me, of a hand with a gold class ring on the finger flying toward my face. I gasped and touched the scar in my eyebrow.

I ignored the customers staring at me as if I were a moron and strode to the kitchen. The feeling stayed with me, hot and heavy. I peered through the window on the kitchen door. The couple that'd just entered the restaurant was talking animatedly to Penney, scowling and pointing toward the kitchen. My gaze swept over the dining room and jerked to a stop on Bridger. I hardly recognized him. He sat leaning forward, as still as granite, his hands balled into fists atop the table. Only his eyes moved as they made their slow way to the kitchen door and met mine. They lingered there, devoid of all expression, and I had the sudden urge to shrink away.

A hot hand grabbed my shoulder. "What you looking at, *mamacita?*"

I practically jumped out of my skin. "Tito! You totally freaked me out. What are you doing?" I put a hand over my stuttering heart.

Tito tilted his head to the side. "Slow night. No dishes to wash."

"Mmm," I agreed, shrugging his damp hand off me. He leered at me and grinned. Taking a deep breath, I went back out to the dining room. Bridger was putting a chip into his mouth, totally focused on his food. If he noticed I'd come back out, he didn't acknowledge it.

As I went about work, things slowly returned to normal—no more crawling skin. Yet I could feel Bridger's preoccupied stare. He followed my every movement, and each time his restless eyes caught mine, they were filled with doubt.

After he sat at his table for an hour without taking more than two bites of food, he waved me over. "I'll pick you up later," he said quietly, pulling car keys from his pocket.

"Are you sure you're all right?"

He shrugged and walked out of the restaurant. On the table was a crisp twenty-dollar bill. I put my hands on my hips and shook my head. Twenty dollars for an eight-dollar plate of nachos that he'd hardly eaten? I had asked Bridger to stop tipping me. Of course, he didn't listen. He always tipped me, and always too much.

My heart was heavy after he left, and the lack of customers did nothing to raise my spirits.

"Wow, nice shirt, *chica*," Penney said during a moment when only one customer was in the restaurant. I don't know if she meant it, or if she was just trying to make small talk, because Penney never seemed interested in anyone's clothes but her own. "Where did you get it?"

I looked down at the shirt—a black, lace-trimmed short-sleeve sweater that was a little tighter than what I usually wore.

"It was Bridger's sister's."

She lifted her eyebrows. "The jeans, too? That brand costs over one hundred dollars a pair."

I looked at my jeans, slightly too long, with a whole new respect. "And the sandals," I clarified.

"So are you and Bridger dating, or what? Because Maria said Walt says that Alex told him you are, but Kat told him you aren't. And you've never mentioned it. And I thought he didn't date local girls."

"We're friends. And you can tell Maria to tell Walt to tell Alex that."

She raised her eyebrows again. "You sure about that friend business? You and Bridger seem tighter than double-D's in a C-cup. And I see how he looks at you when he comes in for dinner—like you're the entrée . . . a bit more than just plain *friendly* to me. If any man ever looks at me the way Bridger looks at you, I'll kiss him so thoroughly he won't know what hit him. Because if we have chemistry, we'll be set for life."

"It's totally not like that with Bridger and me. He made it clear that there would never be anything more than friendship between us," I explained, but the thought of kissing him so thoroughly he wouldn't know what hit him made my breath come a little faster.

"I know what I'm talking about. I'm older than you. I've dated a lot of men, and not one of them looked at me the way he looks at you. If they had, I wouldn't be single," Penney stated. "Believe me or not, but he is totally hot for you."

"I wish," I said under my breath.

"No way! You're in love with him, too!" she exclaimed, grabbing my hand.

"I try not to be," I said stonily, wondering what I had gotten myself into. Penney had a tendency to blab gossip around the restaurant like she was a tabloid. And if she told Maria I was in love with Bridger, Maria might tell Walt. And what if Walt spilled the beans at one of our Ultimate games? "Please don't tell anyone!"

"Oh, honey. You play your side of this pretending not to care a whole lot better than Bridger does. I had no idea! And I won't breathe a word," she said, her Spanish accent thicker than normal. She studied me for a minute. "You know, next time you're real close to him, look him right in the eyes and just lean in halfway, like you are about to kiss him. If he goes the other half, you'll know that I'm right."

I laughed weakly.

"Tell me when it happens," she said and hurried off to refill a drink.

At eight o'clock, José stuck his head out of the kitchen and hollered for Penney and Tito to go home. Tito strode out of the restaurant before José closed his mouth. Penney and I looked at each other and then at José.

"Magdalena hasn't spilled a single thing tonight," he explained at our matching looks of shock. "She's gotten every order right. I think she can handle things on her own tonight."

"That sounds good to me!" Penney said. "My back is killing me." She slipped her feet out of her stilettos and turned to me. "Remember what I said about halfway."

"I am sure it will be on my mind all night."

Even with Penney gone, I never had more than two tables at a time to worry about. To kill time, I washed the front windows, wiped down chairs and booths, swept the floor, anything to make the night pass more quickly. While doing these mundane tasks, I couldn't help but glance at my watch every few minutes, counting the seconds till closing time.

"Watching time pass is watching death approach," Naaly-ehe said. I looked up from the dustpan I was using, surprised to see him out of the kitchen. He tended to avoid the dining room. "If you are an orphan, what happened to your family?" That was the last thing I expected him to say.

"They all died before I was six—aunt, cousin, parents— and then I was alone. A foster child," I said without thinking. I had told that so many times, to so many people, for so many years that it popped out of my mouth in a dainty prewrapped package.

"That man who came looking for you—he said you were a foster child. How could he know that?"

"Well, it wouldn't be hard to find out. It's not like it was a secret or anything," I said sarcastically. "What did they arrest him for, anyway?"

Naalyehe's dark eyes twinkled. "José reported him for loitering. But the warrant I mentioned earlier is keeping him in jail." Naalyehe began wiping a table. A table I'd wiped down five minutes earlier.

I dumped the full dustpan into the nearly empty trash can, then went back to stand beside Naalyehe. We stared at the dark night through the front window.

"So, what was his warrant for?" I asked, struggling to find anything to talk about with a man I had absolutely nothing in common with.

Naalyehe turned to me. I shrank away from the intensity in his wrinkle-lined eyes. "He was caught trying to smuggle the skin of an endangered species into America."

"What kind of animal?"

"A cheetah."

My blood turned to ice. "A cheetah?"

Naalyehe's gray brows furrowed. "No, not a cheetah, a tiger. A Siberian tiger. The police believe Rolf is a big-cat poacher."

My stomach lurched. "What do you think, Naalyehe?"

"I think the police are wrong. They also found this in his car." He pulled a folded piece of paper out of his pocket and handed it to me. It was a worn envelope with an address and stamp on it—an address I knew well. I'd lived at it for nine months. I knew the handwriting, too. It was mine.

With trembling fingers, I slid the letter out, but I already knew what it said.

Jenny Sue,

Stop worrying. I'm good. I live with a sweet older woman in the southern part of the state. I got a job at a restaurant called the Navajo Mexican. Totally weird name, I know, but the food rocks.

Thanks for warning me about Mr. Creepy. I'll keep an eye out, but don't worry. I can take care of myself.

—MM

"So that's how he found me," I whispered, trying not to freak out.

Just then the front door opened, ringing the bell that hangs above it. A young couple, older than me but hardly, stood by the door.

"I will be in the kitchen," Naalyehe said, taking the letter and patting my arm.

I took a deep, shaky breath and forced a smile to my face.

"A table for two tonight?" I asked cheerily, though dread was making it hard to keep from falling to my knees.

∾ 25 ∾

"What is the matter?" Bridger asked the instant I opened the car door. He had been sitting in his idling car in front of the restaurant for almost an hour, watching me through the window.

My hands shook on my seat belt, making the metal clip rattle when I hooked it.

Bridger grabbed my hand. "You feel like ice!" He turned the heater on in spite of the warm night and pointed all the vents at me. "Why?"

I studied his face, wondering what to say. I absolutely could not tell him the truth—that I was a freak of nature who turned into an animal and apparently a poacher was hunting me—but I wanted to with all my heart.

"Maggie! I am freaking out here! What happened tonight?" he practically yelled. I could see the fear in his eyes and knew it mirrored my own.

"Nothing's wrong," I lied. "Just take me home."

He put the car into drive and it lurched into the dark night.

I turned and searched the darkness behind us, though I don't know what I was looking for. All of a sudden I had the terrifying suspicion that my secret wasn't as secret as I thought. Rolf Heinrich knew about me.

Bridger sped to Mrs. Carpenter's house and screeched to a stop in her driveway. I unhooked my seat belt and he unhooked his.

"Bridger, I can walk myself to the door." He looked at me with haunted eyes. I opened my door and stepped into the dark, hostile night. Bridger's door slammed and in half a second he was on my side of the car, his arms open, and then wrapped warmly around me.

I leaned into him, pressed my face against the soft cotton of his T-shirt, and tried not to cry. My arms snaked around his waist and I held on with all my strength.

"How can you stand it?" he asked after a long silence.

I loosened my hold enough to look at his face, shadowed by the newly risen sickle moon, but I wasn't willing to let go of him. Not yet. Not when I suddenly felt like everything would turn out all right.

"How can I stand what?" I asked.

"This fear! It's making me sick." He glanced at the shadows looming on the edges of Mrs. Carpenter's property. "You don't get it, Maggie. I felt your fear when I was at *home*. That's how strong it is."

I put my head back on his chest, closed my eyes, and listened to the breath moving in and out of his lungs. If I could stop time . . .

"Maggie, I won't leave until I know what's wrong. I'll stand guard at your bedroom door all night if I have to." His arms tightened.

"Would you really?"

"Unless I can talk you into staying at my house?" he asked tentatively. "We've got a great security system, and more than one guest bedroom—you could have your choice."

I thought of his huge, empty house. Then I thought of Kat watching my every move, always disapproving. I would never be able to sleep comfortably there. And I still had to feed the dogs and chickens, and check on Mrs. Carpenter. "No. It's not so bad, really." It wasn't! The man, the poacher, was locked away in jail. Seriously, what could happen?

"*What's* not so bad?" he asked, linking his hands behind my back so I could lean into them and look up at his face.

"Well, it's just that some guy has been looking for me."

"I remember you mentioned that at the park. Who is it?"

I shrugged. "No clue. But he knows . . . stuff . . . about me. And he's in jail, so I don't know why I'm so scared." There. I had done it, told Bridger enough of the truth that he could fathom my fear.

"That's everything?" He moved a stray piece of hair out of my eyes.

I nodded. Very noncommittal.

He pulled me to him again, his hand holding my head over his heart. "I have never felt this scared in my life," he whispered. His cheek pressed down on top of my head. I closed my eyes and my body softened against his. Crickets chirped and a cool breeze stirred the warm air, whispering through the juniper ring. I sighed and tried to remember every smell, sound, the way my body fit against Bridger's, the thump of his heart beneath my ear. One day he'd leave me. And when that day came, I'd need all the good memories of him I could muster up.

"That's better," Bridger said, pushing me gently away so

he could see my face. "Now go to bed. But please lock your door."

"I always do," I assured him. His arms dropped and I was out of his embrace. "Thanks, Bridger," I said, trying to force myself to feel happy and strong and calm instead of so thoroughly disappointed not to be leaning against his chest any longer. I craved his touch more and more every day.

"We still on for biking in the morning?" he asked.

"I am if you are. Did you resolve things with your dad?"

Bridger was silent for a long moment. Finally he said, "He asked me to call when I got home."

"Good luck. I hope everything turns out all right."

"Me, too."

" 'Night."

"I'll see you in the morning."

I watched him pull out of the driveway and then went into Mrs. Carpenter's dark house.

"Did I see right?" I jumped at the sound of her voice. She was sitting on the love seat in the dark. "Did that boy give you a long good-night hug?" I didn't need to turn on the light to know she was smiling. I could hear it in her voice.

I tucked invisible hair behind my ears before I remembered it was in a ponytail. "Yeah," I said, smiling myself. Thank you, Rolf Heinrich, for making Bridger hug me. "Can I get you anything? Or help you to bed, Mrs. Carpenter?"

A light flashed on, the new lamp beside the love seat. "No, I think I'll sit up and read for a bit. I can manage." Mrs. Carpenter winked at me and then opened her book. A book with a half-clothed white woman being embraced from behind by a shirtless Native American man.

"Sleep well," I said, turning to the door.

"You, too. Pleasant dreams, Maggie Mae."

Pleasant was an understatement.

I maneuvered the bike out of the barn and shivered. The morning air was cold on my shoulders. I glanced at my tank top and jogging shorts—both hand-me-downs from Kat O'Connell—and wondered if I should grab a sweatshirt.

I propped the bike against the barn and turned to shut the door. Shash looked at me and whined. He'd been whining at me from the moment I pushed him off my feet so I could get out of bed.

"You big baby. I don't have the luxury of lazing in bed until noon, like you." He lay down and rested his head between his paws, and I shut the door.

I climbed onto my bike, about to ride it to the end of the driveway where Bridger picked me up, but paused. A car door slammed, a sound as out of place as bees swarming at midnight—Bridger always waited in his car until I came to the road. I squeezed the bike's brakes and stared down the driveway, thoughts of the night before, of what Naalyehe had said about the poacher, fresh in my mind.

Then another sound reached my ears—footsteps. Running along the gravel driveway. Toward me.

My heart exploded in my chest. I climbed off the bike and threw it to the ground, then clenched my fists and balanced on the balls of my feet. If the poacher wanted to kill me, he'd have to fight me first.

Adrenaline flooding my body, I stared toward the road, ready to face my fate. Bridger came running around the corner of Mrs. Carpenter's house, his eyes wide with my reciprocated fear.

I ran at him and leaped into his arms, wrapping my legs around his waist and burying my face in his neck. I clung to his hard shoulders and forced the prickling tears to stay in my eyes.

"I thought you were someone else!" I gasped.

"Shh," Bridger whispered, running a hand over my hair. "I didn't mean to scare you, Maggie. It's okay." I felt more than heard the quiet laughter rumbling deep in his throat and realized he was holding me and I felt like a complete dork. I'd never been so close to a man.

I pulled away from his neck and stared into his dusky eyes, wondering if he could feel my embarrassment. He grinned and laughed louder, yet made no move to put me down. I unhooked my ankles, which had been anchoring my legs around him, and he lowered me to the ground. But instead of releasing me, his hands braced the small of my back and pulled me against him. He stared down into my eyes.

"You know . . . I love you," he whispered.

The morning seemed to go silent, all sound squelched by my thundering heart. I wondered if Bridger could feel my heart hammering against his chest as I stared up at him in shocked silence. Had I heard him right? Did he really say he loved me?

He must have realized what he'd said. His hands loosened their hold and his eyes narrowed.

Warmth pulsed through my body, making me suddenly, uncommonly brave. I slipped my hand into his obsidian hair and, looking right into his eyes, pulled his face halfway toward mine.

Bridger froze. His eyes studied mine, like a wild animal's

searching for danger. A million different emotions traveled over his face too fast for me to guess what any of them meant. And then, so slowly I thought I might die, one of his hands inched its way up my back and into my loose hair. Still scared, still unsure, he moved his face closer to mine and paused. But then his hand tightened in the roots of my hair and his mouth found mine.

His lips were hesitant, as unsure and wary as his eyes had been, as gentle as a butterfly's wings. But they felt so right on mine, like the missing link to my existence. I stood on my tiptoes, pushed my body against his, and wrapped my arms around his neck. Finally he realized I needed him like I needed air.

His arms pulled me against him so tight I could hardly breathe. I didn't mind—breathing is highly overrated. I couldn't get close enough to him, couldn't touch enough of him, though my fingers were learning every angle of his face, knotting in his hair, sneaking into the short sleeves of his T-shirt, and discovering exactly how his muscles felt as they tensed beneath my touch.

His hands moved over every inch of my back, clinging to my tank top.

"Maggie." He breathed into my mouth.

I growled deep in my throat—couldn't help it! I was like an animal giving in completely to instinct. He pulled away, searching my face with eyes full of questions. Then his hold tightened around my waist and once again he leaned down and kissed me. For the second time I wrapped my arms around his neck, refusing to relinquish his mouth, his closeness. Him.

Silver City, New Mexico, seemed to disappear. Only Bridger existed in my universe. And if my Wiccan foster mother had been right and my stars needed to line up, there was probably a new constellation in the sky of a boy and a girl sharing a first kiss. In that instant, I knew I loved him more than I had loved anything or anyone in my entire life.

And then I remembered.

He would never be mine.

And I could never be his. His family would never let me be.

My heart clenched and my universe shattered. My stars sped way out of orbit.

His hands slowed their touching and his lips froze on mine. He pulled away and looked into my eyes. "Why are you crying?" he whispered, resting his forehead against mine and trying to catch his breath.

I closed my eyes in an attempt to stop the tears threatening to escape. "I'm a *local* girl."

"Maggie, I'm sorry," he whispered. "I'm so sorry. I shouldn't have done that."

I opened my eyes and saw my pain mirrored in his, the glistening of unshed tears. Slowly, he took a step back, distancing himself.

"I can't be with you for a couple of weeks. I came to tell you good-bye. After I talked to my dad last night . . ." He shoved his hands into his jeans pockets and waited for me to say something, anything, but I didn't—just stared at him and wondered why my life seemed to be eternally cursed. And wondered how a suffocating wall of tension had sprung up between us. Then I knew. I had crossed an uncrossable line. *We* had crossed that line. He was guilty, too.

"Are you going to be all right without me?" he asked.

I clenched my teeth and folded my arms over my chest. "You are so arrogant. Of course I'll be all right without you.

I don't need you to survive because I learned how to do that when I was five years old."

"Promise me you won't walk home from work at night. I don't want to worry about you."

"Then just don't think about it, because I'll walk home if I want," I retorted. I was mad and *wanted* him to worry. He didn't deserve my anger—the kiss was my idea—but I could tell he regretted that kiss, and that made me want to hurt him. "Are you leaving town?" I asked a little too sharply.

"I've just got to take care of some family stuff." He studied me for a moment before looking down at his brown leather shoes. When his eyes met mine again, they were empty, the cold eyes of a statue. "I'm not sure when I'll see you next." There was a certain finality in his voice that made bile rise in my throat. I'd heard that finality in so many other voices, so many times in my life. And every time I'd heard it, I was shipped to a new foster home within days. I couldn't talk.

"Screw this," he whispered. He took a step forward and caught my face in his hands, looking right into my eyes. "You've got to trust me. And I'm sorry." He leaned down and kissed me again—hard and fast.

Without another word, he turned and left.

I stood in the shadow of the barn for a long, long time. I had just experienced one of the best moments of my life.

Immediately followed by one of the worst.

26

I played Scrabble with Mrs. Carpenter most of the day. If she wondered why I kept spelling words like "bleak," "sorrow," "regret," and "kiss," and lost three games in a row, she didn't ask. All she asked was, "Why aren't you and Bridger out riding bikes?"

I swallowed a lump that lodged in my throat. "He can't hang out today."

"Do you need a ride to work? My leg's feeling pretty decent today."

"Um. Yeah, I guess I do."

She nodded, studying me.

When it was nearly time for me to go to work, I went to my room and put on jeans and a black shirt that smelled the faintest bit of Bridger.

I needed to get him out of my mind. I strode out of my room and groaned. Even his sister's mountain bike was a reminder, propped up beside the chicken coop. It was then that the idea came to me. Even though I didn't have to cross any mountain paths to get to work, I figured, why not? Riding the bike to work would save Mrs. Carpenter the chore of driving me. She said her leg didn't hurt, but I knew better.

I walked the bike out of the barn and propped it up against the front porch, then stuck my head into the air-conditioned house. Mrs. Carpenter was stretched out on the love seat, her leg propped up on a stack of pillows, a crochet hook and yarn flying in her hands.

"I'm going to ride my bike, so you don't have to drive me to work," I said.

She looked up from her crocheting and frowned. "What about getting the bike home? Will it fit in Bridger's car?"

I cringed inside. "He can't pick me up tonight. In fact, won't be around for a couple of weeks. But I don't mind riding the bike to and from work—it has a headlight I can use after sunset so I won't get hit by a car."

Mrs. Carpenter frowned. "I don't like the thought of you riding home alone in the dark. Not with wolves and wild dogs in the area. I'll pick you up. You can put the bike in the back of the truck." She focused on her hands again, winding yarn on her fingers and sweeping it off with the crochet hook faster than an old woman should have been able to move.

"Are you sure?" I asked, relief welling up in my chest.

"You know I am," she said, giving me the same look her son had given me when he wouldn't take no for an answer.

"I'll see you tonight, then."

As I stepped out onto the front porch, I glanced at the barn and relived the memory of Bridger's lips on mine. I pinched myself. Hard. "Stop thinking about that," I whispered, "or you'll go crazy!"

Cranky as a badger, I yanked the helmet from the bike handle, and as I strapped it beneath my chin, I noticed a huge bird circling overhead. I watched the bird, wondering if it was a carrion eater that had found something dead. In spite of the hot day, a chill shivered down my spine. I picked up a fist-sized rock and chucked it at the bird. The rock soared harmlessly through the air and the bird flew out of view.

"Stupid bird," I mumbled, swinging my leg over the bike.

I got to work, windblown and sweaty, in less than twenty minutes. It helped that the ride was downhill. José let me park the bike just inside the back door and stood eyeing it as if ogling a sports car.

"I think I'm paying you too much," he said, running his hand over the angular blue bike frame. "This is a Gary Fisher HiFi Pro Carbon bike. Don't these cost, like, thousands?" José looked up at me for an answer. Naalyehe peered at me from his place at the cutting board.

"I'm just borrowing it," I said as I tied a white, bleach-scented apron around my hips. I hurried out to the dining room and my feet skidded to a halt. Every booth was full.

José had said New Mexico summers brought tourists to town. You could tell the tourists, too, because they had a certain look about them, like city people trying to look southwestern. They wore brand-new cowboy boots that had probably never touched horseflesh, had on cowboy hats without a trace of sweat on them, and their sunburned noses looked like glossy red peppers. They tipped well, at least.

In addition to the tourists, the summer semester at the university had started, so college kids, a few at least, decided to come in out of the evening heat for a cold beer and some of the best Navajo Mexican food in the world.

It was outdoor eating season, too. Strands of white Christmas lights hung on giant umbrellas over the outdoor tables so customers could enjoy their evening meals in the cool night air, at the steel tables set up on the sidewalk. Tonight necessity made some of them sit at those tables. The restaurant was packed.

Somehow, I got assigned to wait on the outdoor tables. Yana and Penney were better servers, but I got the hard tables. I was back and forth through the restaurant's glass front door so many times, it was a miracle I didn't spill anything.

When the sun started to dip behind Wind Mountain, turning the sky a brilliant orange, I had to stop for a breather. All my customers were taken care of for the moment, so I figured it was all right to lean against the brick restaurant and watch the sky fade to black. One thing about being so busy—I could almost forget about Bridger. Almost.

A breeze lifted the stray hairs around my face and cooled my sweaty back. That was one of the nice things about Silver City. Its elevation was high, almost six thousand feet, so though the days were hot, the nights cooled to the point of being chilly.

I closed my eyes and breathed in the smells of juniper and dust, then looked up at the sky again. My breath caught in my throat. The twilit sky outlined a dark shape. A bird, broad winged and floating eerily on the breeze, soared directly overhead. The second one I had seen that day. I hurried into the restaurant and practically ran through the dining room.

"Naalyehe!" I gasped, sticking my head in through the kitchen door. "There's a bird outside. I've seen it twice today and want to know if it means something significant."

Naalyehe set two steaming plates of food down and followed

me to the front of the restaurant. Outside, we peered at the purple sky.

"There," I said, pointing.

Naalyehe squinted up at the sky, his face following the path of the bird as it flew away from the fading horizon and out of view. "Atash," Naalyehe whispered. "Flying to the east." He looked at me, his eyes full of curiosity.

"Is it bad?" I asked, fighting a surge of dread.

"Is there a reason you need protection?"

"What do you mean?"

"That is a golden eagle. The eagle . . . Atash . . . is a symbol of protection. That can be good. Or bad. What do you need to be protected from?"

"The poacher, Rolf Heinrich," I whispered.

Naalyehe nodded. "Be safe."

"Thanks," I said, hoping he couldn't hear the tremble in my voice.

Around ten o'clock, things died down. Everyone decided to go home—or to their hotel rooms—which was fine with me. My apron was heavy with tips, my shoulders heavy with exhaustion, and my brain running on overload. I wanted to think about kissing Bridger and what happened after. My gut told me it was a mistake, but my heart and lips longed for more. And now the eagle. How much danger was I in?

"So, how are you and Bridger?" Penney asked with a gleam in her eye. She and I were carrying a bulging bag of trash out to the Dumpster together.

"I don't know. Not good."

She let go of her half of the bag and it fell against me, splattering my designer jeans.

"No! What happened?"

"I kissed him." My cheeks started to burn. "And then he apologized."

"Well, that's not necessarily bad. You'll see. He probably just wanted it more romantic. Or maybe he's sorry he didn't have the *cojones* to kiss you first."

"Maybe," I said. But I'd heard the regret in his voice and seen it in his eyes.

"Don't worry too much. With the way Bridger looks at you, I have no doubt he'll come to his senses. You'll see."

I nodded, hoping she was right, but not daring to believe too strongly. It would hurt less if I never truly hoped.

"So, is he picking you up tonight?"

"No. He's taking care of some family stuff."

"He's probably hunting. The O'Connells are really big into hunting," Penney said, picking up her half of the garbage bag again. "They use the abandoned mine as their own personal shooting range. You can hear the guns echo clear over here sometimes. I heard Bridger is a perfect shot and the army tried to recruit him to be a sniper the very day he turned eighteen. And the CIA, too. But I don't know if that is true."

A wave of unease washed over me. "Really? He's never mentioned anything about guns or hunting to me before."

"Are you serious? He and his dad seemed to *live* to hunt before his dad moved. When Bridger was in elementary school, he wore camouflage clothes every day, and at recess he had the other students pretend to be wild animals and he'd pretend to shoot them. Kind of creepy, if you ask me. But I suppose, if you have a buttload of money, you can afford to be creepy." She must have seen something in my face. "Oh, Magdalena, I'm not saying he's creepy. Just that his love of hunting is."

I smiled, though it was strained. "Whatever. I don't think Bridger's creepy."

When the restaurant was put back to rights, I got my bike and walked it through the kitchen.

"Is your boyfriend picking you up tonight?" José asked jovially, glancing up from the pot of beans he was stirring.

"He's not my boyfriend and Mrs. Carpenter is picking me up."

"Be safe, Magdalena," Naalyehe said.

"I will," I promised.

Mrs. Carpenter was thrilled by my desire to play games every day. "I miss Bridger, even miss Katie sometimes," she said, laying her Scrabble tile onto the board. "But there's nothing like spending time with you, Maggie Mae. Just the two of us. And you're getting so good at Scrabble, you might be able to give me a run for my money before Bridger comes back."

On Thursday afternoon, I went to the park an hour before I was scheduled to work and watched the guys play Ultimate. Deep down I hoped Bridger would be there. He wasn't. Walt seemed happy enough to see me and said if they were ever short a player he'd put me in.

It was miserable, having Bridger suddenly removed from my life. I wondered, at times, if his presence had been a really great dream and I'd just now woken up to reality.

But then I'd think of Kat's icy blue eyes watching me, or take one look at the clothes crammed into my closet, hardly worn name-brand clothes, and knew he was for real. Plus, I couldn't have dreamed up that kiss.

I missed him so thoroughly that any time I saw a tall, dark-haired man in the grocery store, at the park, or in the restaurant, my heart would jump to life as I strained to glimpse his face. Living in a city populated with Hispanic and Navajo men, my heart was fluttering on a very regular basis.

Though the Navajo guys I'd played Ultimate with started coming into the Navajo Mexican every day for lunch, I never saw Bridger.

Since I had discovered what life was like with a friend, life without one felt even lonelier, as if Bridger had increased the depth of loneliness I was capable of experiencing. It sucked big time. I felt as if the best part of me was missing.

∾ 27 ∾

I could feel the pull of the full moon when I rolled out of bed. Shash looked at me and whined.

"I've got to make Mrs. Carpenter breakfast," I said. He wagged his tail and spread out in my bed.

It was Monday and I was scheduled to work both the lunch and dinner shifts. I pulled on a pair of jeans and a black T-shirt and took a deep breath before I could stop myself.

"Is his smell ever going to wash out of my clothes?" I asked. The dog opened a bleary eye and peered at me.

Ten agonizingly slow days had passed since the morning Bridger and I kissed. Every time Mrs. Carpenter's phone rang, my heart went ballistic. But when I answered, Bridger's voice was never on the other end of the line. I'd been tempted to call him just to hear his voice, but didn't. If he wanted to talk, he'd be calling me.

I made Mrs. Carpenter's bed and then cooked oatmeal and boiled eggs for breakfast. She'd told me several times that I didn't need to take care of her anymore, that she was feeling great. But being with her and doing things for her chased away some of my loneliness.

I stood over the sink, cracking a hard-boiled egg beneath cold running water, when I heard her cane thump into the kitchen.

"Is Bridger back yet?" she asked, as if maybe she missed him as much as I did.

"Um. He's still gone. But he should be back any day." I couldn't meet her eyes, just stared at the half-peeled egg and wished my fingers would stop shaking. Would he be back? No one ever came back into my life once they'd left it.

"I don't need a ride tonight," I said, scooping oatmeal into a bowl.

Her eyes narrowed. "And why is that? Tonight is the full moon."

"Yeah, I know. I'm going to shift and explore the countryside."

"Do you think that's wise?" Mrs. Carpenter asked. "What if the wolves are out? Or the wild dogs?"

"I'll go somewhere far away. Like the old mine. It seems like a safe place."

Mrs. Carpenter barked a laugh. "The old mine? Safe? That thing is a disaster waiting to happen! What if you fall into a mine shaft?"

"I can see in the dark. I won't fall," I said.

"You let me know the minute you get home! And just to warn you, some of the Quilting Bee ladies are coming over tonight, so don't come knocking in your birthday suit!"

I laughed. "All right."

"Do you want me to drive you to work?" she asked.

I shook my head. "Thanks, but walking clears my head. And it's a nice day."

"Suit yourself."

As I shut the front door, I wondered at the dread curling in my stomach. Surely the mine would be safe—I was just overre-acting to Mrs. Carpenter's concern.

A thick layer of clouds hid the late morning sun, making the air thick and heavy. Overhead, the golden eagle circled, its feathers a dark reminder that I needed protection. I shivered and kept glancing up as I walked to work. The bird stayed over-head, always circling.

On the emptiest stretch of road, the mile-long expanse with no houses and hardly any cars, the hair on the back of my neck started to prickle. I stopped walking and tilted my head to the side, listening. The air was still. No swishing leaves, no droning bees. Not even a bird chirping.

I resumed my steady pace, but before I'd taken three steps, I paused, peering into the sparse woods that framed the roadside. I'd heard something—a stick cracking, or dry weeds rustling, the noise a snake makes as it slithers through the underbrush. For a long moment I stared into the woods, holding my breath. Maybe I should have ridden the bike, I thought, wiping my sweaty palms down the front of my jeans. I faced forward again and made myself walk.

Not ten steps later, I heard the rustling yet again. This time, though, it was on the far side of the road. I had the eerie feeling that if I started running, I'd be chased. I walked as fast as I could, trying to ignore the instinct to bolt.

But then I heard it again.

I stopped dead and slowly turned, peering into the wild, scraggly underbrush hugging the edge of the road where the noise had come from—from right beside me—so close I could have reached out and touched the source of that sound. I tried to quiet my ragged breathing, for I couldn't hear anything over my own noise. I couldn't see anything in the weeds, yet I knew I was being followed. Every cell in my body was screaming a warning.

As slow as I could manage, I crouched down and peered into the underbrush. Rocks and dry soil littered the ground beneath shrubby green-and-brown plants loaded with thorns. Cactus plants spotted the dirt in places, little tiny things hardly bigger than my palm, and a little ways back, pines shadowed the weeds. My human eyes saw nothing, my human nose smelled nothing out of place, but I heard the rustling again, now right in front of me.

A flash of movement caught the corner of my eye, something darting out of the underbrush. I made the mistake of turning to see what it was. And that was when the bushes in front of me exploded.

A bird shrieked and a snarling, snapping weight hit me, knocking me to my back. I threw my hands in front of my face and grappled with fur and paws, trying to get a look at the animal attacking me. It wasn't that big, just a scrawny coyote, but it was smart and it was fast. Yellow teeth snapped at my nose just as I thrust my arm in the way. I squeezed my eyes shut, waiting for the teeth to sink into my flesh. When they barely grazed the skin, I opened my eyes.

The coyote lunged away, pushing off from my stomach with its hind legs. The piercing screech of a bird echoed as a dark mass passed over me, so close that its giant wings fanned a gust of dusty air into my face.

I rolled to my stomach just in time to see the eagle clutch the coyote in its long, sharp talons. The bird of prey held the animal for a heartbeat and flapped its giant wings before dropping it. The coyote thumped against the pavement and yelped. It got to its feet and started to run, but the eagle dove in again.

I didn't see more, for a mass of coyotes seemed to appear out of nowhere, standing up in grass only a few inches tall, or walking out from behind a tree trunk no wider than my wrist. They yelped and howled and started running frantically, clumsily, in the opposite direction of the bird—away from me. Two glossy golden animals burst out of the underbrush on the other side of the road, two muscular cougars. They sprinted past me, flush on the heels of the coyote pack.

I jumped to my feet and ran, making it to the restaurant long before my shift was scheduled to start.

It didn't hit me until I stood outside the restaurant trying to catch my breath, my back pressed against the brick building. Naalyehe had been wrong. The eagle wasn't a symbol of protection—not for me anyway. It had been tracking a pack of coyotes. That made me wonder how long the pack had been around, because, looking back, I had seen that eagle every single time I went to work for the past week.

But why would a pack of coyotes be following me?

∞ 28 ∞

The mood at José's was tense. Business had been good—so good, we were low on refried beans, and what self-respecting Navajo Mexican restaurant doesn't have refried beans?

Once again, the restaurant was packed with tourists. This time, instead of cowboy boots and hats, they all had on similar chokers, three strands of turquoise beads fitted snugly around their necks.

The restaurant was so busy with tourists that I did not get my customary two-hour lunch break—I worked straight through lunch and right into dinner. To make up for it, Naalyehe gave me a plate of steaming blue corn and beef enchiladas—minus the refried beans—and let me eat it in the kitchen.

Customers came and went, some of them familiar, most of them not. Maybe it was my imagination, or maybe the stress of the full moon was making me paranoid, but it seemed like the tourists patronizing the restaurant today were paying special attention to me. They watched my every move, trying to make small talk, asking where I was from, how old I was, what my last name was. Maybe I was so lonely for male attention I was imagining it or making more of their lingering glances and small talk than I should. But it wasn't only the men. The women were staring, too.

I shook it off and went about my business, concentrating on not messing up orders or spilling anything.

And then Yana pulled me aside.

"Dude. What's going on with you? Do you know any of these people?"

"No. Why?" I asked, but I already knew the answer.

"They keep staring at you and asking me questions, like how old you are and where you're from," Yana explained. "I thought it was just *one* of my tables at first, thought maybe the guy was going to ask for your number, even though he was totally too old. But then I noticed it's more than just him. It's everyone."

As I glanced around the restaurant, at all the eyes staring at me, the air seemed too heavy to breathe. *It's the lingering fear of the coyote incident,* I told myself.

"Are you okay?" Yana asked. "You're really pale. Paler than usual, even."

"Totally fine," I lied, wiping my sweaty palms on my apron.

"Did you notice their chokers?" She nodded to the nearest table of tourists.

"Yeah. What are they?"

"*Heishe* beads. Have you ever heard of them?"

I shook my head, studying the strands of turquoise on the closest customer.

"I don't know why all these white guys are wearing them, but the Navajo wear them for one of two reasons. Either to prove they are telling the truth—if they lie the choker strangles them. Or"—her voice dropped to a whisper—"they wear it to keep a secret. If a witch gets caught, his *heishe* chokes him before he can name others like him."

"Witch?" I asked, studying Yana to see if she was teasing me. She glared at me. "Not so loud!" she hissed. "Forget I said that. Let me know if anyone gives you crap or anything, and I'll kick his butt." She strode off.

"Excuse me!" a woman called, waving her hand at me. I forced half a smile to my face. She wasn't a tourist, but a little old lady that ate at the restaurant every Monday night.

"Yes, ma'am?" She always ate alone. I assumed she was a widow.

"I ordered coffee with my flan, but Penney must have forgotten to bring it out," she said, patting my wrist with her cool, frail hand.

"Coming right up, ma'am," I told her, glad that fate hadn't destined me to wait on her. She was nice, I'll give her that, but she tipped only fifty cents, two shiny quarters, every single time. I suppose in her day fifty cents was probably a generous tip.

I hurried toward the kitchen when the bell over the front door rang. I'd get the coffee after I seated the latest customers. Turning to the door, I froze.

Hovering in the doorway was the one person I thought I'd never see again. I looked around the dining room, hoping Yana or Penney would decide to seat the latest customers, because I wasn't sure if I should.

But then she smiled, a soft, shy smile. I took a deep breath and walked to the front of the restaurant.

"Hi. Table for three?" I asked.

"Yes, please."

I walked toward the only empty booth and wondered if a knife was going to be thrust into my back. One glance over my shoulder told me how absurd that was. Danni Williams could hardly walk.

When we reached the empty booth, her parents sat. But Danni put a chilly hand on my elbow and leaned in close.

"Being on the brink of death makes a girl think." She glanced at her parents. Her mom held a grocery bag out to her and smiled at me. "I'm sorry about school, what I did," she said. She took the bag from her mom and pressed it into my hands. "It's another jacket, same as yours minus the bloodstains and being cut in two."

"Wow. Thanks." I took the bag from her scarred hand.

"And Bridger's scum," she said, venom in her voice. That came out of nowhere.

"Scum? Didn't he save you that night?" I asked, utterly confused.

She frowned. "What night? Save me from what?"

"The, uh"—I lowered my voice—"really big dogs?"

She studied me like I was crazy. "You mean the night I got attacked at your house?"

I nodded.

"Bridger wasn't there. He was at graduation. Or maybe he was out with his French girlfriend. I mean, I'd always heard the rumors about her, but—" She shrugged and sat down beside her mom.

I frowned.

"So, are we cool?"

"Yeah. Totally cool, but I thought—"

"Coffee?" a wavering voice called out.

I looked around and remembered the little old lady. I'd have to ask Danni what she was talking about later.

"Coffee's coming right up." I walked to the kitchen for the

coffeepot and a mug. When I pushed through the swinging door, I paused.

The kitchen was packed. José, his three part-time cooks, Tito the dishwasher, Penney, Yana, and Walt from Ultimate were all standing in a huddle, like a group of football players discussing their next move in the middle of the big game. When they noticed me, they all shut up.

"What now?" I asked, my body sagging as if I'd been deflated. José and Naalyehe looked at each other, an unspoken agreement passing between them.

"How is your arm?" Naalyehe asked, coming over to examine where the coyote's teeth had grazed it. When I'd come into work that morning, he had seen the scratch and put chewed-up tobacco on it.

As he picked up my hand and made a show of examining my arm, everyone left the kitchen. Even the cooks.

"Don't draw it out, Naalyehe. Just tell me. Is that poacher guy out of jail, or what?"

"The coyote is the trickster."

I looked at him, trying to figure out what this had to do with anything.

"It is not a good omen," he continued. "It means your life is going to change in unexpected ways."

"And this has to do with . . ."

He cleared his throat. "Bridger is back. Jorgé, one of the part-time cooks, saw him at the seafood restaurant two days ago and Walt saw him at the health food store today."

"Oh my gosh! Really?" Helium seemed to expand my deflated body. I started fussing with my hair, trying to tuck the stray wisps back into the ponytail. "He might come in tonight to see me . . . I mean for dinner. . . . What is it, Naalyehe?"

Naalyehe was looking down at his scuffed black shoes. A frown creased his mouth. "He was not alone."

I swallowed hard. "What? Who was he with? Alex? Or Kat?"

"Walt has never seen her before. Neither has Jorgé."

Her?

"You and Bridger, you were just friends, right?" Naalyehe said, studying my face.

Were just friends? He said it as if Bridger's and my past was just that: past. "We *are* friends."

"Good. Because Walt said he and this woman, they acted . . . they were kissing in the health food store." Naalyehe scratched his head. "And she had her arms wrapped around his waist and was . . . nuzzling . . . Bridger's neck while he examined the organic produce. Magdalena?"

I was gasping for air.

"Maggie Mae?" Naalyehe said, using my real name for the first time since he had employed me. "You said you and Bridger are just friends!"

I nodded and forced my mouth to curve up. "We were. Friends. I'm glad. To know, though. About Bridger. And . . . her. Thanks. For telling me," I blurted between gasps.

I turned my back to Naalyehe and took two deep, calming breaths, then tossed the grocery bag with the new jacket to the side of the kitchen. I grabbed the coffeepot and walked out into the packed dining room like a robot. That's how I was the rest of the night—doing my job, but going through the movements mechanically, as if my conscious mind had shut off and I was on autopilot. Otherwise, I might have broken down in the packed dining room and turned into a puddle of tears.

And if the tourists were still staring at me, I was oblivious.

When José called me aside to send me home, I didn't glance

at my watch, so I had no idea what time it was when I walked out of the restaurant carrying my new jacket in its plastic bag. All I knew was my heart felt dead and the moon was pulling at me. Of the two, the broken heart was stronger.

That is when the tears finally started.

I wandered a full mile sobbing, completely oblivious to my surroundings, before I realized that I had missed my turn. I sank to the sidewalk and cradled my head in my hands.

"What is the matter with you, Maggie Mae Mortensen?" I scolded loudly, not caring if anyone was around to hear. With the hem of my shirt, I wiped the tears from my cheeks. "You have been through so much worse than this crap! So he has a girlfriend! So what? Pick up your feet and stop moping."

I stood and started backtracking. After fifteen minutes of wandering I realized I was way lost. The urge to sit down on the sidewalk again and just stop existing made it nearly impossible to think. I wanted to die.

The will to survive is one of the strongest instincts a person has. Stronger, I found out, than the desire to die of a broken heart. At that moment, I thought death would have been an easy alternative to what I was suffering. I decided to shift before the moon forced the change out of me. That's what ended up testing my will.

I stepped into the nearest front yard. The flowers were fragrant and the bushes were thick. I stripped behind those bushes. After putting my clothes into the plastic bag with my new jacket, I stood for a long minute, just feeling the cool, dry, dusty breeze on my naked skin. Then I shifted into the one animal that could make me forget about a broken heart, because when I ran, my aching heart became an afterthought, overpowered by the feel of the world rushing by.

I became a tall, sleek, spotted cheetah, my long tail whipping slowly back and forth, and the world became clear. Instantly I knew how to get home. In fact, I could sense directions, north, east, south, and west. If I wanted to, I could run in a perfectly straight line to anywhere—the North Pole, Bridger's house, even the mine. I just *knew* where everything was.

With the grocery bag in my mouth, I dug my hind claws into the grass and ran.

For a brief second I thought I was the luckiest girl alive.

༄ 29 ༄

Night thrived at the mine. Moonlight reflected from the small, abandoned cement buildings on the mountainside. An owl hooted and an intermittent breeze whistled through juniper boughs.

I set my bag of clothes beneath a tree and, on padded paws, slunk between the cement buildings. What I smelled there excited my animal side and chilled my human mind. Traces of blood spattered the ground. I glided from building to building looking for the animal it belonged to, but found nothing.

Hugging the shadows, I loped to the dirt road, sniffed, and found my own scent—human, weak, and almost forgotten. Then I found Bridger's scent, new and strong, along with another. It was female, masked by perfume, hair spray, and lotion. A low growl rumbled deep in my throat. I ran from that scent.

The night slipped by as I wandered the eerie terrain, discovering the giant holes where the mine had caved in, swallowing the earth's crust. The holes were dark and silent, yet icy wind poured out of them as if the earth were a living, breathing thing, its breath crying out from haunted depths.

When the moon had moved halfway across the sky, I

climbed to the mountaintop that overshadowed the mine and sat with my tail wrapped around my paws, looking down at the small, sparkling city far below. People were the cause of those lights—normal, mundane, happy people who slept, ate, played, worked, and never turned into something as impossible as a cheetah. They got married and started families, went to school, played with friends, had aunts and uncles and grandparents who came over on Thanksgiving and Christmas.

My tail whipped about restlessly. I was so different. Why was I an animal? Had my parents shifted? Did something happen to them because of it? Did other people shift, but were too scared to tell?

For hours I sat on top of that mountain, savoring the feel of the night wind in my fur and staring down at a world that looked so simple from up high. Finally, when I'd had enough solitude, I leaped from the mountaintop and began a downward sprint, ready to go home.

At the mountain's base, I turned instinctively in the direction of my bag of clothes and started to lope toward it. Tree branches rustled in a breeze that blew from the north. The wind shifted and the world seemed to crumble beneath my paws. I crouched low to the ground and growled an ear-splintering roar that shuddered off the side of the mountain and echoed back.

Something was tainting the air, an odor that turned me into a quivering mass of fear. I had smelled that horrible stench before, the night I'd been attacked by the pack of wild dogs.

In that moment, I should have run. Instead I cowered. And the mine came alive with crawling movement. Dark, slinking shadows materialized from under trees, behind rocks, out of thickets—stalking me on all sides.

Beneath the glow of the full moon, they appeared to be animals. But I knew better. They moved too stiffly, as if stumbling around on legs without joints. Where their eyes should have been were black, opaque shadows that absorbed the moon's light instead of reflecting it. Unlike their eyes, their sharp teeth caught the light.

There were groups of wild boars, coyotes, foxes, mountain lions, dogs . . . When I saw the wolves walking on their hind legs like men, my blood seemed to thicken and freeze beneath my skin. Werewolves were not the fictional creatures I had always imagined them to be!

As the circle of beasts tightened around me, they began to pant and whine and smack their chops. It was like reliving the day Danni got half the school to turn against me, times one hundred. And this time I wasn't going to cower.

One animal, a boar with swordlike tusks reflecting moonlight, slipped from the circle and darted toward me. My muscles tensed, ready for a fight, but one of the werewolves pounced on it, picking it up in its front paws and tearing at the boar's throat with its teeth. The night came alive with the cries of a hundred frenzied animals. As quickly as the noise started, it deadened into silence. The wolf held the boar out and dropped it. Its dead body smacked wetly to the ground, and the scent of fresh blood wafted on the air.

A memory flashed into my head, something so terrible that it had been buried in my brain for thirteen years. My aunt, Effie Reynolds, and her daughter, Lucy, were attacked by a pack of Russian boar when I was five years old. The only reason they hadn't attacked me, too, is because Aunt Effie pushed me up into the boughs of a sturdy pine. When she tried to push Lucy up, Aunt Effie was gored in the back. I still remember thinking that the tusk that went completely through her was more like a sword than something jutting out of a giant pig's face.

Lucy fell to the ground when her mom was gored. The boar killed her instantly. I started screaming and was found within minutes, but it was not soon enough for Aunt Effie to pull through. She hung on to life and died three days later in the hospital. That was the worst day of my life. And the day I met Mr. Petersen.

The memory flashed through my brain in less than a second. I knew these animals. They were the same type of creatures that had killed my family, and now they had found me. Fighting was out of the question. I needed to get away or be slaughtered.

I dug my back paws into the ground, crouched low, and prepared to leap. The deep, gravelly growl of a big cat vibrated in the air and my muscles went slack with fear.

Three huge striped tigers joined the circle of animals, two behind me and one in front. They stood amidst the smaller animals and devoured me with their eyes. The other animals, natural prey of these massive cats, showed no fear. They seemed to be bowing. Even the wolves no longer stood on their hind legs, but hunched low to the ground, groveling. My stomach clenched.

The odds of me surviving till sunrise were growing smaller by the second. I could outrun one tiger—at least I hoped I could. But three? And what happened if one got in front of me while the other two were on my flanks? I was a cheetah, made for speed, lean and long. Compared to the bulky, muscular tigers, I was scrawny as a chicken.

The three tigers, as if of one mind, started slowly, silently, to close in on me. Their eyes did not gleam in the moonlight like their glossy coats, but I knew they were staring at me. The weight of that stare was suffocating. With every predatory step they took, my time was running out. Looking at the tigers, I could imagine being scratched to shreds, gnawed to pieces. I was about to die.

And, broken heart or not, I was not ready.

Once again, my hind legs dug into the earth, my claws cutting the ground for purchase. Muscles bunched and strained, and with every ounce of strength I possessed, I leaped, gliding in a giant, soaring arc past the perimeter of the animals. One tiger had anticipated my reaction, moving at the exact same instant I had. My body came down on top of it. It felt like landing on stone. Maybe it expected me to fight, because when I pushed off its back to leap again and ran into the trees, it didn't follow.

Faster than I'd ever run before, I sprinted down the clearest path, a forgotten, wind-rutted dirt road. I heard no pursuit from behind but didn't dare turn to check—my instincts warned against it. I had to run or die. The road curved to the right, and I followed, though my legs were begging for a rest and fire filled my lungs with every inhale.

In the shapeless shadow of an ancient pine, I paused and scanned my surroundings, desperate for a way to stay alive to see the sunrise. Above a giant hill of dirt, a red flag flapped feebly. I was in the wide juniper valley that stretched below Evening Hill—the place Bridger and I had had a picnic. A burst of hope gave me the courage to go on.

I ran toward that hill, for I had a plan.

At the top, the scent of Bridger became so strong and fresh, I actually feared for his life. I would fight the tigers to keep him safe. But he wasn't there.

I stood atop Evening Hill and awaited my three hunters, luring them toward me. Like noiseless shadows they appeared at the foot of the hill, their dark eyes unnatural voids on their moonlit faces. I tensed to run, but instead of coming up after me like I'd hoped, the tigers split up, flanking me on three sides. That's when I realized *tigers* were not chasing me—I mean, they were, but they had human minds.

Just.

Like.

Me.

Shock overwhelmed my fear. I was not the only human being who could turn into an animal at will. But that meant the boars that killed Aunt Effie and Lucy were not animals. They were beings that possessed a conscience and the ability to know right from wrong. Humans had murdered Aunt Effie and Lucy.

I was about to be murdered by *humans.*

As one, all three tigers lunged. I was their target. The chase was on.

My hind legs bunched and pushed, and I leaped through the air. A pair of gleaming, outstretched claws thrust upward and raked harmlessly through my fur, mere millimeters from flesh, but then I was free, bolting across the dirt road toward a gaping black rent in the earth.

I gauged the distance across the massive fissure, slowed my pace, and when the tigers were practically on top of me, leaped, gliding through a wall of icy air that hovered above that yawning hole. I did not leap straight across the long, skinny mine shaft, but at an angle, hoping the tigers would do the same. They were heavier. If I was right, they couldn't leap as far.

I misjudged the distance and came down too soon. As my

hind half entered the mine shaft, my front legs flew outward, claws extended and searching for purchase in the rocky ground. My body slammed to a painful stop, so hard that my claws almost lost their tentative hold in stone. Yet they held. A swoosh of air ruffled my fur as a tiger missed the edge of the mine shaft and plummeted to its death far, far below.

I managed to heave my aching body up a few inches and sink my claws into the thick, tough bark of a gnarled tree root when fire exploded in my back. A pair of claws was entrenched in my flesh. They clung there, supporting the massive weight of a tiger.

I screamed. The sound echoed to the depths of the shaft and back. The tiger clung desperately to my skin, just as my claws clung to the tree root. Inch by inch, those claws ripped downward through my flesh as gravity dragged down the tiger's body. I screamed again, almost willing to give up my hold on the tree root and plummet into the shaft below if it meant the end of pain. But then the claws slipped from my skin. Frigid air blew against my fur as the tiger plunged into the hole. The third and final tiger, though, did not stir the air around me.

A shadow, almost impossible to see even beneath the full moon, silently crept around the edge of the sunken mine shaft. Fear gave me the energy I needed to scramble up out of the shaft, though my back burned in agony every time I moved so much as a claw.

The moment I stood on solid ground, the last tiger jumped. My ribs strained and cracked as the monstrous beast landed atop my slight body, its momentum rolling me onto my back. Before its whole weight settled, its teeth sank into my shoulder. I screamed and clamped my mouth down onto the tiger's neck, biting as hard as I could.

My teeth sank into fur and met flesh, but the tiger shook me off as if I were a cub. It studied me with midnight eyes, showing me its fearsome teeth, giving me a glimpse of its power.

A noise shattered the night—gunfire. The tiger, about to take my life with its jaws, jerked up and looked in the direction of the echoing shot. And I, with the last bit of strength I possessed, lifted my front leg, thrust out my glorious claws, and swung up and into the tiger's throat.

Like a hangnail snagging on silk, the tiger's skin caught under my claws. It wasn't until hot blood poured over me that I realized I had actually done any damage. And then, as lifeless as a sack of feed, the tiger collapsed on me. A spasm tore through its body as it struggled to breathe.

I clawed my way out from under the beast. Every bit of me hurt, except the tip of my tail. My ribs were broken, my shoulder was bleeding, and the skin on my back was sliced to shreds and streaming blood—I could smell my own blood mingling with the stench of other human blood. I began licking the disgusting foreign blood off my golden fur. I didn't know what else to do, I was in such a state of raw animal instinct. Just sat there and licked and licked and licked.

I probably would have sat there till the sun came up if I hadn't been snapped back to reality. Gunshots, three in a row and getting closer, reminded me of my humanity.

I turned to take one last look at the tiger, but it was gone. What I saw shattered my already broken heart.

Lying naked atop the giant striped skin of a tiger was a muscular middle-aged man with thinning brown hair. I had seen him once before, in the mug shot the police had given Naalyehe of the man who'd been loitering in front of his store and searching for me—Rolf Heinrich. Blue tinted his dead lips and the moon reflected brightly against his glazed, frozen eyes. Blood coated his neck and half his torso, blood from three jagged wounds slashed in his neck by a pair of razor-sharp claws. Mine. And barely visible in all the blood was a turquoise choker digging into his flesh.

Panic overwhelmed my better senses. I clamped down on the ankle of the naked corpse, felt my teeth slide into the cool skin, and pulled. It didn't take much to drag the body to the mine shaft and nudge it over the edge. The empty tiger pelt followed. And then, as easy as sprinting the fifty-yard dash, all evidence of murder was gone.

❧ 30 ❧

I don't know how I made it home, but somehow, with the sun just above the horizon, I found myself wandering aimlessly around Mrs. Carpenter's property, searching for an animal to eat. Shash was barking inside the barn. I was still a cheetah and my wounds were about to drive the lingering bit of sanity I possessed right out of reach. I yearned to be me again.

I almost couldn't change back. It took a lot of energy, I guess, and mine was almost gone—had bled out of my body through the gashes on my back. Had I not been so scared of staying a cheetah forever, I never would have been able to use that last, tiny bit of adrenaline surging through my blood to make the change possible—even so, it just barely made the difference.

Naked, blood covered, and shivering, I skulked into the barn, to the joy of Shash, and stumbled toward the stairs. And then I realized . . . I had left my clothes and my key near the mine. Big lazy tears began making their sleepy way down my cheeks. Then I remembered: I'd replaced the spare key under the bottom step.

With shaking hands, I groped through cobwebs and dirt till I felt cold metal. It took two tries to get the key into the narrow lock, but I did.

In six stumbling steps, I was across the room and staring at my body in the mirror. My shoulder had four tiny puncture scabs. Four long, blood-framed welts shone on my pale back, like I had been whipped. But my skin was whole. I remembered the night Mrs. Carpenter had found me after I was attacked by dogs. I had healed before her eyes. This morning, it was the same. As I watched, the welts on my back faded and then disappeared. My broken ribs were the same. They just stopped hurting, as if they had never been cracked. And the tooth punctures on my shoulder? Gone.

I fell onto the bed, buried myself in blankets, and slept.

When next I opened my eyes, it was dark. I sat up in bed, frantic, and stumbled dizzily across the room to the light switch.

The light blinded me, making it impossible to see for a moment. When I could finally keep my eyes open, I looked at my watch: 9:57. I had missed my shift at work.

My gaze moved from my watch to my naked body, and I gasped. I was covered with brittle brown blood and dried mud. I ran to the bathroom and turned on the shower. Not waiting for the water to heat up, I stepped into the icy onslaught.

I scrubbed every inch of my skin with an entire bottle of body wash, then the entire bottle of shampoo, and still I didn't feel clean. My skin seemed permanently tainted. I couldn't breathe, couldn't move as panic set in. I sank down to the shower floor and huddled there with my head leaning sideways against the wall. Tears mingled with the water dripping down my face as I realized it was the end of the world, the end of *my* world. The world I had known. I had killed someone. And he had tried to kill me. Nothing would ever be the same and I could never go back to how things used to be.

When I finally regained control of myself, the hot water had run out. Cold water pelted my skin and I was shivering. I got out of the shower, wrapped myself up in a towel, and stumbled back into my bedroom.

Hunger pangs clenched at my hollow stomach. If I didn't eat, I thought I might die. And I smelled food. On the dresser, beside the bowl of ash, sat a plate with scrambled eggs and two pieces of toast on top of a handwritten note. Ignoring the note, I grabbed the plate. The eggs were cold and rubbery, the toast hard, but nothing in my life had ever tasted better.

With my belly nearly full, I picked up the piece of paper.

> Maggie Mae,
>   I worried sick about you all night because you forgot to tell me when you got home! I almost called the police to go up to the mine and look for you. I tried to wake you, but you hardly stirred, so I thought I'd leave some breakfast.
>   Glad you're home safe.
>   —Mrs. C.
>   P.S. I forgive you. Just never forget to wake me again!

The thought of her coming up and down the stairs to my room made my heart hurt. She had done so much for me, and yet I was the reason she was injured—because I was being hunted. And based on the graduation night attack, the creatures knew where I lived. Mrs. Carpenter had already been attacked once.

What if they came to the house looking for me and found her again instead?

I climbed from the bed and went to the window. Pulling the curtain aside, I peered into the dark night. Moon shadows shivered over the yard. Past Mrs. Carpenter's house, something gleamed, like the flash of animal eyes, but when I looked harder, I saw nothing but shadows.

I put my right hand on my left wrist, expecting to feel the juniper bracelet—for the *yo-ih*, Naalyehe's gift of protection, was a gift worth more than he'd ever know. But the bracelet was gone, left at the mine in the bag with my clothes. I clenched my teeth. How could I have been so stupid? Protection was what I desperately wanted. But it was Mrs. Carpenter who desperately needed it. Because I, at least, could fight back.

I got dressed and scribbled a quick note. Mrs. Carpenter would be safe as long as she stayed away from me. I just needed to ensure she kept her distance.

> Mrs. C.,
>   I think I've caught something, maybe the flu, and I don't want you to catch it, so I'll be staying away from you for the next couple of days. Don't worry about the chickens. I'll take care of them. And Shash. And thanks for the scrambled eggs. I've got a few things up here to eat, so don't worry about feeding me! I don't have much appetite anyway.
>   —MM

I left the bedroom and crept through the barn, out the door, and to the front porch. Folding the note, I taped it to the edge of the front door so when Mrs. Carpenter let Duke out, she'd see it.

Next, I stuck to the shadows and made my way to the edge of the property, to the ring of protection. And then, one by one, I took the bleached animal skulls from between the trees and put them around the entire perimeter of the house, making Mrs. Carpenter her own snug ring of protection.

When I finished, I lay down in bed and listened. With the skulls only encircling the house, the barn was now accessible to my hunters. I knew they would come for me sooner or later. I prayed it would be never.

∾ 31 ∾

Wal-Mart at seven a.m. is not particularly busy. At least not on a Wednesday morning. I was grateful for the lack of customers and hoped no one would steal the Gary Fisher bike I'd hidden behind giant bags of water-softening salt sitting on the front curb of the store.

I'd hardly slept since moving the ring of protection to encircle Mrs. Carpenter's house, and the only things stronger than my exhaustion were my fear, my guilt, and, more importantly, the hole in my stomach. Even though I'd eaten cold eggs and toast last night, my body felt as if I hadn't eaten for a month. I needed calories ASAP, but didn't dare get food from Mrs. Carpenter's house. Too dangerous—for her. And the note I sent her, about me having food, was a lie.

Plus, my skin still felt tainted with Rolf Heinrich's blood. I desperately needed more soap.

Slouching behind a shopping cart, I hung my head and started toward the beauty supplies section. Hardly anyone passed me in the empty aisles, and when they did, they didn't even look my way. I was invisible again.

I turned my cart down the soap aisle and was reaching for a bulk-sized body wash when I heard a woman's twinkling, false laugh. You know the laugh—what a woman does when she's pretending something is funny to impress the guy she's with. I rolled my eyes—glad I never did that stupid, fake laugh—and picked up two huge bottles of the cheapest body wash.

I heard the laugh again, closer now, and hurried away to find shampoo. I wasn't in the mood to see the woman out giggling and shopping at seven on a Wednesday morning. And besides, I could feel a panic attack looming in my near future.

I scanned the shampoo section for the cheapest stuff. When I found what I was looking for, I heard that stupid laugh again. I grabbed a bottle of shampoo and started to walk away, but heard a familiar, low chuckle. And then the high-pitched laugh again. My feet turned to stone and my ears strained to hear the mumbled conversation going on one aisle over.

"—was so good!" the woman was saying. She had an accent, definitely not Spanish, and definitely not Navajo.

"I know. Tara's does make exquisite food, but, you know, the irony is, a local fast-food restaurant has much better fried chicken. I'll take you there sometime, if you'd like to try it," Bridger's smooth, deep voice replied.

"*Oui!* Anything you like, Bridger, I would like to try," the woman answered and laughed her chiming laugh.

Call me a glutton for punishment, or maybe a masochist, but I had to look. Everything else in my life was crumbling to ruin, so why not just take a quick peep? Bracing myself, I tip-toed around the corner of the shampoo aisle and peeked down the oral hygiene aisle.

She was beautiful. Long, loosely curled hair the color of

honey, skin like a peach, eyes green as grass, makeup that was so smooth it could almost pass as natural, and a flowing dress cut down low on her chest, emphasizing her full boobs and teeny waist. Wow. And her hand, dainty and sparkling with gold and gemstones, rested comfortably in Bridger's.

To see my best friend, my heart seemed to heal and then break all over again. I put a hand to my chest, trying to ease the pain. His dark hair and stormy eyes were so familiar that I took a step toward him, ready to throw myself into his arms and cry on his shoulder. Ready, even, to tell him the truth about me. I desperately needed someone to tell me everything was going to be okay. I needed serious help.

But I looked at Bridger—dressed in designer jeans and a fitted short-sleeve polo shirt—and the sophisticated woman by his side, and stepped back. They looked good together, like two matching puzzle pieces. How could Bridger love me when he had someone like her?

My heart turned colder, harder, and heavier than a lump of lead.

Bridger yanked his hand from the woman's and began pushing on the bridge of his nose.

"Bridger!" the woman exclaimed, placing her delicate hands on his cheeks and trying to look into his scrunched-shut eyes. *"Est-ce que tu es d'accord? Regarde-moi."*

"Donne-moi juste une minute," he muttered.

I ducked back into the shampoo aisle, which also has a big selection of hair dye, and on impulse found just the right color. Black. So black it was almost blue. The color, I imagined, of a supermassive black hole, a color that swallowed and devoured all the light around it. Because that was how *I* felt.

I tossed the dye in the cart and walked, in robot mode once again, to the food section. I hardly looked at the things I grabbed. Any type of food would do. It's not like I actually tasted it.

From Wal-Mart I biked straight to the Navajo Mexican, hoping Naalyehe or José was in early—Wednesday morning was delivery morning. I rode around to the back of the restaurant and sighed with relief. José's car was in the parking lot.

When I walked into the kitchen with the bike and my two bags of groceries dangling from the handlebars, José whirled around. I must have looked pretty terrible, because when he saw me, he dropped what he was doing and ran over, covering me in a great big, warm, cilantro-scented hug.

"Oh, Magdalena. What's wrong?" he asked gently, patting my back.

I had been expecting wrath. I hadn't shown up for my shift last night.

"I need a few days off." I sobbed into his shoulder. I don't know exactly why I was crying. Bridger? The dead man? José's kindness? Maybe all three combined.

"Sure. But do you need anything else?"

"No." I pushed away from him and wiped my cheeks with the backs of my hands. "I'm so sorry about missing work." I sniffled.

"Oh. It was nothing. Tito didn't show up, either, but we were so slow I ended up having Yana wash dishes and Penney run the dining room. We didn't need you, but we were worried about you."

"The tourists?" I asked, wiping my nose on a dry washcloth José handed to me.

"All gone, like they up and left together."

My stomach dropped. I had a guess what had happened to three of them.

"You're looking a little on the thin side, Magdalena. Let me fix up a plate of food for you to take home."

"Thanks."

I watched him make the fish tacos in silence, wishing I was on my way home, yet staying because I didn't want to make José feel bad by turning down his best entrée.

"Bridger stopped in last night."

My eyes grew round and my blood accelerated at the mere mention of his name. José looked at me over his shoulder. I bit my tongue.

"Don't you want to know why?" he asked.

"No. Not really."

He shrugged. "Suit yourself." He started humming as he got a container of grated cheese out of the fridge.

"Why did Bridger come in?" I didn't mean to speak, but the question snuck out before I could stop it

José dropped a handful of cheese onto my food and said, "He ordered takeout. Fish tacos."

"One plate or two?"

"Two."

I nodded silently. I'd already known that would be the answer.

"He brought something of yours with him. Something a bit . . . awkward." José turned and studied me.

"He did? What was it?"

"I'll get it." José handed me my finished and boxed meal, wiped his hands on his apron, then took a bulging grocery bag from a coat hook. My face turned bright red.

He grinned. "I guess you already know what it is."

It was my shoes, socks, jeans, black shirt, bra, panties, *to-ih*, and jacket from Monday night. He was at the mine that night with a gun. That was my guess, at least. Or, rather, my sinking suspicion.

"So, when can I put you back on the schedule?" José asked.

"Can you manage without me for a week?" I hoped that would be long enough to regain control of my sanity and figure out why I was being hunted. It had to be long enough.

"I'll put you down for next Wednesday's dinner shift. Let me know if that won't work."

I nodded and thanked him for the meal. Without another word, I left.

It was raining. Raining really hard. And for some reason, when it rained in Silver City, tarantulas crawled out of wherever they lived and scrambled all over the road. I tried not to run over them with my bike, because their huge, hairy bodies would pop beneath the tires, making me sick to my stomach. Plus, I'd had enough killing to last a lifetime. Even taking the life of a spider seemed suddenly cruel.

When I got to Mrs. Carpenter's, so wet that even my running shoes had water pooled in them, I took the bike directly to the barn, hoping she wasn't watching me through a window, and threw a quick handful of feed at the chickens. Shash whined at me and paced in front of the barn door.

"No, you can't go out," I snapped. "You'll get soaked."

I went upstairs to hide. Shash didn't follow—wouldn't leave his spot by the barn door even when I called him.

José's fish tacos were gone before my groceries were put away. I stripped out of my wet things and then went to the bathroom and transformed my hair from faded plum to cold, colorless black. I will admit, I *looked* better with lighter hair, but I *felt* better when it was black.

After a hot shower, I went to my room and put on the *yo-ih* and an oversized T-shirt that hung halfway down my thighs. As I flopped down on the bed, I wished, not for the first time, that I could throw my arms around Mrs. Carpenter and tell her what was going on, why I hadn't come to check on her for a couple of days. I could practically hear her.

"Maggie Mae, quit moping and face the future. You did what was necessary, taking that man's life. He was evil if he wanted to kill you! You did the world good, removing him from it. You survived. You'll survive again. So count your blessings and come and have some corn bread and chili."

"I am going crazy," I mumbled. "Not only am I talking to myself, I'm imagining Mrs. Carpenter is talking to me, too."

I lay in bed and felt time drag slowly by. Every minute, every *second*, seemed to last an hour. It felt as if the world had changed and days no longer lasted twenty-four hours, but an entire year. And every moment that passed, my heart seemed to hurt a little more. And insanity seemed a tiny bit closer. And my hold on reality slipped a bit farther from reach.

I closed my eyes and prayed I could fall asleep. During sleep, at least, I was numb.

I woke to the sound of claws on my bedroom door and bolted upright, wondering if they'd finally come for me. This time, maybe I would be ready to die.

A dog yelped and the scratching noise repeated.

"Shash?" I called. A dog whined outside my door and I laughed a shaky laugh of relief. And then the afternoon exploded with a single gunshot.

∾ 32 ∾

I jumped out of bed and pulled some jeans on beneath my T-shirt, slipped my feet into Kat's old flip-flops, and ran into the barn. The chickens flapped their wings at the sight of me and scampered to the far end of the coop.

"Mrs. Carpenter?" I called as I darted past them and out of the barn. Sprinting to the house, I leaped up the steps to the front porch. Shash came with me, whining, ears flat and tail wagging.

"Mrs. Carpenter!" I yelled, twisting the doorknob. It was locked, and in my panic I hadn't brought my house key. The curtains were drawn and the house appeared to be deserted, but her truck was in the driveway. I pounded on the front door with my fist, then leaned on the doorbell, pushing the button over and over again. She didn't answer. Five minutes must have passed, with me pounding on the freshly painted front door until my knuckles were bruised.

I jumped down the porch steps but paused before I'd taken two steps. Something was missing. "No," I muttered, shaking my head and wondering if I'd gone officially insane. I squeezed my eyes shut so hard my head started to hurt, then opened them for another look. The animal skulls—the ring of protection I'd put around her house the night before—were gone.

Sick to my stomach, I ran around back and gasped. A tall, gleaming white mound of animal skulls had been piled beside the back door. All around the pile, the damp ground had been scratched up, the weeds pounded down flat.

I tried the back door, desperate to get in. It was locked, too.

"Mrs. Carpenter!" I yelled, cupping my hands around my mouth. The wind answered me, howling through the junipers and whispering past the animal skulls. If I wanted to get into the house, my house key was my only hope. Turning from the back door, I started sprinting toward the barn, but a crunching sensation beneath my flip-flops made me stop.

I stared down at the ground and wiggled my feet. Shards of glass shimmered in the weeds. I looked at the house. The window to my old bedroom was gone. Only a few fragments of glass clung to the frame. Attached to one of the shards was a clump of yellow fur.

I grabbed a fist-sized rock from the ground and hacked away the jagged glass remnants, then climbed through the broken window. Shash leaped through behind me and trotted into the house.

My feet crunched on more glass. Mrs. Carpenter's bed was trashed, with springs sticking out of the bare mattress. The bedroom door had been scratched to bits and hung lopsided on its hinges, the door frame splintered. Searching the room for a weapon, I gripped the toppled bedside lamp and yanked the plug from the wall. Holding the lamp as if it were a club, I stepped through the busted door frame.

Only the sounds of the wind and the grandfather clock filled the house. I crept down the hall and past the kitchen, my flip-flops silent on the wood floor. As I entered the living room, I paused and held my free hand up, as if catching rain. Tiny white particles settled onto it, like ash from a campfire. White dust floated through the air, trickling downward. It coated the wood floor and furniture. I glanced up and frowned. In the middle of the ceiling was a gaping hole.

I took two steps forward and pressed a hand over my mouth. My body began to convulse uncontrollably. Somehow I managed to stay standing, though my knees were knocking together.

Below the gun case lay Duke, his lifeless body grotesquely twisted, bare patches of bloody skin visible where the copper fur had been torn from flesh. Beside him lay Mrs. Carpenter, face ashen, eyes closed, a rifle in her hands. She looked like a pile of skin, bones, and clothes. Shash lay at her side, his head between his massive paws, and looked up at me with pleading eyes.

"Mrs. Carpenter?" My voice was as shaky as my legs. She didn't move. "Please don't be dead," I whispered. Steeling myself for reality, I crossed the room and knelt at her side.

Her skin was cool beneath my touch, but not cold. "Mrs. Carpenter?" I said, patting her creased cheeks. Her eyelids fluttered open and she hugged the gun to her chest. Her lips moved, but I couldn't hear what she said.

I leaned closer, put my ear by her mouth, and waited. A spasm racked her body and she moaned. I climbed to my rubbery legs, crossed the room to the desk, and dialed 911.

After giving the operator the address, I hung up the phone and sat by Mrs. Carpenter again, brushing her tangled hair away from her face. "An ambulance is coming," I whispered, hardly able to talk over the knot in my throat.

She opened her eyes and looked at me again. Her icy hand found mine and squeezed it. "Ring. Broken." She moaned and closed her eyes again. "Shot the ceiling to get your attention," she mumbled. I looked up at the hole in the ceiling and tears found their way to my eyes. I had been so caught up in my own fear and misery, I had completely let her down. The weight pressing down on my shoulders made it hard to keep my head up.

"I'm so sorry," I said. "I never heard a thing from the barn."

Sirens blared outside and car doors slammed. I unlocked the front door and opened it. Shash jumped to his feet, growled deep in his throat, and started barking. Before I could stop him, he sprinted out the door and disappeared, his crazed bark fading the farther he got from the house.

"Shash!" I called as two paramedics and a police officer came into the house. Shash didn't come back.

I stood with my back against the wall and watched as the paramedics examined Mrs. Carpenter.

"She's dehydrated and her hip is broken," one said. They put an IV into her arm and moved her broken body onto a stretcher. I plugged my ears to block out her feeble scream. Even muted, it was my undoing.

With my arms wrapped around my chest, I stood on the front porch long minutes after the ambulance had driven away.

"Are you all right, ma'am?" Officer Dahl asked me again. It was at least the fifth time he had asked.

Am I all right? I wondered. I hadn't been all right for days.

"Ma'am?"

"Yes, I'm fine," I lied, sniffling.

"You know, a lot of elderly women break their hips. It's the most common injury women suffer after the age of sixty. After a few months in a cast, she'll be fine," Dahl said, patting my shoulder. He probably had kids about my age. "Funny old woman. She called the station last night and said the *ring of protection* had been broken and a pack of cougars was trying to get into her house. Does she suffer from dementia?"

I sank down and sat heavily on the porch step. I thought if I left Mrs. Carpenter alone, so would they. I thought moving the skulls to create a new ring of protection around her house would be a good thing. Obviously I destroyed any power the ring had by altering it. A fresh sob ripped at my chest. In addition to the tigers I'd killed, I was now responsible for the death of Duke and for Mrs. Carpenter's broken hip. I pressed the balls of my hands over my eyes. If I didn't figure out what was going on, who else would get hurt? I needed someone to talk to. Someone who wouldn't judge me. I needed Bridger. He *had* to sense my overwhelming misery. Obviously he didn't care enough to come.

I went back inside, picked up the phone, and dialed a number I'd had memorized for a long time. He answered on the third ring, his voice as familiar as my own. "Hello, Mr. Petersen? It's Maggie Mae," I said, my voice wavering with the effort of holding back a sob.

"Maggie Mae? You only call me when you're in trouble. What's wrong? Another indecent exposure?" he asked. If only it were that simple.

"No. It's Mrs. Carpenter. She fell and broke her hip. She's at the hospital, but I'm worried about her."

There was a moment of silence. "I'll be at the hospital in three hours." He hung up without saying good-bye.

I wiped the tears from my cheeks and went back to the porch. Staring at the foliage around Mrs. Carpenter's property, I let anger fill me. When my blood was at the boiling point, I whispered through gritted teeth, "I'm all alone now. Come and get me." As if something out there heard, a low, distant howl echoed through the air.

Oh, crap, I thought, clutching my suddenly roiling stomach. *Now I've done it.*

Officer Dahl blinked at me and cleared his throat. "Are you sure you're all right?"

"Never been better. Can I go now?" I asked. Panic was setting in, making me too hot, making my skin clammy and my stomach churn. I wanted desperately to be alone before I started hyperventilating.

"I just need you to sign some paperwork," Dahl said, going to his patrol car for a clipboard.

I signed the papers, though my signature was illegible.

With my arms hugging my stomach, I walked stiffly through the muddy yard and back to the barn apartment.

No matter how I tried to calm down, I felt as if the air were growing denser and denser, and no matter that I was gasping it in, I couldn't breathe. Opening my bedroom window, I gulped in a lungful of fresh air.

I fell onto my bed and tried to relax every muscle in my

body, tried to become the bed. While my body gave in to relaxation, my mind refused. A name kept assailing my thoughts.

Rolf Heinrich.

Obviously he had been looking for me for a while. He was the man Jenny Sue warned me about after I'd moved to Silver City. And I was pretty sure I knew why he wanted me, well, before he'd died: my second nature.

But how did he know about it? How had he found me? And why the freak did an entire group of animals—some of them, if not all of them also human—want me dead? I was nothing! No one special! Actually, that wasn't true. I was nothing and no one *important*—had been my whole life. But special? I could turn into an animal at will.

I was beyond special.

I lay on my bed with my hands behind my head, feeling seconds scrape slowly into minutes, waiting for the minutes to pile into hours, waiting for the hour when they would come for me. Because I knew they were coming.

I don't recall feeling sleepy—I was exhausted, but not sleepy—when a noise jerked me awake. A twinkling of stars spattered the small patch of sky I could see through my open window.

I sat up, perched upon the edge of the mattress, and listened. Coyotes were about, yipping and barking. I jumped off the bed and ran to the window, sliding it quietly shut and locking it.

In darkness I stood and listened, peering down at the shadowed ground, searching for anything that would warn me, would confirm my suspicions that the hour had arrived.

Shadows moved below my window, shapes darting to and fro, both low to the ground and standing tall. A howl bellowed through the night and I jumped.

I inched closer to the window and placed my palms against the cool glass. An inky black face appeared, peering right into my eyes. A gray beak gleamed in that horrible face and a hiss penetrated through the glass. I fell backward, scooting away from the window, my fist pressed into my mouth to hold in a scream. Earlier that day, I thought I wanted them to come for me—wanted it all to end. But now I was too terrified to face them.

I don't know how my panicked brain could register anything besides fear, but it did. My blood ran cold as a thought occurred to me. When I had come back to my room after finding Mrs. Carpenter, I had not locked the exterior barn door.

I jumped to my feet and sprinted out of my room. The barn was pitch black, darker, even, than my bedroom had been. The chickens were restless, clucking and flapping their wings. I slowed and felt my way down the steps.

Shapes—distorted and hunched and blacker than the blackness—filled all the corners of the barn. I prayed they were shadows or my eyes playing tricks on me, yet they seemed to move when I caught them in my peripheral vision. Then something did move. A long shaft of charcoal turned to a rectangle of gray as the barn door eased open. A bulky darkness stepped through and the door shut.

I could just make out the darker shape in the barn, floating toward the stairs leading up to my bedroom. The whispery sound of footfalls mingled with the chicken noises. I scuttled toward the other side of the barn.

Crouched low to the ground, I watched the shadow's progress, watched as it climbed the stairs and made it to the entrance of my bedroom, about to enter, about to give me the chance to bolt for the outside door. But it stopped, a black human shape silhouetted in the rectangular door frame. And then, as if this shape knew exactly where I was, it turned toward me.

The creature came down the stairs, strode right to my hiding place, and grabbed my hair.

I didn't scream. I couldn't breathe! My arms lashed out, scratching and clawing with nails on the brink of turning into razor-sharp claws. But then I recognized the smell of the person trying so desperately to ward off my feeble scratching without hurting me.

"Maggie! Stop it!" he hissed, clutching both my wrists in one of his hands.

"Bridger?" I whimpered.

"Shh. Yes, it's me."

I pulled my hands away from his grasp and threw my arms around him, burying my face against his bare chest. His arms encircled me with warmth and for a split second I felt safe. Until I realized Bridger was now likely to be added to my growing list of dead and injured people. My body stiffened in his arms.

"You're terrified," he stated in a whisper so soft I might have imagined it. "I'm sorry. We have to get away from here. Now. Can you walk?"

"No! You can't be here. You—" His finger was on my lips, silencing me.

"Do not make another noise." His voice was hardly louder than an exhaled breath.

I pulled his finger off my lips. "But they're going to kill—"

His palm clamped down on my mouth and his arm wrapped around my waist, pulling my back against his chest. Lips pressed against my ear. "You have to trust me. Now. Shut. Up."

I nodded and his hand left my mouth. Taking my hand in his, he led me to the barn door.

He opened the door a hair and moonlight poured in, illuminating Bridger's face, gleaming off his dark hair and bare chest, and reflecting on something long and shiny in his hand. A big, silver gun. I froze.

Bridger squeezed my hand and pulled me forward a step. He dropped my hand, held the gun by his cheek so it pointed at the ceiling, and cocked it. His eyes were hard, his mouth set in a grim line, and the angles of his face seemed more severe in the blue moonlight.

Grabbing my upper arm, he pulled me so close that I could feel his heart hammering against my shoulder. His lips were on my ear.

"When I open this door, you run to my Cruiser, Maggie, faster than you have ever run in your life. Get in, shut and lock the door, and do not come out. If anything happens to me, drive to the Navajo reservation and tell them Bridger O'Connell sent you."

He didn't give me any warning, just kicked the door out and shoved me into the open. I hesitated long enough to see him lower his gun. And then I ran.

The moon-drenched night throbbed with shadows. I hadn't taken two steps when I heard the sickening sound of a gun with a silencer going off at close range. My arms flew protectively over my head but my frantic pace did not falter. A cougar crashed dead at my feet. I leaped over it and kept running.

Parked in front of Mrs. Carpenter's front porch, the SUV reflected moonlight. My bare feet hardly touched the ground as I sprinted toward it. I heard another muffled shot, barely audible above my panting. A sharp yelp met my ears as a giant Doberman fell to the gravel beside me.

And then I was at the car. I yanked open the door and slammed it shut so hard behind me, the car shuddered.

With my nose pressed against the window, I stared through the blue night at Bridger. Shadows flitted about, hugging the ground so I could just catch them out of the corner of my eye. Bridger wasn't fazed. He strode away from the barn and into the midst of the shadows, his shiny gun swinging back and forth, seemingly unaware of his dire circumstances. Calm as a summer morning, he walked toward me, gun ready, face intent.

One thing was obvious, though—the shadows were scrambling away from Bridger and his big, shiny gun. They feared him. Yet one shadow, hiding in the darkness below the porch, was braver than the others. As Bridger walked past, the shadow wormed along the gravel drive and lunged for his unprotected back. I started to scream a warning, pounding my balled fists against the window. Either he heard me or he heard the creature, because he turned and fired his gun just as a massive silver wolf collided with him.

As one they crashed to the ground, a heap of motionless fur. Then something moved. The wolf rose and was thrown lifelessly aside. Bridger scrambled up from the ground, his chest smeared with blood, and aimed his gun toward the crooked pines at the edge of the yard, as if he hadn't almost died a second before. The shadowy creatures went crazy, scrambling away from Bridger, no longer hiding where the moon did not shine. And finally I saw them. Animals. Lots and lots of animals.

Bridger ran to the car. I unlocked the door and he climbed in, slamming the door before handing me his heavy gun. He smelled like blood and gunpowder.

∾ 33 ∾

The engine revved to life and the SUV lurched forward.

"Seat belt," Bridger snapped, buckling his without taking his eyes off the road or his foot from the gas pedal.

As we sped away, I peered out my window. The night seemed like any other summer night—innocent, starry, warm.

"Who the hell messed with the ring of protection?" he snapped.

I looked at Bridger. Obviously I wasn't very coherent, because the only thing I could think to say was, "Where are your shirt and shoes?"

He glanced at me out of the corner of his eye. "I didn't have time to put them on," he said, as if this should have been obvious. "I would have been too late. And why wasn't the barn locked?"

"W-what?" I couldn't think. My body temperature was plummeting, my teeth chattering uncontrollably.

"Maggie?" Bridger grabbed my hand. He swore under his breath and sped up, his SUV practically flying down Swan Street, till it skidded to a stop at the gated entry to his house.

He pushed his gate remote control and the wrought iron parted. The car lurched forward, then slammed to a stop just past the gates.

Silently, he took the gun from my lap, cocked it, and got out of the car without shutting his door. On a keypad beside the gates, he typed in a few numbers and I felt more than heard the sudden hum of electricity. The gates slid shut and Bridger waited, gun pointed at the gates till they closed completely. When he climbed back into the car, I stared at him wide eyed.

"I'm so sorry. I thought if I left you alone, they'd stop hunting you," he said. "Pretty brilliant." My mouth fell open with shock, but he didn't notice.

Bridger stopped the car in front of the mansion and got out. He pulled his phone from his pants pocket and hit speed dial. Even though the car doors were shut, I could hear every word.

"Alex. We need help. My house." Bridger glanced at me and caught me listening, so continued his conversation in Navajo. "*Ho-nez-da. Al-tah-je-jay yea-go.* Yeah. Lots of them." He put the phone back into his pocket and walked around to my side of the SUV. I stared at him blankly. He opened the door.

"Maggie?" he prodded gently. When I didn't respond, he reached across my lap and unhooked my seat belt. "Come on."

He took my hands and helped me out of the car, then wrapped an arm around my shoulders and guided me toward the house.

It wasn't until we were on the front porch that I snapped out of my trance. I stopped moving, refusing to let him guide me a step farther.

"What is going on?" I asked shakily, trying not to look at the wolf blood drying on his chest.

"You're in shock. That happens to a lot of people when they experience trauma. You need to lie down and—"

"I don't mean what's going on with me!" I shouted. "Why the heck am I being hunted by those animals? Why do they keep trying and trying to kill me? And how are *you* a part of this, Bridger O'Connell?"

Bridger's face hardened. "How many times have they tried to kill you?"

"I don't know! At least two. Or three." I thought for a minute. There had been tonight, the night at the mine, the coyotes on my way to work, the pack of dogs that attacked me the first time I'd shifted in Silver City. "Freaking four times! They have surrounded me four times; I have been physically attacked three. And that's not counting graduation night."

Bridger's hand turned icy cold on my upper arm, and the blood drained from his face. "How have you survived?"

I looked into his eyes and wondered if I could tell him the truth, that I had survived by becoming an animal, just like them. Would he shoot me if he knew that?

"Can we go inside, please?" I asked, for I didn't know what to say.

He opened the front door.

"What? You didn't lock your door, either?" I taunted bitterly.

"Not when I was rushing to save your butt."

"You know, I don't know why you bothered. I sort of thought we weren't friends anymore," I muttered under my breath, but loud enough for him to hear.

He chuckled and shook his head. "As far as I'm concerned, we're not."

That hurt.

He stepped through the front door. I followed him into the room with the giant fireplace.

"So where's your girlfriend?" I asked.

"Maggie, it's not what you think," Bridger said, walking away. When I didn't follow, he turned and grabbed my hand, pulling me through the room.

The next room was some sort of office with floor-to-ceiling windows and a desk in front of them. Cozy leather chairs were in two corners, and deer antler lamps glowed in here, too. The next room was a dining room with a long, narrow table that had to sit at least twenty people in chairs that looked carved out of knotty pine branches, with a deer antler chandelier centered above the table. Then we were in an oversized kitchen with stone countertops and rows of polished wood cupboards. The marble floor was frigid under my bare feet.

Bridger led me to a small round table nestled in a corner by French doors. "Just sit," he instructed. "I'm going to get cleaned up a little bit, then make you something warm to drink." I sat.

At the kitchen sink, he turned on the water and began sponging away the blood that had dried on his chest. Dried blood on human skin brought back unpleasant memories. I closed my eyes.

After a few minutes of splashing, Bridger said, "The blood's gone."

He went about the kitchen getting the things he needed, his bare feet silent on the granite tile, his muscular torso the object of my speculation more often than not. I couldn't pull my eyes away from him. The urge to run to him, throw my arms around his neck, and kiss him for an eternity was almost overwhelming.

Bridger paused and tilted his head to the side, as if listening for something. His eyes met mine and one black eyebrow arched up. A brilliant smile spread across his face. Then he went back about his task, measuring hot chocolate powder into a mug, grinning.

I felt myself blush scarlet. "You know, that is so unfair."

He looked at me devilishly. "I know."

I rubbed my cold hands together and glanced under the table at my bare feet. Not really the time or place to feel under-dressed, but I couldn't help it.

"So, what's her name and how come you aren't with her tonight?" I asked, trying my hardest to squelch the sudden surge of jealousy that made my blood simmer.

"You don't need to be jealous of Angelene." He put the mug into the microwave and pushed some buttons. With his arms crossed over his chest, he leaned against the counter and watched me.

"I'm not jealous," I lied. Bridger grinned. "Where is she? How come you two aren't swapping spit at the health food store?"

"I put her on a plane for France this morning. She's gone home."

"Why'd she go home?"

"Because I completed my part of a family arrangement." He opened the microwave and took out the mug. "It's pretty hot," he warned, setting the cup in front of me. He sat down, put his elbows on the table, and leaned toward me. I took a tentative sip of the hot chocolate. It wasn't too hot, and I realized I was starv-ing. I wrapped my cold hands around the mug and downed it.

When I set the empty mug on the table, Bridger was

watching me with raised eyebrows. "What? No more questions?" he asked.

"I've really missed you," I whispered, looking into my empty mug.

He let out a long breath of air. "Believe me, I know."

I looked at him.

"Maggie, I don't know what's wrong with me—I feel *everything* you feel. Even when you aren't beside me. Even when I'm *asleep*." For the first time I noticed how tired he looked—how miserable. Black half-moons darkened the skin beneath his eyes and his cheeks were almost gaunt and covered with black stubble. "I took Angelene all the way to Deming for dinner, hoping to get you out of my head, but no. All that evening, all I could feel was miserable anguish. *Your* miserable anguish! And this morning at Wal-Mart, it was all I could do not to fall to the floor and cry, your emotions were so strong." He reached his hand across the table and took mine. His eyes turned haunted. "And the night you were at the mine . . ." A shiver racked his body. "What happened? Why were you there?"

"You were there, too," I accused.

"Of course I was there! Your fear—it was just like tonight! I thought you were going to be killed! But I couldn't find you! What happened?"

"I killed three men that night," I whispered, waiting for his look of revulsion, waiting for him to yank his warm hand away from mine. But he didn't—just waited patiently for me to finish. "I killed some men who were trying to kill me," I said, fighting a sudden surge of guilt that left me breathless. "And Mrs. Carpenter. They—"

His hand tightened on mine. "They what?"

"They got into her house again. I thought if I moved the ring of protection around her, she'd be safe, but I was wrong."

"Did they hurt her? The house blessing. It should have kept her safe."

"They didn't hurt her. She fell and broke her hip. But Duke . . ." Tears started pooling in my eyes.

"No more tears!" Bridger insisted loudly, startling the tears into staying put. "And no more guilt! All I have felt for days is your guilt and your sorrow! It has been so hard to get out of bed every day, Maggie, knowing I have to feel what you are feeling and knowing I couldn't be there to help you through it!"

"Why couldn't you? I really needed a friend!"

"Remember I told you I had a fight with my father? It was because of you. I made a deal with him. I *promised* to stay away from you for two weeks."

"Why?" I asked again, unable to hide the hurt in my voice.

"Because I am in love with you!"

34

A jolt of energy passed through me as his words worked their way into my brain. "Well, what does that have to do with anything?"

"It has to do with everything! Once I fall in love, I can't fall *out* of love unless you die or I die. I am bound. To you."

I didn't know whether to jump for joy or slap him across the face. Honestly, was I the worst person in the world to fall in love with? "Well, is that such a bad thing, falling in love with your best friend?" I finally asked.

For a moment he stared at me. Then he was up and around the table in two steps, pulling me to my feet. His eyes looked half mad and fevered as he grabbed my face in his hands and kissed me. There was no hesitation in his lips this time. They were urgent and relentless. And they felt perfect against mine. I breathed in his breath and wrapped my arms firmly around his neck with the intention of never letting him go again. But he pulled his face away from mine long before I'd had enough.

"Maggie, I have missed you so much. There is no person on this planet I would rather love."

I was speechless, in complete shock. The ghost of a grin flickered on his lips an instant before they touched mine. He kissed me slowly this time, a kiss that showed me how he felt more thoroughly than any words could have. And then it ended, with me gasping for breath and wanting more.

"Come on. We need to talk," he said, leading me by the hand to the room at the front of the house. He paused in front of a sleek leather sofa and stuck his hand into his pocket. When he pulled his hand out, it was filled with turquoise.

"What is that?" I asked. He didn't answer. Instead, he wrapped the turquoise around his neck. "Is that a *heishe* choker?" I asked, trying to stifle the warning bell that was dinging in my brain.

"Yeah. How do you know about these?"

"Yana. She said bad men wear them."

Bridger's lips thinned. "So do good men. I'm wearing this so you know that every word that comes out of my mouth is the truth. If I lie, my *heishe* beads will choke me."

He drew me down beside him, wrapping an arm around me and pulling me against his shoulder. This close to him, I found it hard to be rational. Choker momentarily forgotten, I melted into him.

"After not being able to touch you for so long, this feels so good," he said, pressing his cheek against my head. "Why'd you change your hair again?"

"Because it fit my mood."

"It makes your eyes look like liquid gold. You have the most bewitching eyes I have ever seen."

I closed my eyes and listened to his heart for a moment, the slow, calming rhythm.

"Bridger?"

"Hmm?"

"Who is Angelene?" I know this sounds crazy, but I was more interested in her than I was in the things trying to kill me—at least for the moment.

"Angelene was my girlfriend. Last year, I thought she was the one for me. I thought I loved her."

I tried to suppress the sudden jealousy that sprung to life inside of me. "What happened?"

"Well, the summer after junior year, I went to France and lived with my parents' friends. Angelene is their daughter. She and I got incredibly close that summer. I would have sworn then that I loved her. But now I know I never did. Love is so much more than making out and liking how she looks beside me.

"I didn't mean to fall in love with you, Maggie. I even tried not to. I thought if I never touched you and stopped flirting with you, nothing more than friendship could grow between us. I was wrong. From the first moment I saw you, I haven't been able to get you out of my head. When I realized I was hopelessly screwed, I made the mistake of confiding in Katie. She called my dad and told him, in exchange for a plane ticket back to France. My dad told me I was an idiot and Angelene was on a plane for Silver City. My dad said I had to be sure I didn't still love Angelene before I changed my mind about her. She would have been the ideal match for me, in my parents' eyes. So my father and I made the deal I mentioned earlier. I wouldn't see you for two weeks, and during those two weeks I would resume my relationship with Angelene where it had left off. Boyfriend and girlfriend. At the end of those two weeks, if I wasn't madly in love with Angelene again, which my father was certain I would be, I could pursue . . . you."

He looked down at me, searching my face. "Maggie?"

"What?" I whispered.

"Will you forgive me? For not telling you what was going on? For not telling you about Angelene?"

I stared into his dark eyes and nodded. How could I not forgive him?

"Maggie?"

"What?"

"I never want to be away from you again. Does that scare you?"

I looked away from his face, fighting against a sudden shortness of breath. "I'm more scared of losing you than keeping you around."

He sighed and sank onto the sofa. "Good. Because, like it or not, I'm bound to you until one of us dies."

"Wait. You're *what* to me?" I asked.

He shook his head and clamped his lips shut, and then he sighed. "It has to do with my *nah-e-thlai*, my guide. If I fall in love, I can't fall out of love. If you die before me, I will live with a broken heart for the rest of my life. So you'll be stuck with me loving you until the day I die. Does that scare you?"

For the first time in my life, someone who would love me forever? I smiled. "No. Actually, that's pretty cool. But I want something to change between us."

One of his eyebrows shot up. "What?"

"Can I kiss you whenever I want to?"

For an answer, he kissed me. "I'll be upset if you don't," he whispered, leaning his forehead against mine and tangling his hand in my loose hair.

A long, mournful wail echoed outside, shattering the sense of safety that had been forming around me. I sat straight up, clutching Bridger's hand.

"They've found me. They're here," I said, turning my haunted eyes to him.

"They won't come in. They can't."

"How do you know?" I peered out the tall, wide windows into the dark night and glimpsed a shadow darting into the trees.

"The security system. I turned on electric shock wires when we drove in."

"Why do they want me?" I whispered.

"Because of me."

I whipped around to look at him, absolutely shocked.

"What does this have to do with you?"

Bridger's face hardened. "They are trying to find a way to hurt me because of who my father is—because of who I will become. I am truly sorry that you have been dragged into my problems. I can't believe it has come to this."

"Come to what?" I asked, fighting the urge to grab his shoulders and shake him.

"Remember I told you I agreed to date Angelene?"

"Yeah, that was two minutes ago."

"I had my own reason. I hoped if I pretended to lose interest in you, they would stop hunting you."

"Wait a sec. You thought if you dated some French blond hottie, those . . . *things* would stop hunting me? I don't understand what *you* have to do with any of this. I thought they were after me because—" My jaw snapped noisily shut before I could finish my thoughts. I had the sudden compulsion to look at the array of guns decorating the room. There were hundreds of guns: big, small, some ancient and tarnished, some high-tech and shiny. But all of them, without a doubt, deadly.

When I looked back at Bridger, his eyes held the faintest shadow of uncertainty. "You were saying?" he asked.

"They aren't attacking me because of you. They came looking for me before we ever met. Before I moved to Silver City."

His eyes narrowed the slightest bit. "What do you mean?"

"I mean that I need to know what the heck you are talking about so I know how much to tell you! How is it you know all about these things that are following me, and what are they?"

He stood from the sofa and started pacing around the room. "*Yea-naa-gloo-shee*," Bridger whispered. "That's Navajo for 'With it he goes on all four.'"

I opened my mouth to ask him what the heck he'd just said, but his face was so pale, so lost in another world, I didn't make a noise.

"The Navajo call them witches. They steal the skin of an animal and become that animal. They are Skinwalkers." He brought his dark eyes up to meet mine. "I can feel the evil in some of them, and it is the most terrifying thing I have ever experienced in my life." A shiver racked his body. "They do horrible, malicious things in exchange for the power they gain by becoming an animal. And they are smart. Very, *very* smart." His dark eyes seemed to suddenly grasp something. He clenched his jaw and stared at me as if I had made him do something he didn't want to.

"How have you survived four attacks, Maggie Mae?" A light seemed to burn behind his dark eyes. "And how did you kill three men that night at the mine? Did you have a gun? A knife? Are you trained in hand-to-hand combat?"

I swallowed the sudden apprehension filling my throat and took a deep breath, about to tell him my secret. The lights flickered and the house went pitch black before a word left my mouth.

It lasted only a heartbeat, that blackness, for the lights flickered back to warm life. A sudden ringing shattered the silence. I jumped from the sofa and leaped to Bridger's side.

"It's all right," he said, voice shaky. "It's just someone ringing in from the gate."

He walked to the front door and I followed on his heels, but instead of opening the door, he pushed a button on an intercom.

"Who is this?" he demanded.

A sharp jolt of static cracked from the intercom; then a silky smooth female voice came on.

"Release the girl to us," the voice said.

Bridger's eyes turned hard. "Over my dead body," he barked into the intercom.

"Well, wouldn't that be a lovely bonus," the woman said with a laugh. In the background I could hear the chortling and braying of animals. "Bridger, the odds are set highly against you. Don't think we will spare you because of who your father is. You are one; we are legion. You can't keep us at bay forever."

Bridger's voice was steely cold when he spoke. "I will give you a warning. But only one. I won't be alone for long. Leave now or you will all die."

There was a pause before the woman's voice crackled to life. "Those are big words coming from a lone boy, Bridger." She had an accent, something much smoother than the typical American accent. Maybe British. "Now it is my turn to give the warning. We have disarmed your security system. You have ten minutes to decide what to do before we come in and kill you."

Bridger's breath quickened. The small muscles of his jaw flexed and released over and over. His eyes met mine.

"I will not hand her over so that you can murder her," Bridger insisted. He reached for my hand and pulled me into a one-arm embrace.

"Murder her?" the woman asked lightly. "Who said anything about murder? You're the only one who's going to die. We just want her back."

∽ 35 ∽

His hand jerked away from the intercom as if burned, and his body tensed as hard as steel against mine. Slowly, his eyes met mine. Doubt and despair battled across his face. "No, please no," he whispered. "Please say you aren't one of them, Maggie."

I looked down at my bare feet, unable to answer.

"You *are* one of them, aren't you." It wasn't a question. It was a statement. A realization. I looked at him. Obviously my silence was answer enough, for he closed his pain-filled eyes and shook his head slowly back and forth. When he opened his eyes, they were full of repulsion.

Faster than I thought any person could move, Bridger was at a gun case. He opened it and removed a weapon before I had time to wonder what he was doing. And then the cold muzzle pressed against my temple.

In that instant everything became clear. Prom night, Bridger disappeared. I shifted. I heard gunfire. I almost died.

Graduation night, Bridger disappeared. I shifted. Danni, wearing my jacket, almost died.

The night at the mine, I shifted and barely escaped with my life. Bridger was there. With a gun.

The choker, the *heishe* beads he wore, were the same as those worn by Rolf Heinrich. Rolf Heinrich had been hunting me.

Was Bridger hunting me, too?

I closed my eyes and waited for my brain to be blasted out of my skull. The metal trembled against my skin, and Bridger's ragged breath moved noisily in and out of his throat.

"Please tell me you are not one of them," he said in a voice so full of agony that it brought tears to my shut eyes. "Just tell me the truth, Maggie, please."

I looked at him out of the corner of my eye. "I am like them," I admitted in a choked whisper.

The gun pushed harder against my head—not the response I was hoping for, yet the response I knew I would get.

"Bridger, please don't kill me," I begged. "I'm not evil, I swear."

"But you are one of them!" he yelled. I jumped and cringed, waiting for his finger to accidentally slip on the trigger, waiting to die. "They used you to get to me! Were you sent to corrupt me? To make me fall in love with you so I wouldn't be *able* to kill you? So I would trust you? Are you supposed to turn me to their side? You seemed so innocent, so clueless about the whole thing! Your fear. It felt . . . it *feels* so *real!*"

"It *is* real! They are trying to kill me!" I insisted. Tears were streaming down my cheeks. I lifted a hand to wipe them away and the barrel of the gun jammed into my temple, making stars burst before my eyes.

"Don't move," Bridger warned. "Who are your parents?"

I wanted to throw my hands up in exasperation. Of course, I didn't. I'd be shot if I did. "I don't know who they were! They died before I was two, and the aunt who got custody of me never mentioned them. I don't even know their first names!" I cried. Then I had another thought. "Bridger, the Skinwalkers, they have been trying to kill me since I was a child! They want me dead because I am like them, but not like them. They killed my aunt and cousin. For all I know, they killed my parents, too. They've been after me a long time."

I felt the gun falter against my temple for the briefest moment; then the pressure was back. "How do I know you aren't lying to me?"

I wanted to throw my hands up in exasperation again. "You can feel everything I feel, so you tell me . . . am I lying to you? I would never hurt you! Can't you feel that?"

"That doesn't matter! I am the sworn enemy of those who steal an animal's skin to take its form," Bridger said between gritted teeth. "It is my duty to kill you, Maggie, no matter how I feel about you!"

"Steal an animal's skin? But I don't need to steal a skin to change," I said feebly. The gun was off my temple in a flash.

"What?" Bridger asked.

Tentatively, I turned my head to look at him full in the face. Tears were gleaming on his pale, pale cheeks.

"I don't *mean* to change into different animals. It just happens," I said, warily eyeing the gun in his hand.

He lifted the gun toward me, uncertainty plain on his face, though this time he pointed it at my heart instead of holding it against my head. "But you said you turn into *animals*, not *an* animal."

I nodded fervently. "That's right. Animals. But I never needed an animal's skin to do it. I'll show you," I pleaded between sobs. "Just give me a chance to prove myself."

His face wavered between hope and despair, and then all emotion drained from it. He grabbed my upper arm in an icy iron grip and pressed the gun hard against my spine, right between my shoulder blades.

"Walk!" Bridger ordered. I walked. He herded me to a part of the house I had never seen, where all the furniture was covered with sheets. We came to a shadowed stairwell. Carefully I ascended, worried that if I accidentally tripped or stepped wrong, a bullet would shatter through my spine and lodge in my heart. I just couldn't believe it was Bridger who would put it there.

"Do not try anything, Maggie, or I *will* shoot you," Bridger warned when my hand started to rise to wipe away my tears. I let my hand fall.

We went up a second flight of stairs. The house was uncomfortably hot and stuffy on the third floor. It smelled strange, too, like a shoe store or a leather shop. I wanted to rub at my nose, but the gun tapped against my spine, reminding me to keep my hands down.

At the end of a long hall was a dusty, ancient door with an antique brass handle. Beside the door was a modern keypad. Bridger typed in a code and I heard a lock click.

"Open it," Bridger instructed, nodding to the door without taking his eyes from mine. I pushed the antique door inward and stepped into heavy darkness. The strange odor permeating the third floor was so intense, I gagged when I inhaled. When Bridger flipped on the light, I knew why.

My hands flew up to my face. I stood in a large wood-floored room bare of furniture. Centered in the room was a spiral metal staircase leading to a hatch in the ceiling. On the walls, covering every single available spot, were hundreds of animal paws— tiger, wolf, bear, monkey, dog, gorilla, coyote, even the leathery talons of birds. And masks, lots of masks, like the ones that had been in my room.

"This is how many Walkers my family has killed since my great-grandmother married my great-grandfather," Bridger explained quietly. "If you are a Walker, I will mount your hand on this wall, too."

I felt sick to my stomach. "Where are the rest of the animal skins?"

"You think we'd keep them? We burn them! Or throw them into the old mine! They are tainted with evil," he said mockingly. "Now go up." He swung his gun toward the spiral staircase. I walked.

"I want to warn you, I am a perfect shot," Bridger said as my bare foot started up the cold metal stairs. "If you try to run or hurt me in any way—"

"Bridger," I interrupted shakily. "I will never hurt you."

He laughed, a pitiful, sarcastic sound. "It's a little too late for that!"

At the top of the stairs, I opened the hatch and stepped out into warm, fresh air. I stood on a large square balcony built on top of the roof, illuminated in steely moon glow. Telescopes and binoculars were affixed to the railing at every corner, comfortable lounge chairs sat beside low tables, and a tall pole extended up from the center of the balcony, a worn, scratched perch at the top.

Bridger grabbed my arm and pulled me to a corner of the balcony, beside a giant telescope and an even bigger flood-light. I wondered for an instant if he was going to push me to my death. Instead, with the gun aimed at my head and with-out ever taking his eyes from me, he flipped a switch on the light, and the ground far below—just outside the fence sur-rounding his property—glowed as if daylight shone from the floodlight.

"Look," he said, pointing to the sun-bright ground. Dark shapes scattered away from the lit patch of dusty earth, like ants marching away from an ant hole. Bridger swung the light to a different spot. Fur-covered bodies darted from the bright-ness again, running haphazardly toward the dark ring around the perimeter of light. Again he moved the light. Again a multi-tude of scraggly bodies rushed to the darkness.

"I've never seen so many in one place," Bridger whispered. His eyes locked on mine, curious and wary. The light winked out and I was blind.

"This is your choice, Maggie Mae," Bridger said quietly, as if all of his strength had been drained away. "I'm taking you down to my front yard and you are going to shift. You can attack and kill me, then slip through the gates of my driveway and run away with your kind and never come back. Or you can stand in front of the gate where all the Walkers can see you and I will shoot you. And I never miss." Moonlight reflected off of his numb, dead eyes.

"Bridger, please—" He lifted the gun to my lips, its light pressure silencing me.

"Don't say anything," he whispered, closing his eyes for a brief moment. "This is hard enough without your pleading."

Resigned to my fate, I began the walk downstairs. My feet felt so heavy, I could hardly put one in front of the other to move. I didn't even have the energy to try to come up with an escape plan. I was broken. Ready to die.

One choice remained to me in my short life. Did I want to kill Bridger and try to escape the Skinwalkers, or would I rather be killed by him? The answer was simple. I'd take a swift bullet to the heart over killing him any day.

On the front porch, I turned to Bridger. It was all I could do to scrape my gaze from my feet and look up at him. "Please kill me on your first try," I whispered, barely able to breathe, let alone speak. His eyes grew round, then filled once again with ice.

Without a second thought, I removed my *yo-ih* and put it in my pocket, pulled the oversized T-shirt from my head, and slipped out of my jeans. I walked from the porch in my bra and underwear, looking at Bridger one last time. My tears made his face blur. Only the moonlight reflecting off his gun was easy to see in the darkness.

Beneath a tree's shadow, I removed my bra and panties and shifted into a cheetah. Might as well die as my favorite animal.

With the bravery inherent in cats, I slunk smoothly from the trees and faced Bridger. He was still on the porch, gun aimed at me. He motioned me toward the gate. Slowly, with my head hanging low, I padded down the tree-lined driveway, away from the house.

I knew the very moment the hot summer wind carried my scent to the Skinwalkers because the silent night erupted with the shrieking and howling and roaring of hundreds of excited creatures. My steps faltered. Even a cat's bravery has limits.

"Keep going," Bridger ordered. I turned and looked at him again. He was following me. The gun, still up and ready to shoot, gleamed icy blue in the moonlight. I walked forward.

It wasn't long before I could see the gate, but when I actually saw the Skinwalkers, snarling, slobbering, intent on my destruction, I froze. I did not dare take one more step. Already, wolves and hyenas were shoving their heads through the wrought iron, their teeth snapping, foamy saliva flecks dangling from their snarling jaws. But that wasn't the worst part. Amidst the rabid animals stood a woman wearing the hooded cloak of an animal skin. Only the hood was an animal's head, its teeth framing her pretty young face. It took her a moment to see me. When she did, her calm face became consumed with eager anticipation. Her tongue darted out and licked her lips. She wanted me. Whether dead or alive, I couldn't say. But she definitely wanted me.

A strange sensation niggled at the edge of my senses and my ears flicked back, listening, waiting.

"No!" Bridger screamed, his hysterical voice overwhelming the noise of animals.

I whirled around. He was running, pointing his gun at two black shadows careening through the yard, coming straight at me. A gunshot exploded, and the closer shadow, a giant panther corded with muscle, fell dead at my feet. Not a heartbeat later, a mountain lion slammed into me with a force that sent us tumbling through the dirt. Its teeth sank into my flesh. I whipped around, dislodging its teeth, and pinned it to the ground. But it was wily. It slid from beneath my claws and was on me in a flash. We were a giant ball of hissing, growling fur, completely wrapped around each other as we rolled about the dusty ground, seeking to tear the other apart.

I felt the bullet collide with the mountain lion before I heard the shot. The animal's body lurched once and then fell atop me. How Bridger missed me I can't say. But I was still alive. Calmly, I stood. The mountain lion twitched once and then the skin seemed to deflate, as if all the air were being let out of a balloon, and then fell away, revealing a shivering, gasping man. He reached a trembling, tarantula-tattooed hand toward me and anger distorted his familiar face. It was Tito, the dishwasher. Hate filled his dark eyes, and with his last breath, he spit on me.

"Keep going, Maggie," Bridger called, "so they can all see you."

In five short paces I stood before the gate, just out of the Skinwalkers' reach.

The animals were crazed now, throwing themselves against the gate in savage hysterics, rattling the hinges. The woman in their midst smiled eagerly. Like she was hungry and I was her long-awaited dinner. Calm as a cat, I turned my back on them, though I could feel and smell their breath. I faced Bridger, sat, and wrapped my tail around my paws.

He didn't make me wait. I heard the shot a split second after I felt the bullet pass through my golden fur and enter my flesh. The force threw me through the air and slammed me against the gate. I couldn't breathe—air refused to enter my burning lungs. And then I slid from the gate and fell to my side as blood began to drain from my body.

Silence enclosed the night.

Bridger stood at my side. He nudged me with his bare foot, then slipped a heavy bag over my body.

"She's dead," he triumphantly announced.

And the night exploded in noise.

∾ 36 ∾

Consciousness slowly settled over me. I was in a burlap sack. And I was an animal. The sack came away from my face and Bridger peered at me. He reached out a tentative hand, caressed the fur on top of my head, then completely removed the sack from around me.

"Maggie," he whispered with relief. "You're alive. Change. If you are what you say you are, you must change. Now, or you will die!" There was urgency in his whispered words. His hands came down on me, pushing painfully against my chest.

I smelled blood—human blood—and realized it was my own. But I was a giant cat. And for some reason, I lay in a damp, barely lit cement room that smelled like water and rock.

"Maggie! Change! Shift!" He pushed even harder against my chest in an effort to stop my blood from spilling onto the floor. Pain shot through my shoulder and into my lungs. I tried to growl, though it was more like a kitten purring.

"Shh!" he hissed, his eyes frantic. "They are out there listening to make sure you didn't survive," he mouthed.

My ears flattened, straining. The very faint echo of animal cries reached my ears. I growled again, a low, hollow rumble.

"Please, Maggie. If you're not one of them, change back to yourself," Bridger begged.

I looked at his hands, pressed against my chest and covered in blood, and licked them clean. I was so tired, though, I could not change back into my human form. I put my head down on the hard cement and closed my eyes. It hurt to breathe, hurt to move. All I wanted was to die so that I didn't hurt anymore.

"Maggie," Bridger started again, always whispering. "I don't want to live the rest of my life with a broken heart. Please, please change back. Find the strength, or my heart will die with you." Without taking his hands from my chest, he lay down with his head on my ribs. "For me. Please, Maggie."

He was silent a long moment. His next whispered words seemed to wake me from the beginning of a foggy sleep. "Maggie, remember the first day we played Ultimate and Alex kept looking at you? And I put my hand on your shoulder? That was the first time I admitted to myself that I was truly, helplessly in love with you. I wanted to tell you so badly when I walked you to work that day, to kiss you. And every day after that, it took all of my willpower not to touch you, or kiss you good night, or tell you how hard it was to be away from you." He sighed, his breath fanning my whiskers. "And now that I am able to tell you these things, you are choosing to die. I always knew you were strong willed . . . but I never thought you were selfish. Do you realize that if you die, you are taking away the only thing that matters to me?

"Maggie Mae Mortensen, if you won't change for yourself, do it for me."

Somehow Bridger's words sank into my fuzzy brain. Without lifting my head or opening my eyes, I remembered what it felt like to be me. Remembered how my clumsy human legs felt, the taste of fish tacos, the rush of mountain biking down a steep hill, the feeling of being held safe in Bridger's arms, and of loving him and knowing that he loved me back. Slowly, with so much strain I felt like the last little bit of toothpaste being squeezed from the tube, I began to change.

Bridger got to his knees, whispering encouragement. "That's it! Keep going! Come on, Maggie, come on!" His hands were in my fur, touching me, warming me. "Don't stop, just make the shift."

I felt my legs lengthen and my claws disappear; then my fur became bare skin. And with a groan of pain, I was myself again, curled up in a ball on the cold, hard floor. My chest and ribs burned. I looked down and saw a hole in my skin below my right shoulder—watched it start to close up and push out a bullet as big as the top knuckle of my pinky finger. As the bullet clinked onto the floor, all pain disappeared. I was whole.

Bridger grabbed my limp body in his arms and hugged me to him, laughing a whispered laugh. "I truly thought you were one of them at first, but when you said you didn't need a skin to shift, I dared to hope—I *knew* . . ." His voice trailed away to nothing. "That's why I didn't shoot you in the heart—why I didn't shoot to kill. Because I knew you'd heal when you shifted back. Here." He held my T-shirt out to me.

I was too tired to care that I was naked, too tired to pull the T-shirt over my head, so he did it for me, tugging the long shirt down around my thighs. Then he picked me up and moved me from the bloody spot on the cement floor to a cleaner spot. His face, mere inches from mine, absolutely beamed.

"I can't believe it! You're one of us!" he whispered. He laid me down on the floor again, taking care that my head didn't hit the cement. Then his hands were all over me, touching my hair, face, neck, my bare calves and feet, back to my face again, like a mother examining a brand-new baby. "You are one of us!"

"What do you mean?" I whispered.

"You are like me. A Shifter. That has to be why I am so drawn to you!" He put his hands on either side of my face, leaned down, and gently kissed my forehead. "I should have known the first time I saw you run. But I thought I knew every single Shifter in the entire world by name. We are so few, so rare, we never lose contact with each other. But somehow you slipped through our fingers." Bridger was whispering almost faster than I could follow. "Oh, Maggie. If only you'd told me from the beginning. If only things had been different for you."

"If only I knew what I was from the beginning, life would have been so much easier," I whispered, thinking about the past two years. My heavy eyelids slipped shut.

"Your juvenile record is for indecent exposure, isn't it?" I could hear the smile in his voice. My eyes flickered open. "A definite downside of shifting, coming out of it naked. I've had a few close calls myself."

My eyes fell shut again.

"Oh, Maggie. If only you'd told me." His hand stroked my hair and I started to drift off to sleep. His voice jarred me awake. "Don't move," he whispered, as if I had any choice. Even the energy it took to open my eyes and watch him leave the dimly lit room almost hurt.

My eyes flicked around, taking in quick flashes of my surroundings before crashing shut again. I was in some sort of windowless, stone-walled basement. A bomb shelter, maybe? It was an empty room, without so much as a rug on the damp, grimy floor. The only thing in the room besides me was a lightbulb dangling on a lone cord from the ceiling.

Bridger returned with his arms full of stuff. Gently, quietly he set the stuff beside me. I forced my eyes open one last time to see what it was: food, two sleeping bags, water, and a foam pad. He rolled out the foam pad and put a sleeping bag onto it.

"Climb in. You're going to fall asleep any minute. I almost killed you." His eyes were dark and troubled for an instant. Then his face broke into a beautiful, breathtaking smile again.

I looked at the sleeping bag but couldn't move my body. Bridger lifted me onto it and zipped me into its soft warmth. He covered me with the other.

"Eat this," he instructed, holding a granola bar to my mouth. I ate the whole thing in record time. "At least your appetite's not sleepy," he said with a whispered laugh. I sipped some stale water out of the canteen he held to my lips, then lay with my back to him, using my arm for a pillow. Maybe it was the cold, damp floor or maybe I was in shock, but in spite of the sleeping bags I began to shiver.

"You're freezing," Bridger said, his breath on my ear. He climbed into the sleeping bag with me and lifted my head onto his warm, bare chest. Wrapped in his arms, I fell asleep before I heard his heart beat three times.

37

A woman's face, framed by the hood of a tiger's head and teeth, stared at me. She reached through the wrought-iron gate separating us and wrapped her hand in my blacker than black hair, pulling me toward her until our noses almost touched. But when she opened her mouth to speak, she changed, grew taller, with crow-black hair and charcoal eyes.

"I have to kill you now," Bridger whispered, tightening his hand in my hair and thrusting a gun against my chest. He pulled the trigger and pain exploded in my heart. I jolted awake and pressed my hands over my ribs. The pain disappeared, but the memory of Bridger's cold, hard eyes stayed with me. I closed my eyes and tried to catch my breath.

"Maggie!" Bridger's voice hissed. He padded across the cement floor and crouched at my side. "What's wrong?" His hair was damp, he smelled like shaving cream, and he was wearing a pair of pajama bottoms and a black T-shirt.

"Nightmare," I whispered. "Where are we?"

"We're beneath my house."

"How long have I been asleep?"

"Not long. Maybe forty minutes."

"Are we safe yet?" I questioned groggily.

Bridger frowned and shook his head. "No. But close. My father is here. With reinforcements. Some of the Walkers felt uncertain about your death. They're lingering, waiting for any hint that you still live," he explained. "They must believe you are dead or you will never be safe."

I squeezed my eyes shut, trying to sort through my muddled thoughts.

"You're confused," Bridger stated. "And mad."

I opened my eyes and scowled at him. "I know."

"Do you want to talk about it? You can ask me anything you want. Oh, yeah—" He held something out to me, a pair of boxer shorts. I blushed as I shakily pulled them on beneath my long T-shirt. "Sorry—I gave all of my sister's old stuff away and Katie didn't leave a thing behind," he said, raising one eyebrow. "Scoot over."

I scooted and Bridger squeezed into the sleeping bag with me, his face inches from mine, our legs tangled together. He put a hand on the small of my back and pulled me closer so the only part of my body not touching his was my face.

I stared at him for a long moment. He smiled, but I knew there was another side to him—a dark side. I almost felt as if I didn't know him anymore.

"You shot me," I whispered.

The smile fell from his face. "I had no choice. That was the *only* way I could save your life and mine—by making them think you were dead. There were too many Walkers for me to fight alone, and they'd already breached the gate. But if they thought you were dead . . . it was our only chance." I could hear pleading in his whispered voice. I didn't have to sense his feelings to know how much he craved my forgiveness.

I understood what he was saying, but it still made me furious that he'd shot me. I changed the subject.

"You say I'm like you. What do you mean?"

"I shift. I'm a Shifter like you."

For a very long time I stared at him, wondering if I was dreaming. I reached out and placed my hand on his warm neck, gently probing until I found the pulse beating against his skin.

"What are you doing?" he asked, his eyes searching mine.

"Making sure you're real."

"Very real."

"So, when you . . . shift . . . are you a cat, too?"

"I am a golden eagle."

"*Atash?* It was you who saved me from the coyotes?"

"You threw a rock at me, Maggie."

"Sorry. But the moon . . . the night of the full moon. I was at the mine and so were you, but you had a gun. You weren't an animal. Were you?"

"Of course I wasn't. I am a lot deadlier with a semiautomatic weapon than with talons and a beak."

"What about prom night? Why did you leave? And after graduation?"

He took a deep breath. "For the first time in years, I could feel Walkers in Silver City. That was prom night. I could feel them hunting . . . *someone* . . . who they were desperate to catch. I figured it must have been one of their own, a deserter. Now I know it was you." He traced my jawline with his finger. "I'm sorry I left you at the prom, but I had no choice. It was a life-and-death situation. I shot one that night.

"When they attacked Danni at Mrs. C.'s house after graduation, I realized they were targeting you. Danni was wearing your jacket. I assumed that by hurting you, they were trying to get revenge on me for me shooting one of them, so I stayed as close to you as possible to keep you safe. Now I know the real reason they wanted you. You're like me."

"But . . . I can't help but shift when the moon is full," I stammered, thinking maybe he and I weren't quite as similar as he thought. I had been a slave to the moon's will for two years.

"There are so many things you should already know. The only reason you would be forced to change at the full moon is if you haven't shifted since the previous full moon. It's like you get this overflow of energy and have to use it. And for some reason the moon pulls it out."

Well, that explains it, I thought bitterly. Until I moved to Silver City, the only time I *ever* changed was when the moon pulled it out of me.

"I still can't believe the Walkers came after you in broad daylight," he mused. "I thought they did everything under cover of night."

"How do you think they found me?"

"They've known what you were from the very moment your mother conceived you. You're a *be-tas-tni.*"

"A what?" I asked.

"*Be-tas-tni.* A *mirror.* It means you can mirror any animal you see, with a few limitations. It also means—" He closed his eyes and ran a hand through his hair.

"What? It also means what?" I asked, nervous.

"You're a *mix.* All mirrors are a sort of really rare *hybrid.*" He cleared his throat and I stared at him, waiting for the meaning behind his words. "Your mother was a shifter—she had to be. But your father? The only way to make a mirror is to have a Shifter for a mother and a Skinwalker for a father."

My entire body seemed to freeze—my breathing, my heart, my wide eyes. After a long moment I forced a breath of air into my lungs. "What are you saying? That I'm a Skinwalker after all?"

"No. You're the *offspring* of one. And the offspring of a Shifter. Somehow, against all odds, you've evaded the Walkers. Possibly, due to all the foster homes you lived in, they couldn't find you, not with you moving around so much."

"But if they wanted me dead so bad—from birth, if you're right—then why didn't they shoot me as soon as they found me? Like when I walked home from the bus? Why didn't they kidnap and kill me, and leave my body on some deserted dirt road? I mean, they killed all of my family. Why not me?"

"I never said they wanted you dead. You're *be-tas-tni*. I highly doubt their intent was to kill you. Most likely they wanted to capture you—to own you."

"Own me? Why?" I asked, unsure if I wanted to hear the answer.

"Since you have the gifts of both a Walker and a Shifter, you are more powerful than either. You heal instantly and don't need a skin to shift, like me. But, like the Walkers, you can turn into any animal you want. If they caught you and made you believe you were one of them, they'd have the most powerful weapon against the Shifters imaginable. And think of what would happen if you fell in love with one of them." His lips pursed. "Think of what your offspring would be like."

My skin started crawling at the thought of having babies with a Skinwalker.

"And if you didn't side with them, they would probably . . ." Bridger cleared his throat and shook his head the tiniest bit.

"What? They would what?" I demanded.

His body stiffened against mine. "Trust me. You don't want to know."

"Yes, I do. Tell me or I'll go insane wondering."

He took a deep breath and his eyebrows pulled together in a deep frown. "They could use your skin."

My head started to spin and my blood felt too hot. I needed a major subject change before a panic attack set in. "So," I said, voice trembling. "You can only shift into one thing?"

Bridger nodded. "Yep. Only one. If Shifters even attempt to force themselves into a different shape than they're born to, they die. Except you. Exactly what else *can* you turn into?"

I know he asked simply to take my mind off what he'd just said. But I didn't care. "Anything with fur. Except really small things, like mice, and really big things. I tried to turn into a horse and got stuck with hooves for the night." A small smile broke through my worry. "And once, I tried to turn into a snake. It almost worked. . . . What?" Bridger was staring at me with a look of such terrified shock that I wondered if we were about to be attacked.

"A cold-blooded creature?" he whispered. "And you didn't die?"

"I was covered with weird, scaly dust for a day. That's all."

His hands tightened on the small of my back. "I remember that day. We talked at the park and you were literally glowing."

"Why do we shift at all?" I asked—the question that had plagued me since the first night I had changed.

"The universe must have balance: light matter and dark matter, good and evil, life and death, joy and sorrow. Thousands of years ago a man sold his soul to the devil and became the first Skinwalker. To keep the universe in perfect balance, someone had to offset him—be his opposite—so the first Shifter was born. Otherwise there would be an imbalance in the world and evil would be given the opportunity to conquer good. Since then, lots of men and women have delved into dark, evil things and traded their souls to the devil in exchange for supernatural powers—one of them being the power to wear an animal skin and shift—Skinwalkers. So Shifters have had the need to multiply. Does that answer your question?"

I nodded, but I could hardly believe it. It sounded so . . . fantastical.

"Skinwalkers aren't Navajo, are they?"

"Evil doesn't choose a race or nation. Anyone can follow the witch way and become a Walker," Bridger explained. "In this part of the world, the burden to battle the Walkers has fallen to the Dineh—the Navajo. But in other parts of the world, other races are Shifters. My mother is descended from Bran the Blessed, ancient Druid king of England. His people were the first Shifters in Britain."

Shifters in Britain? My brain was starting to spin and I needed another subject change. "Bridger?"

"Hmm?" His hands moved slowly up and down my back.

"What do you mean when you say you're bound to me?"

His hands paused and his dark eyes lit up, like the sun burning behind rain clouds, yet he didn't say a word. Tentatively, I put my hand at the nape of his neck and coiled my fingers in his thick hair.

"Shifters have different instincts than humans," he said, as if my touch released his words. "Some can sense danger. You already know I can feel what people around me are feeling."

"Yeah, about that. If you were feeling what I was feeling so strongly, why didn't you feel when I turned into an animal?"

"Actually, I did. I *always* feel you, but you don't feel different when you shift. Whether you're human or animal, you feel like Maggie Mae—there is no difference between the two. A Shifter's instincts are tied—"

"Oh my gosh!" I gasped, gripping the neck of Bridger's shirt.

"What?"

"Tito!" Bridger's eyebrows knit together. "The dishwasher at the Navajo Mexican? He was the mountain lion that attacked me in your front yard. I could totally feel him. Whenever he was around, I got all creeped out. Is that what you mean by instinct?"

"Yes. Exactly."

"So what does that have to do with you being bound to me?"

He pressed a finger against my lips. "If you shut up for five seconds, I'll explain. I shift into an eagle. Eagles . . . stay together for life when they find a mate. Even though I am human, I still have the instincts of an eagle, in some ways. Like my father. Once I fall in love, I cannot fall out of love. I am stuck loving you for the rest of my life. So I hope . . ." His voice trailed off and his finger dropped.

"What?"

"You've never said how you feel about *me*, Maggie."

I rolled onto my back and stared at the hanging lightbulb. I remembered the warmth that coursed through me whenever I met Bridger's eyes, thought of how my heart sped up double-time every time he touched me, thought about kissing him, about watching him ride his bike and throw a Frisbee clear across a giant field. Then I thought how, for the first time in my life, I knew who I was, and in spite of all my flaws, he still loved me. I felt free to be myself in front of Bridger despite my short-comings. I let the warmth from all of those things fill me.

His face appeared above mine and blocked the light from my eyes. "Wow," he whispered. He stared at me for a long time, as if reading in my eyes all the feelings pulsing through me. Slowly, he leaned down. I could feel his breath on my face, feel the warmth radiating from his lips, but before they touched mine, he pulled his face away and sighed, easing out of the sleeping bag.

I sat up, staring at him. "What?"

"That's what," Bridger whispered, looking at the closed door. A heartbeat later the door swung open and a tall, dark man strode into the room. "Dad."

Mr. O'Connell looked past his son and focused on me, accusation burning in his gray eyes.

"Dad, you remember Maggie Mae," Bridger said.

I forced a smile to my face and pulled the sleeping bag to my chest.

"Nice to see you again," Mr. O'Connell said. He wasn't whispering and his voice seemed horribly loud.

"They're gone?" Bridger asked, standing.

"Yes," Mr. O'Connell replied. He cleared his throat and looked down at me again, dark eyes studying me like I was a pebble lodged in his shoe. Unable to hold his gaze, I focused on the ceiling and tried not to cringe. After an uncomfortable moment of silence, Mr. O'Connell said, "She's safe. Move her to a guest room. But give me fifteen minutes to clear out. And I need a quick word with you, son."

Bridger followed his dad from the room and pulled the door shut behind them. Their voices barely resonated through the stone-walled room, completely indecipherable. Call it Shifter instinct, but somehow I knew they were talking about me. I closed my eyes and tried to make sense of their words. When I couldn't, I concentrated on my ears, focusing on making them work like a cat's. Slowly, my ears adjusted, shifted the tiniest bit, and the conversation taking place on the other side of a closed door changed from deep echoes to a conversation that might as well have been being held right in front of me.

". . . because I don't love Angelene! I tried. I really did, Dad, I swear," Bridger argued. "But there's nothing left between Angelene and me."

"You didn't try hard enough," Mr. O'Connell insisted. "Sometimes you have to fan the coals to make a flame."

Bridger groaned. "There aren't even coals left! Just a pile of cold ashes."

"But this other girl—"

"Her name's Maggie Mae."

"She's so ordinary. So unlike us! I don't understand how you formed an attachment to her in the first place. Why you *chose* her," Mr. O'Connell snapped.

My stomach dropped. I'd known all my life how insignificant I was, but it hurt to hear it stated so confidently by someone who didn't even know me.

"I didn't *choose* her! I fell in love with her!" Bridger said, voice tight with anger. "And she's a lot less ordinary than you give her credit for. If you weren't such an elite snob, you might actually be able to see the good in people from other social classes."

"Just don't tell your mother until you're certain this girl is the one," his father replied, voice weary. "It will break her heart."

"I already am certain. Nothing is going to change."

His father sighed. "Move her to a guest room in fifteen minutes."

"I will. And . . . thanks, Dad. For coming."

"It's what we do. Why don't you come upstairs with me. See me out."

Footsteps echoed on the cement floor and faded away.

I snuggled down in my sleeping bag and closed my eyes, content in the knowledge that Bridger loved me no matter what his dad said.

If Bridger came for me fifteen minutes later, he didn't wake me. I spent the whole night in the basement and didn't wake up once.

⤳ 38 ⤳

Two days later, we drove to the deserted mine. Bridger pulled his SUV to the side of the dirt road and we got out. I squinted against the hot afternoon sun and followed him through a sparse copse of trees to a round, fathomless hole in the ground—another place where the parched earth had been swallowed by the mine. Icy air oozed from the hole and crept down my spine.

"Bridger, why did you bring me here?" I asked, rubbing my hands over my arms. The mine was the last place I wanted to be.

Bridger looked at me. A shadow of fear danced in his eyes. "There are *Yea-naa-gloo-shee* here," he whispered.

Dread turned my legs to mush and I grabbed Bridger's arm to keep from falling.

"They're dead, Maggie," he said gently, wrapping his arms around my waist. "My father killed the Walkers that stayed to see if you were dead. Their bodies were disposed of in this sunken mine shaft."

I shivered in spite of the hot afternoon. "Who was the woman at the gate? Is she dead, too?" The woman from my nightmare.

"When the Skinwalkers need to communicate, they have a

designated Speaker—someone who keeps her human form. She was gone before my father arrived, but I described her to my father. He believes she's the Speaker for a Skinwalker named Rolf Heinrich."

I gasped and dug my nails into Bridger's arm. "Did you say Rolf Heinrich?"

Bridger's eyebrows rose. "Do you *know* Rolf Heinrich?"

"He was one of the tigers—the men I told you about—who were hunting me here. I killed him."

All color left Bridger's face. His hands grew clammy against my back, so clammy I could feel them, like ice through the fabric of my T-shirt. "Are you certain he's the man you killed?"

"Yes."

"You killed the Skinwalkers' leader—their most formidable fighter. If I had to guess, I would say the ability to survive against impossible odds is one of your natural instincts." He looked at my hand and began prying it from his arm. My nails had made four half-moon indentations in his skin, right above three wolf-inflicted scars on the back of his wrist.

I thought of Rolf Heinrich's naked corpse lying atop the tiger pelt. "If a Skinwalker dies in the shape of an animal, does he turn back into a human?"

"No. If you kill them instantly, they don't have the power to change back. They are dead animals. If you wound them, they can change back to their human shapes, but they're not like us. They don't heal. Sometimes they still die."

That made sense. Rolf Heinrich didn't die instantly. He shifted back to his natural form and bled to death. My stomach churned and I peered over my shoulder, toward the distant dirt hill topped by a faded red flag.

"What is it?" Bridger asked, his hand slowly moving up and down my back.

"There are three bodies in the mine shaft over there, the one below Evening Hill," I whispered. "Two are animals, but the third one's Rolf Heinrich."

He pulled my head against his chest and ran his fingers through my hair. "He'll never be found. My father is destroying the mine. He wrote an article for the local newspaper claiming it's too dangerous to leave the abandoned mine as it is, which is true, but that isn't the motivation behind his decision. He's disposing of your hunters."

I looped my arms loosely behind his back, content to rest my head against his chest. "How many died?"

"Only a few. Most of them left after you were shot."

"How'd he . . . kill . . . them?"

"My father . . ." I looked up when he didn't continue. His lips were pressed together, as if he couldn't speak another word. He looked at me and took a deep breath. "He had a lot of help—other Shifters."

"Oh. Who?" The house, Bridger's house, had been silent for the two days I'd been holed up in the guest room.

"They left as soon as the bodies were disposed of. While you were still bunking in the basement."

"I would have liked to meet them. To thank them."

"You can't meet them, Maggie."

"Why?"

"Because they don't want you to know who they are. Only Shifters know other Shifters."

"But I *am* a Shifter, Bridger. Why didn't you tell your dad?"

He slowly raised an eyebrow. "How do you know I didn't tell him?"

Heat flooded my cheeks. "When I was lying down in the basement, I could hear your conversation," I admitted, too ashamed to meet his eyes.

"Huh. You could hear our conversation through a sound-proof door?"

I shrugged. "I guess I have good hearing."

"Good hearing? You're such a liar," he said with a laugh.

"But seriously—why *didn't* you tell your dad about me? Is it because I'm a mirror? Because my father was a Skinwalker? Would he think I was evil if he knew?"

Bridger's arms tightened around me. "No! Who your parents are doesn't make you good or evil. It's how you choose to live your life that does."

"But"—I pulled back and looked right into his eyes—"if my mom was a Shifter, why didn't you guys know her? How did you lose track of her? And me?"

"Every once in a while, a Shifter goes rogue and severs all ties with us. Maybe that's what happened. Or—" Doubt filled his eyes and he looked away from me.

"Or what? Tell me. I have a right to know," I said, putting my hand on Bridger's cheek and turning his face so he had to look at me again.

He took a deep breath and continued. "If a Shifter joins the Walkers through marriage, we sever all ties and erase the Shifter from our records—like they never existed. Maybe that's what happened to your mom—she fell in love with a Walker, got married, and got erased. But she must have loved you a lot, Maggie, because somehow she got you away from them—probably died for it. And because of that, you survived. Love is a pretty powerful thing."

I rested my head back on his chest and stared unseeing at the deserted mine. For the first time in my life I felt close to my mother, a woman I never knew.

"One day my father will know the truth about you," Bridger said, tilting my chin up so he could look at me.

"And then he won't care that you . . . like . . . me so much?" I asked.

The corners of Bridger's mouth turned up. "I don't *like* you Maggie. I am in *love* with you. *Madly!*"

A grin flickered across my face. "I do believe I am in the right 'social class' to be your girlfriend."

Bridger kissed my forehead. "Nothing can keep us apart."

Nothing? I hoped that was true. "The Walkers think I'm dead, right?" He nodded. "What happens when they find out I'm not?"

He glanced at the mine shaft. "Hopefully that will never happen. But now that you're with us—the Shifters—they'll think twice about coming after you. Before, when you were alone, you were a prime target."

I stepped out of the safe embrace of his arms and looked down into the depths of the mine shaft again, staring at the impenetrable blackness. Without thinking, I willed my eyes to be those of a cat, made them change, expand, improve, and then, like a movie coming suddenly into focus, the bottom of the mine shaft blurred into view. Dark shapes against darker masses solidified into grotesquely twisted and broken animals.

A gasping intake of breath startled me, and my eyes jerked from the shaft to Bridger. He scrambled away backward, as if I were a demon, and lost his footing. Orange dust swirled as he fell heavily to the ground. I burst out laughing. I'd never seen him trip before—didn't think it was possible.

Slowly, not taking his eyes from mine, he stood and brushed off his pants. A smile crept over his startled face.

"You are definitely a mirror! You have the eyes of a freaking cat," he said, walking back to my side. "But you're *my* cat." He framed my face with his hands and peered down into my eyes. "Even if I'm a bird of prey." Then he kissed me.

⤖ EPILOGUE ⤖

The house felt like a place from my distant past. I hadn't been back since the night Bridger had shot me, four days ago, yet everything seemed different, as if in a matter of days I'd outgrown the place.

Bridger turned off the SUV and I pressed my nose to the window, studying the familiar orange-and-pink-framed skyline—mountains, not skyscrapers—before getting out. As my door slammed shut, Mrs. Carpenter's front door opened.

"Is that you, Maggie Mae?" a deep voice called. I walked toward the front porch where Mr. Petersen stood with his arms folded across his chest. As I approached he smiled and opened his arms and something deep inside of me seemed to wake up. I ran to him and threw my arms around his chest, thinking this must be how it felt to be reunited with a family member after a long time away. He hugged me back, extra tight, and then held me at arm's length. "I think you've grown since I saw you last," he said, eyes twinkling. His hands tightened on my shoulders. "You made it, kiddo. Survived the hardest part of your life and lived to tell!"

My eyes grew round and I wondered how he could possibly know this. "Wait . . . what do you mean?" I asked, hoping he couldn't hear the near-panic in my voice.

"High school," he said with a chuckle. I smiled and laughed a weak laugh. The gravel crunched behind me and Bridger walked slowly up the porch steps. "Bridger O'Connell," Mr. Petersen said, holding his hand out to Bridger. Bridger shook his hand. "Nice to see you, son."

"You, too," Bridger said.

"There's someone inside dying to see you," Mr. Petersen said, looking at me again. "Not *literally* dying, mind you, but she heard the car on the gravel and insisted I get you inside as soon as possible." Mr. Petersen looked down his nose at me, the same stern look he'd give when he found out I'd been caught out on the streets nude.

And all of a sudden I couldn't take a step forward. I'd talked to Mrs. Carpenter every day that she'd been in the hospital—called her from the phone in the O'Connells' guest room—but talking wasn't the same as seeing her. I couldn't help but worry that she'd blame me for everything that had happened—like I blamed myself. What if she hated me?

Bridger looped his arm around my shoulder and put his lips on my ear. "Stop worrying," he said quietly. "She's as eager to see you as you are to see her."

I relaxed a bit and walked through the front door.

"Maggie Mae," Mrs. Carpenter said with a warm smile on her thin face. "How are you, dear?" She lay on a reclined hospital bed in the living room, an IV tube leading to a purple vein in the back of her frail hand.

"I'm good," I answered. She held a hand out to me and I

crossed the room and grabbed it, gently squeezing. "How are you?"

"Better than a woman my age with a broken hip should be. They put a couple of pins in there and now I can practically walk," she said with a smile.

"Not yet, Mother," Mr. Petersen warned in his no-nonsense voice.

Looking around, I felt a sudden pang of homesickness. Things had been put back to normal, thanks to Mr. Petersen— the hole in the ceiling plastered and painted over, the chunks of ceiling swept up off the floor, as if none of it had ever happened.

"John, I need a word with Maggie Mae," Mrs. Carpenter said. "Why don't you go outside and talk to Bridger for a while?"

I looked out the window. Bridger sat on the porch swing, face pointed toward the setting sun, hair glinting black and gold. Mr. Petersen scowled at his mother but said, "Whatever you say."

When the front door shut behind him, Mrs. Carpenter turned to me. "I can see your plans written all over your face," she said with a sad smile.

Tears seeped into my eyes and I nodded. "It's what's best," I explained, wiping my tears away.

"I know it is. Funny thing about doing what's right—it's always the harder road to follow. But you already know that." She sighed. "Now tell me, are you and that O'Connell boy *finally* going steady?"

I blushed and nodded, grinning.

"It's about time! I knew the moment I saw him look at you that there were sparks there—that first day of school." She chuckled. "He's a fine-looking boy, and noble, out there sitting on the swing so that you and I can have a moment alone."

"Mrs. Carpenter?" I hung my head and swayed against a sudden surge of guilt that racked me from my scalp to my toes. "I need to tell you something."

"Well, tell away. I'm not going anywhere."

I looked up into her encouraging, forgiving face. "I broke the ring of protection. I didn't mean to—I thought if I moved it closer to your house you'd be safe." Miserable with guilt, I looked away again and stared down at my shoes. "It was my fault you broke your hip, my fault Duke died and Shash ran away. And I am so, so sorry."

"Maggie?" I looked up at her, blinking against a sheen of tears. "You did nothing wrong. Those creatures—have you figured out what they are?"

I nodded and bit my lip.

"Whatever they are—and I don't want to know the details—they acted of their own will. You had no hand in what happened. The most important thing—are you safe?"

"Yes."

"Good."

Something thumped on the front porch and nails scratched the front door. My eyes met Mrs. Carpenter's fear-filled eyes and a silent question passed between us. *Are they back already?* I turned and faced the front door.

A low growl echoed outside, the door handle turned, and Bridger poked his head inside. "Someone's here to see you two," he said with a mischievous grin. He opened the door wide and Shash, fur dusty and tangled with twigs, slunk inside.

"Shash!" I fell to my knees and clapped my hands, and he trotted across the floor, putting his massive front paws on my shoulders and licking my face until I toppled backward.

"Can I come in now?" Mr. Petersen asked from the doorway.

"Come in, son," Mrs. Carpenter said. At the sound of her voice Shash climbed off me, put his nose on the side of her bed, and whined. "You miserable mutt," Mrs. Carpenter said with a smile. "You're filthy! And I can't vacuum!"

"Maggie, come outside with me for a few minutes," Bridger said, helping me to my feet. I followed him out the front door. "Will you help me rebuild the ring of protection before it gets too dark?"

"I don't think that's a good idea. Why didn't my ring of protection work?"

"Are you Navajo?" Bridger asked. I shook my head. "Did you bless it after you made it?" I shook my head again. "Did you use sage and an eagle feather to strengthen it?"

"All right, I get it," I said. "I don't have the magic touch."

"Exactly."

"Mrs. Carpenter won't need the ring of protection anymore," I said quietly, stepping off the porch.

"She won't?" Bridger asked, surprised.

"Not because of me, at least. There's no way I'll put her in danger again. I'm moving out." I took Bridger's hand and we walked toward the back of the house where the skulls had been piled. A warm breeze blew, stirring the boughs of a crooked pine and blowing my hair away from my face.

Bridger pulled me to a stop. "You're moving?" he asked, slipping his hands around to the small of my back and looking at me with curious eyes. "Won't Mrs. Carpenter need you around to help her out?"

I shook my head. "When I talked to Mrs. Carpenter this morning, she told me her granddaughter is moving into the upstairs bedroom to take care of her. Her granddaughter's a nurse. It's time for me to move on."

"Where are you going to go?" he asked. I could hear the real question in the concerned tone of his voice.

"Don't worry—I'm actually moving *closer* to you," I explained. "Naalyehe has a studio apartment above the restaurant. He says he'll give me a good price on rent if I want to fix it up a bit—paint the walls and clean it up and stuff. I gave him a deposit during my shift today. I can move in tomorrow. If . . ." I put my hands behind Bridger's neck and ran my fingers through his hair.

His eyes narrowed. "If what?" he asked suspiciously.

I shrugged. "If someone with a car can help me move my stuff?"

He frowned and shook his head. "Too bad I own an SUV and not a *car*. Otherwise I'd have been just the guy for the job."

I laughed and shoved him, but his hands tightened on the small of my back and pulled me closer. He rested his forehead on mine. "You've got to get over this inability to ask people for help," he whispered, his nose bumping mine. I closed my eyes and brushed my lips over his, inhaling his exhaled air. He sighed, his body melting into me, his heart drumming against mine.

"Bridger, will you help me?" I whispered against his mouth, opening my eyes.

He took a deep breath and, without opening his eyes, nodded. "Always and forever. Whatever you need, I'll be here." His lips started moving against mine, gently insistent, making my brain swirl and my heart explode. I smiled against his mouth and kissed him, adjusting my body to line up with his like we were constructed for each other, two halves of a bigger whole.

I closed my eyes, and in that instant, my world seemed to shift, as if all the screwed-up crap I'd gone through over the past years clicked into place, locking together to form a bigger picture than I'd ever seen before—me, right here, right now. Every day, every minute, leading to this moment, bringing me to this point in time where everything was all right.

This place where I'd never be alone again.

ACKNOWLEDGMENTS

Thanks to the best agent in the universe, Marlene Stringer, for falling in love with Maggie Mae enough to take a risk on me. Without you, Marlene, this book never would have made it. And a huge thank-you to Emily Easton for believing in me, and for her unending patience and wisdom!

Thank you, Mom and Dad, my sisters Tiffiny, Brittany, and Natalie, and my brother, Matt, for reading and loving my book, even in its early stages.

Thanks to my beta readers, Nicole, Cyndi, Shelly, Kelli, Elana, Michelle, Bonny, Sarah, Heidi, and Janie, for loving the story enough to read it until the wee hours of the morning. And thanks to Pat and Cole for telling me the story was good enough, even when I was in the depths of self-doubt.

Thanks to my kids, for not giving me funny looks when I'd zone off in the middle of dinner or start vocalizing dialogue between two characters while we drove around town.

To the woman who made me realize that deep down inside, I am a writer—my sister and accomplice-in-writing, Suzette Saxton—thanks for daring me to start!

Last of all, with overflowing love and gratitude, I'd like to thank my husband, Jaime, for dealing with me staying up night after night, sometimes till dawn, to get the madness of this story down on paper.